SUSANNA AND SATAN

The Elder Shuttleworth had asked Susanna to come down from the wheat field and fetch a rope rigging from the barn to where he was at work in the shed.

Her thoughts were of the impending marriage to Brigham Young, a stern leader of his flock, but kind to his women. And he alone had the power to rescue her from the Elder. It was not passion. Her passion lay buried in an unmarked grave. Yet she would try to be a good wife.

She reached the shed but it was barred shut. She went to the rear toward a back entrance and suddenly there was a rustle behind her and then a hard blunt weapon struck and felled her.

Consciousness returned in degrees—and horror with it. She was inside the shed, bound spread-eagle fashion to wooden posts. Her skirts had been flung back and, approaching her was the grotesque figure of Shuttleworth, bowie knife in one hand and a long wickedly pointed stake in the other.

"The Lord demands vengeance, slut of Satan," he whispered. Then she knew his madness and knew she was lost . . .

A Love to Match These Mountains

Nancy Elaine Pindrus

A DELL/JAMES A. BRYANS BOOK

Published by

Dell Publishing Co., Inc.
1 Dag Hammarskjold Plaza
New York, New York 10017

Dell ® TM 681510, Dell Publishing Co.

ISBN: 0-440-00163-3

Printed in the United States of America

First printing—February 1979

To Paul E. Jeans and Anne Conover Heller

PART ONE

BOOK I
The First Journey

1

A FEW RAYS of afternoon sunlight filtered through the
dusty windowpanes of the tiny draper's shop. Behind
the counter, Susanna Hungerford Jones sighed and
closed her eyes a moment, and felt that brief, welcome
light warm her cheeks and catch the edges of her pale
curls. Summers never stayed long in Liverpool—just
long enough to ease the damp a little bit, to give a
few moments of gold in the afternoon, like now, before
the narrow street would be swallowed again in shadow.

The brash jangle of bells interrupted her reverie,
and the street door swung wide to admit two men.
They swaggered in, stamping their feet like restive
horses. *Muddy boots,* she thought furiously. *And there's
more sweeping for me.*

"Rogues!" she exclaimed. "Have you no manners at
all, or is't the street you call your home?" The taller
man, his blue eyes gleaming with amusement, approached the counter and regarded her lazily from a
great height.

Susanna began to fidget under his gaze. He seemed
to tower over her so! His presence was out of place
and threatened the safety—nay, even the sanctity of
the little shop. The custom here were gentlefolk. It was
a shop of women, with one potbellied merchant who

9

used soft-spoken words made all of numbers to bargain her mother's prices.

"Fetch your mistress, girl," the tall man commanded abruptly.

The girl blushed and shot him a defiant look. "My mother is entertaining a visitor," she declared hotly, "and I'm in charge of the shop."

"You look like you could be a mite o' entertainment yourself, sweetheart," said the smaller man, with a wide-mouthed snigger that revealed several gaps where teeth should be. He was an ugly little man, with grizzled whiskers and a thick, broad nose that turned too much to one side. His eyes, small and bloodshot, were leering. She loftily ignored him.

The other, for all his brusque manner, was a pleasanter contrast. He had a pirate look, to be sure, but it was a hale and well-formed pirate. His shirt was opened carelessly to reveal a tanned naked chest. *And too much hair,* she thought confusedly. *Too much maleness.*

"Fair." He was remarking her now. "But too bossy, Brock. Aye, and too young for aught but teasing," he added, noting how she shrank from his companion.

Curtains he wanted, for his ship's cabins. To be delivered to the *Star Victory,* moored at Waterloo Dock. She was sailing on the next afternoon's tide, bound for America.

"By noon, little mistress." His eyes swept briefly over her white throat—then lower, across her breasts. "And see you don't dally with the dockhands and bring the stuff late, or I'll worry your backside myself."

She flushed with outrage at his insolence and stammered an angry reply, but they had already left.

Susanna found herself staring at the invoice in her hand. *Captain Jed Taylor* the bold signature read. *Curse him,* she thought, *but he's a handsome, mocking devil.* She could still feel his eyes on her, causing shivers where she had been flushed a moment before.

A look like that, why, it's like he was touching me, she thought in wonder. Those feelings which had increased in intensity lately overtook her now. It had something to do with the changes in her body. Her breasts had grown fuller and stood out like ripe young fruit. Her hips and flanks had changed as well. They were rounder now, swelling out from her narrow waist. And her hands at night sometimes stole to that most secret place between her legs, where it seemed the sweetest pleasure imaginable lay centered.

She knew it was all part of the thing girls whispered about in little groups—thrilling, forbidden whispers that caused Susanna to glance furtively sometimes at the trousers of the boys she used to play with. It was so confusing, this growing up, and distressing, too, on occasion—the looks that men gave her. And sometimes —like now, she had to confess—a bit exciting, too.

"Daydreaming again, Susanna?" Her mother's sharp voice caused her to start, guiltily dismissing those vague but delightful imaginings.

Without further words, her mother swept past, escorting her grave and lordly visitor to the shop's front door. He was dressed in a rusty-brown frock coat and a peculiarly tall black hat. He inspected her fleetingly as he passed, his eyes a cool and penetrating gray, his silver hair lending an additional dignity to his form.

"Reverend," her mother said, offering the stranger her hand in parting. "I cannot thank you enough, and especially for the book."

"It is my calling, sister," he replied. "Bless you, and may we see you soon among our brethren!"

"What does he mean by that, Mother?" Susanna asked. This man had spent the entire morning closeted with her mother in the back parlor, and Mistress Jones had a stiff look about her that signified a mind made up, some great decision reached.

"Susanna," she said, with the aid of imparting a matter of utmost gravity, "today did I commit myself to join the Church of the Latter-Day Saints."

Susanna accepted the news unmoved. Her mother had a penchant for religion and had already converted and then departed from three other churches. She had lately and zealously attended the meetings of the godly sect new in England—the Mormons—of whom this last august reverend had been a missionary.

Their religious observances were quite in keeping with the Nonconformist air sweeping England in the year 1846. But one shadow of scandal attached to them. It was rumored these godly men practiced polygamy in America. And that Joseph Smith, their martyred founder, had taken to himself a score of brides, and had bred by them threescore children.

Her mother's thin, bony face seemed drawn and worried. "Your stepfather will oppose me in this," she told her daughter. She chose her words carefully. "He will take it as an affront and may be in a temper."

Puzzled by her words, Susanna attended now, nervously smoothing her hands over the fabric of her dress.

"When he's in his cups, he can be . . . difficult. And list, daughter. If he should threaten you in any way, you must run and call for help."

Mistress Jones had never minded her daughter much; but on this, the day of her planned departure, she felt compelled, in part by guilt and part by nature, to regard this offspring of hers. Susanna was just seventeen, just awakening to the power of her own womanhood.

Susanna had been born the undesired product of her mother's youthful indiscretion, a brief affair with the son of a noble house. Mistress Jones was then in the spring of her own years, a sweet, buxom lass newly in service. And she had been undone by first the compliments and later the caresses of Jonathan Hungerford, the younger son.

She's a bit like I was then. the older woman mused. *But nay, 'tis his gold curls and stubborn jaw. His eyes too, green like emeralds and slanty like a cat's. She's a quick word for the boys already. and a figure to match. Aye, and no one to watch her when I go.*

Well, I've done the best I could. She's had more schooling than ever I had—she can read and write and cipher as good as any. And she'll have the shop for her living if her father never sends for her. For a brief instant only, she indulged herself with the vision of another figure with tousled curls and brilliant eyes. But that was long past, and served no purpose now.

"Daughter," she spoke, sounding suddenly weary, and placed her hand on Susanna's arm. "Take care of yourself, and mind you guard yourself about the men. There's many as would take advantage of you, being so young and unknowing." She sighed heavily, her speech made. "Go now and rest."

Relieved of her duties to the store, Susanna padded through the back parlor and noted the heavy black book, a gift to her mother from the missionary. She paused for a moment and ran her fingers over the smooth black binding. Embossed on the impressive cover was the title: *The Book of Mormon.*

The heavy volume lay atop an opened letter, and she was startled to note the first letters of her own name exposed on the face of the envelope. She seized it in amazement, only to be shocked further by its contents. The letter was brief and courteous:

It grieves us to inform you of the untimely passing of your father's elder brother, the former Earl of Wye. We are presently ascertaining the whereabouts of Jonathan Hungerford as his immediate presence is required for his proper succession to the Earldom and Family Estates. Our offices cite him last on the Eastern coast of America, and our search will continue from there.

Your quarterly cheque has been honored in good order, and we hope your studies continue to progress.

Very sincerely &c.

M. W. Leighton & Sons,

Executors for the Estate of Wye

For a moment, the room spun before her eyes. Susanna righted herself and slowly began to comprehend the meaning. *She* had never received cheques from her father's estate. *She* had known nothing of his background—nay, little but his name, which she shared despite her bastardy.

Her eyes focused now on the dingy curtain that separated the back parlor from the shop front, which her mother now tended. Susanna was suddenly quite still and sober as her mind worked to assimilate this new and terrible knowledge of unquestionable betrayal.

She has let me grow up unfit ever to be my father's daughter. She has stolen from me my birthright, kept me ignorant of all I might have been. Her green eyes blazed with passionate hate for a long moment, then suddenly squeezed shut against hot tears. *And she's the only one I ever had. All these years, she's the only one was true kin to me, and she never cared about me. All this time, she's never cared.*

Susanna carefully seated herself in a stuffed chair and remained there as the long evening shadows gave way to dark. Her mother had locked the shop and passed without seeing her sitting still as stone a few feet away. The events of the day had been too much. She wanted only the peace of darkness and silence around her.

Later there were voices raised in anger, sounding from the upstairs bedroom. Somewhere a door slammed and footsteps came hurriedly down the stairs. A light was switched on. Roused from her fitful dozing, Susanna awakened to find her mother gathering some papers from the table. The missionary's book was too heavy, the older woman decided. She'd have to send for it later. Then she saw her daughter, and for an instant, neither spoke. Susanna stared at the suitcase on the floor.

"I go to join the mission, Susanna." Her mother's voice was agitated. She flashed her daughter a brief pleading look, like an apology. Then she was gone.

I don't care, Susanna thought fiercely. *I don't care a whit. It doesn't matter anymore. No more can happen now.* But she chilled on hearing a heavy tread on the floor above her head. Her stepfather was coming down the stairs.

Martin Jones was a disappointed man. A wounded man, deserted by his own proper wife. He nicely ignored the fact that he had married her because she was connected to a wealthy house, because she received four handsome cheques each year, and because she had bought this shop with her savings. For those small considerations he had wedded her in her lowly state and given her bastard his honorable name. He poured another tumblerful of whiskey and mumbled to himself of the injustice of the world. That *this* should be the reward for his philanthropy.

His thoughts strayed now to Susanna, who had stayed all night downstairs and strangely quiet. Aye, she'd plumped out these recent months like a pretty piece of pastry. He'd never got proper hold of her, though, with his wife around. Martin Jones found himself drunkenly grinning and started for the stairs.

There might be some consolation for him after all.

* * *

Susanna had not stirred from the chair. Her throat was very dry, the muscles of her back and legs strained with tension. Her cap was undone and hung loose around her neck. The solitary lamp cast little light and made the objects it touched seem even shabbier. All except Susanna's hair, which, like a separate presence, caught and reflected the lamplight in a show of glory, like a field of ripe wheat in the early morning sun.

The light offered no warmth, and the ashes behind the hearth's iron grating were cold. As cold as her body, caught in a frozen panic as her stepfather half-stumbled into the parlor and seated himself with ridiculous pomp upon the sofa.

His almost clownish coordination did not fool her. Once before, when he'd come late from his pub and drunk as a lord, he'd staggered into her bedroom and had thrown himself atop her, smothering her sleep-befuddled face with slobbering sour-mouthed kisses. When she began to resist and kick at him, he'd slapped her face, leaving a purple bruise that had lasted days. He had pretended surprise and shock when his wife appeared, roused from sleep by the sounds of struggle. He'd lied and laughed, saying he was so drunk he'd mistaken the bedroom for his own, and Susanna for his own sweet wife.

Susanna did not gainsay him. Her mother would not have believed her.

"Your mother's left us," he said, in the voice of an honorable man wronged. "She's going to America is what she's aiming. She tried to book passage on that Mormon ship, the *Star Victory*, but they was full up and couldn'a take her. Now she's run to the mission to wait the next ship." He expelled a long sigh that carried the stench of his whiskey-sodden breath to Susanna, sitting a frighteningly short distance away. "There's just the two of us now, daughter," he continued, eyeing her hungrily. "Now come give your old dad a kiss, for he's sorely tried this night and in need of a bit of comforting-like."

"I've no comfort to give you, for I'll be leaving myself come morning." Susanna's voice sounded thin and high in her own ears.

"Nay and I couldn't be letting you do that, now. For there's ill come to a young girl left to her own devices. What kind of proper father would I be, leaving my poor stepdaughter to the cruel hardships of the world?" He wetted his lips and licked the spittle from the corners of his mouth. His bleary eyes focused themselves on the soft curve of her blouse. "Now, daughter . . ."

"A proper father would not eye his daughter so," she snapped, caught between fear and outrage.

His face took on an ugly look. The mask of sincerity slipped from his bloated face. His heavy jowls tightened. He stood up, lurched and righted himself, muttering oaths and invectives. His face screwed up in a hideous sneer.

"And what airs are you putting on, *my lady?* Think I'm not good enough for your high-and-mighty bastard blue-blood? Thinking to give naught to me who's fed and sheltered you these past six years? And what do you give your boyfriends, pray? A bit for them, to be sure. I know the wiles of you young wenches. A feel or two, if not more, and they do nothing to keep you, do they?" He was coming closer. "Just what do you think is so precious under your shimmy, heh? Well, we'll just find out."

Susanna had slid from the chair and was backing toward the door, her mind bent only on getting away. In two surprisingly quick steps, he caught her, locking her arms at her sides in a powerful grip. He proceeded to drag her, struggling for breath, toward the couch. Flinging her down, he held her hands in one brutal fist above her head, and subdued her wildly kicking legs with the weight of his body. With his free hand, he seized the hem of her skirt and raised it waist-high, laying her smooth thighs bare and exposing her flimsy cotton drawers. Her body twisted and thrashed madly in a futile effort to shake him off. He struck her fiercely, and she quieted suddenly, as if in resignation. "There's a good lass," he said, his eyes glinting with lust. He released her hands and she lay all but motionless, her eyes following his actions with the look of a trapped bird. He turned aside, certain of her now, and both his hands went to the buckle of his belt.

In his single moment of relaxed wariness, Susanna acted. Her body was a blur of movement as she leaped from the couch. But he was still between her and the door! He had swung round and was advancing, his expression vicious. Her hands searched blindly for a weapon and encountered the heavy black book her mother had left behind. Terror lent strength to her and she lifted the book high over her head.

Martin Jones took on a look of shocked amazement just before *The Book of Mormon* slammed against the side of his head.

Susanna had fallen back from the effort of her swing. Slowly she raised herself to her knees, banding her arms tightly across her chest, her body trembling. She knew that, for the present at least, she was safe, and gradually her shivering stopped and her sensibilities returned to normal. She regarded the prostrate figure of her stepfather with undisguised loathing. *The pig,* she thought, shivering at the narrowness of her escape. *The filthy loathsome pig.* Then her eyes caught sight of a small splash of crimson on the hearthstones near his head.

She crept forward, unsure of him. His eyes still held a fixed and glassy stare, his brows still raised up in that final surprise, like a hideous caricature. Susanna gave an anguished cry and shook her hand like a rag. Her fingers were sticky with blood.

Her thoughts were wild, chaotic. *I've got to run,* she thought in frenzy. *Get away. Now. No, in the morning.* Her mind was frantic, disjointed. *I've killed him, God, oh, God, help me. God won't help me, I've murdered him. I didn't mean him to die, Lord, I didn't mean . . . But I'm glad. I'm glad he's dead. He would have— Oh, God, I can't stay here—they'll come for me and they'll hang me in the town square—they'll put a rope around my neck—I can't stay here and where can I go—where. . . ?"*

Her eyes, racing like her thoughts, stopped at the sight of an unfamiliar parcel, bulkily wrapped in brown paper. The ship's curtains—the ship, moored at Waterloo Dock and bound for America! And her father was there—or at least he might be. And even if he wasn't, she had to be somewhere—somewhere out of Liverpool, even out of England. They'd come looking for her. They'd track her down.

Suppressing her panic, she grasped the parcel and fled into the empty street.

Stumbling, almost dazed, she made her way toward the harbor. She hid in a darkened alleyway as a copper strolled by on patrol, then continued hurriedly when he was safely past. Somehow she arrived at the docks and spent the night huddled among some crates stored at the side of a warehouse.

With the first gray light of morning, the ships stood out in silhouette. The brigs far out in the harbor bobbed gently in the Mersey tide. A few tugs squatted close to the docks. And at Waterloo the silent *Star Victory,* lashed to the dock by snakelike hawsers, weaved in the water where tiny waves lapped and whispered against her sides. Susanna regarded her with awe. She was a magnificent vessel with her tall masts in stark relief towering against the sky.

Within the hour, the sun was well up, and navvies were busy loading the ships with cargo. Fascination overcoming her fear, Susanna watched as crates of chickens and geese, sacks of potatoes, ripe apples, flour, sugar, and tea, and casks full of ale were ported across the narrow gangplank of the *Star Victory*. She heard laughter and saw a pig on a broken tether chased up the platform with young Tom Austin, a local laboring boy, armed with a stick and close behind.

Susanna started to sidle away, not wanting Tom to see her, but she was too late. Cupping his hands to his mouth, he called to her, then threw up his hand in greeting.

"You're up early, Susanna," he exclaimed, "And what fancy brings you to the docks?" Tom had always liked Susanna.

"No fancy, Tom," she answered, a trifle nervously. She gestured to the parcel in her arms. "I'm delivering an order to the captain of this ship ahead. Lace curtains for the cabins."

"Aye," Tom nodded, "that would be Mr. Taylor, the American of the *Star Victory*. 'Tis warranted he's a good-looking gentleman," he added, noticing how she flushed on hearing his name. "Ah, Susanna," the boy addressed her with mock reproach. "How will us local boys have a chance with you against the charms of foreign gentlemen? Why haven't you ever come dancing with me, lass? No, don't bother with reasons now. 'Tis too late for the best of it."

"What do you mean, *too late?*" Susanna asked nervously. "Too late for what?"

"Why, and haven't you heard? Our town's best band is off to America. Captain Pitts and his brass players were converted all in a lump by that missionary chap. They're all Mormons now, and off like the rest to some new land in West America. The whole ship's been chartered to them, didn't you know? All full of those funny tall caps and sober dresses, they are.

"But stay a bit, won't you, after you've done your errand? Captain Pitts has promised a dockside concert before he leaves. It would be great fun to hear it with you."

"I'm sorry, Tom, truly," she began. Her voice broke. "Oh, Tom, you've always been kind to me . . ."

"Why, sweet, what's the matter?" His freckled face clouded with concern. "Come, you're all a-shiver now. Tell me what the trouble is. Is't running away you're about?"

He held her to himself while she sobbed out the events of the night before. Her story told, she regarded him pleadingly, her emerald eyes awash with the brilliant sheen of tears. "I must be on that ship, Tom," she said in desperation. "I must get away to America. Will you help me?"

"Aye," he said, regarding her fair form with a private longing that he took some pains to hide. In the sunshine her milk-white skin took on the translucence of alabaster. Her eyes had darkened like rich beryl under the pale gold lashes. Her head scarcely cleared his shoulder—just a slip of a girl she was. But brave, and just now, in sore trouble.

"I'll have to help you up to the lifeboat," he told her, pointing to several rows of small craft secured to the ship's starboard side. "You can hide there till the ship is under way." Two men had appeared on the ship's deck. "As soon as they pass," he whispered.

Holding her arm, he guided her quickly along the pier where the *Star Victory* lay secured. "Taylor will throw you off if you're found in port," he said. "It's best you stay hidden for the first day's sailing. I'm going to secure the canvas, so rap on the boat tomorrow and someone will release you. And give me those bloody curtains." He took the parcel from her arms and led her across the plank.

The way across the deck was easy. They rounded the rear mast and passed a small hatchway. But Susanna's heart sank at the sight of the lifeboat itself, raised high on its davits. The gunwale was well over her head. Tom Austin paid no heed to her dismay, but scrambled up to release the tarpaulin, secured by its grommets and tied with heavy knots. In seconds he'd pried loose a knot and opened a flap of canvas. Stepping down to help Susanna, he noticed her good crinoline skirt with its wire hoops for the first time.

"By the mass," he swore, "did you think you were going to tea?"

Susanna looked down mutely at her skirts. Tom drew a knife from his back pocket, and in a single motion, slit the offending garment from waist to hem, tossing it into the boat. Except for her short white bloomers cut wide at the thigh, she was naked from the waist down. His hands flew to her thighs and she cast a terrified look over her shoulder to see that no navvies hung about to witness the scene. Yet her legs felt strangely free and unencumbered, naked in the air, with the wind from the river caressing her flesh. For an instant, frozen like a photograph in time and space, she stood proudly like a gallant little statue, facing the roiling water with the wind blowing through her hair.

Then Tom swung her around, his hands almost rough on her shoulders, to face him squarely. "Susanna!" he said desperately. "Is this what you really want? Must you go off so far?" His voice hesitated—then the words came all in a rush. "Will you not stay, Susanna? I could hide you and we'd leave together later . . . " His speech trailed off. She was shaking her head sadly.

"I must go on this ship," she said finally. "I am truly sorry, Tom."

He recovered quickly. "Step up then, my lady," he

said, cupping his hand for her foot. "This way to America." With that he lifted her up until she could grasp the side of the boat and pull herself in. He followed, climbing quickly, and leaned toward the boat to secure the canvas once more.

"You'll be all right," he assured the frightened girl. "There's a water cask and my bit of lunch in the fore-peak, and the drain in the stern is open—there'll be air to breathe." He looked at her anxiously, and she pulled his arm toward her, raising his hand to her mouth." He straightened up, smiled a shy farewell, and pulled the canvas shut. "God keep you safe, Susanna," he whispered.

Climbing down, he thought he heard male laughter, and somewhere behind him, the slam of a tankard. The door of the rear hatchway closed, and footsteps rounded the corner.

Brock Cowler, second mate of the ship *Star Victory*, appeared to have enjoyed his beer early this morning. He belched loudly and contentedly, but scowled at the sight of Tom Austin, standing nonchalantly on ship-deck, with a package of some sort in his arm.

"What have you got there?" he demanded, glaring up at Tom. He hated looking up at other men.

"For your captain," Tom answered evenly. "I have these for him from the Jones Family Drapers."

Brock continued to eye him suspiciously. "And what of the girl," he asked slyly. "Her what's supposed to do the delivering?"

"I don't know," Tom replied. "I met her at the dock, and she asked me to please bring them on board."

"They ain't paid for, you know," Brock offered.

"I'll see that the money's delivered—that is, if your captain honors his debts. The girl seemed in a hurry to go somewhere."

Brock snorted. "Sounds like her, the snippety bag-gage. Scared to get her rump wet—you know what I

mean?" He leered in Tom's direction. "Yeah, I see you
do. . . ."

"Taylor pays his way, all right. Here's your money
and hand them over, boy. You'll be wanting to get off
the ship. Otherwise you'll get yourself snaggled by a
a Mormon." He snickered.

As Tom turned to leave the ship, Brock called after
him. "Oh, and—when you see her—give the little filly
old Brock's best." He laughed as though he'd just
finished telling a splendid joke.

2

HOURS HAD PASSED. Susanna crouched inside the lifeboat, miserably aware of the damp, hard wood of the boat's floor pressing against her knees. The belly of the boat was deep, but not deep enough to permit her to stand. The canvas covering stopped all but the thinnest rays of light, and she had long discarded thoughts of sight. Touching and hearing—that was all.

At first her spirit had suffered in the dark, and for a time, she feared madness. The boat was a wooden cage with fetid air, and the canvas bound across it made her a prisoner. She doubted she could reach the knots even if she'd dared to try. She felt screams rising from her belly, and she rocked back and forth on her knees in what seemed an ever decreasing box of black space.

But she'd forced herself to breath deeply, fighting the lure of hysteria, the awful need to scream and beat back the walls. After a while she began to listen, straining her ears for the voices and activities outside her vision. She wooed her sanity with amusements and made up images to go with the sounds around her.

A steady tramp of feet signaled the boarding of passengers. There would be forty, she remembered Tom saying. The loudest was a female voice. Its owner had apparently dropped her parasol, and she swore mightily at it. On its evident return, however, the voice took on a sweet, coquettish air. "Thank you, reverend," it had said. "You're a darb."

A firm, precise baritone passed her hideout, but footsteps, echoing hollowly on the ship deck, carried it swiftly out of range. Susanna thought she recognized the captain, Jed Taylor. Even the bold booted tread sounded like him.

By this time, Susanna had thought of using her ruined crinoline as a cushion of sorts, on top of the stuffed canvas bolsters she'd discovered on the floor of the boat. But nothing could keep her dry. Her skin was slick with sweat from the close, stale air. Even her cotton drawers were damp and clung to her thighs and seat. It was hot and almost foul, but at intervals she would lift her face close to the edge of the tarp and suck in sweet, fresh air.

While newly converted Mormons entertained her with their conversations, Susanna managed to stretch out along the floor of the boat. To relieve her cramped muscles, she began bending her elbows and knees, lifting her arms and legs up toward the canvas top. She tried to remember the contortions she'd performed (along with eighteen other hapless girls) at Miss Phipps' Academy, and giggled to herself at the recollection. At least her activities were keeping her calm.

Finally she heard the heavy engines of the great ship start up and felt the *Star Victory* lurching backward. The engines bellowed as they reversed and pulled her forward down the river.

Susanna's heart leaped as the first pull relaxed and the ship began to glide like some gigantic and matronly sea creature. America would be a new world to her, and she would be all-new in it. She would find her real father there, and he would love her and keep her with him. Contrary thoughts came. That she would fail to find him, or worse still, that he would not want her if she succeeded.

Her musing wandered from the dismal to the practical. She was hungry. By feeling her way to the forepeak, she was able to lay hands on Tom's paper lunch bag, which contained two sandwiches soaked in bacon drippings, a whole ripe tomato, and several biscuits. She devoured the sandwiches gratefully, licking the grease from her fingers, and made short work of the tomato, which she ate like an apple, letting the juices drip unheeded down her chin. Two men were speaking from some place very close by. She tried to muffle the crunch of her teeth on the biscuits. Finally, for safety's sake, she stopped eating.

The first voice was incredulous. "Do you mean you've not heard what they done to Joseph Smith?" The speaker paused for emphasis. *"They cut his bloody head right off, is what they done.* Sliced through at the neck and rolled clear off his body. Why, if we was Catholics 'stead of Mormons, Joseph Smith would be a saint well as a martyr!"

Susanna felt faint. She tasted bile in her mouth, and suppressed the need to vomit. *Decapitated.* Susanna could only think of John the Baptist and the beautiful, wicked Salome, dancing, dancing all night, dancing out her licentious pleasures and corruptions on a stage that held a throne.

But the headless victim—this Joseph Smith—this piece of history struck nearer than any Bible story. This was a recent horror of her own time.

Susanna actually knew very little about the Mormons. The people around her addressed each other as "brother" and "sister," and spoke reverently of Brigham Young, who, ever since Smith's death, had led the Mormons. Susanna knew of Young because he'd preached recently in England and her mother had gone to hear him. She said he was a man of greatness. A man of vision.

Another pair of converts, more sober than the first speakers, engaged in talk close by. "Do you think we'll have peace yet awhile in Nauvoo?" a woman's voice asked.

"We must trust Elder Shuttleworth's word that we will," her companion replied, adding grimly, "If not, well, the church has the means to defend itself."

The first woman spoke again disapprovingly. "The reverend longs for women more than battle at the moment, I do believe. See him with that awful woman yonder!"

It seemed that the reverend and Elder Shuttleworth were the same man—an American missionary for the Mormons. Susanna recalled the solemn gray-haired stranger who had visited her mother. Could that be the man?

The rest of the things she overhead—church politics and church prejudices—she held to little account. They had nothing to do with her. She found herself straining to catch the sound of a particular man's voice, a particular booted walk. But she guessed he was spending most of his time in the forecastle, directing course, not gossiping like the passengers wandering about the deck.

She was anxious to reveal herself, and stand upright among the other people, but she held the temptation in check. Tom had told her she'd be safe in the morning, and she resigned herself to waiting in her cramped little space.

Gradually the voices and footfalls drifted away. It was evidently growing darker, and even in the lifeboat, Susanna could feel the air was much chillier. She was grateful for the passage of the hours. And she had been without sleep so long.

Her last drowsy thoughts were of the captain, thoughts that inspired a sweet curve on her lips. She had a feeling there would be order and some measure of security for her aboard his ship.

She had no inkling how wrong she would be.

First there was a blast of cool air. Then, before her eyes could focus in the unaccustomed moonlight, a man's hand clamped her lips against her teeth. Before she could struggle upright, Brock Cowler, second mate of the *Star Victory,* had straddled her, pinning her prone under his own body. "I thought you was in here when I saw the boy a-foolin' with the tarp," he said jeering. "Just couldn't keep away from old Brock, could ya now, darlin'?" She whimpered helplessly against his hand, trying to open her mouth, trying to bite. He saw the trick and ripped a piece of fabric from her crinoline, then stuffed it into her mouth.

Her eyes blazed with dread and shame. She was panic-stricken by her almost-nakedness, and half-crushed under his body. His eyes missed nothing from her soft white thighs to the fragile buttons of her blouse, damp and clinging to her breasts. He bent his head so close that she could feel the sharp bristles of his unshaven cheek scratching the tender skin of her neck. She gathered herself in a concerted effort to dislodge him, but again he forestalled her. He bent one arm behind her back and pressed it upward. Any movement would result in agony. "Tut, tut," he said insidiously, "don't fret yourself, little bagage. Don't be so *anxious.* Old Brock is gonna give you what you've been wanting."

Tears sprang unbidden from her eyes. Here was no weapon, no escape. His voice was fraught with malice; his words doomed her.

He was enjoying his little game. "D'you know how our fine captain deals with stowaways?" He gave her no opportunity to reply. "You want to be flogged and then *keelhauled?*" He saw the look on her face and gloated. "Not a pretty way to die, by the keelhaul."

He was muttering now, close to her ear. "So you'll just be real nice to old Brock."

His free hand unfastened his breeches and pulled them to his thighs. He almost willed her to watch his actions, but she averted her eyes. He fell upon her blouse. The buttons gave easily. Her nipples tightened from the shock of exposure, and she sobbed, helpless even to shield herself. The pressure on her right arm made her whimper with pain. He was reminding her.

His callused hand scraped back and forth over her thigh. "Your turn, missy," he said, and grabbing the edge of her final garment, tore it from her body. Now she was all naked. In torment, she clenched her legs tightly together, but Brock was through playing.

His knee kicked brutally against her thigh. "Spread 'em!" he growled.

He grunted obscenely on his first attempt to storm her virgin passage. Trapped beneath him, terrified into acquiescence, Susanna tried to dismiss her mind from her body, tried to deny the violations being practiced upon her. She closed her eyes upon tears and prayed for oblivion.

Instead, she felt the tearing of tissues inside her as Brock succeeded in his vile assault. Even the gag could not silence her heart-rending moans of pain and degradation. All heedless, Brock plunged viciously forward in a final thrust—and finished.

Her teeth had worked their way around the gag, and her lips were bleeding, almost bitten through. She tried to scream and his palm descended, forcing its way into her mouth and pushing the cloth against the back of her throat.

Her eyes bulged as she choked, and she saw he was very drunk, his eyes unfocused, his pupils shrunk to pinpoints. His hand, seemingly ungoverned, was suffocating her. The thought that she might die—that he could kill her—brought her back to her senses. Moving slowly, she pulled her arm from his slackened grip and brought it to the hand that was choking her. She tugged at his wrist and his eyes began to focus on his actions. His hand shifted from her mouth to her naked breast, and he spoke in honeyed tones. "Now, now," he said, "you're not going to do any screaming, are you?"

She lay utterly silent.

"You liked that, didn't you, missy?"

A voice that was not hers answered dully, "Yes."

He waded up her blouse and drawers and tossed them into her lap. "You can get dressed—in a minute."

His hand probed at the juncture of her thighs. There was no protest. Her expression was fathomless, like that of a stone face. "You're a sweet one," he was saying, moving his hand over and across her violated sex. "All slick and goosey-like."

"I'll be leaving now," he said, releasing her. Just like nothing happened.

"So you just stay tight and cozy, little missy, and wait for old Brock. He'll take good care of you." At this he sniggered meaningfully. "I'll bring you some grub tomorrow," he added from outside the boat. "You'll keep till then."

With that he pulled the canvas taut, retied the grommet ropes, and descended.

Alone again in the black hole of the boat, Susan bent to examine herself. The insides of her thighs were stained with Brock's discharge mingled with her virgin blood. And it hurt there, when she tried to wipe herself. She choked off a whimper. She felt torn and ravaged inside, but she couldn't cry out. After what had happened, there was no one to help her.

What would her father ever think of her, sullied and used as she was? What a fine lady his daughter would make, the whore of dirty scum. She brought her hands up slowly to her face, feeling the salty trails of tears along her cheeks. Her own wrists were smudged from the grime of his hands. Now she needed a bathroom, and irrationally, that struck her the hardest of all. She began to crawl, scarcely troubling to mute the wracking sobs that shook her slender frame. Reaching the stern, she squatted as close as she could to the opened drain.

She continued her toilet at the fore of the craft. Dampening her rag of crinoline with water from the cask, she dabbed gingerly at her wounded groin, and wiped her thighs clean. But her breasts and shoulders were dirty, too—befouled by Brock's slobbering kisses.

Her control suddenly snapped, and, wailing, she upturned the cask and showered her naked body with the remaining water. With both hands she began scouring her flesh, scrubbing until her skin was chafed and raw. She had to force herself to put on her damp, soiled garments. At last she curled up on her side against the canvas cushions, and, like a miracle of mercy, exhaustion brought her sleep.

3

She was back in the draper's shop, but things looked very different. A wedding ceremony was taking place in the back parlor, which had swelled to mammoth proportions, and Susanna was the bride. The tall Mormon reverend who had converted Mistress Jones was asking her, "Do you take this man . . . ?" but he gestured toward a platter which held a hideous bloody head.

Shrieking, she fled, pursued by some horrid creature which detached itself from the gaping throng. It looked like a monstrous vulture, but had the ugly, jeering face of Brock. She stumbled up a steep and rocky mountain path and saw her father in mortal combat with a grizzly bear. Missing her footing, she fell upon the cold stone floor of a morgue. Her mother, standing a few feet away, was assuring the policeman, who was Captain Jed Taylor, that Susanna was indeed the murderer of Martin Jones, whose ghastly corpse she fondled as she spoke. Susanna must be caught and brought to justice, she said.

Then she was standing at the gallows steps, prodded forward by heavy arms at her back. They placed a hood over her head, but slipped the noose under her bare foot and up between her legs. The crowd cheered and pelted her with offal, and Brock taunted her, saying she'd be hanged where it would do the most good.

She saw her father urge the grizzly bear forward to attack her.

Her own screams roused her.

The consciousness to which she woke was little better than her nightmare. Voices were murmuring all around her hiding place.

"I tell you there's someone trapped in that top boat. I heard screams . . ."

"—Send for a crewman!"

"—Where's the captain?"

"Stand to one side. I'm going to find out," a male voice said. "Whoever or whatever it is might be hurt." Susanna heard the footsteps climbing toward her, and resigned herself to her fate.

The sunlight blinded her and for long moments she could not see the face of her rescuer. She felt a soft beard—it was reddish-brown—curling forward from his chin and brushing her forehead. His hands had reached for her waist and helped her from the boat. Now she clung to him for support as they carefully made their way down.

Some fifteen onlookers had gathered by now, milling about the deck, curious and eager to have a look at her.

Pathetic in defeat, she faced them all. Too sick with the humiliation of past events, she hadn't strength to care that her crinoline was in tatters or that half the buttons from her blouse were gone. She turned to thank her benefactor, who bowed to her and doffed his tall Mormon hat as though she were a lady. "I'm James Leverton, my dear," he informed her, extending his hand.

"Susanna . . . Hungerford," she replied in turn, firmly resolving to put all that was Martin Jones behind her.

For all his apparent agility, James Leverton had weathered over fifty years. His features had a craggy look about them, set in an almost-homely face. Though his hair was thinning, his beard was thick and handsomely groomed. His eyes, a brownish-hazel, regarded her kindly. "If you have need of assistance, please remember me." He had taken fleeting stock of her condition. "Forlorn little lass," he'd added silently.

A figure of obvious authority approached, and Susanna was dismayed to recognize the captain. "What the hell is going on here?" he demanded curtly. Then he saw Susanna, on display before the crowd. He swore softly, recognizing her. "Well, I'll be damned—the draper's girl!" His steely-blue eyes raked over her noting the skirt slit to the waist, the disheveled blouse, the tangled mass of gold hair. She was mortified under his scrutiny, recognizing for the first time how she must appear, what he must be thinking. "A bit older than I thought at first," he commented tartly.

She hated him for his thoughts, his lofty judgments. But feeling any emotion at all came hard to her, numbed as she was by so many horrors in so brief a time. Any moment now they would bind her and throw her overboard to drown in the wake of the ship. He—*he* would order it done, and no one would stop him. He was the captain. She tried to gather her strength, to approach her execution with some manner of dignity. But the strength was all quite gone, and the sun suddenly seemed to dim in her eyes. She swayed . . .

Moments later, when she came to, she was being carried down the dark entryway of the forecastle hatch. She could scarcely warrant it. She was in Jed Taylor's arms. *Where was he taking her?*

Her cheek lay quietly against the fresh linen of his shirt, and when she breathed, she caught the scent of spicy soap mixed with the masculine odors of his body. Strangely, she found herself dreading the moment that he would set her down.

It came soon enough. He kicked open a cabin door

and dropped her unceremoniously upon the narrow cot. Seconds later, a boy's head appeared in the doorway. He seemed to wait on the captain, who gestured him forward. Stiff and proper as an admiral he was, saluting the captain smartly. And scarcely twelve years old.

"Sir?" The voice was half-tenor, half-soprano.

A little smile softened the captain's face. "Fetch Maidie Cross, Davy," he told the lad. "Bring her here."

"You have an admirer, sir," Susanna remarked, trying to engage the captain in conversation.

His eyes turned a darker blue to glare at her, and he responded in a tone laced with sarcasm. "But not so *many* as you. May I presume to request, madam, that should you ever decide to stow-away on one of my ships again, you will kindly dress yourself in a manner that will not incite a riot among my passengers!"

She was spared answering by the arrival of Maidie Cross. The girl who now entered was a few years older than Susanna, and very plain except for a magnificent mane of bright red hair. She shuffled awkwardly into the room, but her pace quickened when she saw Susanna on the cot. Turning to Davy, she said sharply, "Call for a tub and tell the cook to heat some water." Her attention returned to Susanna. "Poor thing, she's all cut up and bruised."

"Just see to her quick," Taylor said tersely. "Clean her up. I suppose she can sleep the afternoon in your quarters. We'll bunk her in the brig with Davy tonight." He turned quickly on his heel and slammed the door behind him.

It wasn't till long after the bath, and after she had gently ministered ointment to Susanna's scrapes and bruises that Maidie left her. By then, Susanna, her body clean and snug in a fresh flannel nightdress, was curled up on her side asleep in Maidie's bed. Maidie waited for a time at the side of the bed, content to watch the sleeping figure that looked so peaceful now in repose. Not at all like the terrified chewed-up little creature of an hour before. *What a perfect little beauty,* she thought, noticing the sweet curve of her cheek, the gold cloud of hair against the pillow. But though her hands had washed and tended, Maidie did not reach out to touch her slender guest. That was a sleep she would not disturb.

When Susanna awoke, it was almost dusk of the second day's sailing. Several people were tramping about in the small corridor. Maidie rushed in, delighted to find Susanna awake. "Oh, you must come on deck," she said. Her eyes were shiny with excitement. "Captain Pitts and his band are giving a special concert, just because some of the passengers missed the one dockside yesterday. Oh, *do* come!" she urged. "It's going to be lovely."

Rejuvenated by sleep and comforted by Maidie's kindness, Susanna let her new friend coax her into a borrowed shift, and together the two girls joined the crowd waiting amidships for the music.

Except for the cooks preparing supper in the kitchens, almost everyone on the ship was in attendance. Susanna found she recognized the man called Elder Shuttleworth as the missionary in her mother's shop. He seemed to command the rapt attendance of small clusters of people, and, indeed, there were some who followed him as he strolled about, visiting various groups. She overheard a matronly convert say, "He is such a wonderfully *intense* man. His faith is a potent force among us."

Captain Taylor apparently was not so susceptible to the reverend's "potent force." The two men stood off to the side of the gathering. They seemed to be arguing. Susanna, who was not far from them, heard the reverend mutter, "Gentile!" as Taylor, after a mocking bow, departed. His crew had fetched his guitar, and were calling for him to start the entertainment. It seemed he was a favorite singer among his crew. It was odd, somehow to hear those rough sea-dog voices calling for music, but there they were—

"—A song, cap'n!"

"—Aye, Sir, gi'e us a ballad, sir!"

And, almost boyishly, the black-haired pirate consented. The guitar in his hand was of fine Spanish crafting, its table a fine spruce, the rosette inlaid in the most translucent mother-of-pearl. Bending his ear toward the guitar's belly, he tuned the strings. The people quieted. He whispered something to Captain Pitts, who nodded and turned to his string players. The violins began softly and the guitar joined them to carry the song. It was a much-loved ballad in England, attributed to Sir Walter Scott:

> *I have wandered all the day,*
> *Do not bid me farther stray.*
> *Gentle hearts of gentle kin,*
> *Take the wand'ring harper in!*
> *All my strength and all my art,*
> *Is to touch the gentle heart.*

It was a tender, sweet song and he sang it well. The crowd was touched. And they wanted another. Susanna's voice mingled with the others, calling for just one more. For a fleeting instant, his deep azure eyes seemed to seek her out, to capture her gaze. But it happened so quickly that she suspected her imagination. This was a traditional love song, and most of the passengers joined in the chorus. Even the Americans who didn't know the words managed to hum along.

> *Greensleeves was all my joy,*
> *And Greensleeves was my delight.*

There was no doubting it this time: he *was* looking at her. And smiling at her blushes.

> *Greensleeves was my heart of gold,*
> *And who but my lady Greensleeves?*

He sang through the verses, but left immediately after the song. Susanna found herself painfully aware of him —his looks, his physical presence that both alarmed and attracted her.

The balladeer having vanished, Captain Pitts advanced to the center. As always, his khaki uniform was spotless, and as he bowed to the eager assembly, the sun flared off the polished brass buttons of his jacket. Cut double-breasted and fitted in military fashion, it shaped his stocky torso like a corset.

"Friends," he began, his jovial smile extending toward them. "Captain Taylor has been so kind as to give us a bit of our England. Now, we are going to America, and they, too, have their songs!"

With that brief introduction, he addressed his players. The violinists had switched to banjos, which set the tone of the song with their merry strumming. The English all thought the tune jolly, and laughed at the silly simple words. Before long, they were trying to sing along, giggling and stumbling over the lyrics:

> *I come from Alabama wi' my banjo on my knee;*
> *I'se goin' to Lou'siana my true love for to see.*
> *It rained all night the day I left, the weather*
> *It was dry,*
> *The sun so hot, I froze to death,*
> *Susanna don't you cry.*

Much later, the song would take on personal meaning for many who listened to it for the first time that night. They would learn to sing it for courage and strength, with the wonderful folly of people who sang mockeries at hardships, while in the midst of them.

Susanna especially enjoyed the ditty, which honored her own name. Here she was, after all, on her way to America, and an American song seemed already to welcome her. She couldn't account for her own good fortune; she had anticipated a frightful death this morning, and this evening she was standing, clean and refreshed, in happy camaraderie with her fellow passengers.

The last chorus was ending:

Oh, Susanna! Oh, don't you cry for me,
For I come from Alabama with my banjo on my knee.

Susanna dismissed her apprehensions. She wanted to savor the hour.

The time passed too quickly. "Fellow passengers," called Captain Pitts. "Fellow pilgrims, brothers and sisters, it would give me great pleasure to close this concert with a hymn of our new church, 'Adam Ondi-Ahman.' Let us all sing together."

Violins introduced the joyous melody. The brasses were muted, and voices swelled up from the faithful, joining their spirits to the hymn. They sang of Eden with reverence and hope, and a feeling of brotherhood came to them with the song.

The cooks were screaming for supper to be served, and the company broke up, passing to the mess still singing softly and smiling to their fellows.

When Elder Shuttleworth rose to speak a few words before the meal, his talent for the converting of souls became evident. He was a powerful speaker, preaching the gospel of repentance in a voice ringing with conviction. The deep resonance of his oratory, the glow that seemed to fire in his gray eyes made it easy to imagine God passing on His own words through the worthy vessel of the reverend Elder. Susanna, raptly attending, resolved to learn more about this new religion.

Later, inside Maidie's cabin, Susanna could hear her hostess arguing with someone in the corridor. "It's damp in the brig," she was insisting, "and unhealthy." The other sounded like the captain. "There's no other room to spare, and I'll not have her roaming about all over the ship!"

"She'll stay in my quarters," Maidie countered. "I'm nursing Sister Willoughby, and I'll make up a pallet for myself when I come in." The captain swore roughly, but agreed.

Maidie was going to America to marry her Mormon fiancé. She confessed to Susanna that she was a "mail-order" bride. "I'd like to have babes," she confided, adding wryly, "if he'd still have the likes of me once he'd seen me."

She was adamant that Susanna should wear the white peignoir she'd brought for her own wedding night. It was a delicate lacy thing, though a little large and cut low over her breasts.

"It's way too hot for the flannel," Maidie said, gathering some remedies for Sister Willoughby. "I'll be late. You catch up on your sleep."

Susanna thought it was Maidie returning when, hours later, a key turned in the lock. She raised her head in sleepy greeting—

Jed Taylor entered and closed the door behind him.

She was shocked awake. So *that* was why she'd been spared. It all seemed suddenly startlingly clear: that in return for her life, the honorable captain had other payments to draw.

She didn't scream. Too much had happened to her. And the captain's word was law on the ship; she would find no redress. Her green eyes narrowed to slits of hate. "Beast!" she cried. He was approaching the cot.

"Why, what matter, little mistress?" he said mockingly. "When I've just come a-visiting." He sat boldly on the edge of her bed and stared down. Then, calmly and deliberately, he drew the bedcovers from her body, revealed in rosy hues against white lace. His fingers traced the edging on the bodice of her gown. "I was thinking," he whispered softly, "to more closely appreciate those charms that you see so fit to display."

He was kissing her breast through the fabric of the gown, but she was stiff, unyielding. The lacerating pain of her encounter with Brock was still fresh in her mind. Oh, but she didn't want to die! Offering no resistance, she lay back, dreading. She only hoped it would not hurt so much, that he would be done quickly.

He seemed in no great hurry. With the same sure motions as before, he pulled down the straps of her gown and undid the satin ribbon. The bodice slipped to her waist. His vision fixed on her breasts. "Pretty," he murmured, stroking the softness of them. Then he was watching her face, which betrayed nothing.

"Don't you like me, Susanna?" he whispered against her ear.

Her eyes blazed up hot with fury and fear. *"I hate you!"* she shrilled. She pounded with her fists against his chest, and he laughed. Laughed and pinned her wrists against the bedding, then pressed his smiling lips against her throat. He was kneeling above her on the bed and chuckling. "Perhaps you'll change your mind."

His hands grew bolder, his lips more demanding. He lifted the nightdress above her waist to reveal the smooth white belly, the softly rounded hips and trembling thighs. She was warm there, flushed with distress at being thus exposed and mortified by her own unaccountable responses. His hands seemed to draw fire from her flesh.

He stripped off his shirt and breeches in short order,

tossing them carelessly to the floor. He was as naked now as she, the ultimate item of his manhood standing well out from his body. And he was covering her, his hands exploring her intimately, drawing back the fleece that guarded her female secrets. She moaned, feeling him penetrate that most private passage.

But what was this feeling in her belly that came so piercing sweet and not like pain at all? Her hands that had been clenched into fists opened of their own accord and instinctively drew him closer. Her mouth was all slack and moist. Her lips parted under his urging. And he was all inside her now. They were moving together in some pulsating primal rhythm that could only climb higher and faster, sweeping them both toward the same inevitable conclusion. For her, it came in rising, undulating waves that tightened into uncontrollable spasms. Her hips arched to meet him, drawn irresistibly toward that final satisfaction. He finished in hard, short strokes that pressed her back against the bed.

Then it was over. His body lay quiet and spent, his cheek resting between her breasts. Moments later, reluctantly, he rose to dress, examining her with eyes brilliant like a hawk's, proud and proprietary. Undone by her own wantonness, she lashed out at him.

"You animal!" she hissed, cursing him for his attentions that had provoked her own shameful responses. "You're all alike—there's no honor in you!" she shrieked. "No decency!"

Stunned by her invectives, he countered harshly, his face suddenly altered to a tight mask of anger. "Why you hypocritical little bitch!" he said scathingly. "And not five minutes ago—or did I mistake it, lady?—was it not you crying out like a cat in heat?

"You're a hot little piece, all right," he continued, needling her further. "And you'll beg for it before this voyage ends," he added grimly.

He stalked out of the cabin, slamming the door behind him.

Maidie was exhausted when she returned and quickly made her pallet on the floor. Undressing in the dark, she never noticed the tiny motions of the bedcovers that held a silently weeping form.

4

THE SUN NEVER rose the next day, and both girls stayed late in their beds. On rising, Susanna peered through the tiny porthole to view a solid sheet of gray, ocean married to sky in one murky, sullen haze. A sudden toss of the ship sent her spinning from her perch, and Maidie, already awake and quietly plying her needle, looked up and laughed merrily.

"You've never been on a ship before, Susanna," she remarked, giggling at her companion's befuddled expression, "or you'd know you never sit yourself without something to latch on to." She stole a brief glance out the porthole. "This now isn't so bad. It may get worse though, before long."

"Have you been much about ships, then?" Susanna inquired, looking up from her less precarious seat on the floor.

"Oh, aye. My father was a fisherman, and he used to take me with him on the short runs, when I was a little 'un. He used to say he'd make a sailor of me"—the voice hesitated—"but the sea made a corpse of him instead. The *Maidie Lea*—he'd named her for me—she bellied up on the rocks one day, and that was that."

"Oh, Maidie, I'm sorry!"

" 'Tis the way of that life," Maidie told her. "And all who choose it know. I have it in my head some-

times that he would've been pleased going that way—
he was like that, you know, always bellowing a laugh
to the winds when they rose fierce and daring the
lightning down." A smile played about her lips, remembering the jaunty rolling walk, the great bear hugs of
greeting, the beard, full and red as her own bright hair,
and always stiff from salt.

"Anyway," she continued, "my mum didn't take
much to widowhood and runned off with a butcher to
set up housekeeping. I kept the flat and took in laun-
dry from the sailors. Could do a bit of nursing, too, I
learned from our parson's wife. My mum used to say,
'Them as can't get by on their looks had better learn
to be useful.' "

"Why, you're not ugly!" Susanna protested, rising to
her friend's defense. "You have beautiful hair and a
lovely figure!" Actually, Maidie carried herself with a
plodding awkwardness that made her body less attractive than it might otherwise have been. She was a big
girl, of robust build, with meaty hips and a full bosom
that, carried well, could easily excite desire.

Now Maidie's sallow skin blushed. She admitted
shyly, "I haven't been much about men. I mean, my
dad and the sailors and all, of course, but not—
that way."

"I think men are all scoundrels!" Susanna declared
passionately, thinking with embarrassed confusion of
the night before. How Captain Taylor had taken advantage of her, spared her only to satisfy his animal
cravings! And the humiliating words he had tossed at
her—"like a cat in heat!"—*Oh, damn him!* she thought
angrily. *He* made *me behave like that!*

A knock sounded on the cabin door, and Susanna
started, her heart suddenly thudding against her ribs.
It was he!

She quickly draped herself in bedding while Maidie

opened the door to the little blond urchin who'd run errands the day before.

"I have a message from the captain," he announced, standing properly straight while his brown eyes widened at the sight of all the mysterious girl-things—laces and needles, boxes and powders and sachet—that made this place so different from the sailors' quarters. "Passengers are forbidden the deck until the sea is quiet. He's hoping it'll blow south of us, but it's too soon yet to tell."

Susanna smiled with relief at the identity of their visitor. "Would you like a biscuit, Davy?" she offered.

The staunch little figure unbent and became a boy. "Yes, please!"

Tom Austin's lunch bag had not weathered well, and the two remaining biscuits were soggy. But for Davy, such treats were rare, and he accepted them gratefully.

"The captain said you're to work in the kitchens with me," he told Susanna. "He said that as you hadn't the fare, you could earn your keep that way."

As though he hadn't exacted payment from her already, she fumed. Not that she'd mind the kitchen work. And perhaps this meant he would leave her alone.

She left with Davy soon after, and Maidie, off to check on her patient of last night, accompanied them partway. In the stairwell at one turning, a solitary figure loitered, waiting, like a scavenger awaiting its spoils.

He doffed his cap to the ladies in a parody of manners. "Why, good morning to you, ladies," he said in greeting, concentrating his attentions on Susanna who recoiled, visibly trembling.

Maidie was puzzled to see her react so. Why, Brock had bragged to all the crew about his conquest, and practically everyone knew Susanna'd lain with him. Maidie herself, never having been asked, refused to judge Susanna, although she had thought Brock a poor choice. But if what Brock had said was true, why did the girl appear so frightened? She eyed the mate suspiciously. That he was a braggart and a swillpot she knew. But that he might be guilty of much worse, she had not suspected. Until now.

She waited while Susanna and Davy passed, then turned to confront him. "What've you done to that girl, Brock?" she demanded. "If you harmed her I'll see you get yours in good measure!"

"Why, we just had our bit of fun, Maidie-girl," he answered, soothingly. "She liked it. Told me so herself, she did, right after I'd finished giving it to 'er proper—you know what I mean." Elated to note her discomposure, he went in for the kill. "And what's all this to you, Maidie Cross?" he asked with the face of earnest inquiry. *"Could it be you're sweet on our Susanna?"*

It was with great satisfaction that he watched her, the round face mortified and drained of color, the stocky form turning and fleeing down the hall. "There's one up for old Brock-o," he congratulated himself, skipping a few steps gleefully as he headed to his post.

Susanna worked hard in the steamy kitchen, scouring the heavy black iron pans that Davy carried from the ship's huge ovens. But it was pleasant labor for all that. The kitchen help were already teasing her with friendly banter. They liked her pretty, modest ways, and her willing hands helping to relieve their own labor. And she was a lovely thing, a regular pocket Venus with her sweet gold curls tucked under her cap and her skin like an English rose. So small she had to stand on a box to reach the washing basin.

Relief came in good time. Her hands were beginning to burn from the lye soap and hot water. A slick coating of grease gave a sheen to her skin and clung to her hair—there was grease everywhere in the kitchen—and she looked forward eagerly to a warm, soapy bath. Released from work, Davy followed her like a puppy until she turned and said, "I think Maidie's fixed a tea, Davy. Would you like to come and make it a party?" He grinned delightedly. Susanna couldn't resist ruffling his blond hair where it fell forward, half-covering his eyes. "Maybe we can even find shears to trim that mop of yours," she said.

The three of them made a merry company. Susanna squatted on the floor with Davy, whose ears rang with her admonitions. "Be still, you imp—the bowl is slipping!" she cried. "Now where's the shears? Oh, do stop chewing—you're moving your head too much!" Meanwhile Maidie served the tea, and smiled from her corner seat. "I think the left side's a bit higher than the right," she offered. Susanna groaned in frustration, and Davy wriggled away, handing her back the bowl and diving for the biscuit tin. They were all orphans in their own way. But together they formed something very like a family.

"How did you come to be on this ship, Davy?" Maidie asked.

"I ran away," the boy said in satisfaction. "I was 'prenticed to a cobbler's shop in Islington, and the master there beat us for the littlest excuse.

"So I thought to go to sea, and one night I crept down to the South Bank and hid in a wooden crate that was waiting to be loaded. The cook unpacked me —he thought I was potatoes—and he sent for the captain—that was Mr. Taylor. But the ship was the *Sea Falcon.*"

"You mean you *stowed away?*" Susanna asked incredulously. "And you weren't . . . punished. Or— threatened with keelhauling?"

"Oh, no!" Davy replied. "The captain, he took care

of me. And I've been the Captain's boy ever since. He calls me his adg—adju—"

"Adjutant?" suggested Maidie.

"That's right," Davy said proudly. "Like the generals have to sort of look after them."

Maidie thought it all a huge joke. "Susanna, *keelhauled!* Where did you ever get such an absurd idea?" Then sobering, she asked sharply, "Who told you that? Susanna, *was it Brock?*"

Susanna's face paled. "No!" she whispered. "It was just—something I read somewhere." But Maidie needed no more than that stricken look to confirm her already aroused suspicions. "Susanna, you must go to the captain," she said gently.

"Never!" she cried. "Maidie, you must promise to tell no one of this. *Least of all the captain.* Promise me right now, or I shall never forgive you."

Reluctantly, Maidie gave her word.

"But what did Brock do?" Davy asked, and both girls hastened to satisfy him.

"Brock was mean to Susanna," Maidie explained carefully. "He wanted to frighten her."

"And so he told her about keelhauling?" Davy said slowly.

"That's right, Davy," Maidie said. "Like telling somebody a scary story."

"I don't like him, either," Davy announced. "He worries the deckhands, too. Treats them like dirt."

Tea had been late, and the supper bell was already sounding. Susanna was relieved to end the conversation. She realized with chagrin that the captain had not threatened her life. She had submitted from the first, under the delusion that to refuse him meant to die. He must have thought her a tart—such an easy conquest! Recalling the scene in her mind, she emerged disgraced. He had aroused her, made her cry out. To suffer his actions had been wrong enough. But that wasn't the worst. That she had answered the beast in him with a beast of her own—this was the unacceptable, the scarlet, unwashable sin. Not that he had taken her—but that she had wanted him to.

They met briefly at supper. His greeting was cool and very proper, as though their coupling in the dark on that narrow cot had never been. *Perhaps because he's had so many,* she thought, dismayed. *And what am I but another doxy who's admitted him so lightly to her bed? With not a bit of fuss, and at the end*—at this her mind recoiled, willing itself not to remember, but the thought would not be halted—And at the end she had clutched at his shoulders, drawing him down to her even closer, deeper, answering a need that could only be met by more of him. Now she kept her eyes low to hide the turbulence of her emotions, and stammered a quick "good even."

The Reverend Shuttleworth, flanked by two rough-looking characters, arrived soon after and announced that as it was Sunday, a brief sermon would be offered. Susanna had not seen the elder's companions before, but they had savage faces, and one of them was so big he had to duck inside the doorway. Their jackets were crude buckskin, and they wore guns on their hips, which caused some unrest among the passengers. Murmurs passed back and forth, and Susanna thought she heard fat, pigeon-breasted Sister Willoughby whisper the word "Danites!"

At this point the captain rose and announced with unruffled composure that passengers were not permitted to bear arms aboard ship. At a nod from the reverend, the two ruffians shrugged and removed their weapons. The crowd seemed to breathe easier.

Elder Shuttleworth's sermon was both brief and inspired. "My brethren," he began quietly. "Satan is among us!"

His eyes only glanced at the pages as he read. "O

that ye would awake; awake from a deep sleep, yea, even from the sleep of hell, and shake off the awful chains by which ye are bound, which are the chains which bind the children of men, that they are carried away captive down to the eternal gulf of misery and woe."

He looked up, transfixing the audience with his penetrating gaze, and his voice rang forth like booming thunder. "We are all black with sin!" he cried. "Toppled from the state of grace, brought low by corruption and licentiousness."

Susanna shrank back in her seat. He seemed to be speaking directly to her. "But there is hope, my friends," he said, more gently now. "For in repentance lies salvation. Repent! and ye shall be washed clean of the blackest sin and received by God's angels into the Kingdom of Heaven."

Susanna thrilled to the words of comfort and felt a heavy cloud lift from her mind. There was hope for her to expiate her sins. She would repent. She would pray for the soul of her stepfather, govern the distracted heat of her blood, put from her all unclean thoughts. With these happy resolutions, she attended the last of the sermon, supped with great relish, and assiduously avoided the black-haired knave who headed the captain's table.

She was honored later by the elder's attentions. Passing her in the corridor, he dismissed his henchmen and fell to walking with her. "I know you, mistress, do I not?" he asked, a faint puzzlement in his tone, as though he could not place her.

"Aye, sir," she answered shyly. "In my mother's shop, that's Jones's Drapers in Liverpool. You converted my mother, sir."

"Of course!" he exclaimed. "The worthy Mistress Jones. A fine woman, devout—she'll be an excellent member of the church.

"But what of you, child?" he inquired, regarding her with benevolent concern. She certainly was attractive with that dewy skin and that incredible crown of hair capping her head like a halo. "We left your mother waiting the next ship. And did you not say your name was Susanna *Hungerford?*"

Susanna bit her lip. "My mum wasn't married to my true father, sir. And I'm going to America to find him."

"America's a big place, Sister Susanna," he commented dryly. "And where do you hope to find him?"

"I—I'm not exactly sure," she admitted hesitantly. "But I had a letter that said he'd been heard of in the East. I guess I'll start looking in East America."

"Even that's too big a space for a young lady all alone," he informed her shrewdly. "There are some members of our church still in New York. I could make inquiries for you." How delicious she was in her gratitude, those eyes shining like twin perfect gems, that mouth like a flower bud half-opened! It was a face that could turn a man foolish, but the Reverend Horatio Shuttleworth was anything but a fool. On the contrary, he was a man of most unusual perceptions. And he could be very, very patient.

Susanna returned to her room in the highest spirits. How helpful these good people were! The reverend's offer gave her greater hope than ever of finding her father, and even the burdens of guilt she'd carried seemed dissipated. *I'll learn to be pious*, she decided. *And spiritual. And I'll not let another man touch me! No, I'll not even think of those things.*

With such righteous determinations, she yawned happily and undressed for bed. But somewhere in the dark she felt herself grow restless. Her body rolled and twisted with vague yearning. It was at least an hour before she slept, and then the nightmare returned. Only this time the head the reverend offered was a face she recognized with growing horror. It was the face of Captain Taylor.

Maidie woke to her cries and thrashings and rushed to comfort the pitiful girl. "Hush, Susanna," she whispered soothingly, stroking the flaxen curls that clung damply to her head. Slowly she quieted, and Maidie slipped into bed beside her, gently cradling the girl's head against her own full, warm breast. With that unaccustomed comfort, Susanna seemed to relax, and finally, peacefully slept.

The storm had indeed passed south, and the following day dawned in great streaks of gold light. Susanna woke with no memory of her nightmare.

As usual, Maidie was already up and about.

"Up with you, lazybones!" she called to her friend. "We have us a project this morning." An opened trunk was set in the middle of the floor, and Maidie proceeded to pelt Susanna with various garments. When a pair of oversized pantaloons encircled her head, Susanna began sending them back, resulting in the wardrobe equivalent of a pillow fight and ending with two hysterical females clutching themselves with laughter and rolling around on the floor.

"This is ridiculous," announced Maidie, panting from her most recent outburst of giggles. She worked to achieve sobriety. "I want to cut these down for you," she told Susanna, indicating some of the clothing missiles. "We can start with a shimmy, and work up from there."

She dismissed Susanna's protest with a wave of her hand. "We certainly can't have you always wearing a single shift with its hem hanging down and getting all full of that kitchen grease. And what will you be wearing while that's washing, pray? Your blouse is all we could salvage from what you brought with you, and won't you be a sight going to supper in aught but that!"

Under such a barrage of arguments, Susanna submitted, standing docilely while Maidie, her mouth full of pins, skillfully tucked and measured. Someone began knocking on the door. Susanna wrapped herself in a robe, thinking it must be Davy, but for the second time she guessed wrong. Their guest was James Leverton, who'd brought her down from the lifeboat that first morning.

He pulled off his tall Mormon hat and smiled apologetically. "I hope I haven't interrupted," he began. "My room is just across the hall, and I heard you laughing. So I thought I'd invite you two charming happy ladies for tea. I do love company with my tea."

"I've had mine, thanks, but take Susanna," Maidie suggested, trying to pull the pins from her mouth. "Get on with you," she insisted, shooing them both to the door. "I can do this up like nothing."

Thus bullied by her friend, Susanna padded barefoot across the hall to their neighbor's cabin. It was actually larger than Maidie's quarters, but appeared much smaller because of the crates and stacks of books that lined the walls, cluttered the table, and peered out from beneath the cot.

"I'm afraid, my dear," her host said, fidgeting a bit, "you are viewing my greatest indulgence in its very worst state. Usually they're shelved in a library, and nominally, at least, under my control. But traveling in such narrow quarters, they are constantly dropping off things and scattering about, appearing everywhere underfoot and never the one I'm looking for." He sighed in annoyance, but his eyes held a merry twinkle. "Really," he said, "it's most frustrating!"

He watched with great delight as Susanna explored among his treasures. She was awed by their number. She'd never seen so many books owned by one man. And they were all so different—huge folios and sets of books, bound manuscripts, and tiny volumes, exquisitely bound in leather and edged with gilt. "Would you care to borrow one, Mistress Susanna?" he asked graciously. "Pick one you'd like, and I'll give you others when you're finished. There's poetry in this pile," he said, pointing to a row of slender works. "And history over here. I have the complete plays of Mr. Shakespeare, too, along with some novels young ladies seem to enjoy." He beamed as she reexamined them, narrowing the field. At last she showed him her choice; a thick little volume by Jane Austen.

"An excellent choice, my dear!" He paused to clear some journals off the tiny table, only to store them immediately beneath it. "But let's have some tea, shall we?" He drew a hot kettle from behind him on the floor, and produced, as if by magic, two dainty cups and saucers, exquisitely formed with fluted golden borders.

They had not been long enjoying their steeped hot tea when three quick raps on the door announced another guest. Leverton opened the door. "Oh, come in, captain," he exclaimed hospitably, "My dear neighbor and I are just having a cup of tea. Please join us."

The tall, dark-haired man towering in the doorway looked past James Leverton to Susanna, anxiously gripping her borrowed robe more closely around her. His dark brows knit above his glaring eyes, taking in every detail of her dishabille, even to her bare feet poking out from beneath her robe.

"You're due in the kitchens in fifteen minutes, miss," he remarked tersely. His eyes still raked over her in frosty judgment.

Taking leave of his host, he said only, "We can have our game later, *Mister* Leverton. I wouldn't interrupt your—*tea!*" With that he bowed carelessly to them both and quickly made his exit.

Leverton returned to his seat on the cot totally unperturbed by his friend's sudden departure. In fact, he smiled to himself, rather pleased and flattered to be the object of such jealousy, however ill-founded. It made him feel quite young again.

He lit his pipe with infinite care until it was drawing well, then remarked mildly, "The captain is an impetuous young man. But one must forgive him. He plays an excellent game of chess." Leverton found nothing so delectable as romance, and the good captain was quite evidently taken with his little stowaway. He eyed her discreetly, noting her charming face, all blushes. But she was actually upset, he realized with concern. Indeed, she was on the verge of tears.

"Now, now, Susanna," he said, patting her hand, "if I may take the liberty. There's no need to take on so. He'll be back before long. You'll see."

"I hope he never comes near me again!" she cried, surprising him with her vehemence, which was part pain and part fury.

Ah, but predictable, he thought to himself, remembering his own hot youth and the convoluted roads that passion often took. Well, this would be an exciting event unfolding in the ship's long hours of sailing—a subject outside of his books for pleasant musing.

He absently stroked his curly beard, keeping to himself that innocent amusement, the delight of wise old men who see the ending before the tale begins. Who have already lived it, known it, lost it before ever they sit and sagely prophesy. So did James Leverton sit and gather from Susanna to himself traces of lost pleasures —youth and bravado, and the warm breath of desire.

He stooped to pull out a wooden box, that held thirty-two ivory figures. "Would you like to learn chess, my dear—?"

Their morning visits rapidly became a habit in the days that followed. Often Maidie and Davy would come, too, happy to sit about sipping tea and listening to Leverton's stories. As neither of them could read very well, he gave them lessons sometimes in the later afternoons, while Susanna performed her duties in the kitchen. Susanna herself had a quick mind and soon exchanged her first book for a second, then a third. She had a wonderful memory for detail, and as her knowledge increased, she delighted much in sharing it. To Davy she read poems that sang like lullabies by Mr. William Blake. She kept Maidie informed of current inventions. "Maidie, d'you know that America has strung wire that can talk, from one town to the next? It's called a telegraph. Think of it!"

The days seemed to pass in stately order, and Susanna took some pains to assure that they continued. She carefully avoided any places Brock might find her, and seldom walked about except in company. A few times in the kitchen and once in the hall just outside her room, he came upon her. Always there had been others around. And always Susanna felt the same stab of terror as when he first attacked her. It made her skin crawl to be reminded by his unwashed flesh, his grizzled face, the hideous lecherous smile with which he greeted her each time, as though they understood each other well.

Of Captain Taylor she saw little—indeed, almost as if he were avoiding her. At supper he would bow with a cold and studied politeness that became for Susanna harder to bear than insults. She could not help stealing glances at him sometimes, when he was laughing that rich, mellow laugh with his head thrown back and his dark curls dancing. She watched him walk and later her memory would recall those hard, muscled thighs against her thighs. *Am I so debauched,* she thought distractedly, *that I pine for his kisses and feel my breasts burning for his touch?*

Her daily resolutions could not comfort her in the dark. She tried to remember the words of Reverend Shuttleworth's sermon, but she could not think past the image of that tall booted figure, that dark-haired devil. One part of her cried out for him to touch her with his blunt male hands, while the other recoiled in horror at her desires. Her hand would reach to quiet those demands awakened from that wild night of loving. But often her own caresses would leave her with a curiously empty feeling, as though she had been a long time without food.

She woke one night in a steamy sweat with the walls of the cabin seeming to close about her. The air was oppressive in the small compartment. It was stifling her. She dressed in the dark and hurried out the door racing through the corridor as though to flee her own fever.

The dense night was very still, and the full moon shone down on the quiet deck where Susanna now stood, drinking in great breaths of the freshened sea air. Moonlight crowned her head with silver, giving her the look of some fairy creature born not of the earth but of the air.

The illusion faded as she began to pace. The blood still pounding at her temples demanded action. A great despondency mingled with her agitation.

If only he would come. If he came to her now, she would go with him, willingly. If he would only come to her now, silently, asking no questions, then she would, without questioning, follow him. But her eyes burned with the warning sting of tears. She knew he would not come. That night that had branded her consciousness and set the seal on her desires had been nothing to him but a passing amusement, and she no more than a hundred other wenches who had parted their legs to receive him. The tears spilled from her eyes unchecked, wetting her face to cool her burning cheeks. How should he come when she was nothing to him? Of course he would not come.

A thousand thousand stars set against the black of

night blinked and watched, but kept their counsel. After a time, Susanna retired, walking slowly now, each heavy footfall sounding on the deck an echo of her despair.

5

IF JAMES LEVERTON was puzzled by the captain's morning absences, he gave no outward sign. Jed Taylor had returned for the match, but not until later, when Susanna was in the kitchens. And if Leverton occasionally chanced to mention this or that about Susanna, he was answered in monosyllables that discouraged further mention. Not a man to interfere with what he termed "matters of mating," the burly scholar watched and bided his time.

Susanna, too, had undergone a change these recent weeks. Her looks were more sober, her actions slower and less spontaneous than they had been at first. And seldom now did anyone hear those silvery peals of merry laughter issuing from her lips. The unspoken sadness that hung about her like a cloak set an aura of dignity about her dainty form, which Leverton found disquieting. Dignity was for matrons, not for the children of spring. Those wonderful green eyes so capable of flashing fire now at best glowed like small candles, easily put out.

Too, she was often to be seen consulting the Reverend Elder Shuttleworth, asking questions about the church and listening with seemingly rapt attention to the answers that came to her in grave, sonorous tones from the Mormon preacher. And this for some unknown reason, outside the realm of base or logic—this Leverton found the most discomfiting of all.

Not that he knew any scandal attached to Shuttleworth—he had never met the man before this voyage. Since then he'd learned little. That Shuttleworth had been twice widowed of young wives, Leverton—who had seen Nauvoo the Beautiful in its fever-infested swamp beginnings—knew meant nothing. That he was perhaps a great preacher of the Mormon doctrine, that he was a powerful and persuasive speaker—this, too, meant nothing. Or perhaps it did. Because fanaticism was a bedfellow of madness—this, too, Leverton recognized.

And feared.

He chanced to make mention one night to Taylor of his misgivings about the preacher. They had been playing a game of chess.

"Aye, and I'm with you there," the captain answered. "I've not liked his looks or ways since he stepped aboard. And as for Clem Hogans and Tasker Blake, those two sidekicks of his—"

"—They've kept quiet, have they not?"

"Quiet, yes. But it's the quiet of funerals. I'd just as soon feed them to the deep as carry them on a ship I captain."

"The reverend is making no small progress with our fair Susanna," the scholar observed, leaning forward to shift his bishop.

Taylor, who had been spared hearing her name of late, scowled. "I wish him much success," he said sarcastically. "When she was first aboard he wanted charge of her—another soul for his bonnet, I suppose. I should have let him. 'Twould have spared me trouble for certain.

"So let him ply her spirits with salvation. If he can convert the baggage into an honest female, I'll call him a miracle worker myself." He bungled his next play and swore feelingly.

While planning his move, Leverton took time to examine his opponent as well as the board. Jed Taylor was an astute man in his own right, a man of keen sensibilities. And he was headstrong—that came of youth—the captain was just thirty-four. Tall, handsomely formed, abounding in health and vigor, and possessed of a probing questioning mind. Could it be he was unaware?

Leverton stirred to take the white queen with his bishop. "Mate in two moves," he said raising his eyes to his partner's face and adding almost casually. "It's appeared to me more like courtship than conversion."

Shock registered on the captain's face. "What makes you say so?" he demanded.

"Our honorable reverend is known to have an eye for a pretty face," Leverton began mildly. "He's a widower, you know. Not that that would halt a Mormon wooing—they believe polygamy to be divinely inspired. Though oddly enough adultery is held among the deadliest of sins, subject to severe chastisement by the church.

"But I'm digressing. As for Shuttleworth, he's quite simply spending a lot of time with her. More than he spends with Amy Willoughby or the Davis sisters, for instance, who are always tugging at his sleeve. And Susanna is young, impressionable.

"For God's sake, man!" Leverton's voice rose, exasperated. "What do you expect me to tell you? He's not a man for exchanging posies and kissing in dark corners. *But he wants her!* I've seen it plain on his face, though the girl I'd swear has never seen it. Shuttleworth is shrewd. Too shrewd to tip his hand."

The captain took time to digest this piece of news. But at last he commented angrily that if she were to marry, 'twas no concern of his, except to pity the husband. "For she's a troublemaking bit of fluff if ever one was!"

James Leverton did not answer him directly, but instead picked up the delicate, slender chess piece that had cost his guest the match. "There was only one piece protecting your queen from my bishop," he observed standing the white queen upright. "When you moved that piece away, you lost her."

He proceeded to pour two brandies into fat round snifters, signaling the close of the evening. The two men toasted each other silently and drank. Leverton was gratified to see the thoughtful, brooding look in his friend's eyes.

"Good night, Captain Taylor," he said softly.

Jed Taylor bowed, then made as if to speak. He stopped himself before a word was loosed, and left, shaking his head and frowning.

James Leverton permitted himself a little smile of satisfaction. *Nothing like a game of chess for ordering one's thinking.*

Every female aboard the *Star Victory* from stooped old Mrs. Witherspoon to little Janey Bates was in a dither of preparation. In celebration of approaching the great port of New Orleans, Captain Taylor had suggested a dance. Captain Pitts had generously consented to play "all night or as long as the ladies' feet will hold them up." The crew planned to clear the long dining tables and chairs from the mess adjacent to the ship's galley. They would serve a light, early supper, and begin the music thereafter.

Jed Taylor had his own reasons for offering a lively evening's entertainment. The *Star Victory* had been out now forty-eight days sailing. His men were restless, inclined to temper, strung like the gut on an archer's bow. They wanted liquor and hot women, and

Jed Taylor knew the delays he would face if he docked in New Orleans. It would be days before the rummies would be sobered up and out of pocket. Before the lusty ones would wear the luster off the dark-eyed Creole women who had golden skin and lips so full and sweet a man would bite them, expecting the taste of honey.

New Orleans was a crown jewel brought from the great heads of Europe, a glittering courtesan entertaining power, a shining white city, with streaks of black like the marble that built her great houses. And she offered pleasures for every palate, any satisfaction guaranteed. You could still buy a white girl in New Orleans, provided the package was for shipping. And even young boys came to the docks, ready to be harlots for the crew. After weeks or months asea, a man was not always particular.

It was Taylor's plan to avoid stopping in the great city, other than to clear customs. And if his crew had a night to party a bit on board, there would be fewer gripes and mutters about going straightway up the broad Mississippi to Nauvoo. Besides, if what he'd heard about Nauvoo were true, his men would find entertainment there aplenty.

So it was that the girls were airing their best frocks, the carpenters were busy constructing a makeshift platform for the band—even the old biddies were planning the decorations and refreshment. In some inspired fit of generosity, Sister Willoughby had given Susanna a gown, several sizes too large for her delicate frame, but outgrown by its ever-expanding original owner. The fabric was lovely—a soft flowing green muslin, almost sheer, with a lacy slip sewn inside from bodice to hem. With Maidie's help, Susanna cut the length and tightened the bodice. Well over a yard they drew from the great full skirt—enough to make a gauzy shawl of single weave to cover the bare white shoulders.

Now Maidie stepped back surveying the results with a critical eye. Thank goodness Susanna's shoes had survived her adventures, for no one on the ship had such tiny feet. And they were pretty, with their dainty heels and bright silver buckles. The hem was just a little high, exposing slender ankles. Not at all unattractive, Maidie decided. The fit was perfect—drawn provocatively over the breasts and tight at the waist, falling in soft folds over the hips and legs. The lack of wire hoop was really a blessing, as the gently flaring skirt had a grace not found in those rigid bulky dresses. The shawl was the final stroke of genius—it wrapped caressingly about the shoulders and above the low, sweeping neckline, satisfying modesty without concealing the loveliness of the form beneath.

And above it all that rosy little face, the eyes that caught the color of the dress in a green as deep as pine forests. They sparkled, searching eagerly into the mirror of Maidie's eyes. "Well, say something, Maidie, before I burst. . . . How do I look?"

Maidie's voice broke slightly, as though her throat were dry. "You look—like a princess in a fairy tale, Susanna," she said. "Come, let's show this masterpiece to Mr. Leverton."

At that moment, Leverton was attempting to light his pipe while a large opened book balanced precariously over his lap. It clattered noisily to the floor when he rose, hearing the girls outside. His face delighted at the sight of his favorite, clad in her gossamer gown. "Ah, you're a perfect flower, my dear." he sighed, "and the dress is your beautiful stem. You must remember me for a dance tonight. And you too, Maidie, I'll not let you beg off in fear of your toes." He returned to his pipe and matches and picked up the fallen book, bringing it briefly to his lips.

Susanna caught the gesture. "Why do you do that?" she asked curiously.

"It's an old custom among the Hebrews," the scholar replied, "that if you drop something holy, you kiss it when you pick it up. Like an apology."

Susanna recognized the volume now—*The Book of Mormon*—just like the one given to her mother. "You've never told us how you came to be a Mormon," she said.

"You mean I don't fit very well with your idea of a proper Saint?" he asked teasingly.

"It's true—you're not like the others," offered Maidie. "They're all hushed and sober, and you're so jolly."

"Well, ladies, I can only tell you you've not seen all of the Church of Saints." He blew a perfect wreath of smoke that rose lazily in a circle above his head.

"You see," he began, "I happened to be traveling on the Mississippi several years ago, and my curiosity led me to stop at the site of a new town, called Nauvoo the Beautiful by its founders.

"The town wasn't beautiful. Most of it wasn't even built. The chief occupation was dying, and second to that, digging graves. There were so few healthy that even the children—those that were able—helped break the ground to bury the dead. Folks roundabout called it 'Commerce Graveyard.' "

Maidie shivered. "How dreadful! But *why* were they dying?"

"It was called 'swamp fever' by the natives," Leverton explained. "At home we call it malaria. Nauvoo was built on a stinking quagmire full of infecting miasmas. The people set about to drain the area, but all through the labor they were dying like flies. And there was Joseph Smith, rising from his own sickbed to heal his followers with the laying on of hands."

Maidie's eyes were like saucers. "You knew him

then? The prophet himself? Pray, what was he like?"

Leverton laughed at the recollection. "Not what you would think of as your classic biblical prophet," he said provokingly. "Rather crude if the truth be known. Big and blond and openhearted, friendly. A warm eye for women. And something of wonder about him, too," he said in a different tone. "Something many people missed who were put off by his rough back-country ways. I believe he was a sincere man. I think that indeed he had the gift."

Both girls listened fascinated. "And is that when you converted, sir?" Susanna asked.

"No, my dear. No, I returned to England, to my chair at Cambridge, continuing my teaching duties. But I had been struck by those people—there was something brave and fine in their pioneering and their unity in faith. They had been massacred, dispossessed, driven from their homes and lands—yet still they hung together, building again, and always with the firm belief that they were right and would prevail.

"So it was with pleasure that I followed the progress of my semiadopted Saints. If what I read and heard is true, Nauvoo became a great city in Illinois. There's been recent trouble though, ever since Smith was murdered. It's been rumored the faithful are being forced out again."

"—I asked Reverend Shuttleworth about Nauvoo," Susanna interjected. "He said we must wait till the journey's end and keep our faith in the Lord. Does that mean we'll have to move from there?"

"Why, Susanna," Maidie said with delight, "this is the first I've heard that you're going with us!"

Susanna smiled happily. "The reverend elder has offered me a position in his household," she told them. "I was feeling so sad about leaving the two of you, and I wasn't really sure where I would go or how. And he's going to make inquiries for my father! Isn't that fine?"

Leverton pursed his lips, but kept his thoughts silent. Maidie was pleased beyond measure, embracing her friend as though at a reunion. Something lodged in Leverton's mind. Susanna's father. Hungerford.

"Susanna," he asked suddenly. "Did your father have estates in Hampshire?"

Susanna swung round, her face a mixture of hope and disbelief. "That's what the letter said. The earldom of Wye. Oh, sir, d'you know of it? D'you know aught of my father?"

"Please be calm, my dear—an old man's memory. But I believe I taught the heir of Wye, Robert was it? Or Roland? Alas, child, it was years ago." He shrugged his shoulders, regretfully.

Susanna tried to hide her disappointment. In a small voice, she drew the conversation back. "You still haven't told how you came to join the church," she reminded him.

"Well," he said, "that can be brief and honestly told to you, my two dear friends. I have been widowed of a good wife these past ten years, and that is an old grief —I have lived with it long. But we had one daughter, and she was, you might say, the remaining structure of my hopes and plans. She was to be delivered of a child last year, but the child came untimely early. The birthing came hard—too hard—she was such a delicate thing, her heart gave after two days labor. And the babe that would have been my grandson never drew breath."

He passed the tale of his loss quickly, as though the wounds were yet too recent and tender to bear for long. Now he breathed deeply and went on. "I believe a body needs something outside himself to build on. In youth it's not a thing of great concern, perhaps because the building is ahead. But what we construct then in our fruitful time of life is the support for later. I shall have no grandchildren about me, so I am a Mormon, and a pilgrim of sorts. And so are we all on board this vessel, though for many different reasons. It's off to a new life, ladies, and a new home.

"And look, here we are—the three of us, and both of you like my children. Am I not blessed after all?" He opened his arms and both girls ran to embrace him.

"Now, now," he said, a trifle embarrassed at his own emotions. "It's getting late. The supper bell will ring at any moment. Susanna, you must change your gown, or risk gravy on your skirt." His arms still about them, he walked them to the door. "And remember my dances!" he called.

The mess hall was festooned with banners of brightly colored paper, the lights softened by skirts of donated fabric, formed into shades with baling-wire armatures. Captain Pitts and his players were tuning up and people milled about, self-conscious in their finery. The gentlemen were dressed in their best frock coats and suits, the women garbed in their gayest dresses. Three kegs of ale had been brought from the last of the ship's stores, along with steaming caldrons of tea from the kitchen to go with the little cakes and sandwiches. For one night the ship became a flating ballroom, its hull ringing with merriment—songs, voices, dancing feet.

Maidie looked lovely tonight in her best dyed silk, a soft rose color that brought warmth to her complexion. Her flaming mane of hair fell well back from her face and almost to her waist, and it rippled in great waves of red as she danced the lively Kerry Dance from Ireland. James Leverton had taken his promised dances, and now circulated in his gentlemanly manner among the older matrons. He dared a gallopade with Sister Willoughby, who had poured her ample self into a stiff gold brocade with flashing crimson petticoats. Davy, in clean short pants and a sailor's blouse, was helping Sisters Marwick and Witherspoon to serve the tea, and casting mournful gazes at the plate of sweets set just beyond his grasp. Even Clem Hogans and Tasker Blake, clad in coarse homespun, were each swinging a girl in the mad whirlings of the country dances. Their savagery seemed to have been channeled into a different energy, the high-spirited larking of farm boys at a local frolic.

Susanna was a vision in her flowing muslin. Maidie had secured her yellow curls to the top of her head, letting the ends fall softly back in rolls. They swung and bounced against her neck as she twirled and bowed and glided in response to the music.

There was a hand at her elbow. That slow, infuriating smile, the light of deviltry in those brilliant blue eyes. Susanna had tried not to think of it, that he would touch her again. And in the last long weeks, she thought she had succeeded. She had prayed much and repented much under the kind guidance of Reverend Shuttleworth. She thought herself well in control, disenchanted. Then how was it at a mere touch those feelings, unbidden and unwanted, could return full force, running a course like fire through her veins?

She forced herself to smile politely, nod, and take his arm. And she was careful not to tremble, not to stumble as the music was introduced and he led her to the floor. It was a gliding dance with the partners close together—a waltz by Johann Strauss.

His arms held her as lightly as a bird, but she could feel the heat and strength of his body, subtle, graceful as a panther, and equally dangerous. His hands drew her inexorably closer. She could feel his heart beat against her own flesh.

And that taunting, wicked mouth resting just above her ear. Whispering. "The dance is exciting you, Susanna. I can feel your heart like a little bird trapped in a cage of bones." He was holding her firmly with his hand at her waist, pressing her up against him until a hair could not pass between them. His thigh intruded between hers as they turned, and she could feel his demanding hardness through the thin cloth of her gown. She caught her breath, all the fine resolutions overthrown. She was giving way, yielding under the onslaught of his raw male domination.

The voice continued, insolent, suggestive. "I'm afraid this waltzing has you quite undone, Susanna. You're panting like a little puppy." His fingers brushed the arched peaks of her breasts. She gasped and would have stumbled had he not caught her. Her green eyes blazing with heat slanted toward his face, but he continued in the same maddening way. "You must not be so transparent, mistress. These good people will think you a wanton, flashing those hot and hungry looks at their honorable captain. If you must have a kiss," he said turning at the next step, "here's a nice shadowy corner."

She was pressed back against the wall, and his face shut out the light so that his mouth found hers in darkness. He caught her lower lip between his teeth and bit until she moaned and her mouth fell slack. From the corner of his eye he saw a tall grim figure approaching and acting quickly, almost before Susanna could get her footing, he had her fast in his arms, gliding past the glaring reverend elder to dance the last bars of the waltz.

They applauded the gratified Captain Pitts from the center of the floor, and Taylor again saw that thin specter parting the crowd and coming toward them. "There's Shuttleworth come to rescue his little lamb." His tone became serious—"Keep clear of Shuttleworth, Susanna." Louder, he said only, "I claim the last dance, mistress," and left her.

"Keep clear of Shuttleworth," she thought in ragged confusion. As though he were *ordering* her. And the reverend himself must be thinking no good of her, compromising herself so blatantly. Oh, what had she been thinking of to swoon in that pirate's arms like some round-heeled hussy! The tall elder was almost beside her already, and what could she say, how defend herself? The reverend bowed stiffly and offered his arm. Amazed, Susanna folowed as he placed a dry hand at her waist and led her through the next dance number.

The band was playing "Gypsie Laddie," an English country song. The elder's formal coat smelled of must and camphor, and his deep-set eyes stared at her strangely. His expression was so stern, impassive as they stepped an awkward pattern around the room. Susanna was relieved when the last strains sounded, ready to excuse herself. His looks this night made her uncomfortable.

He acknowledged her pardon and said, "I must speak with you soon, Sister Susanna, on a matter of some import."

She nodded vaguely and began weaving through the crowd of dancers. Someone tapped her on the back. It was Davy, released from his tea-serving, come to claim a dance.

At twelve, he was almost as tall as Susanna, and if his dancing was somewhat incompatible with the beat, it made up in enthusiasm what it lacked in accuracy. She found herself infected by his good spirits, laughing as she hadn't laughed in weeks. It was a magic evening after all, lighted by soft colors, the air full of music. She shook off her misgivings and took up singing, for they were playing her song again, the banjos were strumming, "Oh, Susanna."

Maidie stood in the circle, tapping her feet with the others, closing her eyes and remembering the young sailor who, an hour before, had walked her to the deck and kissed her there. It was her first real kiss, and she hugged it to herself like a cat with its belly full of cream.

Susanna found her beautiful shawl, long forgotten and trampled beneath a chair. A few older people were returning to their cabins, but the young group had feet of iron, to tap all night upon the hollow floor. Susanna decided to leave the shawl in her room. The dance would go on for hours yet.

She heard nothing until she was descending the hatchway. The sudden sound of running steps, a shadow in the stairwell right behind her, and midway through her scream, his hand whipped up the side of her face, almost knocking her senseless. When they could focus, her eyes wished themselves blind.

Brock had his own plans for the evening's entertainment.

After the first time, she had played so coy, that naughty girl. Brock had begun to despair of having a second round of play. And now here she was, the little flirt, alone at last, just as if she were following his instructions.

Her face was bright red where he'd struck her, and her lip was bleeding. He could see her shuddering as he came nearer, gazing at his face with trapped animal eyes.

"I don't think you'll scream again, missy. Doubt as anybody'd hear you if you did. Besides, you don't want to get old Brock angry with you, 'cause he just wants to give you a little fun. It's always better after the first time," he said almost cackling. "But I guess you've already found that out for yourself, now. Haven't you?

"So just you come with me, litle filly. You're gonna invite me to your room." One hand trapped her wrists behind her back, the other grabbed a fistful of curls, and he marched her down the corridor. She suddenly flung her weight back against him, shoving him against the wall, and for a split-second, she was free. It was only that long before he had clawed at her shoulder, swung her around, and cuffed her across the breasts.

She doubled up, covering them with her arms and moaning.

Inside the cabin he threw her down across the bed, and casually drew a knife from his belt. Deliberately, he began to pick his teeth as she stared at the gleaming blade, her mind thinking of death. She wanted him to be dead, like any foul thing. Or let him kill her. But not the other, no—the things he would do she could not bear again—the degrading and devastating ugliness of it. No, better to be quiet and dead and out of it all.

He waved the knife and smiled at her. "Come on over to Brock now, darlin'," he coaxed. She was already standing before him when he said, "We're just going to slice you out of that cover-up and then you're going to open your pretty little mouth and Brock'll feed you some sugar."

Standing before him, Susanna knew with a sudden and terrible knowledge that she could not throw herself upon the knife as she had intended. In a wild and heedless despair she screamed before Brock could move to stop her—screamed like a rabbit under a pack of hounds. An instant later, a young boy's voice cried "Susanna!" and Davy burst into the room.

She just had a chance to bite Brock's hand, until she tasted blood and heard the knife clatter to the floor. His other hand struck her jaw a heavy blow and she went down.

Then Davy was upon him, his fists flailing punches at the tough, wiry body. It was no match at all. Brock had the weight and was used to street fighting. His thumbs went round to Davy's throat and squeezed, holding the boy up by the neck, and shaking him furiously. Susanna came to and staggered toward him, her eyes on the knife, and Brock flung the boy away to land in a crumpled heap across the threshold. Brock set his jackboot over the knife just as Taylor, aroused by the screams, broke in on the scene.

Five other faces crowded the doorway, but Maidie Cross managed to press her way inside to kneel with the captain by Davy's body. When Taylor rose, Brock could feel his blood turn chill. It was too late for the knife. He raised his fists for what he already knew was the last time. Brock had seen murder in men before, and this man, he knew, would carry it out.

Brock tried to gain an edge by closing quickly and aiming a swift low jab at his opponent's middle. Taylor spun aside, avoiding the brunt of the blow, and brought both hands down hard on Brock's shoulders. He half-lifted the fallen man with one hand and in icy satisfaction slammed his fist against the other's face. He was rewarded by the sound of cracking bones.

Brock desperately tried to kick the captain's groin, but Taylor forestalled him by clutching at Brock's body and binding it against his own. He stumbled back a few paces with his adversary in his arms, the two figures frozen together like demon creatures performing some macabre dance step. But the illusion faded rapidly.

Like a wolf to the scent of blood, Taylor closed to finish. The last of it went quickly. Brock was already unconscious when his body was pinned against the floor. The captain, whose fury made a monster of him, knelt over his victim and pulled the yellowing face with its blank distended eyes up from the floor, only to slam it down again, over and over again. Leverton tried to pull Taylor's arms, but the man was beyond stopping. Not until the eyes rolled back in the grizzled face, and blood gushed from the ears and mouth was his ferocious bloodlust abated. He seemed literally to shrink to human size again, stepping over the broken corpse and returning to the boy. Davy was still unconscious. But he was alive.

"Clear out," his hoarse voice told the onlookers. Then when they did not stir, he shouted, *"Clear out!*

All of you, back to your cabins!" Two crew members quickly dragged Brock's body from the chamber.

Jed Taylor's arms cradled the boy's back, shifting him up to carry. He was so light, the little lad. "You'll tend the boy in my cabin," he told Maidie, who was already running for hot water and bandages.

His gaze shifted to Susanna, who stared glassy-eyed with shock. She could scarcely see his face, but the parting words came forth distinctly, each like a blow thick with rancor and disgust.

"Slut!" he hissed. "The boy's like this because of you." With his face like an iron mask, he turned away, bearing the precious burden still cradled in his arms.

It was a long, silent vigil all night in the dark, tiny cabin, but Susanna scarcely stirred from her seat on the floor. Her arms and legs seemed to stiffen after a time and lock themselves in place. At times she became confused and thought herself back in the draper's shop. She was still hollow-eyed and awake when Maidie returned in the morning and told her the boy would live.

6

IT WAS STRANGE to see land off either side of the ship after so long an ocean journey. Susanna spent most of her free time leaning over the deck rail watching the brown muddy waters of the great Mississippi swirl below. Thick tangled underbrush choked much of the earth along the steep wet banks. But willows and cottonwoods grew in profusion and tracts of land had been cleared for farming and boat docks. And there were always a few people about, sitting with their bamboo poles waiting for a fish to strike. She watched a boy about Davy's age haul up a huge ugly fish, then throw it back in disgust. One of the crew told her it was a catfish, so called for the long whiskers on its face, and that it got spoiled during hot weather, feeding as it did in the slime of the river bottom.

There was a good deal of traffic on the broad waterway. Paddlewheels lifted the water in small cascades. Barges floated past heavy with their goods. Small ferryboats, carrying people and livestock from one side to the other, darted like dragonflies around the larger craft.

There had been no peace for Susanna since the night of Brock's death. He was not mourned, though Reverend Shuttleworth had given words of peace before his

body was cast in the Gulf. Davy was almost well, still
tended by Maidie in the captain's quarters.

But for Susanna there was damage to her soul, a
damage she was hard put to repair. First there had
been her stepfather, almost surely dead. Then Brock,
and Davy's injuries. And the captain, whose words were
somehow the most damning of all. She *was* the cause
of these events. Her very existence had precipitated
the actions of the others—Martin Jones's attack, and
Brock's. Davy's brave and costly rush to save her—
even the captain's seduction and the blood now on *his*
hands. It was blood on her hands as well. She wanted
desperately to be off the *Star Victory* and at the journey's end, away from all the ghosts that seemed to lurk
in every corner of the ship.

As though by prearrangement, she and Captain Taylor avoided one another. He ate supper in his own cabin
now, with Davy. And though once in the evening, he
sang for the assembly, he did not sing to her or look
as he had done that other night that now seemed cen-
turies ago. James Leverton told her she must stop blaming herself, and Maidie encouraged her to other pur-
suits. The Reverend Shuttleworth, though, encouraged
her repentance, and urged her toward further embrace
of the Mormon doctrine.

"Christ loves the children of despair, my child," the
elder would say. "Repent of your sins, renounce the
carnal appetites, and accept God into your heart. Then
shall you be washed clean." Susanna was finding herself more and more in the reverend's company these
days. He generally sought her table at supper, and
talked long with her after meals, instructing her, guiding her as he put it "into the path of Right."

It seemed to offer the only comfort she could accept. She wanted no more destructive passions, no more
vanities. Only peace, and some measure of relief from

the unbearable guilt she'd carried since the night of the celebration dance.

He had called on her early this morning, walked with her around and around the upper deck, while the Mississippi stretched out all around them. He thought she should be baptized before they docked in Nauvoo. Gesturing toward the broad powerful waters, he spoke of the soul-cleansing effects of immersion, the feelings of levity and rebirth. He would perform the baptism, he said, this very evening after supper. She would come to his chamber as a penitent to the Lord.

Susanna had long dismissed her strange forebodings suffered the night of the fateful ball. The gaunt minister had proved himself her true friend and guide, helping her to overcome her wickedness and misfortune. She longed so to be that other Susanna, that young, untouched Susanna who had served custom in her mother's shop on West Grove Road in Liverpool.

She had dressed carefully in the most demure blue shift with a round white collar and white buttons down the front. A little timidly, she made her way to the reverend's quarters at the forward end of the ship.

He looked so formal when he opened the door. His thin frame was clothed in a long black frock coat that almost rustled with stiffness, and he held *The Book of Mormon* in his hands. The chamber was almost twice the size of hers and Maidie's, and in the center of the room was what looked like a small dais with a barrel standing upright in the middle.

The barrel was filled with water.

Susanna looked around dismayed. There were only herself and the reverend, who had brought forth a thin white robe, doubtlessly the garb of the newly baptized soul. The girl's lips trembled before she could form words. "Do we not need witnesses, Elder Shuttleworth?" She prayed for Maidie, even Sister Willoughby.

"One moment, sister," he replied and stepped into the

hall. In a few moments, Clem Hogans and Tasker Blake shuffled into the room and took their places against a wall that faced the baptismal platform. Hogans's heavy jaw was unshaven, and his grin seemed to suggest that baptism witnessing was his favorite sport. Tasker Blake, a huge man who never smiled and hardly ever talked, stood with his arms stiff at his sides and his head cocked back so that his eyes looked down through half-shut lids at the center stage.

Susanna looked at Elder Shuttleworth with panic-stricken eyes. He held command, he had to help her now!

His voice was tight. His eyes were a fiery gray. "The witnesses will turn their backs until the penitent is immersed," he announced, never taking his eyes from her. And he made her turn her back to them as well, to face the single step that led up to the rim of the wooden barrel. For himself, he only reminded her, in the deepest, most solemn tones, that a man of God was not moved by temptations of the flesh.

It didn't seem holy to her as she stood on the platform. It seemed like—an exhibition. Her fingers lifted tentatively to the buttons of the dress. But she had to do it! He had told her to place her trust in him and in the Lord. Perhaps this was a test of faith.

Still, she almost wept when the shift slid to her feet. Her hands trembled at the hooks and could scarcely undo them. Now the shoes and hose, and the stare of those eyes at her back. She was so awkward, finally pulling off the long white bloomers, so exposed, lifting her thigh from the step to the rim of the barrel.

Oh, God!—he made her stop there, poised over the water while he asked the Question of the Faith. The water was an icy relief.

She raised just her head from the bath, and obediently replied "aye" to the questions he put to her. He was holding the robe and a drying cloth in his hands. She desperately wanted that robe.

To her dismay, he helped her from the water, then handed her the towel and ordered the witnesses out. But Clem Hogans caught a full picture before he sauntered through the door.

Susanna shivered, but it was over. Dressed now, she prayed only that the thing was right and accomplished. Shuttleworth gestured her to a seat and stood himself several feet away. "I have given much thought," he informed her gravely, "to the further good of your soul."

She needed much instruction. She was subject to temptations, pitifully weak in her resolves. With help she could overcome her sinful nature. She could learn to embrace the True Word.

He proposed to marry her and save her soul.

She couldn't have understood. Did he mean *man and wife*?

"You will be my bride, sister, in the ways of the Mormon church."

He spoke with such finality, as though the thing were already done. "It will be a celestial marriage, during which we will pray for our spirits to unite, that we may thus be bound for eternity."

Susanna's mind worked desperately, trying to comprehend. Spiritual brides clearly must not be meant for carnal relations. Was it thus he had been inspired to help her renounce the earthly pleasures? Her head nodded. It must be so. What better way to avert sins of the flesh than to commit oneself to a spiritual marriage?

"I'll arrange it for the day after tomorrow," he continued, assuming her consent. "I mean you to step forth in Nauvoo as newly baptized *and* my bride."

"Will we—live together?" she asked in a tiny voice.

His answer came with sober reassurance. "We shall

be living in the same house, Sister Susanna, but you
shall have your private quarters."

She returned to her cabin in a kind of fog, wondering
just what had befallen her. And Maidie, who had
worried at her being so late, accosted her with questions. What was the news? Why was she dressed like
that?

"I'm going to wed with Elder Shuttleworth," she
said in a dead, calm voice. "I'm to be united with him
in spiritual marriage."

Maidie stared at her in disbelief. How was it her
lovely young Susanna—and Elder Shuttleworth? Why,
he was a dry skinny spider of a man! How could
he. . . ?

But she could learn nothing more.

James Leverton heard of it next morning. His lips
tightened almost imperceptibly. "Does she seem happy,
Maidie?" he asked.

Maidie was distraught. "She doesna' seem *anything,*
sir! She's all hazy and will say nothing of it. Except
that she'll be married in the white penitent's robe. Mr.
Leverton, is there nothing we can do?"

"We can only be her friends, Maidie. Who love her."
He stroked her long red hair and cupped his fingers
under her chin. "You must watch out for our Susanna
in Nauvoo."

More bewilderment. "But you'll be there with us—
won't you?"

His words came slower than his thoughts. "I—have
some business, Maidie Cross. I shall return to New
Orleans when the *Star Victory* leaves."

Maidie left shaking her head. She had expected—
at least hoped for—some great plan of action that
would overturn the coming event. She had no quarrel
with Reverend Shuttleworth—she admired him as a
preacher. But the thought of him wedding Susanna—it
was like grafting a fresh new flower to a withered stem.

But at least Davy was a bit of sunshine this morning. He was already well enough to champ and complain at being "confined to quarters." His cuts had healed, and the bruises around his throat had changed from purple to a dull yellow. His spells of dizziness, too, were all but gone. And he had a twelve-year-old's solution to the problem of Susanna's coming marriage. "You and I, Maidie, we could do it easy," he insisted. "Both of us'd sort of sidle up to him on deck. You know, one on either side—"

"Davy, we don't want to *kill* him!" Maidie cried.

"*I* do," asserted the boy. "I think he's worse than Brock."

"You think that only because he's trying to wed Susanna. And he's just too old for her. Why, he must be past sixty."

"It's not just that. Why, Mr. Leverton's old, too, but I don't feel like that about him.

"You think I don't know anything," he accused. "You think I don't know about things, but I know. I've seen him look at women—you too, Maidie—when you're not looking at him. And it's not just the looks such as I've seen men give when they want to—you know—lie with a lady."

Maidie's blushes went unnoticed as Davy continued. "There's a glittery look to him, along with the other, I've seen it before." His wan face frowned. "It's like—when I was little, living with my mum, there was a butcher as had a shop in Penton Street. And people used to say he was the best, you know, and would come on market days with their lambs and geese and such for him to fix.

"My mum used to send me when we were to have fowl, to bring it to him for slaughtering. One day my friend Tim and me, we both sneaked in to watch how it was he butchered the larger animals. We figured there'd be dressed carcasses, you know, but he hadn't slaughtered any yet. There was just a tight little pen in the back with four lambs in it, and one little calf, all crying and bawling like they was hurt. When we peeped over the edge of the pen we saw why. They was hamstrung, every one of them.

"So there they were all crying pitiful and trying to drag themselves around. And Tim and me—we had to hide because the master was coming in, and he was whistling. The animals went mad and all dragged themselves to the darkest corner, just piling atop each other, when he opened the gate and pulled a lamb out by its neck. He laid it on the stone floor and set his knee over its forelegs. And all the time the lamb was bleating and crying, its back legs just hanging loose—"

"Oh, Davy, do stop it!" Maidie exclaimed. "You're just trying to frighten me. Why this has nothing to do with the Reverend Shuttleworth."

"It was the *look*," Davy insisted. "Don't you understand? He just held it down on the floor with a great, sharp cleaver in his hand, and he had this look about him all the time that little creature was crying.

"What I'm trying to tell you is, that's the look the elder has. Besides the regular one, I mean."

"Davy, he's a holy man," Maidie said. "You're imagining this. I don't want him to marry Susanna any more than you, but you mustn't spread such tales about the reverend and a—a butcher! If you ask me, it's Susanna who's gone mad. Don't you have any better ideas than throwing him off the ship?"

"Feeding him some rat poison?" the boy offered hopefully.

Sometimes little boys were impossible. Maidie sighed and left after they had promised each other to share any ideas that came to mind. She almost collided with Captain Taylor in the corridor. She blurted out the news all in a breath, but the captain was chillingly unmoved.

"Why do you dislike her so?" Maidie asked, confused. "I thought—"

"You thought *what,* Maidie Cross?" he said impatiently.

"I saw you dancing at the ball," she replied. "I thought you—cared for Susanna."

"Care for her?" he said sarcastically. "I despise her. She has brought nothing but grief to this ship. Her lover Brock is dead of her witcheries. And Davy almost killed. And you ask—"

But Maidie was bearing down on him like some red-haired Valkyrie. "Her lover? *Brock?*" she shrieked. "Oh, you fool! You blind, stupid fool! D'you see the likes of Susanna choosing the likes of him? Brock, her lover?—*Brock raped her!*

"Aye, you may well stare," she continued without pause, " 'twas a maid she was when she came on board. Brock ravaged her that first night in the lifeboat, and locked her back in there. And it's a fine one you are to judge, hiring a crew of such slime as that."

Taylor's whole demeanor had altered radically, from flushed red anger to an ashen paleness. He remembered it seeming odd for Brock to offer the girl to him like a piece of cake. But he'd wanted the lass, and, desiring did not question his own fulfillment.

Maidie was still seething invectives against both himself and Brock. "Enough, Maidie Cross," he said wearily. "You say the wedding's tomorrow?"

At her nod, he dismissed her. "Leave me awhile, woman. What you've said has been all news." Shaking his head, he turned away.

Susanna herself viewed the coming ceremony not as a marriage, but as a kind of final expiation. No one seemed to understand this, except the reverend himself, of course. James Leverton was upset by it, and Maidie openly disapproving. But it was the bargain she had made, and she would not go back on it.

As the day wore on, her thoughts drifted to incidents both recent and long-forgotten, as lifetimes are supposed to pass before the dying, or as a nun might reflect on the eve of taking her final vows. When she was a little girl, her mother's hair had been rich and brown, as curly as her own. How different her mother had been, before she'd grown bent and gray and dry and bitter. She'd had time to hold her daughter then, to tuck her into the truckle bed at night and tell her stories.

And Susanna recalled the flowers given her by a market boy. Daffodils they were, the first of spring, sun-bright and sun-yellow, still wet with dew from the field. She could almost touch them, so clear they were, the velvet smoothness of the petals, the dusty pollen that had clung to her fingers. She conjured up the images of boys who had smiled at her, men whose looks had said they wanted her, the few introductory probings that had proceeded her time aboard the *Star Victory*—as though to bid them all good-bye. Her life would be very different from now on.

And good-bye to the dark-haired captain, who had marked her most deeply of all. They shared Brock's death between them. They had shared a bed one night, and his cruel, sweet mouth had branded her with kisses. And was it not strange that as she sought to put from herself the act of passion, the act itself ceased to be so shameful. The reckoning was her bid for peace, for absolution. The price was marriage without a wedding night.

Reverend Elder Shuttleworth took the opportunity at supper to announce his imminent marriage to Sister Susanna Hungerford. The gathering buzzed like a nest of drones and Susanna was troubled to find herself the unchallenged center of attention. Everyone had something to say—if not to her, then about her. Many offered their congratulations. Maidie and Davy maintained a stony silence while the felicitations came forth.

After a time, most of the people had returned to their cabins or gone above for a walk about deck. Captain Taylor remained. Susanna noticed and worked to compose herself. It was all right. She was only a little shaky.

To any of the scattered observers across the room, he had taken her hand and was wishing her well. But his hand held hers tightly—so tightly it almost hurt—and his words were not of wishes, but of urgent command.

"Meet me, Susanna. Here. An hour before midnight." He let go her hand, and without even waiting an answer he was gone.

What incredible folly was this? What madness? An assignation on the eve of her marriage? Yet here was her giddy heart all fluttering, the hand that he had gripped so tightly raised to her lips, if only to feel the last impressions of his fingers. It was quite impossible— she could not go, of course—but tomorrow it would all be over and never, never to come again and there was only tonight. And if she sinned and followed this unreasoning passion tonight, was there not her whole life to atone for it? Only tonight. Only tonight. Or never, and nothing at all.

Did a smile break out from those sad, quiet lips like the sunshine through a bank of clouds? And was the lazy Mississippi evening suddenly too lazy and too long? There was a sudden glow about her, more heightened for its being so rare of late. And her dainty feet could scarcely keep themselves from dancing or running or kicking out in some coltish display of spirits. She would go. For certain, she would go. Now she must see the evening through, and then—

Maidie was appalled. A bath at this hour? Was she daft? But Susanna waved away her dire threats of con-

sumption or influenza. She would have her bath this
very hour, and Maidie would be splashed for her in-
terference. Afterward, she brushed her hair until it
crackled and sparked against the bristles. Maidie, who
was reading in her painstaking fashion, looked up in
bewildered disapproval. "Susanna Hungerford, you'll
comb yourself bald at this rate, and deserving of it you
are, you bird-witted wench!" But her tone was more
indulgent than her words, for it was a glad relief to
see this sparkling bubbly child replace the too-quiet
creature of the recent month. If she suspected the man
who had waited for her friend was the strapping handsome captain, she would not seek that knowledge. It
was enough that Susanna was happy tonight.

The intervening hours passed with stubborn sloth.
The tickings of the ship's clock, like runners on a
treadmill, were constantly active but seemed to go
nowhere. And would Maidie ever sleep? She was reading unusually late. It was already ten o'clock when she
finally said goodnight. Susanna had been under the
covers almost an hour, fidgety from feigning sleep herself. At last her friend was asleep. At last she could
pull back the covers and spring to her feet, as eager as
a child on Christmas morning.

She borrowed a dark gray cloak and threw it about
her shoulders. There was no question of dress, not on
this night's business. Under the shroud of the cape she
wore Maidie's satiny peignoir. Under that she was
naked.

The moon was close to full again, beaming a silver
ribbon upon the quiet water. The air was cool, with just
a hint of autumn, and a soft breeze buffeted the folds
of her gown. It played about her legs and ankles, making her all the more aware how little she wore. The
deck and passageway were fairly quiet; by now most of
the watch were stealing sleep in hidden corners.

She was conscious of him emerging from a seemingly

empty shadow and coming toward her. She knew what
he was coming for—so fierce and quick that he almost
frightened her. One step more and he would be touching her. Her legs were so weak. Her eys stared at his
hands—broad, powerful hands that in another instant
would reach for her. She swayed on her feet, certain
that if he touched her she would surely die.

But no, his arms were warm around her, drawing
her toward a makeshift bed of flour sacks, drawing her
down to lie against him. They made a warm nest of
their bodies, twining about each other, making little
knots of limbs. Their seeking was of a single nature,
answered in touches and kisses, not words. Susanna
found her hands returning his caresses. His kisses
drifted along the soft underside of her jaw up to her
ear and changed to whispers. Her fingers traced the
lines of his face and closed upon his mouth until he
was kissing her hands as she lured him back to her
mouth. It was like drinking, yielding to his kisses. It
was like being drunk.

He lifted her from the cloak and their bodies rolled
together. His hand slipped to the hem of her nightdress
and drew it up, pausing at each new revelation to feel
and explore. Up and over her head—he was insistent.
He wanted her all naked.

His own things took longer—hose and boots and
buttoned breeches, but soon they formed their own
heap on the floor. She wanted to touch this almost-
stranger. Her strokings were tentative, shy. But how
lovely, this curling pelt of hair across his chest, the
smooth tautness of his belly, the lean hips and hard,
well-muscled thighs. Her fingers traced a jagged scar
across his ribs where no hair grew, wondering at the
history this body hinted at. There was a thin scar that
ran along the back of his right hand, and an old punc-
ture wound at his shoulder. But whatever mishaps or

misdeeds they bespoke only made her hold him closer, this passionate and dangerous creature.

His mouth grazed her thighs and nudged them open while he searched the folds and discovered the secret places, the soft naked parts that lay hidden. She moaned as he continued his attentions and tried to draw her legs together. But he would hold them firm until he could feel the tremor in her limbs, the almost unbearable frenzy rising fast for the peak. Her whole body stiffened, arched hard against him, then fell back.

And he was brazen. He pulled her into the light to see her better, her breasts glowing like pale, lush moons, her hair catching errant streaks of sliver like a crown about her. He stood and began to excite her again, working his fingers over her swollen nipples, pausing to stroke her thighs, storming her wet mouth with kisses. She couldn't stand any longer. Her blood was too aroused, her limbs too languorous.

He was sure of her now—she had surrendered. He lay her back against the floury cushions and worked the fires hotter, teasing her flesh with the barest caresses, holding himself back until she cried out for him to touch her. He was provoking her now, supreme in his conceit. "Do you beg me, lady?" he whispered against her ear. She cried again, but he waited until she'd given in and managed a scarcely audible "Please!" And he made her say it again, and louder, until the pleas were strung together in a wailing little singsong that grew shrill as he entered her.

He lay above her, making only the slightest movements inside her. He was watching her face, her eyes soft and liquid with the green of hidden marsh ferns, her skin flushed rosy with the stirrings of passion. She felt the soft heat in her belly make ripples of excitement and carry her floatingly like moving in water. He moved against her, drawing her with him, building so slowly, so effortlessly yet always deeper, nearer to the vortex of sensation that would bring them both over the edge. Her eyes closed at last, shutting out all but this joining, this sweet coupling of their bodies.

In the dim half-light, the two merging forms glowed softly, rolling from light to shadow and back again. They began to move faster, clinging in need, in heat, seeking the end of the climb. Susanna's thighs were warm ivory, open to receive him, wanting only more of him, deeper and closer. She was nearing the finish. She was ending and he was with her, caught up in the same irresistible frenzy. She felt her own convulsive heavings joined by a flood of liquid warmth that came of his spending. It ran a course of heat through her body.

For a long time they lay together, their bodies completing each other. The captain's lean, handsome face rested itself in the hollow of her throat and Susanna's hands smoothed the damp unruly curls that clung to the back of his neck.

She became aware that the light had altered, was growing pink. It would be dawn soon, and with that knowledge came the other thoughts. It was the last day on this ship.

It was her wedding day.

She didn't want to cry. She kept her head very still and quiet as the tears gathered of their own accord in the corners of her eyes and overflowed in watery paths down her cheeks. They were icy wet, but she didn't stir to wipe them away, because he was so peaceful, so unutterably beautiful lying with her in the calm stillness of after-love.

For all her attempts at hiding, he discovered it. He raised himself on one elbow and hesitantly, his other hand extended its fingers toward her cheek, touching its wetness lightly.

"What's this?" he said softly. "Come, sweet, why do you cry?" He smiled suddenly, mischievously. "You cannot say you didn't like it, mistress. What, did it not suffice to cool your blood a little?" He reached to stroke her breast, idly playing the nipple with his fingers. "Is it more you'd be wanting?"

She drew away a little. "No, no, it's not for more," she said, gathering control to stop the foolish weeping. "It's . . . it's the last, is all." The tears began again, and she turned to hide her face. "Forgive me, it makes me sad."

He regarded her in a wonder of confusion. "What can you mean, *the last?*" His brows drew tight together as recognition dawned. "You don't mean—surely you can't mean you're still to marry?" His voice was incredulous.

She nodded mutely, wiping her eyes with the edge of the lacy nightdress. "I must," she said. "I've promised."

"I must. I've promised," he repeated in harsh mocking tones, his entire aspect altered. "And what, pray, is the promise of *this?*" he demanded, squeezing her breast rudely. "And this?" as he forced her onto her back and pulled her legs apart. He stared long at the naked bud that formed at the juncture of her thighs, and his eyes had no trace of softness in them now. She struggled for release, and he thrust her from him.

"Aye," he said, unstopped, "you're a lady full of promises. I should have seen that sooner. There's a big white house I know in New Orleans, and at least two dozen ladies there of promise. Some of them as promise twenty times in a single night. They keep tickets of the tally in their corsets. You'd do very well there, mistress. It's promises as would suit you I'll be bound.

"The good reverend has his share of devils, sweetheart," he continued, "but I'll wager he's met his match in you. And to think you'd have it hard—" At this he laughed, but it was a cold and ugly laugh, with not a trace of humor in it. "I'm sure it's a novel idea, setting the bridegroom early to his horns. Why, I've a mind to convert myself and become a Saint, take me a bevy of wives. Can't see as it'd be much different from life as a single man.

"I see it all clear now. Old Shuttleworth'll have the head of a ten-point buck—you'll see to that, won't you? Poor fool, he'll scarcely squeeze his antlers through the doorway. Well, how about another promise for me, sweet Susanna? Are you busy a month from Thursday?—or do you book more in advance? Do you give tickets, lady? Or sell—"

She had shrunk to a tight ball of grief and shame, begging him in ravaged tones, "Please stop. Please, say no more!"

"Stop?" he repeated innocently. "But my dear, how you've changed your way of speaking. Just a short time ago, it was 'Please, more!' wasn't it? And clutching and clinging like a baby possum, weren't you? Even a few 'I love yous' for the added sugar."

"Oh, please!" she moaned. "I meant it, it was true—"

"Oh, stop your mouth!" he said coldly. "The words are light as air—they billow up and vanish. You needn't fear I'd hold you to them, understanding now that you are a lady of promises."

His eyes noticed the light briefly, and they both heard the shuffling of feet above. "You'd best return," he said finally. "It wouldn't do to be late to the wedding, little blushing bride."

She wrapped herself in the garments, beseeching him with her eyes wet. But his looks were stony and scornful. They damned her and she fled.

At least Maidie was still sleeping soundly when Susanna stole back in. The dawn was streaking in through the porthole with a pure glory that Susanna could share no part of. How could a single night carry her to such extremes—from the dizzying heights of fulfillment to the most wretched loss and degradation. The conflict of those violent emotions had wrung her dry. She wanted nothing more than to sink down on the vacant bed and sleep. But there was no time. If she once lay down, she didn't know that she could rise again. Oblivion was too tempting. Her duty lay elsewhere.

She had mangled the one full night of loving she had known. What was there left but the path of repentance to which she'd committed herself? That and a loveless marriage, and an empty mariage bed.

For Jed Taylor, the night's events filled him with the turmoil of hot fury and intense frustration. Damn the witch, that she could affect him so. He wondered what there was in her that drew forth such unbridled senseless passions. He had known countless women, some more beautiful than she, many more skilled in the sensual arts. She was pretty, to be sure, but that was a superficial matter, and little enough to cause a man this harsh and wracking torment of the mind.

There was something else with her, something quite different—a sense of delicacy, a kind of *discovery*—she made the common carnal act all new, as though it had never happened before, and there it lay like a gift and a secret between themselves.

But it was all a lie. And he cursed himself for falling victim to it, like some green schoolboy out for his first piece, who makes a white virgin of a whore. The girls with whom he'd pleasured were not good women. But they were honest females all, and what they gave and what they took in exchange was all direct. Like Louisa, his sloe-eyed Cajun mistress, herself the toast of half the gallants in Louisiana. And when he was away, those dandies paid her well for the favors of her tawny, supple hide. And when he returned, as he intended soon, she would make the time and place, with the usual flurry of broken engagements, to frolic on the silken sheets and feather mattress of her grand fourposter bed.

His thoughts drifted idly to the incident four years

before, when some curiosity or wanderlust had led him across the great American West in company with fur trappers who knew the mountain passes. He had met them in the bayou, trading great stores of fur—marten, lynx, beaver, and well-cured deerhides. They had bellies full of liquor and heads full of tales. And most strangely, when he had made up his mind to go, Louisa had desired him to take her. It was absurd, of course, and he had refused out of hand. It would have been like taking an exotic hothouse flower and planting it in the desert, where only cactus thrive. She was a natural courtesan, nurtured by civilized wealth and decadent appetites. If there had been anything deeper in her odd request, neither had ever spoken of it. They understood each other well.

Not like this sly vixen Susanna, he thought, his musings come full-circle. Impossible to understand *her*—a young girl all pink face and gold curls, sweet, beguiling. A conniving harridan who would attend her own wedding with her flesh still hot from illicit and wanton embraces. Cheap, he judged furiouhly. Cheap and false— the type that could sell her maidenhead twelve times over and make shift to bleed each time. He reached to his shelf for a bottle and a glass, and poured himself a generous shot of whiskey. He'd had enough of Mistress Hungerford. She'd be gone today, and good riddance.

Susanna was dressed as had been planned, in the thin white gown of her baptism. Her undergarments had been sent by Elder Shuttleworth. They were hand-woven, also white, and embroidered with a tiny emblem in the corner, a sign of the Mormon church. Her husband-to-be addressed a few words of faith to the company asesmbled to witness the marriage, and the ceremony proceeded without incident.

Except that Captain Jed Taylor had sent his excuses and spent the morning in his quarters.

7

THE PASSENGERS WHO had watched from the foredeck had their first glimpse of Nauvoo from a distance of twenty-five miles. Maidie had raced down to the cabin and pulled Susanna from her packing. "It's the steeple," she had cried. "You can see the top of the temple!" And indeed, it rose loftily above the highest trees and lesser buildings like an airy beacon, drawing the seekers to its gates.

The town itself came into view as they maneuvered a river bend about five miles from the city wharf. By that time almost all of the passengers were leaning against the deck rail, listing the ship by their communal weight, craning their neck starboard to the Illinois side for closer glimpses of their new home.

The temple, built of gleaming white limestone, crowned a gently rising knoll. All the shops and townhouses surounded it like honored sentinels. The streets seemed laid out in careful order, and small garden plots could be vaguely discerned, attached to many of the houses. Maidie was perhaps the most anxious and agitated of all who scanned the village streets. Brother Martin Brauer, a farmer of twenty-eight, was somewhere in that place, possibly even now approaching the landing wharf to meet the ship that carried his foreign bride. Would he really meet the ship? How would she

know him if he did? He had dark hair, she remembered
from a letter. He was not tall. And yes, he limped
slightly—a horse had kicked his left leg, and it had
never healed quite right. . . .

As it was, Maidie could have saved herself the worry.
Only three people awaited the ship as she discharged
her living cargo onto solid land and a new continent
after the long voyage. Martin Brauer was the first,
walking among them, calling Maidie's name. The second was Dr. John Bernhisel, slender, courteous, a little
stooped under the rigors of his long, unflagging service
to the Mormon cause. And a gray-haired woman of
some forty years named Prudence Shuttleworth, first
wife to the reverend elder.

Whispers of hesitancy circulated among tht converts.
The town was beautiful. But so quiet. Not a dog barking, no merchants aboard on the streets. Dr. Bernhisel
had requested them all to convene at the great temple,
and the crowd of some forty-odd pilgrims moved slowly
along the main thoroughfares. The smithy was closed,
and the stable. On close inspection, the gardens were
untended, and farther off there were fields of grain and
corn rotting unharvested. Cherry and apple trees had
dropped their fruit, and only the birds had eaten it.
The doors to several homes stood carelessly ajar.

They continued their walk toward the meeting place,
treading softly on the paved boulevards and uttering
their misgivings in hushed tones, as though they feared
awaking ghosts. For Nauvoo lay like a dead city, em-
balmed but unburied, or like a place enchanted by a
fairy spell which had forgotten time and motion.

Susanna had not been totally unprepared for the appearance of Prudence Shuttleworth. This unusual custom of the Mormons certainly excited notoriety; and
while she wished she had been informed before, she was
relieved to find that the thin, weary-looking woman ac-

cepted her without question. It had been hard times
these many months, the older woman told her husband.
Brigham's party had begun the trek in February, and
all who could left with him. Only the lame, the ill, the
aged had remained with those, like herself, who awaited
family. And of course good Dr. Bernhisel kept them
together as best he could. But the raids and bombard-
ments had been vicious and continued even now, with
so few of them left. The Brooks home had been fired,
and thirteen other dwellings. Little Tommy Blackstone
and his father had both been ruthlessly murdered. And
rabble had moved into the southern section—they
made hovels of good people's homes and terrorized the
remaining inhabitants with drunken looting and plun-
dering. Shadrach, she informed him, was out nights with
the other boys, dealing out their own singular ven-
geances. She feared for him, but couldn't control him.
So far he had been lucky.

They were almost to the church when she excused
herself to return home. Maryann was canning, she explained, and needed help with sealing. The harvest had
been poor with so few hands to tend. She'd get a meal
laid out.

Susanna asked her new husband if this meant they
would be leaving Nauvoo, too. He told her it was too
soon yet to tell. But fall was a bad time to travel on
long journeys. They would meet with winter before
they met their destination.

Inside the church was evidence of desecration;
shrines despoiled and cornices hacked with blades. A
beautifully carved marble basin, itself supported by
twelve life-sized marble oxen, had been sullied with
human sewage—the apostates had marked their scenes
of victory like dogs staking out territory with a lifted
hindquarter. Susanna had to hold her breath against
the stench as she passed. The elder, in a grim voice,

told her that the twelve oxen represented the twelve apostles of Joseph, upon whom the security of the church depended.

Dr. Bernhisel gently informed those newly arrived of the events that led to Brigham Young's departure. The Gentiles had been tireless and had managed to secure a warrant against Brigham Young and his apostles. The charge was counterfeiting currency, and federal troops in New Orleans had only been waiting a thaw in the river to travel upstream and make the arrest. The Saints had been long preparing for the exodus, though they had hoped to wait until spring. So it was they departed early with winter still hard upon them. Word had come they were encamped in Winter Quarters, a site in Iowa, and that they had established a happy peace with the native Omaha Indians.

Newcomers would find food and lodging—this he promised. The Saints remaining in Nauvoo were living humbly and half in hiding from the hordes of pillagers that had descended on their once-splendid city. Many brothers and sisters were bivouacked in tents and makeshift shelters across the river to escape the ravages of the mob. But fever had taken hold there. For tonight, he suggested, they would be safest to take refuge in those deserted dwellings set farthest from the main streets north of the town. A man would be assigned to each house to keep watch. Food would be distributed from the church vestibule at five o'clock. They must light no fires or lamps to attract attention after sundown. Those to whom Nauvoo the Beautiful had fallen were, like predatory beasts, most dangerous at night.

Meanwhile, the *Star Victory* still lay at anchor. The crew that had left so eagerly soon returned, more than a little disgruntled. What whore's trick was this, they complained vociferously, to grant them play about in a ghost town, dry as a snake's rattle and as void of pleasure women as the ship's own galley? Not a glass of small beer, not a female over six who was not also over fifty.

Jed Taylor looked at the sky and did some rapid calculations. It was too late now to navigate downriver, but they would weigh anchor at first light and head back to New Orleans. He promised them an extra day's pay to make up for the dearth of entertainment tonight. "Think, lads," he said grinning, "how much hotter she'll be for having missed your attentions this day." The joke and promise of recompense appeased the men, and the captain heaved a sigh of relief. He had seen trouble with crews for less reason than these men had. And he'd be glad himself to see that bright, wicked city again. This trip had left a taste like ashes in his mouth. First Brock's death and Davy's injuries—he'd have to file a report of that. And to top it off that last night with the girl who'd played him like a gull—a dumb puppet with the strings all in her hands. Well, she'd have to be content to ply the elder's strings now; there'd be no more come-hithers to him. He was strangely irked that the thought did not much please him.

With his mind so occupied, he did not notice James Leverton approach until he felt a hand on his shoulder. "Captain Taylor," his friend said cordially, "can you spare a few moments for a glass of port?"

"Of course," Taylor answered, returning the greeting.

"To my cabin, then," said Leverton. "There is a matter I would discuss with you. I think we have mutual friends. We'll have us a good bottle, and I'll have my pipe, and we can reflect upon the future."

They were settled in comfortably sipping the heavy sweet wine before Leverton made any move to speak. At last he ceased stroking his coppery beard, drew the

pipe stem from his mouth and leaned toward his guest.
"I'm meeting a man in New Orleans on Friday. Colonel Melvin Wayne—I believe you know him?"

Taylor's eyes lit at the mention. "Mel Wayne! Tall,
ginger-haired, scar down his cheek?" Leverton nodded.
"Why, that sneaky old mountain devil!" Taylor exclaimed. "You know how he got that scar? 'Twas a
starving grizzly clawing his face in the great Sierra
Mountains. He was with Fremont's explorers at the
time, and I'd met up with them and traveled with them
for a bit. Fremont drew up a bead on that bear cool
as you please just as the beast was about to relieve old
Mel of his head." His eyes blazed at the recollection.
"So he's become an army gentleman, you say? A colonel?"

"He always has been an army man," Leverton explained. "And very much an American, though his
mother had insisted he be educated at Cambridge.
That's how I knew of him." At this point, Leverton
was forced to smile. "And a more bone-headed scholar
one could scarcely hope to find. I remember telling him
years ago he had made a providential decision in
choosing the army for his career. Certainly he'd never
make a priest!"

Taylor laughed heartily, with prior knowledge. "No,"
he agreed, "he's too much life in his trousers for that!
Now, professor, you've pricked my curiosity. What is
your business with Wayne?"

Leverton took his time, pausing to refill his pipe
with fragrant tobacco, tamping it expertly, refitting it
to his mouth. "You commented when we began our
voyage, captain, on the weight and bulk of my books.
Twenty-five boxes, I think I have in the hold." At his
companion's nod, he continued. "Only five of them con-
tain books. The others," he said meaningfully, "the
other twenty cases are all English guns and rifles."

If shock were his intent, he had succeeded. Taylor's

eyes widened; then his face became grim. "It's late for me to say I'm not pleased with that subterfuge, Leverton. Was Wayne in on this with you? Just what kind of a game are you playing?"

"No longer chess, Captain Taylor," Leverton said seriously. "The deception was considered a necessary precaution—and not my idea, I assure you. But let it suffice that I had means to dispose of the arms should circumstances require it, and neither you nor your people were in jeopardy. Any responsibility would have fallen on my head and that of Carl Whittaker, who owns the *Star Victory*."

Again the captain started. Whittaker, too? "You are indeed a man of surprises, Mr. Leverton," he said at last. "And damn me for being duped all around. Can you tell me what might be my part in all this intrigue?"

"Colonel Wayne needs a courier. The arms are to be delivered to a Mexican purchaser—" Leverton noted Taylor's raised eyebrow and smiled reassuringly. "They are *special* guns, captain. Something to give American troops a certain edge when it comes to battle. I cannot give you all the details now. Many of them I don't know myself. But if you agree to meet with Colonel Wayne in New Orleans, I think he'll be able to satisfy any questions you might have."

"I'll meet with Mel," the captain said, "but I promise nothing more. He stood, regarding James Leverton with a puzzled, almost sheepish look. "There's more to you than you care to show," he said. "You're an Englishman. What is all this to you?"

"There's more than one thing to any man, Jed Taylor, if he's a man at all. This is my adopted country now, my new home," Leverton said softly. "I've little to lose in being of some small service to her. When this is done, I hope to follow the Mormons. That has been my real intention from the start."

It became apparent a few days later that Leverton

was not the only one interested in the Mormon trek. "They're a perfect cover for you, Jed," the Colonel said. "The gun wagon'll be just one of hundreds, as I read it—you can journey with them as far west as they go. That may be in this rough land—the Great Basin, maybe all the way to California."

The intervening years had done little to change Mel Wayne. He still stood tall and walked heavily, a great bear of a man. He had grown a bushy red-blond moustache, which covered part of the grizzly scar. And he was in the uniform of the U.S. Army. Aside from that, he was the same eager hellion, the same keen-spirited wit and incisive mind that Taylor had known in the hard western mountains.

The three men—Taylor, Wayne, and Leverton—stepped into a long, empty courtyard. Wayne reached for an opened case and drew out a new rifle. He handed it to Taylor with a box of ammunition. "Load it," he said.

Then he gestured Taylor to an empty run bounded by a wooden barricade. The rifle shot perfectly.

The performance was repeated six times. On the seventh shot it failed. And continued failing.

"The workings are for your protection," Wayne related. "The Mexican will undoubtedly insist on trying the weapons at the exchange. And every one will go at least four times before it fails. We figure somewhere between four and ten shots will go. Then nothing. See here." He opened the rifle expertly and showed the two men a small broken metal pin. "Each firing pin has been broken, then weak-soldered." He pulled out another rifle to demonstrate. "Even if they took the gun apart, it's unlikely they'd notice. And ammunition is precious to them now. They won't waste it in repeated trials. The gun, she works," he said grinning. "The Mex, they buy. The money they pay for the guns will be yours,

Jed, to sweeten the pie a little. The government doesn't want the profit—only the delivery.

"And," he added significantly, "every rifle that dies is worth at least one American life. Probably more. If the timing comes off as planned, there will be more than these passed off down there." He looked for Taylor's reaction. "What do you think, Jed? Can you fancy yourself a gunrunner?"

"I'm waiting to hear the rest of it," Taylor said evenly. "Where do we make the exchange?"

"Come into my office," Wayne said. "I'll show you."

He pulled out a map and pointed first to a huge lake in the land referred to as the Great Basin. "If the Mormons stop here, you can catch the old Spanish trail just south of the lake. Fremont used it, too—I can give you copies of his maps. If they continue west, it'll probably be all the way to Los Angeles, which is your destination anyway. Garcia will be sending men to meet you. You'll be escorted a little ways south to a port they call San Diego de Alcalá. That's the final exchange point, and also the most dangerous part of your job. They can be tricky dealers and it's their territory. I understand the Mormons are moving slow. Young is supposed to be heading a group some twenty thousand strong. There's plenty of time for you to make the rendezvous, and if you have to desert the train to do it, go ahead. But you're safer and less identifiable with them, so bear that in mind.

"Now, before I pull out a bottle of my best rotgut whiskey, I need an answer. Are we toasting to old times or new times, Jed?"

Taylor looked from Wayne to Leverton and sighed at length. "I don't think a man stands much chance against the two of you." His face broke into a sudden grin, wide and sunny. "Pour it up, Wayne," he said. "The army's newest gunrunner has a powerful thirst!"

They soon agreed that Leverton would take charge of Davy and bring him by ship to Los Angeles. The arduous overland trek would be too difficult, and the "captain's boy" would not be left behind.

"By the way, colonel," Leverton said, "you have the fastest carriers in this part of the country. I need to send an inquiry to England, an old student of mine—"

"Anyone I know?" Wayne asked.

"No, he's before your time. He was in America, but there's recently come an estate, and I've reason to believe he may be already back in Hampshire. He had a daughter out of wedlock some eighteen years ago. She's with the Mormon group, but she came here expressly to look for him."

Wayne frowned slightly. "I can get it fast to New York and back—it's traveling over water takes the time. But look—I can forward the message by ship to you on the western coast. It's the quickest route by far."

Taylor, recognizing that they spoke of Susanna, scowled meaningfully but said nothing. She was nothing to him—a bit of blond fluff, a deceiving little bitch. Still, he could not deny that it would add a measure of interest traveling with the Mormons if she would be among them. He might even find some opportunity to balance the scales with her.

Taylor was soon outfitted in typical army fashion. They gave him a wagon that looked more like a buckboard, a horse that looked more like a mule, and an Oriental wagon-driver who was nicknamed Hoppy because of his rapid jerky walk. But if anyone thought the name comical, Hoppy had a renowned expertise with the double-bladed butcher's knife which he kept sheathed on his belt. And the look on his face when he unsheathed that knife was not comical at all. A man with a finely distinguished sense of honor was

Hoppy, and men thereabouts accorded both him and his knife a fitting respect.

"You'll begin to move as soon as we have word the trek is beginning from their Winter Quarters," Colonel Wayne told him.

He went whoring with Melvin Wayne that night, and, as they had done once in a frontier trading post, they changed women halfway through the evening. Mel had chosen a plump bouncy blonde from Madame Lorraine's. Babette was juicy-fleshed and eager to please. Her fat little bottom jounced as sweet against a mattress as it did against the tight cloth of her gown. Jed had brought Louisa, who found nothing amusing in the idea of changing partners. Her beautiful dark eyes were first angry, then reproachful. Jed Taylor sat hot in his liquor, insistent, commanding. He came toward her laughing, but there was a chill in his laugh. He swung her onto the bed and over his lap, and picked up a hairbrush to spank her. And he did until it hurt and she was screaming. He let her up and pulling a small purse of gold from his pocket, thrust it into her hand. *"You're paid for,"* he growled. Half-drunk, he was finding a cruel satisfaction in abusing her. He took her by the shoulders and shoved her out toward the door to Wayne's room. "Go on!" he charged, urging her relentlessly, pushing her from him until she whirled on him crying fiercely, "You're getting your own streak of poison meanness, Jed Taylor!" Head down, she crossed the corridor to the colonel's room, and disappeared within.

A few moments later, sweet, chubby Babette appeared, and Taylor set her rapidly on her back. He took her swiftly, brutally, as though the game of love were a battle and he the attacker. She was soft and he sank into her flesh. But he persisted in lancing her until she had had enough and then too much. Though afterwards she had curled about him appealingly, he had frightened her a little. There was too much power in him, mixed too much with anger.

He was thinking all the while of Reverend Shuttleworth's new wife.

Susanna had not slept well that first night in Nauvoo. She had been given her own bedroom on the second floor, a small, sparsely furnished chamber with a single window that faced the river. The night was quiet, dark, empty. There were no stars, no moon. Little traffic rippled the river water; few signs of life interrupted the strange country silence.

But later she had heard coarse voices shouting and singing. She saw torches at the southern end of the city. They were moving toward the temple. She saw a bonfire start in the empty courtyard, heard the splintering sound of shattered bottles. She felt small and lost and lonely, and turned away from the window.

Stories had circulated describing the actions of these "Gentiles" who so hated the Mormon people. They had strung up young men of the city after beating them bloody, as "examples" to the citizens. They had fired fields and houses. Five people in a single home had been burned alive. The mob had constructed barricades to prevent the victims from escaping.

Nauvoo was a town in siege, a town in the grip of horror. Shuttleworth and Bernhisel had conferred for several hours after supper, planning flight for the remaining Saints. There would be no peace to winter here. Many of their fields had been destroyed, and much of what remained was rotting for lack of harvest hands. Food was growing scarce. Winter would bring certain famine. The little livestock that was left was kept hidden in cellars and lost flesh for lack of fodder.

Shadrach Shuttleworth, the elder's son, had not returned that night. Shadrach had joined with the Danites, a Mormon vigilante group who believed in the ancient

justice of repaying the enemy with the same mercy as
they themselves were shown. There was unbridled
savagery on both sides.

Too, Susanna had met Maryann Shuttleworth, whom
she at first believed to be the reverend's daughter, but
who turned out to be his second wife. Maryann had
immediately regarded Susanna with a singular and un-
compromising hatred that came of viewing her rightful
place usurped by a foreign tart, an interloper. Prudence was accorded first place, but she was old. Maryann was young, still in her twenties, and pretty in a
drawn-out way. She had dark brown hair that hung
raggedly about her face, fair skin, blue eyes. Her breasts
were rather small, her hips and legs very thin. She had
been wed three years and had borne no children. Children were very important to Mormons and Susanna
had already begun to fear that Elder Shuttleworth might
forget his tacit agreement that they not share a common bed. That he, having only one son, might try to
breed further issue from her. Prudence was too old.
Maryann was barren.

But at the moment babes and bedposts were the
least of the elder's concerns. Survival for those already
here was the worry that kept him from sleep. He
worked long into the night in a heavily curtained room,
drawing plans and figuring necessities for the imminent
journey.

They could not leave for at least a week. It would
take all of that to gather what foodstuffs there were,
assemble the wagons, break the teams that had been
left to forage on the most meager grasses. A few thin
draft horses, a tiny herd of starving oxen that were
hidden in the woods were all that remained of the
abundant livestock that had nurtured Nauvoo in its
prime. That, and the scattering of milk cows and pigs
that were secreted in cellars and woodsheds.

Maidie had been wed that same day to Martin

Brauer. She had worn a pretty white poplin gown, tight at the bodice and flowing full over her ample hips and strong legs. Her husband, though he stood only a few inches above her shoulder, seemed well pleased with the match, and Maidie herself was a radiant bride. Her eyes glowed with a sense of belonging as Dr. Bernhisel blessed her, placing his hands on her brow, and united the two in holy wedlock. It was a sign, he said, that the church would stand since it had in its flock the fruitful continuations of celestial marriage. Maidie was especially gratified, however, that Martin Brauer had no other wife.

Were they even now, Susanna wondered, consummating the marriage contract? Was Maidie clad in the same white satin she herself had worn to meet her captain? She wished her friend joy and pleasure, remembering with a sudden pang the cruel, angry words that had ended her last night with Jed Taylor. She put the thought from her and recalled instead that moment he had held her so tenderly in his arms—so safe, so protected—as though within the embrace of his body was the home she had so longed for and never found. This she held to herself as a comfort. It gave her peace for sleeping on that dry straw mattress in that cold and lonely room.

The worthy Reverend Shuttleworth took command early the next morning. Susanna was assigned to several chores and duties, and Prudence explained the tasks. Every member of the household had work. When he returned, Shadrach was subjected to a heavy tongue-lashing, which culminated in the reverend's shouting, "I keep order in this house!" Then he raised his hand and struck his son full in the face.

At twenty-one, Shadrach was a tall, husky youth with a breadth and largeness of bone almost twice that of his father's. He wore his straight brown hair long at the shoulder, like an Indian, and there was a stub-

born set to his jaw. He had stood unflinching under his
father's heavy hand, but in the moment of silence that
hung between them, Susanna sensed a tightly controlled
fury in the younger man, that might have set him
against his own father. She was relieved when he
turned and stormed out of the room.

"You've been away many months," Prudence said,
trying to placate her husband. "The boy's become bold,
it's true, but there's hardness needed in these times."

"He's my son," Shuttleworth countered angrily. "He
owes obedience to his father. I'll tolerate nothing less."

There were two cows hidden in the root cellar, and
Susanna was set to milk them. Both were pitifully bony,
bawling in the dark confines. The black and white one
kicked, and Prudence helped her hobble the beast. The
two together yielded less than a quart of milk.

"That's all there is?" Prudence asked, sighing heavily. "Well, then there's naught we can do to force the
beasts. But if this keeps on, we'll have to slaughter
them. Their meat is shrinking every day. We only
stand to lose by keeping the creatures alive." Her gray-
ing hair was loosed in wisps from her bun, and her
mild eyes were half-teary. "I raised them from heifers.
They used to be the best milk cows in Nauvoo." Her
eyes fell to her own thin work-worn hands, callused
and dry. Old-looking. "I guess," she said softly, almost
to herself, "we've all of us seen better days."

She looked up at Susanna, her smile too quick and
bright. "Now be a good lass and fetch up some kindling.
I'll have to start the stove going soon."

A thin grove of trees separated the Shuttleworth
house from its nearest neighbor. Susanna could spy her
husband conversing with a teen-aged boy who sat splay-
legged on a wooden piling, casually whittling a block
of wood. "Where's Shadrach?" the elder demanded
with quiet authority.

The boy grinned sideways at the older man, revealing strong buck teeth. "I believe he's gone to make some catfish bait. Seems to me I saw old Shad pull out a leather necklace and head for the swamp. Said them damn catfish was so hungry they was jumping up from the mud bottom and meowing for some meat. Guess Shad didn't want to see them starving. Clem and Tasker was with him."

Shuttleworth grabbed the boy by his shirt collar and dragged him to his feet. "Now you listen here, and you listen good. When you see my son you tell him— this show-off butchering's got to stop! You think nobody sees a man in a boat cutting the guts out of another body? You think he's going to get away clean every time? If it's killing he's after, let him use a gun and get away fast. This is no boys' game! You hear me?"

The boy had grown pale and shaky under the hand of the formidable elder. "Yessir," he said quickly. "I'll tell him."

Susanna shuddered. This was a raw and barbarous land, a land steeped in blood. People killed without compunction, as though murder were no sin. As though there were no law. She returned hurriedly to her chores.

Afternoon found her near the main street of the town when a line of painted wagons drew up. The first carriage was a huge and stately affair, drawn by two magnificent white horses. The red paint on the sides had chipped and weathered in places, but Susanna could make out the large gold letters that spelled MABIE & HOWES CIRCUS.

The dapper ringmaster jumped from the seat of the wagon he drove, surveying the empty town with undisguised dismay. He looked sadly at three little boys who gazed wide-eyed at the caravan. "We've played this city for four years and more," he told them. "But there'll be no performances now, not now. I'm sorry, lads. Sorry for all of us." The animals remained caged, the brilliant costumes unpacked. The performers did not leave their wagons. A few minutes later, the train moved on.

Nothing in Nauvoo was as before. Only the shells of buildings and the pavings of the empty streets marked what it had been before the exodus. Susanna ended the day digging potatoes in the cold earth and pulling onions where they could be found. These she gathered in sacks and brought to the root cellar for storage. Her fingernails were encrusted with dirt, her face beginning to burn from the unaccustomed labor in the sun. She had been given three of Maryann's dresses, one of which was already stained with sweat and field soil.

Maryann had vehemently protested the loss of her garments, and this time it was Prudence who raised her voice, admonishing the girl for her selfishness. "It's well enough of trouble we've got without your making things still harder with your pettiness," she said. "Now quiet your tongue!" Maryann had shot Susanna a look of pure venom. With a sinking feeling, Susanna realized she had an enemy in the household, one who would actively wish her ill.

Elder Shuttleworth's second wife was already in disgrace; she had lost three nesting hens that morning. The broody birds had secreted their eggs in some craftily hidden corner and would not be discovered. Susanna had overheard Clem Hogans laugh and say there'd be some reckoning come Saturday. But she had heard so much that was new that she didn't pause to question its meaning.

Shadrach had returned for supper and Shuttleworth, subdued in part by Prudence's intervention, talked with him after the meal, laying plans and dividing labor in preparation for the journey. Shad stole out before sunrise the next day, moving the livestock through the woods to a sheltered pasture. He set a boy to watch them and returned to begin assembling wagons. One of the milk cows was butchered that day, and the meat hung in storage. Activity was almost frenzied in the daylight hours because the Saints went into hiding after sundown, locking themselves in their houses.

Dr. Bernhisel made daily rounds of the sick and injured, even to crossing the river to the fever-infested dwellings of the dying. Maidie, eager to assist the kindly man, went with him often. Sometimes when he took the ferry, he left her to attend the city families, giving her part of his drug supply and instructions for their use. Martin Brauer, working with the other men of the town, prepared their household for departure.

In the few first days of her marriage, Maidie had blossomed. For all the sly jokes about "Maidie's little man," Martin Brauer was a worthy partner, gentle, industrious, and delighted with his bride. He had treated her tenderly on their wedding night. Considerate of her virginity, he had taken his time, arousing her body until she was more than ready—aching to begin this new adventure. It showed on her daily face. She smiled easily; her complexion glowed. Her walk was more assured, unconsciously sensual, feminine. Her demeanor bore the mark of a woman satisfied and complete.

It was only when she saw Maidie that Susanna was reminded of Jed Taylor. Most days she worked too hard; most nights she was exhausted and sank immediately to sleep. Maidie reminded her; she beamed with the same sweet brightness that Susanna herself had felt. But only once, and only for a little time.

This afternoon Shadrach had startled her, coming up suddenly and standing over her, much too close as she straightened up from gathering wood. His bold eyes assessed her like a piece of beef, his full, sensual lips curled into a smile. And he trapped her against the shed with his arms stretched on either side of her.

"I don't think my father's taking proper care of you,

sister," he drawled. "A pretty thing like you—needs a man in bed nights, don't you?" His hand brushed against her pale gold curls. She shook him away angrily.

"Lively little missus, ain't you, now?" he continued, unperturbed. "I like the kind that fight—they're the hottest at the end. I'll bet you'd howl like a she-wolf when the moon's full. Yes, I'll bet you would."

He taunted her further while she shrank back against the wall of the shed. Finally, he let her go. She was terribly shaken at this new threat. There was no one she could tell. Prudence, who was the kindest to her, was Shadrach's mother. Susanna herself might be accused of encouraging his attentions. *She was his father's wife!* But clearly there was no immunity in her status. Still, she didn't believe he'd dare go too far. Even he held the reverend in some awe.

Saturday began like any other day, until the midday meal, during which Elder Shuttleworth seemed to be taking an unusual interest in Maryann. The thin, dark girl was agitated, apprehensive. She scarcely touched her plate. When the dishes had been cleared away, the reverend addressed her. "There's the matter of the hens to be reckoned, madam," he announced. Maryann paled visibly and lowered her eyes. "Prudence, Susanna —I'll expect the three of you back in the barn directly." With that he pulled the napkin from his lap and left the table.

The three of them assembled as directed. The last stall in the barn stood empty except for a section of a huge tree trunk lying on its side and positioned slightly back from the wall. Its bark had been removed, and its oak surface was polished smooth. At certain intervals, stakes had been driven into the soft dirt floor; two set on the near and two on the far side of the curious wooden structure.

The elder bid Maryann assume a humiliating position on her knees and bent well over the log bolster, so that her face was to the wall and her hips arched out toward the small assembly. He motioned to Prudence, who without instruction began to bind Maryann's ankles to the nearer stakes, set about two feet apart. Then she proceeded to tie the girl's wrists to the farther pair.

Susanna looked away in disgust, her husband's firm, proper voice brought her back, and his words held a trace of menace. "Sister Susanna, this is also for your enlightenment. You will give it your attention."

Thus she was forced to witness the degrading preparations.

At a gesture from Shuttleworth, Prudence drew Maryann's skirt well up so that the hem now hung about her neck and shoulders, leaving her fully exposed from the waist down. Her buttocks stood out tight against the coarse cotton drawers, and with an almost theatrical gesture, Shuttleworth himself pulled at the flimsy covering until the fastenings gave and the last garment slid to her ankles. His right hand held a short braided leather whip.

Now he stepped back and spoke to his trussed victim directly for the first time since the meal. "Sister," he intoned. "You have through sinful laxity lost us our sure sustenance, for which you must be punished. For each of the hens that is gone, you will receive three lashes. Do you repent?"

The reply came like a well-rehearsed litany. "I repent of my sins and I beg you to chastise my body that I may account for my misdeeds and be redeemed in the sight of my husband and the Lord."

The first lash came down.

For a moment there was nothing but the angry *thwack* of leather against flesh. Then Maryann screamed. Susanna looked on, frozen, as an angry weal appeared along the soft white curve of the buttock. The girl's legs, held in their bindings, were shaking uncontrollably, anticipating the next blow. Each succeeding stroke seemed to come with increasing ferocity, but the reverend spaced them out, pausing between each lash to wait for the welt to raise, as if to judge the quality and depth of the wound inflicted. The girl's whimperings became loud sobs as the whip bit into the tender flesh, carving its punishments across her naked buttocks.

At last the castigation was completed, and the avenging patriarch put up his scourge. He paused for a moment and gazed with an unholy satisfaction upon his handiwork. Maryann's buttocks were lacerated with deep, fiery welts, as were the backs of her thighs. He nodded to Prudence that she might now release the girl. Still bound, Maryann wailed, writhing and twisting in pain. The reverend turned on his heel and left the barn.

Her eyes full of pity and horror, Susanna rushed to help Prudence undo the bindings. Maryann seemed oblivious to all but the burning agony of her flesh, and made no protest as the two women lifted and half-carried her back to the house. "How can he do this?" Susanna cried. "Why does no one stop him?"

Prudence answered her with calm, sad resignation. "The reverend holds that a woman's like a child, and has to be reckoned with regular, to keep her on the path of Right. Don't fret so, child. She'll be up and about by supper. And who are we to argufy with a man, him that's our husband and our keeper in the eyes of the Lord?"

Yet a short time later, Prudence called Susanna to the kitchen with a brief warning. "You must take care not to rile the elder, Susanna. Man of God he may be, but he owns a fierce temper. Sary Lynn sassed him once too pert and he hauled her out back on a Saturday evening. Buck naked he had her, too. And when he'd finished a'reckoning her, he invited Clem and Tasker to whup her some more. Clem's his sister's boy, you know, and thick that family is.

"The boys was both in their likker, and when I finally got to carrying her back in here, she was laid up for five days, crying fierce with every move. And there was blood down there didn't come from no licking," she added darkly, "though I ain't saying nothing, mind."

The evening meal passed silently, without incident, and Susanna and Maryann both retired early. Susanna herself felt marked by the occurrence of the afternoon. She sensed an evil in this place and wished she'd never come. There was no one to comfort her, and she was frightened. This house, this place among these stern, religious-minded folk was foreign, sinister.

Susanna could not sleep that night. Sounds came to her through the thin walls that separated her bed-chamber from Maryann's. The sounds came clearly—the door that opened and closed, the rustle of clothing, followed by the quick, heavy breathing, the stifled moans and hoarse gruntings that spelled an unmistakable cadence.

The Reverend Horatio Shuttleworth was exercising his marital privileges upon his recently chastised second wife.

BOOK II
The Exodus

8

THE TOWN HAD taken up a cry that began as a murmur and swelled as the news spread from home to field to barn and street—everywhere residents of the city could be found. Porter Rockwell was back in Nauvoo.

He had been held in jail for most of the summer, accused of the attempted assassination of Governor Lilburn W. Boggs, archenemy of the Mormon people, the man Joseph Smith had predicted would die violently within one year. Porter, who loved Joseph, was a prime suspect, the man most likely to take on the task of prophecy-fulfillment.

Yet when his case had finally come to trial, not a man rose to point a finger. And with good reason. Porter Rockwell was probably the deadliest man on the western frontier. His name was synonymous with the fearsome sons of Dan, Danites, Daughters of Zion—whatever one chose to call them. He had been personal bodyguard to Joseph Smith; now he was the avenging angel of the Mormon persecutions. He was the man Joseph Smith had promised no bullet would ever touch, and he wore his hair long in remembrance—a fashion that Shad and a host of other Mormon youths followed slavishly.

His figure belied his reputation. He was short, squat, round-faced, with a high voice that often broke like an adolescent boy's. But when he walked down a crowded street, men parted to make way for him and raised whispers in his wake.

The night raids on Nauvoo had intensified. The Mormon-haters descended like armies laying siege, broke into houses, held drunken orgies in the temple. The people had taken to hiding the most helpless of their brethren in the tall grasses, to escape threats, interrogations, and beatings. Rabble had descended on the Brauer house last night, and Maidie and her husband had hidden in the cellar while above their heads their furniture was broken, food stolen, and articles of clothing ripped with bayonets and knives.

Now Porter Rockwell had come back to Nauvoo. And though he had yawned and drawled in his high voice that he only wanted a little rest from the poor accommodations of the Liberty jail and some time with his sweet wife who awaited him, the townfolk all breathed a little easier, and the Danite vigilantes only waited the call to arms.

Elder Shuttleworth had officially put his house up for sale, but there were few and meager offers. A wonderful brick home of two stories, set on five acres of land, had gone for only $15 in gold. A Gentile speculator had offered the reverend $200 for his home—but his currency had been false. When the elder called his attention to the matter, the man had laughed in an ugly way and retorted he was only giving back Mormon money to the Mormons. Gold was needed—reputable, solid coin. And in these times, gold was rare.

Gentile women came like scavengers, offering a pittance to the Shuttleworth wives for solid furniture, good iron stoves, treasured linens. And their troubles dictated that the unfair price would be accepted. Prudence stood by while her precious cut-glass goblets were snatched up, her imported china vases pawed over by the bargain-seekers. She watched silently as the women stuffed their sacks with the precious luxuries of her accumulated days. It had all happened before; it had happened more than once. They would start again, in another place. They always did.

Maryann was not as hardened to loss, and she wept at giving up the mahogany china closet, the silver candlesticks, the soapstone carving—they had been wedding gifts from her family in New York. She lashed out at Susanna, who kept quietly to one side. "You've got no reason to be sad, do you, sister?" she hissed. "You've brought nothing to this house, so you've nothing to lose!"

Susanna had no answer.

The house and land was finally sold to an immigrant family newly arrived and seduced by the fertile soil and well-built structure of home and barn. What they had heard and seen of trouble did not deter them, knowing the Mormons were preparing to leave and assuming that the fracas would then end. They paid $85 in good money, and were promised possession within the week.

Shuttleworth immediately went dealing with the riverboat merchants, buying up stores of flour and sugar, rope, two new rifles, a fresh yoke of oxen, and one fat sow—some on cash and some on faith. He heaved a mighty sigh of relief—his household, though not well equipped, was better off than most.

The women spent their evenings sewing tents and wagon covers, and the days were busy with pickling, salting beef, baking hard biscuits, and drying fruits and vegetables.

Susanna met Maidie on the street, and the two were delighted to have a chance to talk. Martin Brauer had been long preparing for the trek. His livestock had fared better than most, because he had gathered grain and field grasses by hand for their fodder each day. He was a handy wagon-builder, too. The axles were of stout hickory soaked in brine; the wheels were sturdy and turned well under tested weight. They had been terrified the night of the raid. Both were anxious to be on their way. She had, she admitted, been drinking a draught to prevent conception every night. She didn't want to bear a child on the trail. When the Saints reached Zion would be time enough to start a babe. She would give Susanna a supply of the draught if she wished. But Susanna, flushing hot under her friend's scrutiny, said it wasn't needed.

In turn, Susanna told Maidie of the successful sale of the Shuttleworth home, her husband's bargaining for supplies, the busy labor of the house. She mentioned neither Maryann's whipping nor Shadrach's approaches, held silent by some peculiar sense of wedded loyalty.

Maidie offered a juicy tidbit concerning Dr. Bernhisel. For forty-six years, the good doctor had maintained his contented bachelorhood against the church's dictate by neatly sealing unto himself ten proper unwedded women, all of them safely quiet and buried in Mormon graves. A bit over a year ago, he had at last yielded to ecclesiastic pressure and married a living widow, Sister Julia van Orden. And since then, unknown to Sister Julia, had added five others. The last of these, Elizabeth Barker, was just seventeen, "and the change she makes in him, Susanna, you never would believe." Maidie giggled. "He seems so strict and proper, but he's like a puppy around her—so anxious, so eager to please.

"It does seem a pity that he has to visit her in secret, she makes him so happy. Wouldn't it be nicer if he had just her for wife? I only hope Martin isn't pressed to wed another."

"Why, Maidie, he is so clearly content with you," Susanna said comfortingly. "I can't imagine him taking another wife!"

"Aye," Maidie sighed, "but there's so many widows

about, Susanna, and Brother Brigham has said they must be sheltered in earthly marriages for time. You know he himself has married nine of the prophet's widows!"

The girls continued walking arm in arm awhile. Neither mentioned the time aboard the *Star Victory* that had brought them to this place, but Susanna's thoughts were full of Captain Taylor. She wondered if he ever thought of her, and dismally decided not. If she closed her eyes, she could almost see him, standing so tall above her, eyes mocking, his hands poised to reach for her. Blushing at her own thoughts, she forced herself to attend her errands and bid Maidie good-day.

Six wagons arrived late that afternoon, sent from Winter Quarters by Brigham Young himself to assist the departing Mormons. The men who delivered the wagons brought news. President Polk had sent an order for the Mormons to raise a battalion of 500 men to aid the U.S. Army against the Mexicans. The Saints themselves had been stubborn and wrathful that the nation that had allowed them to be so persecuted and driven from their homes would dare to enlist their aid.

But Brigham Young, with the astute political mind that was to mark his greatness as a Mormon leader, had exhorted, cajoled, and threatened his stubborn flock to obey the presidential command. He had finally warned that he would send women and old men if the youth refused to volunteer. The Mormons were already pitifully short of supplies, cash, and adequate health to continue the journey. Winter was setting in. The Mormon soldiers would be outfitted at army expense, paid in solid currency, and even allowed their women to travel with them as laundresses, cooks, and nurses.

And never one to be bested in a bargain, Young had traded his battalion in exchange for legal right to camp on Indian land—the land of the Omaha nation—where they had already built the cabins and plowed the fields—the very site already known as Winter Quarters. On the whole, it was a very convenient arrangement.

It may have been this news, coupled with the aid of the wagons and men and Porter Rockwell's return that lulled the town into a false sense of security. But lamps were lit that night, and precautions relaxed as families crowded to hear the stories from Brigham's messengers and speak in soft voices of their hopes for Zion.

Most were already sleeping when shortly after midnight a line of boats, lighted by torches, made their way along the river. They docked at the city wharf. A hundred—perhaps two hundred men descended on the sleeping city. Clem Hogans and Shadrach Shuttleworth had been up late, sharing jokes and tales and whiskey with Porter Rockwell. They were the first ones to see and hear the approaching attackers.

Shad and Clem were quick to reach for rifles, but Porter held them off. "There's five times as many of them, or more," he said. "It's not the time. Quick and quiet now, to all the houses! Get all the people to the cellars or the fields. Tell them to bring arms, but stay quiet, for their lives. Else it'll be suicide and morning'll see us all dead."

The young men, who would have chafed and fought under anyone else's orders, leapt to follow Porter's dictates. Susanna huddled on the dirt floor of the cellar, together with Prudence and Maryann. Elder Shuttleworth and Shadrach were rousing other homes, hiding the infirm, and carrying the precious food supplies toward the swamps.

They were too late for Jeremiah Talbert and his wife, who had sailed from Liverpool on the *Star Victory* with Susanna and Maidie. The Talberts had chosen a house fatally close to the temple. Jeremiah had been shot six times in the chest and face. His wife Melinda, six months gone with child, was found on a bed of blood, her belly ripped open by a bayonet. One of the men who found them hurried outside and retched then returned to help cover the bodies.

With Porter's command and fast warnings, the Talberts were the only deaths, but it was a night of black horror. The temple was the main object of desecration —the temple each man had tithed for, the temple upon which Joseph Smith had said depended their salvation, the temple of the Mormon endowments and religious mysteries. Those hidden in sheds and under houses could hear the raucous laughter of vulgar women, brought in to further profane the altars with lewd sporting. They could hear curses and saloon songs adding their insults to the night. Axes worked at the wooden fittings, and robes used in the Mormon rites were consigned to the flames.

Those who had fled to the woods watched the night sky glow like day from the three huge bonfires that had been lit. Furnishings stolen from the Nauvoo households served to feed the flames, and the flames burned all night long.

It was close to dawn that they heard the cannon blast. The infidels were firing the temple. Then at last— at long last—the invaders crept back to their boats and were gone.

In a slow, deathly silence, the Nauvoo inhabitants came forth from their hiding places. In the same silence, they prepared the bodies of the Talberts for burial. Close to sixty people, all who could walk, attended the hurried funeral. Reverend Shuttleworth consigned their souls to God, and six strong youths set their earthly remains in the ground.

Porter Rockwell, bristling and grim, spoke softly to a group of some twenty young men, including the six newly arrived from Winter Quarters. "Hide your women tonight," he said, "and dust your petticoats. See that your bowies are sharp." The men all nodded, unsmiling, and dispersed to the labors of the day. They were all due to leave Nauvoo the next morning.

All was in readiness. The last of the wagons had been assembled, well hidden in the swamps. What teams they had only waited the yoke. Supplies had been inventoried, packed in the wagons. Susanna and Maryann were set to sew the final coverings while Prudence helped load the last of the household goods. Maryann made no effort to conceal her hatred for Susanna. "I wish it had been you!" she said harshly, referring to the death of Melinda Talbert. "You seduced my husband, bitch! Couldn't you find another man who'd consent to have you?" She stuck herself with the needle and screeched. "Now see what you've made me do!"

She looked ridiculous, really, petulantly sucking her finger and complaining. But Susanna felt only that unearned hatred. She would have gone from her place, from the Shuttleworth house, if she could. But there was nowhere to go. "I'm sorry, Maryann, that I've hurt you," she said quietly. She picked up the canvas she was working on and went to another room.

Shadrach was clothed in his mother's housedress. There was paint on his face, a rifle in his hand, a long knife at his belt. His father observed him silently for a moment and said, "Wait here a minute." He went out back and returned with one of the new rifles he had just purchased. This he gave to his son. "Use it well," he said. "God go with you."

Night was coming earlier these days. All of Nauvoo not with Porter had hidden away as they had the night before, anxious, waiting the outcome of the coming battle. There was no doubt the Gentiles would return after their success the previous night. But tonight there were more than twenty well-armed men in women's skirts, whose faces were painted like Indians for war.

Porter had secreted his men well and cunningly. They

would not be casually discovered. And he was firm in
his commands. Most of the night would be spent in
waiting—they were too few to attack like soldiers.
They must attack like wolves.

So they waited and held back their arms. They
waited while the enemy whored in their temple and
sacked their homes. They listened to exhortations of
Mormon cowardice, challenges that went unanswered.
They watched the infidels drink themselves stupid and
all night they watched the bonfires burn, fed by their
property, the fruits of their long labors, the crafts of
their hands. Beds and bureaus were used for kindling;
precious kerosene from their homes made the flames
leap high. And the enemy celebrated their little victories of destruction, toasting each other with whiskey
and moonshine. And gradually, they fell into stupor,
sleeping, snoring in their drunkenness, in what was to
be their final sleep.

With a rustle of their women's skirts, the Daughters
of Zion crept forth from their hiding places, stalking
the enemy on bare feet, as quiet as the night. The fires
crackled and flickered, casting ominous light over the
feast of slaughter. The first carefully removed their
opponents' weapons, in case any should wake. They
used leather thongs for quick strangling and knives that
plunged deep and true to their marks. So ordered, so
careful were they in their butchery that a half-naked
slut still wheezed and snored, oblivious to the fact that
the arm which encircled her body belonged to a dead
man.

The moon set and began to fade against the coming
dawn. Eighty men lay dead where they had slept. The
whores were spared, and many had begun to wake and
scatter in blind panic. The Saints began using their
rifles, cutting down the men who fled toward the river.
Like a hunter after game, Shadrach followed a man
he had wounded, a man who now crawled on his hands,

desperately dragging useless legs along the ground. With his assailant hard upon him, he stopped and cringed, blubbering at Shadrach's feet, pleading for his life. So cowering, so undone in defeat, the man's bladder let loose and stained the front of his trousers. Shadrach observed it all in gleeful triumph and thrust the bayonet home.

Still the stockyard drama continued, turning the streets around the temple into a field of carnage. Their ferocity was boundless and totally without remorse. It was a bloodlust grown of weeks and months and years of persecution, and for this night it was a thorough revenge they took. With the sun well up, they counted 136 dead. Only two of their number had suffered wounds, neither of them fatal.

They had gathered a store of many weapons from their victims. Now they took up axes and hatchets and made their way among the dead, in the last hideous ritual of their victory. From each of his kills, every man cut a token and tossed it into a sack.

They called their families out from hiding, and the people emerged, gathering in upon the square in joyful disorder. The enemy had been routed; the infidel had paid in blood. They were leaving Nauvoo today, but they were leaving a town that, however briefly, was in their possession again.

Their warriors reeked with blood—their hands and faces and women's garments all splashed crimson. It looked like a scene from hell. Several women, not so toughened to the sight of slaughter, fainted dead away. Shadrach Shuttleworth, gory and proud as any young dog wolf whose jaws foam after a successful hunt, embraced his father and gave him the sack that contained his battle trophies. It had, after all, been the elder's idea.

Elder Shuttleworth stepped to the brightest of the

three bonfires, which still burned in the early morning light. His passionate and stormy voice rang out like a clarion in the still air. "The Lord in his wisdom had seen fit to grant us vengeance on our enemies, the enemies of His chosen people!" he cried. "The hands of the Gentile would smite us—here then, are the hands of the Gentiles!"

With a great flourish, he raised the sack above the flames and let fall its contents. One by one, the Danites followed suit, offering their tokens to the fire until the air turned brown with the stench of burning flesh. The Mormon victory fire was fed by 136 dismembered Gentile hands.

Overwhelmed and sickened, Susanna fled the scene, running back to the Shuttleworth house. Prudence followed close by and called to her. Together they made their way back, and the older Shuttleworth wife tried to comfort the younger girl. "This is the worst of it, Susanna," she said. "In an hour or two we shall be on our way out of this place, and pray God we shall find rest and an end of these persecutions."

"How can you speak of God and rest in the wake of *that?*" Susanna cried, shuddering and gesturing back toward the exulting crowd.

"We have not been warlike, child, except that others have warred against us," Prudence answered. "You have been among us only a little time, Susanna. Too little a time to judge us. Come now, we must prepare."

It took them most of the day to make the eight miles to Sugar Creek, first camp on the way to Winter Quarters. Twenty-seven wagons, light and wide-bodied were laden with food, supplies, household goods, and farm tools. The three Shuttleworth wives shared the back of the wagon with four chickens—three hens and one yellow-feathered rooster, who flapped and crowed for most of the day.

Ah, but it was good to be gone from Nauvoo, the city of horror. The day indeed was a fine one—crisp, clear, sunny weather with just a hint of coolness.

Fording the Mississippi was by far the hardest task. Everything the wagons held had to be unloaded and crossed on barges, flatboats, and lighters. The livestock balked. Two oxen slid down the bank like simple children, surprised at their predicament. The Shuttleworths' new sow had to be carried, protesting all the way, by three strong men. On the opposite bank, teams were doubled and tripled to ease the wagons up to solid ground. Susanna strained with the others at the heavy wheels that clung tenaciously to the Mississippi mud.

But there was a fine satisfaction in the labor. The pilgrims were united in the need to get from where they were and the desire to get where they were going. Reverend Shuttleworth had promised a celebration tonight, and weary as they were from the sleepless night of vigil, their hearts were light and full of hope.

The road to Sugar Creek was a mud-rutted track. Wagons were cleared of passengers, and only the chickens continued to ride in the Shuttleworth carriage. It was close to sundown when they reached the camp, where their twenty-seven wagons were greeted by some sixty more, already settled for the night.

Much of the woods had been cleared by previous camps, and all around them spread stands of oak and hickory, elm, black walnut and maple. Several children ran to gather nuts in the fading twilight. The men set up tents and the women began the organization of outdoor cooking over the small campfires. Mormons who had gone ahead came looking for friends in delighted reunion, though some were already pitifully thin and weary.

Dr. Bernhisel had stayed in Nauvoo, determined to meet the last boat of converts still due from Europe. He had given Maidie a good supply of drugs; quinine to treat swamp fever, draughts for dysentery and chilblains, spirit of opium for pain. Maidie had told Susanna that five women in their group were already far gone in pregnancy. Could Susanna help when their time came? Susanna was quick to agree, though she had never seen a birthing. Sister Willoughby had offered, too, and she was experienced in these matters, as was Prudence, Shuttleworth's first wife.

A great fire was started in the center clearing, and Captain Pitts and his boys, glad to exercise their long-silenced instruments, were already tuning up. Shadrach dove into the wagon and emerged with a long bamboo fishing pole. He shuffled impatiently while his mother rummaged for pins, which she gave him for hooks. Gear in hand, he raced for the creek. Susanna watched him go, unable to reconcile this eager, simple youth with the blood-covered savage who only last night had severed the hands from the lifeless bodies of his victims.

Indeed, the entire face of the camp seemed to have altered in some magical way. In Nauvoo, people had walked with their heads down, defensive, alert to the slightest threat. Here they raised their faces to the dying sun, laughed easily, joked, sang, and attended their duties in a brand-new spirit. Close by the band, a young girl stood. She had dark eyes and milk-white skin and sang a beautiful soprano that had been trained in the great city of New York. She offered a hymn, which in its lyric beauty, full of faith and hope, seemed the essence of this happy change in the Mormon character.

Now let us rejoice in the day of salvation,
No longer as strangers on earth need we roam,
Good tidings are sounding to us and each nation,
And shortly the hour of redemption will come.

A circle of voices joined her softly.

When all that was promised the Saints will be given,
And none will molest them from morning until ev'n,
And earth will appear as the garden of Eden,
And Jesus will say to all Israel, "Come Home."

With the last bars of the song, Susanna felt for the
first time a certain oneness with these strangers to
whom chance had joined her. For she was like them—
what they sought was the same as what she was seeking, had been seeking from the time she had crawled
into the lifeboat at the Liverpool harbor: a place to
rest at the end of the journey. A home that offered
safety, warmth, affection. And she hoped, in a spirit
not unlike those other travelers, who had, as James
Leverton had said, all become pilgrims for their own
reasons, that somewhere in this new land there would
be a place for her.

For the first time in weeks, she thought of her
mother, a small woman stooped and gray before her
time, beset with work and worry—a woman not unlike Elder Shuttleworth's first wife. How had it been
for her—burdened with a child out of wedlock, married to a man without warmth or sympathy? Had her
mother also been seeking in the shelters of those various religions a place for herself? Was she a pilgrim,
too?

She hoped her mother would join them soon on this
wonderful, impossible journey. There was so much she
wanted to say, so much she had learned from the
hardships she had already known. It would be like
beginning again, with a new and better understanding
between them.

She could not know that the ship upon which Mistress Jones had sailed had been badly provisioned and
ill-fated from the start. That midway through the ocean

journey, disease would strike, and that Mistress Jones, weak to begin with, would be among the first afflicted. She could not know that her mother's journey had already ended, and that she had, full weeks before, received the final consecration of her new faith.

And what of her father, that shadowy unknown figure in her life? Had her husband, as he had promised, sent inquiries to New York? The vastness of this America had already awed her; but she clung to her hope as surely as these others clung to their faith. Somewhere Jonathan Hungerford lived and knew he had a daughter. And someday—perhaps someday soon —the two of them would meet. She determined to question her husband at the earliest opportunity.

But now supper was being laid out on long wooden tables, and the band was beginning to play the lively tunes of country dances. Already Porter Rockwell was whirling his pretty wife, whom he had abducted at gunpoint from her first husband, a local tavern-keeper. Shadrach had bowed to Maryann; Sister Willoughby sported with Elder Bedweather. Maidie and Martin Brauer, arms locked and eyes lit with pleasure, turned and spun in time to the music. The caller kept them dancing with never a pause.

> Greet your partner, do-si-do,
> Bow to the left, but don't let go.
> Promenade your sweetie-pie,
> Swing her round and lift her high!

The men quenched their thirst with beer and liquor; the women had tea or sweet wine. A huge quarter of beef turned on the spit. Breads and jellies were set on the table along with roasted corn, sweet potatoes, late berries, and apples that only waited to be eaten—all contributed to the holiday air, the feeling of abundance that comes at the harvest season. They could have been back aboard ship, or in a palace or a neighbor's barn. The spirit was jubilation. They were on their way to Zion.

The band stopped playing to join in the feasting. Susanna and Maidie were giggling together, their lips and fingers dripping with the savory juices of the delicious fresh-charred beef. Even Tasker Blake had unbent from his usual stony silence and was flirting with the lovely singer who had lately led them in the hymn.

"You may start worrying," Susanna teased her friend. "Sister Willoughby has your Martin hard in tow."

"She may have him all night," Maidie countered, "and I'll know he's safe. He told me she reminds him of your husband's new sow, all ready to give birth to piglets!"

"Oh, she's not even pregnant, Maidie Cross Brauer!"

"She doesn't have to be. But she owns enough bulk for a litter of six."

They gorged themselves at the well-laden table. Soon the band had returned to its place, ready to help them dance off the heavy meal. Martin Brauer, having disengaged himself from the overwhelming embrace of Sister Willoughby, came to claim his wife. Susanna moved to the edge of the dancers while the band struck up her song. By now even those just come from England could sing it without mistake.

Oh, Susanna! Oh don't you cry for me,
For I come from Alabama with my banjo on my knee!

She could hear Maidie calling her name over the music. Dear Maidie, because it was Susanna's song. But suddenly Susanna could take no more of the revelers, the whirling figures, the bursts of laughter. Suddenly it was like that other dance, but this time there was no dark-haired captain to waltz her into shadows, no strong hands to claim her. No, she didn't want to dance tonight.

She wandered to a small grove of pine and sank down upon the fragrant needles of the forest floor. She heard the banjos and the merrymakers, but her thoughts were somewhere else—with a tall man who had drawn her down to a bed of flour sacks, who had played her body like a piece of music.

She stayed a long time, until the ground was too chilly to sit, then made her way back to the tents. The fires were lower, but many of the company still danced, their bare feet stirring up clouds of dust in the clearing. Male voices boasted various exploits in whiskey-sodden tones, and these Susanna gave wide berth. She couldn't see Maidie. Most of the women not engaged in the music's tireless swinging had already gone to bed.

Reverend Shuttleworth watched her progress from the grove with a particular satisfaction that bordered on relish. Since returning to Nauvoo, he'd been beset with burdensome practicalities—he'd had no time to spare for the prize he had so neatly and so cleverly won for his own. Now the Mormons were at last on their way. Now he would have leisure to enjoy the charms of his new little bride.

The faded plaid dress, he observed, though long on her, fit tightly over her hips and breasts. Maryann was thin. But Susanna, while dainty, was possessed of full sweet curves that strained against the cheap gingham fabric. Tonight, he decided, that dewy young body would lie under him.

Oblivious to the plans being made for her, Susanna undressed quickly, shivering in the coolness inside the tent. She donned the flannel nightdress Maidie had given her, grateful for its cozy warmth. It seemed a long time since last she'd slept, and the limp bedding on the tent floor looked increasingly inviting. She crawled under the blanket and chafed her arms and legs until her body heat spread to the covers, making a warm cocoon.

Outside the tent, Elder Shuttleworth opened the flap of the shelter and bent his tall, thin frame to enter. Alarmed, Susanna stared up at him. He did not even bother to greet her; his presence and purpose were obvious enough.

Only her face and hands showed above the covers—her green eyes apprehensive, her dainty fingers clutching at the bedding. Altogether, her husband decided, a very desirable picture. He would see more in a moment.

He knew she was not virgin and wasted little time with preliminaries. He paused to partially disrobe—it was too cold to undress completely. As he approached, he saw she was stiff and taut as a frightened doe, which added a certain piquancy to the proceedings. She remained still and docile as he lifted her nightdress. He placed her legs out just so and patted her thighs as though to remind them of their place.

"Just lie still, very still," he told her. "I'm not going to hurt you." She closed her eyes as she felt him mount her and stifled a sob in her throat. It was just as she had feared, but that fear had dissipated as the days had passed and he had let her be. She thought then he would keep his bargain. But he had betrayed her. He was her legal husband, acting within his rights. Oh, she'd been such a fool! And now he would have her as he chose.

His movements were curious; never varying, except that at the end he moved faster—all in the same pattern and position, rising and falling like a dark shadow above her. Nor did he seem to seek any response from her, for which she was grateful. No doubt he considered desire in women a sin.

But how was it then she felt more shame in lying

thus beneath her wedded husband than she had felt
the night before her marriage, all wanton in Jed Taylor's arms? This man—her husband—did not kiss her,
whispered no endearments. Indeed, he seemed not
even to look at her while performing this most intimate
act. It was for use, not love, that he had come to her.
And when he finished, he straightened his clothing,
wished her a brief goodnight, and left.

Susanna made a point of seeing Maidie early the
next morning to get the contraceptive draught.

9

THE FINE WEATHER lasted for the better part of a week as though to bid them godspeed on their journey. Rising at dawn and breaking camp, the Saints were able to make twelve miles in a single day, no little accomplishment for some eighty wagons, driving or leading livestock, often with women and children walking beside. Their skin burned, blistered, and finally tanned in the sun. All around them the trees took on their autumn glory, red to the maple and gold to the oak, mixed with earth browns and russets, and the deep green of pine.

The roads, too, were well trampled by those who had come before, hard-packed dry earth, easy on their oxen. They followed the Des Moines River, fording it on the third day and camping at a settlement called Bonaparte Mills, whose single industry depended on the quick-running stream. Thousands had already come before them, and sheltering the Mormon travelers had become a second livelihood for the residents, who viewed the steadily passing caravans with something of awe and something of the indulgence extended to people who are thought a trifle mad.

Beyond Bonaparte, the capricious weather changed, and there was rain. The wheels groaned and mired in the mud. The oxen strained and stalled on uphill ridges.

Sometimes it seemed the rains came from the east and would depart. Then clouds would form ahead and deliver more rain. They slept in tents with damp bedding, awaking to dress in clothes that had not dried from the previous day. The nights grew ever more chill, and several of their party were taken sick.

Reverend Shuttleworth, evidently satisfied with his first visit, had availed himself of his new wife twice more in the first week. Each time it was the same, but still Susanna could not resign herself to his perfunctory attentions. Many nights she lay in dread of his anticipated entrance. He was so cold!—his very lust was a cold and isolated act, uncaring and unconnected. His gray eyes shone with a steely glint as he lay above her, almost daring her to move, to object, to question his use of her. But she never did. It was as though some deeply buried instinct warned her against such folly. She was his wife, she repeated to herself as she submitted to his passionless embrace. And sometimes afterward, after he was gone, she would cry a little, lying just as he had left her, her legs separated just so, to assist his penetration, her body stiff and unmoving, her eyes glazed with tears and staring blankly at the canvas roof. He left her feeling so unclean. And so terribly alone.

In the morning she would bathe in icy streams, resolutely washing away the remainders of her encounter with the elder. Each night without fail she would drink the bitter draught, that he get no child from her. She nurtured a forlorn little hope that if she failed to conceive, he might tire of her and finally let her be.

There were no secrets in the camp. One day as Susanna, fresh bathed from the river, made her way to the tents, she heard Porter Rockwell talking about her to Shad. The two men were lounging at the edge of the site, idly tossing their bowies at a wooden target some twenty feet away. Porter's eyes had sparkled at the sight of her emerging from the trees. He noted the cap of pale gold hair, the tanned golden skin, the delicate ankles and bare feet that padded softly across the leafy ground. Turning to his companion, he said, "Looks like your papa finally found himself a replacement for Priscilla."

Shadrach studied the retreating figure and agreed. "Yup, you're right, Port, now that I think on it." He grinned at the shorter man, as though sharing a joke. "This one's prettier, though. Still, the old man needs one more to make it even again. A black-haired hussy like Sary Lynn."

"Your old man hasn't had much luck keeping his women, has he?" Porter said in passing. "If'n he wants some lessons, you tell him old Port'll be more than glad to help him with his ladies!" They both laughed and returned to their game.

The rains that had let up briefly began again, coming this time with torrents of icy wind. Several tents blew down under the onslaught, and for two nights the Shuttleworth women slept in the wagon, crowded among the crates and tools and squawking chickens. Susanna did not mind—it kept the elder from her bed.

But the unrelenting damp was taking its toll. Bushels of seeds, brought with such high expectations from Nauvoo, were rotting in their sacks. The best-weathered wood of the wagons was beginning to swell. One wagon had already broken its axle and was a day's delay in being repaired. Dry wood of any kind was at a premium, and fires became a luxury. They woke each day with sore joints and aching muscles, cramped with cold, and had to put on clothes that, despite all attempts, never got dry. Everyone had colds. Prudence had a dry hacking cough that lasted well into the night. At last Maidie gave her a mild sleeping potion made from poppies that seemed to give her rest.

Their progress had shrunk from the admirable

twelve-mile days to scant three and four miles that seemed to go forward by inches. It took them one full day to cross a stretch of boggy marsh no more than eighty yards across. Their oxen were belly-deep in mud and heaving dangerously as though at any moment they might die in their traces. Even with tripling the teams and taking one wagon at a time, the beasts and laborers both suffered loss of health and strength. Susanna and Prudence strained at the spokes of the wheels, slipping knee-deep in the sopping muck which clung in great clods to their feet and legs. Shadrach and Maryann worked the other side while Shuttleworth himself whipped, goaded, and urged the teams on. Three of the weakest beasts fell that day and did not rise. The families who owned them had to butcher them where they lay.

It was late into the second week on a night when the winds were howling like wolves on the hunt that Sister Willoughby came running and panting to the Shuttleworth wagon. "Quick!" she cried, gasping for breath. "Maidie Brauer says to come right away if you've a mind to help—Julie Stockton's hard in labor!"

Prudence reached for her clothes, but Susanna stayed her. "You're just getting over your sickness," she said. "The three of us ought to be enough. We'll send word if more help's needed." Protesting feebly, Prudence remained behind. What Susanna said was true. Her cough had only just begun to ease, and a night out in this storm would bring certain relapse.

The rain was pelting furiously against the wagon cover, and inwardly Susanna groaned. The Stockton babe had chosen the worst of times to make its grand entrance. They had been three days without fire. She threw on a dress and together with Sister Willoughby raced through the downpour to the Stockton camp.

They found Jay Stockton working in the shelter of

his wagon, desperately hacking up a heavy oaken chest. They needed fire, he explained, and this was the only dry wood he had. While three men lifted a canvas to keep off the rain, he piled up the kindling and tore leaves from an old book to place under it. On this he poured kerosene and set a match to it. Twice the shifting winds put down his efforts. He added more fuel. At last it caught, and a bucket was suspended over it for boiling. Maidie had torn a sheet into strips and some of these she gave the men to boil with the water.

The tent itself was a rude affair; just old canvas hung on poles and buffeted by the merciless winds. The roof, patched with tree bark, did little to keep the rain from dripping down inside where the covering was worn. The interior was lit with a single lantern, and at first Susanna could barely discern the shadowy figures within. But there was Maidie, kneeling at the foot of a crude pallet on which lay Julie Stockton, whose great swollen belly formed the center stage of the drama about to ensue.

The girl was pale and frightened—her child was close to a month before its time—and despite the frigid cold, she was drenched in sweat. It formed in tiny beads above her upper lip and soaked her brow in icy wetness. Sister Willoughby picked up a clean linen, went to her head, and wiped her face with gentle caressing motions. Susanna stood over her, holding bowls to catch the roof leaks that otherwise would have soaked her body.

Brother Stockton put his head inside to offer the bucket of hot water. Maidie reached for the bucket and summarily sent him out. This was a ceremony of women—their peculiar female domain. No man might enter now.

The timely pains now wracked the young girl's frame again, and even through the blankets that still covered her, Susanna could see the lurching contractions of her distended womb. Working quickly, Maidie removed the blankets and raised the shift to examine the rigid laboring girth. She pressed gently against a bulge low on the protruding belly. "That's the wee one's head," she told them softly. "Aye, that's good. It's coming down just right." She propped the girl's legs with cushions and used the blankets to cover her thighs which looked thin and pitifully inadequate below the massive expanded paunch.

Now she moved to the head and drew the girl's arms out, joining her hands to Sister Willoughby's, palm against palm. "As soon as the next one hits," she told the girl, "you push! Push against those hands, push down and out and help your baby come. Breathe slow and deep—that'll help."

Maidie raced back to her place, but not before the spasms came on again. She had to position the legs once more, and then she was probing deftly, delicately, at her very insides. "It's coming! Now push down," she cried, and the girl heaved to obey.

Susanna watched spellbound as a tiny red form appeared at the opening between the girl's legs, with Maidie stretching the passage to give it room. "That's good," she said soothingly. "That's just fine now. This is an easy one for a hard night. Come we're almost clear now—once more, push down!"

And there it was, so tiny Maidie could hold it in one hand. A new little person, covered with blood and mucus, its wrinkled face already screwed up for its first tiny wail. With a warm cloth, Maidie cleaned it and lay it on the driest towels they had been able to find. "It's a son," she announced smiling.

Susanna held an empty bucket for the afterbirth, waiting until the last of the blood and spent tissue had emerged. Sister Willoughby cleaned and toweled the girl's thighs and groin while Maidie drew a clean sharp knife and cut the shrunken umbilical cord. Sister Julie bared a heavy-laden breast as Maidie set the tiny mite in his mother's arms.

From outside the tent, voices shouted frenzied questions scarcely heard against the wind, which, with the crisis passed, seemed to have redoubled its efforts. They covered the new mother quickly, and Maidie opened the flap of the tent to allow Brother Stockton, now a father, entry to greet his newborn son. The men outside shouted loud hurrahs from this newest member of their party, the first of what would be many births on the long journey west.

As though some unkind hand had only waited to balance the scales, they suffered their first casualty two days later. Little Janey Bates, who for two days had complained of a pain in her belly, developed a sudden fever and died. Her mother was inconsolable, saying over and over again that she'd thought it simple indigestion, had given the child a purge, and sent her to bed. She had awakened early on the second day to find her daughter writhing, soaked with sweat, her eyes all glassy with fever. When Maidie was summoned, she could do nothing but give the child a soothing syrup to quiet the pains. She comforted the bereaved mother as best she could, saying that even if she'd come sooner, there was little she could have done. She suspected a tumor, but she had no skill at surgery and in all their group there was no one else to call.

Men worked the muddy ground with shovels, and Tasker Blake, who was handy with tools, built a narrow coffin. Elder Bedweather, a stocky, sweet-faced man, presided over the burial. They had little time to spare in mourning. The ill-fated weather had set them back, and already provisions were running dangerously low. They must push forward to Winter Quarters.

For Maidie, who had weathered out the first weeks' difficulties with a careless ease born of pure happiness, there was suddenly much more than the day-to-day hardships to bear. Her husband had taken ill.

It had begun as a simple cough, much like the ailment Prudence Shuttleworth had suffered—a minor annoyance, nothing more. But Martin Brauer had not heeded the warning signals—the shortness of breath, occasional dizziness, the flashes of heat that sometimes overcame him. Each day he rose, put his chilled feet into sodden, misshapen shoes that refused to dry, donned clothes always damp from the day before, and began the morning's labor. He still gathered feed for his stock by hand, cut wood for fires when it was dry, bore the brunt of unloading and reloading all their goods when they had crossings—and when Maidie scolded him for overworking, he only patted her hand and said he was all right.

Now it was only too clear that he was *not* all right. Worried and alarmed, Maidie had taken him hard to task. "Now what is all the good of your mule-headed laboring," she shouted angrily, "if you leave me a widow by and by to do it all alone?" And he had just laughed and retorted that if she had a mind to turn shrew he would have to marry a docile widow to balance her sharp tongue. Their jesting was all too short-lived. He fainted that afternoon while unyoking the team of oxen.

Maidie made space in the wagon for a makeshift couch, so that he could ride and sleep while she herself drove the wagon. She nursed and fussed like a broody hen with one chick, and for a day or two, he seemed to be on the mend. Then suddenly his cough worsened and the fever started. Susanna brought them pots of good hot broth from Prudence. Fellow travelers were kind, helping Maidie with the heaviest work and bringing gifts of food to tide them over. But Martin had little appetite now, and his ever-slight frame grew even thinner.

Maidie admonished him no more about making her a widow—the threat had become too real. Then one night while he was sleeping, she moved to straighten the bedding and discovered the handkerchiefs where he had hidden them. They were spotted with blood. For a time they kept up a double pretense. Martin continued to hide the now-much-bloodied linens, and Maidie went on as though she knew nothing of it. But often at night she would walk out through the woods beyond the camp, weeping until no more tears would come and she could return with a smiling face. There was nothing in her arts or drugs to cure him. His flesh was wasting daily, and those warm, dark, kindly eyes loomed ever larger in his sunken face. His lips were parched and cracked with fever, and he never could have enough to drink.

Nights she slept in the wagon with him now, holding him as gently and as tenderly as a child, as though by holding him she could keep him with her always, could keep him safe. As though as long as she was holding him he could not die.

Then on one rare and sunny afternoon, as Maidie drove the wagon, she thought she heard a choking sound within. Braking the carriage, she leaped from the seat and found Martin struggling for breath. His eyes were glazed. His dry lips moved to say something but said nothing, and suddenly a hideous rattle sounded deep in his throat, and great clots of blood issued from his mouth. She cried out and pulled his head down to her breasts, while the blood poured down the bodice of her gown.

And then there was quiet and she was holding him again in her arms, as though he were her baby and she was only rocking him to sleep.

Drivers from the back wagons came up to seek the reason for delay. Susanna, who had been walking with

the Shuttleworth women a full quarter-mile ahead,
heard the leaders call a halt and looked back at the
crowd already gathered a distance away. Suspecting
the cause at once, she picked up her skirts without a
word and raced to the scene. Coming up on the wagon,
her suspicions were confirmed. Already four men were
digging in a patch of grassy turf a little way from
the trail. Burial must be immediate. There was no
time.

Elder Bedweather emerged from the back of Maidie's wagon, his usually ruddy face pale and confused.
Maidie would not give up the body.

Susanna pushed her way through the crowd and
went swiftly to her friend, who turned with a fierce and
wild-eyed look to face this new intruder. It took long
moments of slow, soothing speech to calm her. She
still clutched her dead husband in her arms. "He's already getting cold—so cold!" she whispered to Susanna. "I have to keep him warm." Now her whole
body seemed to slump back against the wooden frame,
and her voice rose to a strangled cry of despair that
bordered on distraction. "It's cold in the ground, Susanna!"

Her friend answered nothing, but with slow and
infinite patience, she reached for Maidie's hands and
gently disengaged them from the still, rigid form.

Susanna traveled with Maidie most of the day and
reluctantly left her at sundown to rejoin the Shuttleworth camp. People had been kind, as much as they
could spare from worry at their own troubles. Martin
Brauer had been the fifth death that week. Many poorly
provisioned travelers were half-starved, their food supply reduced to hard biscuits and the thick, pasty gruel
made from flour and river water. The constant chill
hung like the threat of death over them. They were
desperate to make Winter Quarters before the snow.

For the next two days, Susanna made innumerable

trips to the Brauer wagon. It was an ironic kind of mercy that so many people were in need of nursing, for it took Maidie somewhat out of herself. But for the rest, it grieved Susanna to see the fine, broad figure bent under the weight of her grief, walking with a tired shuffle as though she lacked energy to lift her feet. Maidie was frozen in lethargy, and Susanna feared the wagon train would leave her at some way station to winter. She had delayed their moving out for the past two mornings, failing to rise and prepare to leave the site. It was as though with Martin Brauer's death had gone all energy, all vitality, all reason to rise at all.

By afternoon of the second day, Susanna had made up her mind. She proposed to Maidie that they travel to Winter Quarters together, divide the labor, and take turns driving the wagon. Maidie roused from her apathy, and if she did not break into a dazzling smile, she was nevertheless very pleased. "I should love to have your company, Susanna," she said. "It's been so lonely nights—" Her voice drifted a little at the last words. Then she asked, "Are you sure Elder Shuttleworth will approve?" Susanna assured her.

In her own mind, his approval had no bearing. She did not ask her husband for permission. She *told* him she was driving with Maidie as far as Winter Quarters. Prudence nodded her approbation. It was a proper act of Christian charity, she said. Maryann was frankly delighted and took no pains to hide it. The elder himself could make no decent objection. His household was large enough to spare Susanna's labor, and the recently bereaved widow would need help. Susanna herself felt a distinct benefit in traveling with Maidie, over and above the comfort to her friend—the reverend would not be making nightly visits to her in Maidie's tent or wagon.

The Brauer wagon was stocked almost as well as the Shuttleworths'. Martin Brauer had been a good and careful provider, and he had been planning the course for months. They had a horse, a milk cow and poultry, farming and building tools, half a ton of flour, ample corn, some coffee, sugar, meat, and dried vegetables. Though the two girls together made an odd team among the numerous households of multiple wives and offspring, they managed very well. Susanna now rose to gather fodder for the livestock, though grass and wild grain was getting more rare in the chilling ground. Maidie started the coffee, broke down the tent, and loaded the wagon. At night they slept like sisters, close together against the cold.

The Mormons received warm welcome at Mount Pisgah a few days later. It was then a way station, built by Brigham Young's first body of wagons. They had arrived in late spring of the previous year in what was then a virtual wilderness of boggy plain. Four weeks later, they left a village of log cabins and cleared fields already sown with grain for those who would follow. Many who found themselves too sick or ill equipped to continue their journey had stopped for the winter, planning to continue on when weather and food conditions improved. There was a great show of visitors and news-seekers crowding the camp, and that evening settlers from miles around came up to hear Captain Pitts and his band in concert. Brother William Clayton, one of the horn players, took up a collection for the entertainment, and the grateful audience offered bushels of corn and flour in payment, which was then distributed among the needy. There was dancing, too, but neither Susanna nor Maidie felt of a spirit to take part. They went to sleep early, warm and dry for once, in a log cabin shared with five other settlers.

It was the last real comfort they were to know. Two days out of Mount Pisgah, a light snow fell, followed by a frost that effectively destroyed any fodder left on the plains. The ground had frozen, and while it made travel easier than on the mud plains, the live-stock were rapidly wasting from lack of feed. All that the Mormons had carried for their stock had gone, and Susanna was reduced to offering them twigs from fallen elms, and cottonwoods. The horse had gnawed at the branches with good-natured practicality, but the milk cow and oxen refused it for days and suffered accordingly. On the fifth day, when Susanna brought forth an armful of twigs, Nelly, the milk cow, shuffled forward. She bent her big broad nose to examine the pitiful feed, snuffled several times, hoping for something better, then slowly began to chew with a somewhat resentful look in her large brown eyes. The oxen followed suit, and Susanna heaved a sigh of relief. It wouldn't keep them hearty, but it would keep them alive.

Late that night, the wind blew down the tent. For the first time since Martin Brauer's death, Maidie laughed. She and Susanna lifted the tent, poles and all, above their heads and shivered and stumbled into the wagon. Inside the wagon cover, they looked at each other and smiled in a peculiar gleeful triumph. In spite of the worst that fate could hand them, they were muddling through.

That night set the tone for the days that followed. Wagon by wagon, the Mormons plodded on, making better time because of the hard earth, and because the cold was driving them. They had to keep moving to stay warm. They had to reach the main camp to stay alive. Funerals had become a luxury on the frozen trail, but the temperature kept the bodies from decomposing. It was no uncommon sight to have the dead as passengers for two days or more before graves could be dug. Five more children had been born, but only three had lived; and Sister Ursula Huxtable, already widowed on the trek, died after almost two days in labor, her still-unborn child with her.

The band still played sometimes in the evening, but the time of barefoot dancing was over. Most of the songs were hymns, and people hummed or sang them as they went about their chores. But sometimes they would break out with the lovely strains of Mendelssohn, and once Susanna heard—carrying high and clear to the very outskirts of the camp—the very same Strauss waltz that she had last danced with Jed Taylor. She angrily brushed aside the tears that came forth, all but freezing on her face. It seemed so long ago and such rank folly, with the icy breath of winter at her back and death a daily visitor, that she would shed tears at the sound of a song.

Maidie had calmed from the worst of her grief, and if she was no longer the blooming bride of Nauvoo, was surviving with a strong will. She made a brave and good companion. Susanna, with her single pair of inadequate evening slippers, was lame for days with frostbite, and Maidie nursed her much as she had the day of her friend's discovery aboard the *Star Victory*. She borrowed a charcoal stove from the Davis sisters, and used it as a foot-warmer inside the wagon where Susanna now rode. When the kindling dried out sufficiently, she made a great fire and heated steaming buckets of water which she brought inside for bathing. Baths had become another of the almost-forgotten luxuries lost in the frosty air of encroaching winter.

But not tonight while the fire flamed well and the little borrowed stove filled the wagon with cheering warmth. Susanna stripped and let Maidie soap her from head to toe. She basked in the unaccustomed pleasure of being cared for, and Maidie's hands were gentle, almost lingering, as though they enjoyed the task.

Then still more water, for Maidie to have a turn. She, too, drew off all her clothes, and her body, bigger and fuller than Susanna's, soon shone from its soapy latherings. "It's a disgrace," she said, gazing down at the now-gray bath water. "What a pair of slop-mullers we've become."

"The weather hasn't exactly encouraged cleaning," Susanna said in excuse. "You know, Sister Willoughby did a washing last week, and you would have died to see it next morning—six pairs of size-twenty bloomers frozen absolutely solid. I could just picture her trying to thaw them out—it really makes you pause."

"Well, we'll put off doing the clothes for a time, I guess. Some say it protects you from cold, and since we haven't enough food to put on fat like the animals, we'll just have to make do with a layer of dirt. Though I must confess I much prefer being this way." She began to rinse off the soap and her hands moved slowly over her belly, squeezing the wet cloth so that the water streamed in little rivers down the length of her front. Her voice became thoughtful. "I wish—"

"You wish what?" Susanna probed gently.

"I wish I'd never drunk that bitter stuff, Susanna," Maidie confessed. "I wish we'd started a babe!" Her voice began to break and strain. "Then there'd be something in sight for me instead of seeing the tomorrows all empty and Martin gone—and we had so little time, Susanna, such a little time for it all to be gone so fast!" She started to cry and buried her face in her hands while her long red hair fell like a veil around her, closing her off in her grief. Susanna came and held her, stroking her heavy mane and drawing it back from her face, wrapping a dry towel around her naked shoulders. After a time the crying stopped, and Maidie wiped her tear-ravaged face on the towel. Her eyes, red-rimmed from weeping, looked gratefully upon her companion. "You're my only friend, Susanna," she said softly. "My only one."

The next day was bright and frosty, and the girls were up at dawn. Susanna, who insisted on doing her share of the work, clumped about in boots outgrown by Shadrach Shuttleworth. Maidie had stuffed them with rags to assist the fitting, and while they were certainly not the latest fashion in elegant footwear, at least they protected her from the biting cold. While the livestock fed, the girls turned toward the pageant in the eastern sky. The land all around them stretched out on a flat, low horizon, dominated by the weight of the clouds above. And where the sun was rising, the clouds were edged in brilliant gold and silvery white, while others hung in dark silhouette. Great beams of light penetrated the haze and touched the earth as though to bless it.

"It minds me of an English sky," Maidie said. "I crossed once on Salisbury Plain, in the south, where the great stones lie in circles. It was flat, like here, and the sky was all a mass of different clouds in sun and shadow."

"Do you miss England, Maidie?" Susanna asked.

"Why, no—I don't think so," Maidie said slowly. "There was nothing to keep me in England—that's why I came here. And there's nothing to make me want to go back . . . nothing to go back *for*. This America —it was Martin's country, of course, and I lost him here; but I had him here, too, and that makes this place more to me than England ever was. I think I'll stay in America till I die. It's home now."

"A home on wheels," remarked Susanna. "And unless I'm much mistaken, we'd better get our home moving before they leave without us!"

It was the last stretch of their journey, and the line of wagons pushed on with a mighty will that was half hope, half desperation. Messengers arrived daily from Winter Quarters. Several men whose wives were with the train came out to greet them and drive the last few miles in. Hosea Stout, the dark, grim chief of the Nauvoo police, also came up and rode among them, seeking news of his sister Anna, who had stopped at

Mount Pisgah. He had gone forth with the first wagons from Nauvoo, and the trip had cost him a wife and both his sons. Not surprisingly, it was a stern and bitter man who edged his thin black gelding among the tents and wagons.

The countryside was changing, and now instead of plains, the travelers saw the rim of forests in the west. To those lacking meat, it meant game. To those who had come this way before, it meant that the shore of the wide Missouri River was just a step beyond. But still it seemed nothing short of a miracle when three advance riders came galloping into camp, whooping like drunken Indians, to spread the word that Winter Quarters was just eight miles away.

Before the day had ended anyone on the train could look to the west and see high wooded ridges on the far bank of the Missouri. Just two miles up at the riverside there was a ferry. Tomorrow it would carry them all to Winter Quarters, the present camp of Zion.

Fatigue, hardship, even death were forgotten that night in camp as people who had become almost strangers to gaiety began a celebration. The last of the wines and spirits filled their cups; precious stores of dried fruits, honey, and sweet biscuits found their way into bowls onto plates, and from there to the mouths of visiting celebrants, some of whom had not eaten so well in weeks. One of the scouts had brought down a four-point buck and the whole of it, skinned and dressed, now hung roasting above a pit fire in the center of the camp. Maidie and Susanna had made the rounds of feasting and drinking, taking glasses of sherry with Evelyn Tasker, and discoursing long with Sister Willoughby on the unquestionable merits of her home-made elderberry wine. By their fifth glass, it had become the uncrowned queen of spirits. By their sixth, Sister Willoughby, who had been tippling well before their visit, began to look a little green. Maidie and

Susanna each took an arm and helped their bilious hostless outside, where she promptly gave up, along with her dinner, most of the much-touted elderberry wine.

By this time the two girls were feeling so good themselves that they bid good night to the good sister and headed away in the wrong direction. When they realized their mistake, they were stumbling and giggling and making little progress in *any* direction. Maidie solemnly declared this very wise, since it meant they could not go far wrong. Susanna chose that very moment to slip and fall against Maidie, who already had her hands full keeping herself in an upright posture. Both girls found themselves quite suddenly seated on the frozen ground.

It seemed a most auspicious time to look for landmarks. That was definitely Sister Willoughby's red wagon, and amazingly, it was only about ten yards away. Thus located, the two friends staggered to their feet and began the long march home. Maidie began to sing "Oh, Susanna," in a trembling soprano that wavered between flat and sharp. Not to be outdone, Susanna joined in this homage to herself, her harmony a little off-key, but at least, she said in self-defense, it was *consistently* off-key.

It took them almost ten minutes to navigate to the wagon, by which time they had admitted to being slightly—that was to say—*politely* inebriated of spirits. The wagon couch, though narrow, was already made up, and understandably, neither girl could see sufficient need or merit in struggling with the complex machinations of setting up the tent. Each in turn lumbered up the running board and fell inside.

Susanna sat on the edge of the pallet, trying to work her feet out of Shadrach's stuffed boots. After much extensive pulling and panting, the right one came off. The left, however, seemed stubbornly fused in place, resisting all efforts of tugging and heaving. Maidie finally lent a hand, positioning the offending boot between her knees, and instructing Susanna to brace her right foot hard against Maidie's backside. The next moment, both Maidie and the boot were sent lurching across the width of the wagon, while Susanna's two unencumbered feet flailed the air and she herself lay back dissolving in a paroxysm of giggles.

Maidie came forward, brandishing the boot like a weapon and stood over Susanna, who still lay in the clutches of her laughing fit. Her fair gold curls fell in disarray around her face, which was still flushed pink from the chilly air. Her eyes were half-shut, curtained by her lashes, and her full red lips were parted, still laughing with unbounded amusement. Maidie dropped the boot and without a word bent forward and stopped her laughter with a kiss.

She knelt on the bed beside her friend and kissed her again full on the mouth, and Susanna felt a strange kind of excitement—a warmth almost forgotten now combining with the giddiness of the wine. Maidie's long red hair fell down over her face and it pressed between their lips in the kisses that followed. Maidie's hands were reaching to undress her, and Susanna did not resist. Where she had gone to school, it was not uncommon for girls to form intimacies much beyond the usual hand-holding and walking arm in arm. It gave vent to their developing sensuality without the risks attendant in playing similar games with boys. Whether through modesty or natural aversion, Susanna had never been tempted by those overtures made her by older girls who sometimes had whispered promises of pleasure in her ear.

But that was before her body had been truly awakened to passion—a passion briefly fulfilled and then abandoned, starved in recent months by the indifferent attentions of her husband's selfish lust. Susanna was aware of Maidie's delight in her, of the warm brown eyes that bespoke desire and pleaded for acceptance. She was aware of her own body's response, aroused to hunger now, warmed by wine and Maidie's kisses.

At first it seemed to differ little from Maidie's usual affections—the care she had taken when Susanna was not well. But slowly, her caress became more concentrated, playing longer about the sweet breasts she had laid bare, daring a kiss to the stiffened nipples. She stroked the almost invisible whorl of down below the navel, marveling at its softness. "You're so pretty, Susanna," she murmured.

Because she was a woman, she knew just where to touch and how to excite, so slowly—her fingers feeling everywhere—now teasing, now satisfying. Her lips followed her hands with hot, eager kisses to which Susanna responded tentatively at the start, and then with blissful abandon. She found pleasure in the fullness of Maidie's breasts pressing in against her own—the rich, generous female body that built passion with an ease, a luxury that took its own time, that lingered over small delights and sought no single end. She felt Maidie's thick shock of hair brush her arms and drape over her belly. The waving tresses fell between her legs and over her legs, like a net spun of red silk. Maidie's knowing fingers provoked the dormant fires to flame, her fingers running delicately up and down the length of Susanna's body, over the rising hills of breasts, the swelling contours of her belly, chafing where the moisture started at the juncture of her thighs. Their bodies began to mesh and strain closer, their torsos glued together in the foaming turbulence of their mutual need. Above and below, the red hair mingled with the gold. Incensed by the musky perfume of their own rapture, they quickened the tempo of their merging, giving over to the consuming fire, the delirious agitation. They uttered the trills and warbling cries which passion sings.

They clung and melded until both had quivered with the final spasms and they lay exhausted in each other's arms.

Susanna awoke the next morning in slow stages, her consciousness seeming to break through thick banks of fog. Her head felt heavy, her mouth dry and foul and cottony from the wine. For once Maidie slept on, her body still and content in sleep, one leg thrown over Susanna's knees. The events of the night before, viewed through a sober mind, left Susanna feeling uneasy. She wondered how Maidie would respond now that this had happened between them. Susanna herself had reacted in a single night's abandon—already starved of sensual delight, she had warmed to Maidie's attentions. But it was not a course she wished to repeat. And she was afraid that for Maidie, it meant a great deal more.

Such thoughts made an effort of the day. Maidie awakened and reached to kiss her friend. Susanna drew away. Her own discomfort made her see advances in Maidie's every gesture, and she told herself she could not stay and travel anymore with her erstwhile companion. The wagons lined up at the ferry, and Susanna knew the Shuttleworths were somewhere up ahead.

Maidie had been hurt already. That was very clear. And now Susanna was gathering her things, reminding her friend that she had promised to travel only as far as Winter Quarters, and Winter Quarters was just across the river.

Maidie tugged at her arm. "Susanna, is it because of last night?" Her round face, freckled by the sun, looked wounded and distraught. "I wouldn't do anything to hurt you, Susanna. I'd never hurt you . . ."

"It's naught to do with last night, Maidie," Susanna answered quickly, too quickly. "I just have to go back now."

Maidie followed her as she turned to go. "Susanna, I'll never touch you again, I promise! Only please stay, Susanna—please stay with me!"

But Susanna was already running, racing through the cold to the shelter of the Shuttleworth wagon.

10

A MAN COULD have too much of a good thing—at least that was the foremost thought in Jed Taylor's mind as he woke amid the soft silks and feather pillows of Louisa Dolarier's bed. He'd been held up in New Orleans for months now, while Mel Wayne plotted for more guns and teased the Mexicans with planted information, casting like a fisherman with twelve lines, waiting for twelve strikes at once.

A pretty housemaid entered bearing a silver tray which held a huge steaming pot of coffee, a basket of hot, buttered croissants, and a single cup and saucer.

"Madame has gone out?" Taylor asked the girl, noting for the hundredth time that the little starched white apron and short black skirt did little to hide the saucy charms of Louisa's servant.

"Oui, m'sieu, madame left for shopping early this morning and left message she would join you for dinner." Her black eyes sparkled and her full lips smiled becomingly. "Would m'sieu care for anything else?"

Jed Taylor smiled back, his blue eyes lazily assessing her. "No, thank you, Minette, that'll be all." But he watched as she left, her hips swinging out under her brief skirt, undulating in a subtle invitation. Louisa liked having pretty things around her, and she had little to fear in the way of competition against her own refined and sensual beauty. This little chambermaid was no more than a tribute to her good taste.

Jed looked around the room, which also bore the unmistakable stamp of its mistress. The bedchamber managed to appear both spacious and intimate. Purple silks hung over the canopy of the bed itself, matching those hangings which decorated the smaller panels. The walls and ceiling were ivory, the inside moldings painted in gold leaf. A largish painting in an ornate gilded frame dominated the far wall. Done in the style of Boucher, it depicted Louisa herself, posing, reclined on purple cushions and unabashedly naked. The entire room was done in purple, ivory, and gold, from the love seat by the corner window to the heavy velvet drapes. Near the door stood a huge beveled mirror, fully nine feet high and set in its own gilded oval frame. In it the mistress of the house was wont to preen herself, both clothed and naked, before receiving any but her servants.

Now as he pulled back the draperies to admit the bright sunshine, Jed Taylor was aware of the softening effects of civilized luxury. The sun was well up—he'd been out late again last night dicing with some of the soldiers from the post. His body felt heavy, dining as he so often did of late on the rich sauces of Creole-French cuisine, the seven-course dinners, the straining buffet tables at supper, laden with pork and spice garlic shrimp, platters of fried potatoes. New Orleans could be a never-ending banquet if one had the appetite to sustain it. He was finding out that he did not.

Not for the first time was he aware of the overpowering femininity of Louisa's favorite chamber. He smelled the fragrance of her jasmine perfume still lingering in the air, but today he found it cloying and oversweet. He would have preferred wildflowers in the ground and mountains at his back. He was not a man of cities.

He poured the pitcher of hot water into the bowl and began to wash, feeling tired before the day had begun. He donned breeches of finely woven wool broadcloth, polished black leather boots, and a freshly laundered linen shirt. As he passed the great oval mirror, he paused for a moment to regard his own image. The lines of dissipation were faint, but nevertheless discernible: a slight thickening at the throat and jaw, eyes still bloodshot from excesses the night before. Too much eating, too much whoring, too much breathing the air breathed by too many others.

He wanted out. He wanted to get on with the job. He wanted—this he had some trouble admitting, even in his most private moments—that towheaded witch. Susanna.

He should have forgotten her five times over by now. But he hadn't. Her image returned to his mind again and again like some capricious ghost bent on mischief. Last week on the boulevard, he had followed a woman seven blocks who, from behind, resembled her, even though he knew it could not be she.

"I must be getting senile," he thought to himself. "Or going balmy." But perhaps seeing her again would be the cure, would end this folly. He could have his fill of her, husband or no, and then be done with this foolishness. He pulled a watch from his pocket and checked the time. He had a noon engagement with Melvin Wayne, and he was determined not to be put off again.

The army post was then situated at the western outskirts of the city, as though New Orleans would put as far as possible from itself all uniforms, all suggestions of imposed order. The city had had the dubious privilege of playing hostess to the soldiers of many nations, but familiarity was no grounds for affection—at least not among the natives.

Walking down the dusty street toward the colonel's

office, Taylor spied Hoppy on the shaded veranda outside the saloon. The little Oriental was seated crosslegged on a wooden crate, opposite another man similarly seated. Between them, a rickety table held three
decks of cards and several silver dollars. Jed paused
briefly to greet the men and left grinning to himself. He
knew which of the two would leave with the silver dollars—Hoppy played a mean game of pinochle.

He found Mel Wayne looking harried and thinner
than he remembered. There was a tense, worried look
about his face, bent over one of his innumerable maps.
He looked up and smiled at his visitor, but Taylor
sensed he was not overjoyed to see him. No doubt Mel
knew the reason he had come.

"Say it out, Jed," the colonel told him wearily.

"You already know it, Mel," Taylor answered. "I've
been piddling about for months. I'm stale."

"I'm stale, too," the other rejoined, smiling tiredly.
"Let's talk over a beer, shall we?"

The two men were soon installed at a table in the
Belle Chat, the army post's only saloon. Two foaming
mugs of ale were brought, and the men drank thirstily.
Mel Wayne was the first to speak, and his tone was
apologetic.

"I could never have foreseen the delays, Jed, when
I first asked you to take this on. You've been on the
payroll since then, though I know that's little compen-
sation for the waiting. If you'll only be patient a while
longer I know we can—"

"Mel, I know none of this is your doing," Taylor interrupted, "but I'm getting out of New Orleans. I've
been thinking about it for two weeks now. Another
month of this kind of living and I'll be no good to you
or myself."

"Trouble with the lovely Louisa?" Mel asked curiously.

Taylor grinned. "Not the kind I'd be likely to run

away from." He hesitated a moment, frowning. "Maybe it's too much of a good thing. But I'm not cut out for the soft life. This whole town is a whore, Mel—soft and sullied and everything in it for sale. I started a brawl the other night—you know the Queen's Parlor?"

Wayne nodded. "The most elegant refreshment parlor in our fair city," he said, as though quoting the words of an advertisement.

Taylor laughed and his blue eyes lit with amusement. "I was something the better for whiskey, and I brought three of my rowdies down there. They tried to—how do you say?—politely discourage our entrance. That big fellow at the door—"

"Otis?" Wayne offered.

"That's the one. He tried to discourage us the most, but there were five or six others, including the maître d' and the headwaiter."

"I noticed your eye was in mourning," Wayne said, referring to the yellowing bruise just above the left eyelid. "But being too polite to ask, I just figured Louisa had skinned you with a perfume bottle. Now you say you've been raising the devil, eh?"

"It's the best time I've had in weeks," Taylor said with conviction. "But its out of place, here, Mel. *I'm* out of place here. I've come to tell you I'm headed out. I'm leaving tomorrow morning."

Wayne sighed and leaned back in his chair. "Not a man to waste time, are you, Jed? Not that I haven't been expecting it. For that matter, I can be honest and say you've been more patient than I thought you'd be.

"Don't think I'm letting you run out on me, though. Your part of the operation has been in the ready all along. If you take the wagon overland, it's going to take you a piece to get to the Mormon encampment anyway.

"Any word of them moving out?" Taylor asked.

"God, no!" They're in the midst of blizzards up there. Don't let our fine Louisiana sunshine make you forget. You know what winters are like on the Missouri."

"They aren't easy to forget. Coyote country. They were the only well-fed creatures up there, and they didn't make appetizing meat."

· Wayne smiled grimly. "A man gets hungry enough, there's nothing he won't eat. But we're getting off the point. I haven't had word on that Canadian shipment yet, but it'll come through soon enough. I'll send a messenger to you at Winter Quarters before they move out, and that won't be till spring. He'll probably ship up the Missouri, and he won't be in uniform. But he'll give you my name.

"By the way. Did I hear you've got hold of Dan Stillwell's bay stallion?"

Taylor's whole face lit with pleasure. "That's right. Won him in a poker match. Stillwell was a jackass for making him a stake, but he's got card fever, and it was a lucky night for me. That horse was sired by a blooded Arab crossed with a Barbary mare. Stillwell wanted to put him up against a thousand in gold, and I said no until I saw him."

"A man could live his whole life and not see the like of that horse," Wayne said. "I know I'm wasting my breath, but I'm going to say it anyway. I wish you'd leave him in New Orleans. There are a hundred men in this town alone who'd gladly slit your throat to own that stallion."

"Mel," Taylor said softly, "that's exactly what they'd have to do. Brushfire's just a four-year-old, and before he and I are both too old to take an interest in the fillies, I'm going to have the sweetest line of fast horses this country's ever seen. And meantime, if you ever see another man riding in on that horse, you'll know to plant lilies for your old friend Jed."

"Sounds like you're fixing to give up sailing," the colonel noted.

His companion grinned. "I'm giving up as little as possible—just adding to it, that's all. But I guess getting that horse has sort of put ideas in my head."

"Just see that the Sioux don't sneak up on you some moonless night, Jed, or you'll be minus your ideas, your horse, *and* your head." Wayne downed his beer and stood. "I'll tell Hoppy to be ready to pull out in the morning. If I don't see you before you go, look for news come spring. And good luck, Jed. Take care of that horse."

Louisa came in early from shopping, bringing with her the same breathless flutterings that butterflies carry with them, or bright-plumed birds. She'd had a most successful day—the jeweler had finished setting her topaz, which she now modeled. It hung from a rich gold chain, falling just between her breasts. Her dressmaker was fitting her with a new gown, raw silk of the creamiest ivory. They were having guests for dinner—three couples—Louisa wanted to show off her new gem. She prattled gaily and Jed Taylor did not interrupt with what he knew would be unwelcome news. Tonight would be soon enough, and he wasn't looking forward to it.

But after the dinner and after the guests and brandies and good-nights there was no way to avoid it. She saw him pull out his buckskins, which she always complained smelled of horses. Without being told, she knew.

It was the longest he had ever stayed with her, and yet the worst. There was a change—nothing she could put her finger on, not with certainty. He had always been a strong man, a powerful man, but now he seemed hard. He was cruel sometimes in ways he'd never been. And just as distressing, at times he had seemed—bored. At first she took it as impatience for this job with the colonel to begin. But it was more. His spirit was repulsed by the life of the city, the luxurious indulgence, the glittering castles and temples built by slave labor under white masters. For Louisa, it was the power and the glory. For Jed Taylor, it was something he was putting aside, like a game he'd finished playing.

"When are you going?" she asked, trying to keep her voice light and easy.

"Tomorrow morning," he answered quietly.

So fast! "I—I thought it would be a month! The colonel said last week—"

"The colonel spoke too soon!" *And too much,* he added to himself. "A dispatch just arrived today. We have to move as soon as possible."

She did not challenge the lie, but accepted it. Just as she accepted the feeling that up to this moment she had vehemently denied—that he would not be coming back, either to the great port city or to her. And because she was a courtesan and knowledgeable in these matters, she knew very well that a man who wished to go could not be held.

So it was she said nothing to him of what these last three weeks she had known for a certainty. She had money; she could retire to the country. She would have him very warm and very close tonight. Her well-practiced lips kissed him deeply, expertly. She yawned delicately and leaned back on the bed, smiling at him meaningfully with all the charm and the assurance of a lady who knows her worth. And as he bent his long, hard body to cover hers, it was like a curtain being drawn over her. She pressed her lips to his ear and said only, "Be sure to wake me in the morning. I want to see you off."

11

THE WOLVES HOWLED every night. Every night their wailing voices carried to each log cabin and tent. Every night they seemed to range closer to the camp itself, closer to the stockade where the livestock huddled, crowded in the narrow space—horses, cattle, oxen, sheep—all prisoners together, all gathered for protection from the nightly dangers rife along the river bottom.

In the morning a thousand cookfires signaled the start of day. At evening watchfires burned, guarded and tended throughout those interminably long frozen winter nights by men who posted themselves in sheltered corners, men who might be clad in anything from buckskin to rags. Sometimes they fell asleep, if there was a building or a tree to lean up against. But always the wind or the wolves would rouse them from the chilly, stolen slumber. One night two of the bold gray hunters had slipped into the stockade itself, inciting the animals to riot. Terror-stricken and confused, they milled about in the narrow confines and covered all the targets while each of the intruders brought down a small bleating lamb and slipped back under the stout rail fence. Now they had fires every three yards around the stockade at night, enough to discourage any but a mad wolf.

They had been at Winter Quarters for two weeks

now. A small party of men had greeted the wagons of Nauvoo at the ferry. One man, separating himself from the others, had come forward to address the first wagons. All granted him deference, and those newly arrived from England craned their necks and crowded closer to see this man who, since the death of Joseph Smith, had held supreme authority in the Mormon church.

"That's him," someone whispered. "That's Brigham Young himself."

The word passed down the line of wagons, and the travelers left their seats to edge forward and hear him speak.

Joseph Smith, the prophet, the founder of the church, had been his mentor. Smith had been the visionary. To Brigham Young had fallen the task of making the visions a reality. He was the organizer, the doer, the natural leader of men. And many believed that the church would have died along with Smith had it not been for Brigham Young.

He was not a tall man. The clothes he wore were plain and sober and worn, and there was less flesh now on his stocky frame than when the journey had begun. But his voice carried clearly to the crowd who circled round to hear him. And something of his strength, his faith and iron will, was passed to everyone assembled there.

Susanna, who had gained an unobstructed view of the Mormon leader, remembered stories she had heard at Nauvoo; how when the church was rudderless and disintegrating from within, this man had stood and spoken, and people had witnessed the image and voice of the martyred Joseph Smith speaking through him. Thus he had assumed the leadership of his people. Thus he had become the patriarch and guardian of twenty thousand souls.

The newcomers were welcomed and warned. Times

were not easy, he told them, and never was their cooperation more needed than now. But there were stout cabins ready to house them, and together, with willing spirits, they would come through this winter and be on their way to Zion in the spring.

"The prophet has spoken to me in my dreams," he said. "We must keep our faith in the Lord and our eyes to the west. There we shall find the place God has chosen for us."

At his signal, the Apostles began to move among the wagons, assigning space and duties to each household. As they crossed the ferry, they were escorted to their dwellings and given the rules in force at the settlement. It was with such quick and marvelous efficiency that the newcomers were assimilated into the community of the Saints at Winter Quarters.

They had peace with the Omaha Indians on the west bank and with the gentle Pottawatamie on the east. Both tribes had promised to warn the Mormons of any danger from their local enemies, the thieving, raiding Pawnees, but so far there had been no trouble.

A thin wailing sounded from a log cabin shelter. Outside, a tall, dark figure paced the entranceway. Hosea Stout's dour, brooding face flinched at every cry. He had already lost two sons. The younger, William Hosea, had perished in his arms. One wife had run away, and now, inside that cabin, his faithful Marinda was dying, too—her insides slowly tearing with each contraction of her labor by an infant grown too large inside her ever to be born. A doctor might have cut the burden from her and saved her life, if not the child's. Miriam Young and his own sister Anna were doing all they could, but that was not sufficient. And God seemed short of miracles to spare for one man's anguish.

The waiting women called him in from his solitary vigil, but only at the end.

In the morning, Sister Eliza Snow would compose yet another eulogy. In the afternoon, there would be another burial; just one more among the hundreds already passed and the hundreds more that would come to pass before the journey's end.

In the Shuttleworth cabin, the women slept on straw piled up for warmth over the dirt floor. Two featherbeds had already been traded at Pointe aux Poules for more necessary food and provisions. They were lucky at that, with so many starving people in the camp. At least they had goods to trade.

Game had grown scarce for the hunters as well as for the wolves and coyotes, and meat of any kind was at a premium. Their survival depended on their livestock, and each morning the beasts were carefully herded out to forage as best they could on the short meager grasses underneath the snow. One householder who had gotten five bushels of Indian corn as fodder for his beasts found himself and his family eating the softer kernels, as horses do, right off the cob. More was made palatable in stews and soups, but little in the end went to his cows and oxen.

But the services continued every morning, and there were concerts and even dancing on the eve of Sabbath. Brigham Young himself had twice begun the dancing, after first kneeling and offering a prayer to the Lord. He rejuvenated the flagging spirits of his flock, exhorting them to dance and gladden their hearts with faith, that this would be most pleasing to the Lord. The president himself had lost so much flesh on the journey that he often laughed and said he could now wrap his greatcoat twice around him, and receive a double warmth.

Susanna had been accepted back into the Shuttleworth camp, without comment, as though her return had never been in question. She kept to herself her now-banished secret hopes that traveling with Maidie might be the beginning of her escape from the Reverend Shuttleworth altogether.

He had resumed his visits almost from the day of her rejoining them, and continued even now, in this cabin of communal sleepers. He had assigned her sleeping space in the very rear corner of the log hut, the darkest part of the single room. Maryann slept close to the door, and Prudence opposite the only window. Usually he took advantage of those nights when Shadrach was out hunting or on the night watch. But Susanna was terrified that one of the two sleeping wives would wake and see her shame, see him making use of her, see how he bared her body, sometimes minimally, sometimes entirely, so that he could see or handle her naked parts just as he chose. She all but stopped breathing to keep silent while he partook of his conjugal pleasures.

One morning as Susanna trudged up carrying water from the sloping and snow-drifted river bottom, a knife whistled past her, just inches from her breast. She gasped, expecting Indians, and turned to see Maryann Shuttleworth coming brazenly toward her to retrieve the weapon.

"Shadrach's teaching me how to throw bowies," she said without apology. "Guess I'm not too good—yet."

"You—you tried to kill me!" Susanna cried.

"You don't know that, missy," Maryann answered warningly. "Actually—I was aiming for this tree. I didn't even see you coming." With forced nonchalance, she bent and picked up the weapon, then retraced her steps to face Susanna. "If you tell the elder, I'll say it was an accident. He might beat me for it anyway, Sister Susanna, but if he does I'll kill you sure, and the coyotes can eat your bones!" She glared at the blond girl with a hatred so virulent, so profound, that Susanna found herself amazed.

"I've never wronged you, Maryann. I've never wished you ill. Why—"

"Oh, you're Little Miss Innocence," the other sneered. "You're just a real angel, Sister Susanna." Her eyes fired with enmity, and her voice came thick with rancor.

"It was *me* he'd come to before you were on the scene, with your fancy accent and your yellow hair." She bit off each word as if it would choke her. "No, you've done nothing but seduce my husband from me with your foreign wiles—hardly a reason to dislike you, sweet sister."

Susanna was as startled by this sudden confession as Maryann would have been disbelieving of the truth —that the reverend's attentions repulsed her. It was no personal hatred of Susanna herself, but a frustrated desire and possessiveness—the earmarks of passion— that drove this bitter vengeance-seeking woman. And just as woman will not see that another might want what she herself does not, even less can she conceive that the object of her affections is undesired by others.

Maryann was in love with the elder! With the sweeping clarity of that insight, Susanna could only wonder how it was she had been blind to the obvious truth for so long. There lay the cause of malice. Had she not been so much the victim of Maryann's passion, Susanna would have been moved to pity.

"Priscilla's hair was yellow too," Maryann remarked insidiously. "Just like yours."

Susanna felt a thrill of fear—a death fear. "Did you kill her? Priscilla?" she asked.

"I didn't have to," Maryann replied contemptuously. "But she died young, Susanna. *And so might you!*"

Maryann's threats made just one more danger, one more reason for caution, one more cause for fear. But there were a dozen ways to die at Winter Quarters, and people fell victim to all of them. There was a scourge of the disease called black canker, which Maidie said was very close to the scurvy she had seen about ships too long at sea. It came from a lack of fruits and such, and Maidie had given the Shuttleworths a supply of plum preserves to fortify them against the sickness. She and Susanna had tried to appear both casual and friendly, but they succeeded only in being uncomfortable.

For this, Susanna was profoundly sorry. The two girls, who from the first had been so close, were so self-conscious now in each other's presence that they could scarcely manage more than the most trivial social exchanges.

But Susanna had her hands full with her own dangers and distresses. She had finally managed to protest to the elder that their activities might be witnessed by other members of the household. But he had put it off as a false modesty. "They sleep soundly," he had told her firmly. "And you ought to consider, sister, that what we do is right and proper in the sight of the Lord, and therefore must be accepted by all."

Susanna knew otherwise. At least one sound sleeper knew of his attentions, possibly even watched and listened throughout, and fed a growing choler toward the recipient of those husbandly regards. The Lord might be accepting of their connubial alliance. But Maryann Shuttleworth was not.

Susanna had also asked him pointedly if he had made any of the promised inquiries about her father, and he had actually turned on her in anger. Was it not enough, he said accusingly, that he gave her bed and board in a household of righteous and honorable people, but she must be nagging like a fishwife in the middle of the wilderness where their very survival was a daily question? His temper had waxed furious and he forbade her to speak of it again.

Susanna had suspected as much since his initial betrayal of her, but now it was a certainty. Whatever fond hopes she had nurtured in spite of all were irrevocably dashed. And mingled with her despondency was a deep, abiding anger at her deceiver that chilled her to the very marrow, made her even more disgusted, if possible, more oppressed by his embraces, so that at times she had to grit her teeth to keep from screaming.

So it was that Susanna had little to spare for Maidie, except a fleeting sorrow. She could not guess the full extent of Maidie's loneliness—the long, silent weeping of dark nights, the anguished tossing on the cold straw bedding, the utter desolation of a woman who has discovered within herself all the love in the world to give—and none to give it to.

But people seldom die of loneliness, and the days passed on, marked by snowfalls and crosses on the calender. Sister Eliza Snow kept poetic record of all the great events, which by midwinter were almost always deaths. Their food stores were at the lowest ebb when a five-day blizzard hit, piling up drifts some twelve feet deep into which a man could sink and never emerge. And for days they were literally trapped inside their cabins, many without wood to burn in their fireplaces, and some cut off from their main provisions.

It was shortly after the blizzard that a shrill cry from Maryann broke the silence of the night and roused the neighbors on either side. In the dim light, she seemed to be fighting off an animal of some sort. Shadrach was the first to reach them, and Susanna heard him gasp. "My God!" he cried. "It's Jamie Williamson!"

But the raving thrashing creature he was struggling to control bore little resemblance to the boy who was reported missing during the blizzard and had been assumed dead. He was half-naked, his clothing shredded, his body covered with scratches and frozen wounds. Ice clung to his hair, and his eyes were a ghastly sight—feverish, lurid, with no trace of human reason. He began to rant madly, babbling a disconnected string of foul oaths and invectives which dissolved into incoherent gibberish. How he had ever survived the five-day blizzard at all was to remain an unsolved mystery, for this pitiful mindless savage had not the power to tell it.

Prudence crossed the room to comfort Maryann, who sobbed in the corner holding her right hand to her face. Then Prudence saw the object of the boy's demented attack: the third knuckle of Maryann's middle finger hung loose and bleeding, suspended by a piece of skin. He had been trying to eat her fingers.

Prudence looked to her husband and son, fighting to subdue the boy, and in a voice firmly controlled and curiously gentle she said, "There's no help for him now, Horatio. Take him out of here."

They dragged him, still raving, outside the cabin, where neighbors wakened by the disturbance crowded about. Two other men helped tie the boy to a post a distance from the cabins. They threw him a blanket and left him some food. In the morning he was dead. The food they had left was untouched.

But he had eaten the fingers off both his hands.

The terrible blizzard was the last heavy snow they suffered. A week later some of the snow began to settle, making it possible to travel short distances. Hunters were bringing down game again—turkeys and prairie hens, rabbits, an occasional deer. A few Indians from the friendly neighboring tribes came to trade. One Pottawatamie brave had brought several goods to offer, the last of which was a shocking item to the Mormons who had come to barter. She was a young Indian girl of nine or ten, belonging to an enemy tribe. Her dark eyes were frightened, fawnlike. She had been starved obviously, and beaten. Probably raped. Several of the Mormons took pity. One offered a horse and a sheep. The brave shook his head angrily. Another added two sheep, and another a calf. At last the brave accepted the livestock and left the girl behind.

The intended kindness proved to be more curse than blessing for the dark-eyed Pawnee child. Barely two weeks later, after the Mormon matrons had fussed and fed and dressed her neatly, a group of young men dragged her through the snow to an empty shed, tore off her clean, fresh garments, and used her for their pleasure, one by one.

Her softness, her vulnerable fragility, like that of a small woodland creature, only incited their lust to further debaucheries. She was gagged to prevent her screaming, and they continued their abuses fully half the night before someone was alerted and sounded the alarm. Five boys hitched up their breeches and hurriedly made their escape. Two others, Russell Emery and Clem Hogans, were caught by Hosea Stout. The Pawnee child lay belly-down in a heap of straw, looking for all the world like a sweet wildflower crushed under a careless boot.

The two men refused to identify their companions and were sentenced to be publicly flogged, each to receive twelve lashes. The scandal furnished fresh fodder for wagging gossipy tongues, and for a week it was the chief topic of discussion among the ladies. Over half the camp turned out to watch the whipping. It was rumored that Hosea Stout had threatened to hang both men before mitigating the sentence.

President Brigham Young, who had warned his people to caution and straight dealings with the Indians, now chastised them severely and advised them that just as Indians were held responsible to the Mormons for their activities within the camp, so Mormons committing acts of violence against their Indian neighbors would be subject to Indian justice. This more than anything served to curb the licentiousness of the younger men and to silence the casual joking among the older people, who had laughed at the incident and regarded it as little more than the roistering high spirits of spring come early among their youth.

The girl herself spoke not a word after the assault, but suffered herself to be tended and dressed. Late that night she fled the camp and was not seen again.

An eastern breeze was freshening the land and blowing the stale breath of winter before it. Although the snow remained for weeks, each day found its bulk decreasing in an ever-unequal battle with the sun. Great chunks of ice in the river thawed and separated into little islands that moved with matronly ease along the sluggish river current. The most daring boys employed them as rafts and used poles to guide them skillfully down and across the river. The most definite sign came from the great majestic geese who came from Canada—handsome, graceful birds of brown and green and golden plumage. They had passed through in the fall traveling south. Now they were on their way home, and their coming was a great event in the Mormon camp. It signified more than the availability of game. It meant that the worst of the terrible winter was done, that the children of God had passed yet another test of faith, that soon they might continue on their long journey home and raise a new city of Zion.

Even before the snow was gone, men were pulling out their hoes and forks, sharpening their scythes, cleaning plows. At the sound of a bugle, fifty men would begin felling trees. They stripped the bark and split the trunks into planks. They made pins from the branches and raised new cabins to house more Saints who would follow along that trail. There were thought to be some ten thousand souls behind them, some so poor they carried their goods in handcarts and traveled on foot. For them these stout log cabins would be shelter. For them the fields would be plowed and

planted with rich, golden grain that would sustain them
as they answered the summons of Brigham Young and
the Twelve Apostles of the church to join them in the
wilderness and build a temple to the Lord.

There were still small squabbles and incidents. William Dawes was accused of selling whiskey to the Indians. Evelyn Tasker lost a milk cow and blamed an
Omaha youth for stealing it. Sister Willoughby ha-
rassed Mr. P. A. Sarpy for better trade on her silver
serving dishes.

But every cookfire had meat to roast, and their heaviest woolens and red flannels were being aired and
packed away. A band of little children in the mad ex-
uberance of spring had kicked off their shoes and
splashed about in fine deep mud puddles, perfect for
wading, sitting, and sailing small wooden boats.

The men gathered in the evenings and spoke of
planting. Most of them were farmers, and for them the
turning of the soil and the laying in of seed was the
ceremony of their sustenance, their common bond to
the earth. So they scratched their chins and spoke of
the wind and the fields and the fullness of the moon
and discussed—half in wisdom, half in superstition—
when to plant the wheat and when the potatoes, which
land to clear and which to plow—and it made no difference that they would not be present at the harvest.
Land was to be tilled and man was to labor and husband the growth of the fields. Without it the fine, solid
structure of their existence would break down, become
rootless and confused. Within it, they knew where they
stood: they were the men who made things grow.

At the same time, Brigham Young, too, was tasting
the promise of spring in the air. He watched the slowly
setting sun as though that fiery beacon would light the
path to the new land, free of jealousy and intolerance,
of political entanglements and Gentile persecution. He
was hand-picking a body of men numbering twelve

times twelve, trusted, proven men to lead the expedition. And he had hired several Gentile scouts who knew the rugged western regions to guide the first wagons. It would take several weeks longer to outfit the wagons, but what, after all, was several weeks after seventeen years of seeking Zion?

The hardiest of the trees were sending up new buds; the young men were courting after prayer meetings. At last the ceremonies of marriage were outnumbering the funerals, and the dances brought light feet and light hearts to whirl the gay Virginia reels.

One of the new scouts had come into the settlement mounted on a magnificent bay stallion, and the boys were all agog. The beast stood as high as some of their draft horses, but he was built with strong racing lines, long-legged, clean-limbed, his fine head shaped as delicately as a piece of rare porcelain. His owner was a strange-looking man. He was tall and had a full black beard, and though he was not old, he had no hair on his head. Not even any eyebrows. He was camping south of the settlement with an odd little Oriental who managed the wagon.

Susanna, who had never ridden a horse, listened without interest to descriptions of the marvelous beast. Spring itself meant little to her, imprisoned as she was in the Shuttleworth household, trapped by her husband's lust, and burdened with Maryann's unflagging hatred. Too, she was sometimes haunted by the mystery of the elder's two dead wives. She almost never heard them mentioned, and one day, finding herself alone with Prudence, she took the opportunity to ask her about them.

"Well," Prudence had begun, straightening up from the oven, "can't see as it's any secret, 'specially you being family and all. Priscilla, she was a sweet thing, now. Delicate. Too delicate to my way of thinking for the hard ways of our living. But the elder fair doted on her, gay as she was. And such a pretty voice.

"Priscilla used to walk out by herself sometimes, up to a cliff that looked over miles of the countryside— this was before that butcher Boggs got us run out of Missouri, you understand. Anyway, it was a popular spot enough. Boys used to take their gals up there for sparking and carrying on, and nobody ever reckoned on it being dangerous.

"But we could only guess it was on account of a spring thaw that loosened up a boulder overhead. 'Cause some freak thing knocked Priscilla off the cliff, and it took us two days to get that poor girl's body up for a decent burial. The elder took on fierce with grieving. She was with child, you know, so it was a double loss."

"And what about the other one?" Susanna asked. "I hardly ever even hear her name."

"You ain't likely to either—at least not in the elder's presence. Sary Lynn was a child of shame, no doubt about that. He had no business marrying her at all— even less than Priscilla. 'Cause Sary Lynn was one of them gals always wanting things, you know—frills and fripperies and soft living. And we're a humble people, not given over to the wealth of this world.

"So it wasn't no surprise that she was discontented. She complained about the work and often as not refused to do her share. And the reverend's whippings didn't seem to do no good, just roused more of the devil in her. Don't suppose there was many surprised when she finally turned wanton and took up with some slick-talking Eastern fella, a Gentile he was. The reverend was all for letting her go with him and good riddance—she was bad seed among us. But he deserted her at the end—just never showed up when he was supposed to come and take her—and two days after, she took off to the woods with Shadrach's old shotgun, set the barrel in her mouth, and used a stick to pull the trigger."

Prudence shook her head, remembering. "It was an awful mess, Sister Susanna, I can tell you. The elder was tending the fields close to the woods and he heard the shot. He went in curious-like, cause there wasn't no game to speak of in that part, and he found her there with the top of her head blown to hell and half her face shot away. Weren't no pretty ending on top of the grief she'd already caused, and the reverend don't like to hear her name. Can't say as I blame him neither.

"But that's all the mystery, child. Nothing to fret us now."

Susanna questioned her no further, but she wondered sometimes if infidelity was always a matter of the flesh, as it was with Sary Lynn and her Eastern lover. How often did she now close her eyes as the elder lay with her and see in her mind's eye not the gaunt narrow face, the thin lips and piercing gray eyes of her husband, but blue eyes that sparkled and laughed, and thick, curly dark hair and a mouth that planted kisses everywhere. Why, even last night she had dreamed or imagined she heard the strains of an English ballad carrying across the still Missouri air. And she could just see him, singing before the company and the rough ship's crew, but really singing to her, his eyes holding her glance, wooing her. . . . She could almost feel his arms around her, his strong, lean body pressing down against hers. But it was all so long ago. Now it was spring, and she felt too old for it to be spring. All her springs were past.

But the wagons had been covered and repaired, provisions inventoried, and Brigham Young proposed to leave right after the next Sabbath day. Their livestock had fattened on the new grass, and most of the men were in the fields before dawn, tending the last of the planting. It was a fine cool morning with the mist coming up over the river that offered concealment for the long Indian boats slipping across the Missouri, carrying some twenty painted Pawnee braves. Nearly a hundred others, including the warrior whose daughter had been dishonored, were climbing up the eastern shore to the village of the Pottawatamie.

The first Mormon lookout, a lad no more than eighteen, was silenced before he could give warning. The second was more successful, and moments later, the shrill camp bugle rang out the alarm, calling the men in from the fields and the women to shelter.

"Get ammunition!" one man cried. A Danite youth ducked low across the open space and ran for the supply house. Seconds later he snaked back through the barrage of guns and arrows, carrying boxes of cartridges and bullets to the men.

Children were screaming, hauled in from their play. Hosea Stout snatched a toddler from the grass and set it inside the nearest cabin. Horses were stamping and pulling at their tethers in confusion, and three men ran to guard them from the attackers. The camp had been thrown into uproar, yet within minutes armed men stood at their places, and the women and children were within shelter.

Numbering so few, the Pawnee concentrated their attack on that area of the camp where the girl had been abused. They ran low and charged suddenly, leaping out from behind the bushes and trees that marked the edge of the settlement. One tall youth, in the first flush of triumph, knelt to take a trophy from his victim. Porter Rockwell, pressed against the side of a cabin, calmly raised his rifle and shot him in the head.

The entire assault was over within an hour. Driving volleys from the well-armed Saints pushed the raiders back to seek new openings and new victims. Seven braves lay dead where they had fallen, and at last, their knives made useless, their arrows lacking targets, the remaining assailants slipped back to their boats to join the heavier fighting on the east bank of the Missouri.

The women, emerging from the cabins, called out to their men for reassurance. Twelve got no answer. The attack had been so swift, so unexpected, they had been caught so unaware—it was a mercy there were only twelve. But it seemed no mercy to the wailing women who cradled their dead, who shut the eyes of their husbands and covered their broken bodies that the children might not see. Twelve women, who this morning had been wives, of a sudden become twelve widows. For them it was no mercy.

Susanna, walking out with the others, saw something in the bushes that looked like a pile of rags. The rags had been a dress and in that dress a woman and with a hollow feeling of dread at the pit of her stomach she was walking faster and then running until she saw what she feared was true.

Maidie! They must have caught her down by the river—she always fetched water as soon as she'd risen. Perhaps it was to keep her from giving the alarm. But whoever had done it had not left without his battle trophy. The glorious red mane was gone, leaving her poor scalp naked and bleeding in a dozen places. And the knife wound in her chest had left a trail of blood that bespoke the horror of this last hour. She was too weak now even to crawl.

Susanna knelt beside her, heedless of the blood that drenched her skirt. Maidie was still conscious. She opened her eyes once, very wide, then let them flutter down half-shut. "How kind," she said, her voice no more than a broken whisper. "Susanna . . ." Now she gathered herself in some concerted effort, as of a tired lady feeling the need to entertain a visitor. So much of her was already somewhere else. Her hand raised weakly to her head. "Oh, I must look a sight!" She could see Susanna, could see that she was weeping. "I'm glad there's one, Susanna," she said softly. "Don't be too sad, but all the same, I'm glad there's one to mourn me.

"And you can pray for me, Susanna." Her lips turned up in a little smile. "Pray that I won't meet my Martin like this—he loves my hair so . . ."

The voice trailed off, and Susanna was looking through a flooding rain of tears. Maidie's head was suddenly heavy on her lap. The dear, kind face, so drained of color, looked somehow peaceful now. So pale—like a wraith, or like an angel.

She needed help to bear the body to the settlement. A short distance away, two men stood talking. She recognized the portly Elder Bedwether, but the other man, who stood with his back to her, was a stranger. His head was bald and stood out most strangely in the camp of tall-hatted men. He must be the Gentile scout Shadrach had spoken of—the man with the wonderful horse.

As she approached, the elder turned toward her and the other man followed suit. The lower half of his face was hidden beneath a thick full beard. He was looking at her and his eyes were—She stared again, unbelieving. She noted his height; she looked at his body, telling herself it was impossible, it couldn't be.

Both men regarded her questioningly, and she could scarcely trust herself to speak. She struggled to find her voice. "Maidie Brauer is dead," she told them, pointing back toward the bushes where the body lay. Her eyes, awash with tears, went swiftly to the blue-eyed scout. "Maidie's dead!" she repeated. "Maidie *Cross*," so that he would know.

He stepped toward her now, and took her arm.

"You need help then, madam," he said in a curiously formal tone, and guided her back in the direction from which she'd come. His whispered words came low and urgent. "Say nothing, Susanna. Just walk with me."

His expression grew somber when he saw the body, and like Susanna, he knelt a moment beside her. "Poor Maidie Cross," he said, shaking his head. "The fates did weave you a sad life, and a sad death, too." His arms reached under her and lifted her inert form.

Susanna walked beside him. She plied him with questions. Why had he told her to say nothing? Why had he shaved his head and grown a beard? And what was he doing here at all, hiring on with the Mormon train?

He brushed her questions aside, saying only, "I've given my name as Clint Beauchamp. I won't be much about the camp, and there's little chance of any ship's passenger recognizing me as I am. Just don't you give me away, Susanna, or I'll skin the hide right off your pretty body and no mistake. And stop staring at me that way, for God's sake. I saw your husband talking with Young outside of the third cabin, and if anyone's likely to know me, he's the one. Especially if he sees us together and gets curious. Be calm now, and tell me where to lay the body. I'll see you later if I can."

He followed her to the designated cabin, set down his burden, and left, refusing to enlighten her any further.

Brigham Young understood as much about the Indian as most of his hired scouts. He directed several men to port the Pawnee dead to a place close by the river—he knew they would return and try to recover the bodies of their slain. And he expressly forbade any abuse or mutilation of the corpses.

Later on they would learn that the brave of the Pottawatamie, he that had first sold the little maiden, had been found still alive and bound to a tree. He had been cut several times with a knife in such a way that he would never walk, nor ride a horse, nor ever be a man to a woman. Such was the fierce justice of the Pawnee.

12

THERE WAS A broad ancient beech tree that stood in the center of a wooded bluff between the Mormon settlement and the river. Its trunk was peeled smooth of bark, and its greedy, overgrown roots had used up all the soil around it, forming a small clearing underneath. The man who called himself Clint Beauchamp had met Susanna gathering kindling near a grove of cottonwood. He assisted her at the task until they had piled as much as she could carry back to camp. Then he had taken the last of the twigs and branches from her hands and led her to the clearing.

They had at least an hour before she would be missed. He pushed her up against the massive trunk of the beech until she could feel the firm, hard wood pressing into her back. His tall figure towered in front of her, completing the trap. But she sought no escape, uttered no protest, not even when he took her hands in an iron grip and raised them over her head. And for a while he just looked at her.

Her face had aged. Matured might be a better word —it looked now more a woman's face than a girl's. All that she had done and witnessed, all that had been done to her had marked her in some subtle way, firmed the sweet round chin and thinned the cheeks, added a melancholy depth to her brilliant eyes. He wondered briefly at the change. He wondered how she liked her husband, and if there had been others, then censured those thoughts, angry that he should care. What did it matter? Right now she was his for the taking, and he meant to have her.

He could see the heat starting out from her slanting green eyes, the slow pink flush along her throat, and he smiled slowly, lazily, as a hunter might smile at some small animal over whom he is master. He bent to kiss her mouth which trembled more than smiled, but opened easily, willingly to his kiss. He kissed her again and then many times more, until she was pliant and swaying, reaching toward his face, his mouth, his kisses. He released her hands, which clung to him. He began to unbutton her blouse.

For Susanna this meeting had the nature of a dream. Seven months it had been since the *Star Victory* had docked at Nauvoo. Seven months she had not seen him; a hundred times she had remembered and yearned, as though his bodiless presence were haunting her. His nearness now—even this dizzying passion coursing through her—seemed to her a reality so fragile, so delicate, that anything might disturb it, cause it to dissipate, cause her to wake.

She wanted it to be real. She challenged him then. She stopped his hands. She rebelled against the nebulous ease with which he was taking her. She asked him questions; she wanted to know why he was so disguised and how he came to be joined with the Mormon train.

"It seems your charms have drawn me, lady," he said in answer, mocking both her and himself. He looked down at the curve of her breast, exposed where her blouse was undone. His hands parted the neckline further and covered her naked breasts. "Don't fight me, Susanna," he said almost grimly. "You'll be hard put to explain if your clothes are ripped off."

She yielded then, giving herself over to the hands that were undressing her, that caressed as they uncovered, that finally pulled her down to the dark, mossy earth to couple with this almost-stranger whose looks still startled her. She submitted then as though the whole seven months had been nothing more than a waiting—for this moment, and this man.

Afterward they lay together quietly, and Susanna began to accustom herself to the strange appearance of her lover. There was a short, scratchy stubble already started on his tanned and shaven head, and she told him he ought to let it grow again. He laughed and shook his head, declaring that Hoppy would soon barber him clean and smooth. He was setting a new fashion for young men-about-town, didn't she know? Soon it would be the rage.

"Do you find my locks displeasing, then?" he asked, holding her face very close to his.

She stared at him a long time before replying. The absence of hair on his head, the shaven eyebrows, gave him a lean, ascetic look, totally contradicted by his rakish eyes, standing out like hard, bright gems against the darkness of his tan. His thick, full beard looked wild and ungroomed—a very Blackbeard—and his lips, centered within the curly forest of hair, were hot, sensual, demanding. "You look," she said finally, "like a bad man, a bearded outlaw. You look like all the wicked fires of hell, Jed Taylor!"

"Then you're surely bound for the furnace yourself, it seems," he said laughing heartily. He drew her closer. "Well, my pet," he whispered, "since we're doomed to burn for it anyway, I'll give you another taste of the heat that awaits us down below."

They had met only once more since that time, and Susanna's face still burned to recall the episode. It had begun with such joyful anticipation. She had managed to excuse herself for the afternoon, and the

bearded scout had met her a distance from the settlement. He brought her to his campsite, with its rough-
hewn corral that housed the most royal-looking creature
Susanna had ever seen.

Seeing Taylor, the stallion had trotted up expectantly, nudging at hands and pockets until the man laughed
and produced a biscuit. His flaring nostrils were so fine
that Susanna could see the bright blood running just
under the surface. His slick coat glowed like a russet
sun, and strong, hard muscles rippled under his hide.
Taylor clapped his hands and set the beast running,
an easy rhythmic leggy stride that did not begin to tap
the power, the charged potent force of the powerful
body. He trotted back to his visitors and Susanna
reached to stroke the high, arched neck that trembled
at first under her light hand, and then relaxed.

"I'll put you up on him sometime," Taylor promised.
"Anyone traveling in this country should know how to
ride. But you'll go astride if I teach you. None of those
silly sidesaddles the ladies sashay about on." He
grinned wickedly. "He'll be a good bit of horse between your legs, Susanna. He'll warm you up proper
for his master."

The sun made her hair a golden froth, tossed about
on breezes. Her head was low, her hands gently caressing, stroking the velvety dark nose of the stallion. Taylor was suddenly reminded of her body, naked beneath
her clothes; the ivory white breasts, the sweeping curve
of the hip. And recalling this, desire leaped in him,
fierce and urgent. There was a bed of soft deerskins
inside the cabin, and he wanted her! He brought her
in quickly, whispering in her ear that he would show
her how a stallion takes a mare.

Despite her protests, her embarrassment, he made
her kneel and lifted up her skirts. His fingers drew
circles on the soft insides of her thighs and urged
them apart. Then he played between her legs, tugging

gently at the soft curls of her nether hair, moving again to where her hips arched up and out. He could see her body quivering—quivering, he told her, just like a mare with a stallion at her.

With his hands gripping her flanks, he plunged to the very core of her. She could feel his belly pressing at her loins in the thrusts that followed, and she bucked like a pony as he rode her, until she had lost consciousness of all but his hands on her hips and the penetrating animal force of him behind her.

In the closeness that followed, in the circle of his arms, she had begged him to take her away. And with a sardonic kind of pleasure that remembered its own revenge, he had refused.

"Why, madam," he said, feigning surprise, "what of your poor husband?"

The reverend's visit the previous night had only served as a miserable contrast to this meeting with Jed Taylor, only sharpened her desire to escape. "He betrayed me!" she cried. "From the very beginning. He let me believe it was no marriage of the flesh, I was to have private quarters, yet he uses me when he wishes. Only last night—" her voice broke off—"I hate him, he's cold and horrid—"

But Taylor's booming laughter overpowered the words that followed. He shook his head, laughed again, and looked at her as though she were something quite remarkable. At last he managed to say, "It would be such a stupid and ill-conceived lie that I'm hard put not to accept it as true. Which means you would believe a man would marry and not bed you. That makes you the most excessively ignorant female I think I have ever met."

He placed his hands on her shoulders and turned her to face him while his keen blue eyes made a leisurely tour of her undraped figure. "Do you not know what a man sees when he looks at you? What he thinks, what he wants?"

"I look at you and I see you naked as you are under your clothes, flat on your back, my lass, with your legs spread apart and I between them." His hands slipped from her shoulders, began to move over her body. He chuckled softly to feel her trembling under his touch. "And do you really believe, little fool, that other men think differently—see you differently than I?

"Sweet hot little vixen," he taunted, toying with her breasts and enjoying the view of her discomfited excitement. "A female ripe for bedding. And if that's not all you are, my dear," he concluded, "it's a goodly portion of it.

"Not that I overly relish the idea," he admitted in a voice tinged with irony, "of following the path your husband plows. But that's not really my domain. I always thought it was the nature of wives to plead headaches and vapors and such when their husbands' attentions are—less than welcome."

"You don't know him!" Susanna cried. "His is the only law. He *beat* Maryann just for losing some hens! He whipped her and made us all watch—!"

"Well, there's one point your husband and I agree. A bit of leather on the backside would probably do you good." His lips curled up slightly; his eyes laughed at her. "And if you were my woman, you would've felt it by now, on at least a couple of occasions I can recollect." His voice lowered to an insidious murmur. "Though I might guess you'd enjoy my beatings more, Susanna. Am I wrong?"

In return she raised her hand and slapped him full across the face. "There's *that* for your beatings, *Mister* Beauchamp!" she cried furiously.

He did not retaliate as she half-expected he would,

but instead drew away from her, putting a certain distance between them, as though building up a wall. And the words that came after were cool and hard and mocking. "You must tell me, madam, when it comes your turn for a bit of religious instruction. Perhaps I'll come and watch.

"But you needn't waste your breath begging me to be your ticket out of here. When I go and where I'm going there'll be no place for you. If that's your tack, you'd best find yourself another prospect."

For seven months he had waited to refuse her, to spurn her, to negate her. Every time she had intruded into his thoughts, interrupted his pleasures, he had told himself he would have some fun with the elder's little wife, play her as she'd played him, and then refuse her. Let her go. Then why didn't he feel victorious? He felt . . . deflated. Was it because she looked so frail and hurt—damn it—or was she acting?

She was gathering her clothes, readying herself to leave. Already the afternoon sun was lengthening the shadows. She didn't want to stay any longer. But he caught her at the doorway, swung her once around, and told her hoarsely, "You'll come anytime I call you, Susanna. *Because you want me.* If there's nothing else, there's that between us. Whenever I want you—!"

But she was already walking out the door.

They had been on the trail for two weeks now. Susanna had not seen him in all that time, only glimpses at a distance of a tall rider on a great bay horse, sometimes conferring with other riders, but seldom about the wagons themselves.

Just now she was giving Brother William Clayton an hour's relief at his "roadometer," the right front wheel of Heber Kimball's wagon. Brother Clayton had spent a portion of every evening on the trail arguing with other men's guesses as to the distance traveled that day. After much searching and measuring, he had discovered the circumference of Brother Kimball's wagon wheel to be fourteen feet eight inches, which calculated to 360 revolutions per mile. From that day on, having tied a rag on one spoke of the magic circle, poor Brother Clayton had diligently counted off the circles; three hundred and sixty to the mile, for sometimes twenty miles a day. It was an almost fascinatingly monotonous labor, and on several occasions, Susanna had spelled him and been mesmerized by the counting of circles which became for her like the counting of sheep.

Still, it was better than having her mind too free. Her thoughts were all painful it seemed. Her last meeting with Jed Taylor had left her—worse than angry—defeated. His sudden appearance had set her hopes shining. She had believed somehow he would help, would protect her. And he had refused her. Worse than that, she was ashamed for having asked him. What reason had she to trust him, to expect that he would help her? Only fancies and dim longings and the magnetism of their coupling. All of which meant—nothing.

Brother Clayton returned and wrote down Susanna's numbers. For a while she continued walking with him, eased by the rumbling drone of the wheels moving across the hard dusty earth. But after a time her eyes were drawn to the flat, sunken floodplain before them; a land so empty, so unadorned, that its very space pressed in upon her consciousness, made her a small lost thing, caused her to hear a litany in the ever-rolling circle of the wagon wheels. *Alone,* they seemed to be saying, in mechanical chorus. *You're alone . . . alone . . . alone.*

Where was her lover these soft and balmy nights? And where was her friend? One scorned her; the other was dead and buried, out of reach for comfort. Who would ever match the child with her father and the woman with her mate? Who would shield her from her husband's cold embrace which had become like death to her? Or protect her from the jealousies of Maryann? No one.

The wagon wheels kept turning, unconcerned. She managed a poor excuse for a smile and bid Brother Clayton good-day. She had to walk alone; she had to keep herself from crying. There was a wilderness of strangers all around her.

Brigham Young saw her pacing alone beside a grain wagon and thought there was something gallant and a little sad about the slim figure of Elder Shuttleworth's young wife. She was an interesting figure and certainly a pleasure to look at on a fine spring afternoon.

Young was currently bothered by a large party of Indians who had been following the train for three days. Word had been brought that they were some four hundred Pawnee, designs unknown. Late that afternoon, Young ordered a cannon fired, hoping that the fierce explosion, though short of range, would discourage the uninvited observers.

That same night, by suspicious coincidence, the breeze that whistled in from the west carried a faint acrid tinge of smoke. By morning they could see the distant orange blaze of a prairie fire, burning low to the earth in front of them. The wind shifted the fire north, and the wagons were forced to a southerly route along the wet, muddy bank of the Platte River. They camped that night on the nearest high ground, and Wilford Woodruff had another of God's miracles to record when the rain fell and put out the fire.

Three days later, at the Loup Fork, Brother Woodruff in his typical spiritual fashion mired his teams in quicksand trying to ford the shallow but fast-moving waters. Rescuers transferred his load to the revenue cutter, a long leather boat ideal for crossing the toughest water. Porter Rockwell, riding up to the opposite

shore, spit down into the water and laconically remarked it was a good thing Woodruff had the ear of
God for miracles, " 'cause he sure ain't worth the skin
off a fart when it comes to driving a wagon!" The man
who had ridden up beside him, the scout Beauchamp,
agreed and stayed to watch. Woodruff, standing up to
his knees in muck, gestured superfluously from his
place in the middle of the stream, while the men in
the revenue cutter sweated and cursed and heaved as
they maneuvered the heavily laden craft.

On the other bank, more wagons lined up for the
crossing, and a crowd of people waited their turn. The
bearded scout caught sight of a cap of blond hair, and
Susanna emerged from the crowd to get a better view
of the progress. They had not seen each other so close
in two weeks. Their gazes locked for a moment over
the sandy shallow waters. Then Susanna watched as he
wheeled his horse and set off toward his camp. For a
long time she stared after his retreating figure, hating
him, hating him that he could turn so easily away from
her.

The Mormons had suffered a preponderance of ca-
sualties among their horses. Three had been lost to
Pawnee thieves—two were stolen in broad daylight. A
horse belonging to Brigham Young had been secured
improperly and was found choked to death, hanged on
his own tether. But the greatest defiance of laws and
logic occurred when Brother John Brown pulled a coat
from his wagon, caught it on the hammer of his rifle,
and fired a shot through the left foreleg of Joseph
Matthews's horse.

Beauchamp with his "hot racin' stud horse" deigned
to picket his prize with the ill-fated camp horses. He
set his tent about two miles ahead of the Mormon
wagons, which huddled in protective circles in the
evening. The stallion, Beauchamp claimed, was as good
as any watchdog. The strong piercing clarion call of

his neigh announced anyone paying the campsite a call.
Not even Hoppy, coming and going about the tent and
stores, escaped the strident chimes of the stallion's
greeting.

The little Oriental was himself more about the Mor-
man wagons than his companion, who had become
rather taciturn of late. Evenings would often find
Hoppy in company with those of the train whose hearts
were gratified by the sight of a riffling deck of cards.
Pinochle was a friendly game for two or three, but
when more came about, they often switched to poker,
which Hoppy regarded as a phenomenon of tense faces
and hidden cards, fewer grunts of conversation and
more curses at a loss. He accepted his own luck at the
cards with philosophic Eastern calm, even while keeping his senses alert for the disquiet of somone lacking
his peculiar gifts of spiritual transcendance.

He was also aware of certain comments occasionally
whispered at his back that remarked his yellow skin
and slanted black eyes, and any conclusions as to his
character that might thus be drawn—to his detriment.
It was not in any way surprising; indeed, he had en-
countereed it in various degrees everwhere he had been
in this country of white men with black slaves. As a
man whose pigment fell in between, his status was constantly suspect.

He had adapted in his way and within the boundaries
of his private moral code. He did not forgo the company of men as did some others of his race. In his
native farming village, the society of males was an important adult pleasure, whether for games or conversation. He had found a place for himself at the army post,
and these men seemed to differ little except perhaps
that they considered themselves soldiers of their God
rather than their country. At any rate, Hoppy was not
a man who looked for trouble. A man who would not
dare an insult to his face did not require answer.

Susanna had often passed Hoppy about the camp, and each time the little man had paused in his jerky stride to smile warmly and bow his respect. She could not bring herself to ask after his companion, and if she had, Hoppy would have been at a loss to ease her. There was, in essence, nothing to remark. Taylor scouted trails in the daylight, running his stallion whenever he found good ground, and bedded rather early in the evenings—he rode hard and his days were strenuous. Of this yellow-haired lady, he said nothing. Personally, Hoppy felt the man, whom he liked and respected in most things, was better with his horse than with his women. This gold-haired flower who was badly husbanded by the hard gray man deserved better at the captain's hands. But Hoppy saw and thought a great many things he did not say aloud. He had found that unrequested counsel was generally unwelcomed.

The ease of passage along the trail, the swift rolling of the wagon wheels, brought no gladness to Susanna. Indeed, the long, sunny days seemed to feed her loneliness. At the noon stop, she watched William Clayton scrawl his mileage computation on a plank of wood which he set on a mail post some fifteen feet high. Many travelers left letters and messages inserted in notches or weather-safe wooden boxes for friends and family who would come after along the same route. And Susanna, without letters or friends or family, could not but envy those simple gestures of contact and caring, those homey little concerns. She thought of James Leverton, who had left them at Nauvoo to return to New Orleans. But she wouldn't even know where to address a message, and what in all honesty could she say? That she was unhappy, frightened? That her husband used her, as was his right, or that Maryann hated her? What did it mean to anyone? And as kindly as he was, what could Leverton do from wherever he might be now?

The nights were calm and leisurely, with few of the perils that had marked their flight from Nauvoo to Winter Quarters. Her husband visited often at her tent, though mercifully he did not stay long. And when he was gone, the remaining sweetness of the spring night was spoiled for her, only marking by cruel comparison the barrenness of the act just completed. The dark, secret fecundity of the earth outside, the balmy freshening breezes, the incessant chorus of the crickets all conspired to remind her that the quickening, budding fertile season surrounded her, and she was all alone.

She could look to the west and see, at no great distance, the gold and orange flickering light that marked Jed Taylor's watchfire. And her mind's eye would measure the distance, but she herself could make no move—no more than a caged thing who sees freedom beyond its bars. This man had spurned her; yet the longing persisted, leaving her frustrated and distraught. The need would not go away, and he would not come to her. And between those two immutable facts, Susanna's spirit suffered the days and nights in isolated misery.

They had a brief spell of rain, and for a day or two, the wagons creaked and whined struggling through the sandy muck. They had to be hauled quickly, before they had a chance to thoroughly mire in the almost bottomless ooze. But after the first few wagons rolled through, the ground seemed to settle for those that followed.

The rain nourished the thirsty sod, and Elder Bedwether happily remarked you could almost hear the grass sprouting up green and strong in the quiet night. The cattle and oxen fattened, and chickens clucked about picking grain in the early morning before they were caught and cooped and set back in the wagons. The Shuttleworth sow sacrificed one fat piglet to a dinner roast. Game abounded, and there was no need to hoard their meat. The entire company was well stocked, well fed, and merry as any people carrying out their dreams on a cloud of easygoing.

The land was beginning to change. Soon they would leave the rambling whispering waters of the Platte, which the Indians called Nebraska, or Shallow Waters. The Platte had been their companion for hundreds of miles along the trek, but now they could see the foothills of the great mountains rising up in the distance, beckoning them on. Brother Clayton's last marker had ascertained a distance of 472 miles from Winter Quarters.

The Mormons held a celebration with much music and sportive dancing, but Susanna remained on the periphery, having no heart for singing, no role to play in the festivities. She had thought that perhaps the blue-eyed scout would make an appearance, but neither he nor Hoppy was in attendance. Shadrach was dancing with his mother, who whirled and turned like a young girl tonight. Good food and spring weather for traveling had lightened the pinched look she habitually wore, erasing the lines of worry around her eyes and mouth. Her family was alive and well and together on this pilgrimage, and the worst all seemed far behind. The elder danced with Maryann, and Brigham Young led his pleasant wife in the first reel, while portly Captain Pitts, in full regalia, led his players in the country tunes so loved by the company.

Susanna heard the banjos strum the introduction to her name song. The last time she had heard it, Maidie had sung it, high and wavering, laughing through the lyrics that were made for just such laughter. Where was the laughter now? Not in Maidie, dead by violence in which she had no part. Nor in Susanna, who heard only the ghosts of other times.

The elder would come to her tonight. She knew, as surely as she had felt the cold stare of his gray eyes following her a short time ago. The moon was full, the breath of spring was balmy, and it was a night for love —not for what he would do to her.

He had begun to take particular pleasure in positioning her for his attentions; placing her arms out from her body to expose her breasts, bending her knees while her thighs remained apart, that more of her was revealed to his sight. He seldom caressed those parts he so ceremoniously laid bare, just fixed his steely gaze on her lying passive and prone before him, waiting for it to be over, for him to be gone.

Sometimes she thought he could not but sense her repulsion, her abhorrence, even as she yielded to him. It was beyond her comprehension that he might enjoy the act of taking what she would have withheld if given choice. That her very reluctance could be a spice beyond the simple act of possession. It was his will triumphant over hers. Her sufferings, her shame and wretchedness, served only to feed his sense of power and his perverted lust.

She was about to turn and head back to her tent, where she might have an hour or more of peace before the reverend would leave the celebration for his final evening's amusement. A man separated himself from the revelers and approached her. Susanna was amazed to recognize Brigham Young himself.

"Would you care to try a round with me, Sister Susanna?" he asked, his usually stern lips smiling. "I have already asked your good husband's permission."

Confused, complimented by his seeking her out, Susanna nodded and gave him her arm. For all his somewhat stocky frame, Brigham Young was an agile dancer, weaving his partner easily in and among the other couples. His broad hand rested lightly on her waist, guiding her through the turns and bows. "You seem unhappy of late, sister," he said, his face bent close to hers. "Is something amiss?"

Was it so obvious now that even this man had noticed? She had to choose her words carefully. "This is a strange land to me, sir. And Maidie Brauer, who died in the Pawnee raid, was my dear friend. This county is so different from England," she added, as further excuse, "so big and lonely-feeling."

"This part of the continent is strange to most of us, sister," he replied, seeking to comfort her. "But it's a new home we are all seeking. And we are all your family. Think on that when you feel lonely." The music had ended and he was standing very close to her. His eyes regarded her warmly, and it came as a sudden shock to Susanna that he would like to kiss her! She edged a distance away, hoping not to offend him. He was kind, and she was so starved for kindness. She excused herself from further dancing, explaining that she was weary and would return to her quarters.

Brigham Young watched her departing figure and frowned in puzzlement. She was sweet—very sweet, pretty and delicate and well mannered. And clearly distressed by some unknown cause. He recalled a rumor he had heard some time back that Shuttleworth's second wife had sworn a feud against the new bride, but he hadn't paid it much heed. The divine inspiration of plural marriage had always caused unrest, particularly among the women. Confronted with it, they prayed and fasted and fasted and prayed. In the end, most of them—those of the true faith—accepted it. He supposed household jealousy could be part of the reason, along with the Brauer woman's death.

His own wife Miriam disliked Elder Shuttleworth, though she had no real foundation. She said his presence was like a cold wind—an ill wind. But then women were forever having these feelings—instinct, they called it, or intuition—and swore by them as though the voice of God had whispered revelations in

their ears. The trouble with his wife's feelings, to
Brigham's pragmatic mind, and what made him at
times a trifle uneasy, was that she was so often right.

Shuttleworth had been with the church for many
years. He had left a small farm in Vermont to join
them a short time after Brigham himself had been converted by Joseph Smith. Since then, he had proven his
worth as a speaker of the Word and a missionary of
the church. His faith was unquestioned. Some men of
authority did not take to him, which may have been
the reason he had never risen to an apostleship. But
no impropriety had ever been attached to him, and a
man could not help his own nature. With a sigh, the
Mormon leader dismissed history and returned to the
festivities around him. As to the future, and particularly the future of Susanna Shuttleworth, he would watch
and see.

Susanna did not have long to wait the inevitable.
Her husband made his way to the tent shortly after
her own departure. She was still clad in the full gathered skirt and cotton blouse she had worn at the
dance. But when she turned her back to her husband
in order to disrobe, he stopped her.

"Face me, madam," he commanded in the icy tones
of authority.

She obeyed numbly, her hands stiff at her sides. His
face was a mask of cruelty. What had she done to
anger him?

"If you will consent to undress, wife," he said, "I
will remain where I am."

Her consent was superfluous, and they both knew
it. Trembling, she moved to obey.

It was like the scene of her baptism aboard the ship
so long ago, but much much worse. Here was no pretense of averted gaze. She felt his gray eyes focused
piercingly, recording her every move. Her legs were
naked, the skirt heaped on the floor. She retrieved it

clumsily and put it away. Her fingers worried over the buttons of her blouse. She was trying to hurry, to get on with it and have done with it. But her own unease hindered her progress. She had to grope at the straps and fastenings of her undergarments. She had to bend and stoop to pull them off. All the while he watched, his eyes gleaming with some unholy light, but disdaining any motion toward the image of loveliness being revealed before him.

He fastened his gaze where he deigned to touch, over the full high, flawless breasts, the narrow waist and outwardly curving hips. Even in her present state of apprehension, she was graceful, dainty—her mouth rich and full, her skin so very fair, her eyes green and darkened with misery, and her hair such a pale gold, such a shining crown.

He stood up and approached her, still examining her coolly, meticulously. She might have been a milk cow that he owned or thought to buy.

"It seems our honorable president looks with favor on you, madam," he said at last, in a faintly sarcastic tone. "Just what about you does he find so pleasing?" This time there was an unmistakable menace in his voice.

Susanna was bewildered. What was he implying? "He only asked me to dance!" she cried. "He said you gave permission—"

She was answered by her husband's heavy hand, striking hard across her face. His voice reached her from somewhere in the distance. "You are a married woman, madam. *You are my wife.*"

It was too ludicrous—her clandestine meetings with Jed Taylor unsuspected, and accusations of sporting with Brigham Young! Her cheek was a flaming splotchy red where he had struck her, and her head was reeling. But she would not grant him the satisfaction of her tears. He was cruel, and stupid in his cruelty. She held back a sudden almost hysterical urge to laugh, to laugh in his face, but the look she gave him was eloquently defiant.

"I fear I sense a wanton in you, madam," he said coldly. "But henceforth you will conduct yourself with the decorum that befits your station." He paused for emphasis. "Or suffer the consequences!"

He did not elaborate on his threat, and Susanna's attitude remained rebellious. Still naked, still standing before him, she waited his next move. Aside from the slap, he had not touched her.

His eyes glittered strangely in some final appraisal, and she was amazed to see him reach for his hat and prepare to exit. "Consider well my words, madam," he said. And then he was gone.

Outside in the camp, the musicians had ceased their songs, and the revelers were retiring. It was late and dawn came early. Sitting quietly inside her tent, Susanna was wide awake, her thoughts grinding like stones in a tumbler. She waited until she was certain that Shuttleworth would not return. Then she reached for her shimmy, her blouse, her skirt and shoes.

The back of her tent faced west, and by lifting the edge of the canvas, she could see, beyond the dark silhouette of wagon wheels and axles, a fire glowing in the distance against the black of night.

For the first time in many long months, Susanna knew exactly where she was going.

The freshening air, cooled by the evening, braced her to her purpose. Hearing the voices of men on the night watch several yards away, she slipped behind her tent and between the wagons that formed the boundary of the Mormon camp.

The taste of freedom was sweet to her, like the wind blowing softly through her hair. She looked west to the fire that was drawing her like a moth to its flames. She held the fine woolen shawl that had been Maidie's tighter about her shoulders and began to walk—a small, brave figure quickly lost to sight in the great sweep of prairie and sky.

The round, full moon gleamed down on the broad, shining land. The grass was thick and springy underfoot. There was a reverent hush in the air, a kind of stillness broken only by the occasional cry of a night bird, or a coyote howling out his eerie song of courtship.

It was farther than she had thought—across the flat landscape, bearing only sparse and stunted brush, distances were deceiving. She began to have misgivings. Above her a myriad of stars made a ceiling for the sky. The fire still glowed ahead, but it was like the moon—seeming so close, yet over out of reach.

And what if—*what if he didn't want her?* She hadn't even thought of that, drawn as she was by instinct and desire, by the flickering lure of his fire and the devil of need for him that would not be exorcised. In the middle of the night, in the middle of the empty land—but he *must* want her! He must let her stay with him, warm, beside the fire. If he wouldn't have her, she might as well continue walking across the prairie until she dropped. Then let it be as Maryann had said, and the coyotes could eat her bones.

She could hear the stallion Brushfire sound a trumpeting neigh from somewhere in the shadows up ahead. She shivered. He would think her mad, but she had to come to him, there was nothing else to do. She needed him to hold her in the circle of his arms, to feel the warmth and the strength of him. And if he did not want her—

A shadow she had not seen among the patchy scrub moved swiftly up behind her. She gasped, feeling an arm lock tight about her neck. Light glinted dully off the gray metal barrel of a pistol pressed against her throat. The shawl fell back from her head, exposing

a tumble of curls that glowed incandescent with moon-
beams. The arm that was choking her dropped suddenly from her throat, and two strong hands gripped
her shoulders to spin her around. Jed Taylor stared
down at her, disbelieving.

"I thought to catch a costumed Indian! Little fool,
what are you doing out here? Are you trying to get
yourself killed? I might have shot you for a horse
thief! What do you want?"

She tried to tell him. Her lips worked to form the
words, but they lay half-strangled in her throat. Her
green eyes finally lifting to his were blazing with hot,
bright tears. And then she was sobbing, sobbing like a
little child who has come a long way to reach uncertain
welcome.

But it was all right, it was all right now, even as
her tears were staining the front of his shirt, because
he was holding her, his arms pressing her close against
him, gentle and tender and giving her everything she
had come there seeking.

He had never expected she would dare so much—
to cross that wild stretch of prairie in the dead of
night. "Hush now, sweet," he whispered. "Hush now,
my brave little lamb. Don't cry." He cupped his fingers
under her chin, kissing the tears from her face, kissing
her with a hunger he had denied these last weeks, even
to himself. Now a fierce gladness took him that she
had come, that she had sought him out, even foolishly
in the dark and over a wild land.

Without a word he picked her up and carried her
to his tent.

13

HE MADE HER return early to the Mormon wagons. Well before dawn, he set her up behind Hoppy mounted on the bony sway-backed nag Mel Wayne had supplied to pull the wagon. Hoppy knew the lookout posts and could be trusted to return her unobserved.

She was still all flushed and rosy with the passion of these last hours. Her lips were dark red, half-bruised by his kisses, and her eyes were soft like sleepy wild things dozing in green forests. There were marks on each side of her hip, where his hands had gripped too tightly. And he himself had not emerged unscratched. He smiled wryly to himself. Her fingernails had bit deep into the flesh of his shoulders and left thin red scratches as souvenirs of their bedding.

He was not pleased to be sending her back at all, and she had given up protesting only because he had promised they would meet soon and that he would take her with him when he left the train. He had decided he could carry her to Los Angeles and leave her in Leverton's care while he finished his business with Garcia. Of this she knew nothing, but it was better so for her. Actually, he would not have minded finishing off her husband for good and all, but those were private thoughts.

He was *not* a private man. He was on the payroll of the U.S. government, though with the charming expedience-mongering of all governments, they would deny it were he to fail and be captured. He was Mel Wayne's gunrunner, and neither the army nor Wayne would look with favor on a killing that would doubtlessly send the whole Mormon camp up in arms. Taylor rather liked Porter Rockwell—he was disciplined, quiet, and deadly—and Taylor had no illusions that given official word, Porter would cheerfully, and without personal malice, seek to cut him down. Rockwell and Blake and Fagan and Stout—the four dark horsemen—would certainly slender out the odds of his survival.

It was wiser to deal by stealth. Let Shuttleworth despair of his runaway wife—he and Susanna would be well gone.

A great deal had changed in those few hours since she had made her private little pilgrimage to his camp, and the one sure thing he knew was that he would not leave her behind.

They say there's one to every man, he was thinking, *and damned if she's not mine—my trouble and my pleasure both. And I'm a wooden Indian if I'll let her get away from me now.*

Last night was for good. He still wondered at his own joy at the feel of her beneath him, the warm, sweet, fragrant skin, the taste of her breasts, her mouth. The way she could cling to him, arms and legs curled around his body, drawing him down to her. Just a slip of a wench, tousled blond curls and little hands—but of all the women he had known, she was the one he wanted to keep.

Susanna hummed as she paced beside the wagon that day and in the days that followed. When he saw her next, Brigham Young could scarcely connect this vibrant young female with the forlorn, distressed-looking lady he'd noticed the week before. She was speaking with the little Chinaman—Beauchamp's shadow, the boys called him, because whenever he drove the wagon, he stayed just behind his partner, the bald-headed scout, who would slow his big bay horse to an easy walk. Susanna's gestures were animated, her face vital, glowing as she posed some question to Hoppy and listened to his answer. When Brigham himself approached she had thanked him prettily for his concern. She was feeling much better now. And so she looked. But then, females had their mysterious ways of altering drastically from one time to the next. At least this was a change for the better.

Indeed, Susanna seemed to have discovered a new energy, a secret well of happiness. Everything was alive to her now, and lovely. She gloried in the cool misty dawns of the higher ground they now traveled, the glowing pink sun that rose and pasteled the edges of flat gray clouds wafting lazily. She watched startled rabbits blink as the wagons rumbled by their burrows, and heard the chittering of birds building nests within the safety of the brambly low bushes that dotted the landscape.

Her days had meaning. Every step she took beside the wagon followed her lover's trail, kept her close to him. And the nights—when Hoppy would have told her where to meet him or when he would come to her —the nights were the reason for the days.

It was not always easy. But Elder Shuttleworth did not come to her as often as he had before. Susanna suspected he was still displeased with her for dancing at the celebration, and if that kept him away, she was very glad of it. He had taken her only once since the night he had commanded her to strip, and it seemed no different than all the other times. She had resolutely closed her eyes and borne it, while imagining it was another man upon her—a strange bald-headed man with a thick black curling beard and eyes the color of warm ocean waters.

Sundays were best for the lovers, for the Mormons would not travel or labor or work their beasts on the Sabbath, and the two of them had long afternoons to let the cedars blow above their heads, to lie drowsy and love-filled in the private sunny nooks he marked while breaking trail. They gamboled like puppies, rolling on the mossy grass, their naked bodies warmed by the sun and refreshed by eddying breezes.

But the sweet unbroken ease of their days was ruptured, and all because of a poker game, a jug of whiskey, and too much luck in Hoppy's cards.

Clem Hogans brought the whiskey, which he'd smuggled in from Fort Laramie, when he joined the card game behind the grain wagon. Hogans didn't like Hoppy—he was one of those men whose half-whispered insults sometimes sounded at Hoppy's turned back—insults which the little Oriental had deigned to answer or even acknowledge. Hoppy had already been in the game for two hours, and Clem Hogans had been drinking for close to the same amount of time—long enough so that after another hour of playing, with Hoppy's luck running to take most of the pots, Clem Hogans was moved to slam his hand down on the last pile of silver and looking straight at the calm, unruffled winner, he spat the words that guttered from his throat, "You cheat!"

No one there would ask Hoppy to prove himself. Every man knew he played a straight hand—he had not even dealt this round. An almost palpable tension emanated from the little wagon driver, whose black eyes, inscrutable, stared into the face of his accuser. "You drink too much, Clem Hogans, for an insult to be wise." The words were spoken softly, as though he were gently chiding. But the men on either side could see his hair bristle dangerously, his back arch slightly like a cat before it springs. "If you seek to dishonor a man, you must expect he will defend his honor."

"A *man?*" Hogans snarled the question, his heavy jowls set with stupid fury, his thick eyebrows knit across his brow. "I don't see me insulting no *man!*" His eyes raked across the Asiatic face, the bland, passive looking features. "All I see is a dirty yellow Chinaman. A chinky-chinky-Chinaman who cheats at cards!"

So Hoppy stood and drew his double-bladed knife and waited calmly while someone lent Hogans a bowie. Hogans was fat and bulky and charged in the unthinking animal manner Hoppy had anticipated. Hoppy gave answer with a movement that resembled nothing so much as the leap of a dancer—a sharp high kick that disposed of the knife in Hogans's hand, and an upswinging arm that thrust forth the razor edges of his own weapon. In a neat downstroke, he sliced Hogans' right arm, drawing a seam that showed scarlet and oozed blood. His aim was to disable, not kill, and the skill he displayed was graphic proof that sparing Hogans was no accident.

But be that as it may, Hogans wanted Hoppy taken care of, and being summarily discouraged from taking him on alone, was insisting he be tried before President Young and a court of the Apostles.

Just before sundown as the trial was to begin, Susanna saw her lover ride into camp looking as grim as death astride his dark gold horse who pranced nervously between the wagons. And every man who saw him pass knew that should harm befall the little Oriental, there would be the devil to pay. And that devil would be Clint Beauchamp.

Owing exclusively to Brigham Young's finesse, bloodshed was averted. Clem Hogans, sober and surly, his right arm in a sling, stood with five of his cronies on one side of a bench around which, on makeshift seats, sat the Apostles. Hoppy, with unshakable dignity, stayed alone on the other side. A distance away,

Porter Rockwell waited for several of the boys to carry out Brother Brigham's rather strange request. With a sharp whining of wheels, the large flat-bottomed wagon that carried the revenue cutter lurched and maneuvered its way behind the Apostles' bench. It was from that high and most unusual platform that Brigham Young intended to speak to the broad assembly gathered before the Mormon leaders.

The business of Hoppy was dispensed with almost before anybody realized it. There were a half-dozen witnesses in agreement as to what befell, and Hogans' wild accusations reduced to regard of Hoppy's deadliness, which Brigham Young handled in brief. Every man in the camp had arms, Young observed, and any arms were deadly. A man who defended his own honor was, in effect, defending himself, and two men equally armed were equally deadly. It was not the matter of fault in the incident, but the *fact* of the incident that was the issue here. And then began one of the most thorough and well-remembered tongue-lashings in all of Brigham's long career.

"When I wake up in the morning," he said, gazing out toward the assembly, "the first thing I hear is some of the brethren jawing at each other. I have let the brethren dance and fiddle and act the nigger night after night to see what they will do.

"Well, they will play cards, they will play checkers, they will play dominoes, and if they had the privilege and were where they could get whiskey, they would be drunk half their time. In one week they would quarrel, get to high words, and draw their knives and kill each other.

"It may be that we have this man to thank," he said, nodding to Hoppy, "that killing it was not.

"Do you suppose that we are going to look out a home for the Saints, a resting place where they can build up the kingdom, with a low, mean, dirty trifling, covetous wicked spirit dwelling in our bosoms?"

He raved and exhorted the company, sharpening his tongue on their guilty misdeeds and indulgences until the faces of men became the faces of little boys, penitent, remorseful, promising to do better. Were they ready to cease their wickedness, their pettiness, and push onward to their godly purpose? Every hand went up.

Young looked meaningfully at Clem Hogans, whose hand rose reluctantly. Hogans had been in disfavor since the incident of the Pawnee maid, and he may have sensed his days in the church were numbered. Two months from now, he would be exiled from the city of the Saints, but at this moment he was subject, like all the rest, to the supreme authority Brigham Young represented. He was a disgruntled but nonetheless obedient member of the clan.

The onlookers and participants shuffled their feet and disbanded in appropriately penitent spirits. Clint Beauchamp, still mounted, wheeled his horse and headed out, satisfied that no revenge would be attempted on his wagon driver. He passed very close to Susanna, who felt relief at the peaceful outcome of the affair mingled with that biting frustration that this man who was her lover and her love must pass her like a stranger. She comforted herself with their shared secrets, their delights, and his promise that soon they would leave this place together.

But it was a cold comfort later that night, when the unwelcome presence of her husband followed her like some dark shadow to her tent.

It was raining outside. She tried to concentrate her thoughts on the splashy percussion of raindrops on the canvas roof, to avoid the hard calculating stare of the elder's eyes, watching her, always watching. He

couldn't complain anymore about Brigham Young—
she'd spoken to him only once, and that was briefly,
a week or more ago. But his silence unnerved her,
made her wonder. Oh, why wouldn't he just leave her
alone! Why did he come and press his cold lust upon
her. Maryann loved him better—why did he not go
to her? Why did he say nothing, not a word, not even
good night? But at least he was going. The calm per-
sistence of the raindrops finally lulled her from her
wondering, her unease. She was grateful that at least
he gave her leave to sleep alone.

The rain continued all the next day, soaking into
the parched earth and forming muddy ruts where the
wagons passed. A chilly wind blew in from the north,
strangely out of season, and further balked the Mormon progress. Susanna rode in the wagon with Prudence and Maryann, who shot her looks of spite. Was
she so aware of the elder's movements, Susanna wondered, or had he spent all the other nights with her?

She was glad Jed Taylor waited until very late, until all the camp was sleeping, before he came to her.
Tonight not even the watchfires would burn. The rain
still held sway in the heavens. But tonight, and very
late, while she waited lying in the bedding, all naked
for her lover, the pelting rain would sound in her ears
like music, heralding his coming. Like chimes, timing
the hours passing, drawing closer to the time when
he would appear, chiming like a thousand tiny clocks
all keeping company with her, waiting.

And he came in all soaked through, his beard full
of raindrops, water squishing in his boots. He grinned
at her appealingly, like a little boy tracking mud into
the kitchen. She pulled at his shirt. "Off with it all!
We'll wring it out at least."

He unbuttoned his shirt and she struggled with the
knot of his bandanna—it was blue like his eyes and
of strong, fine silk. He always wore it now, just like

the broad-brimmed western hat, though the hat had been scant protection tonight against the slanting rain. He was soon as naked as she and nuzzling at her neck while she toweled him down, brushing the rain from the dark pelt on his chest. "Now hold hard, you soggy thing!" she cried. "Wait until I get you dry!"

He said nothing, but toyed with the silk bandanna, forming a knotted loop which he slipped over her head as she bent to wipe his legs. He pulled her up and smiled, his fist casually holding the loop at the pit of her neck.

"Stop your foolishness, knave," she said, shaking the towel at him. "Let me get on."

In answer he tugged at his makeshift tether drawing her face up close to his and nibbling like a rabbit at her chin. "It's a handy thing, a bandanna," he said, smiling mischievously and keeping firm hold of the knotted silk. "A halter when one's needed, or hobbles if it's long enough, to curb a horse from running."

"Now there's horses bred to stable, like my Brushfire, such as train up under gentle handling. And that's the way you treat them."

"Then there's fillies that get a bit of a stubborn streak, maybe from running about too long on the plains." His fingers brushed across her mouth and wedged between her parted lips. "They try to take the bit between their teeth, you see, and lead their masters about, whinnying out their complaints of this and that. They need breaking before they're good for much. They need to know who holds the reins."

Susanna trembled, held by the silken collar. His hands brushed over her flesh as he spoke. He teased the arched peaks of her breasts, flickered across her belly. Her legs were shaking. Her breath was coming fast. She did not know how much longer she could stand.

"Now go lie on the bedding, little filly," he whispered at last, whipping off the blue bandanna. "And show me how you need no hobbles on your feet!"

His flesh was cool and damp against the warm dryness of her skin. His body wedged between her legs until they opened wide to receive him, and her face was wet with the soft damp bristles of his beard. Her eyes were closed; her lips were parted—a blind mouth searching for his kiss, fastening to his mouth, hungrily, greedily. They coupled and rocked to the rain's accompaniment, moist, straining toward each other, meeting, then separating, then lunging to meet again.

Susanna arched upward, moaning to feel his hard chest scrape her nipples. She felt his thighs against her thighs, his strong arms raising her face to his kisses. He was so deep inside her, so hard and strong. And her limbs were so languorous, all melting, all his. Her hands on him tightened suddenly, involuntarily. Vaguely she was aware that her fingers were digging hard into his flesh. Then she felt the stirring, tingling mount in her belly, dissolving all else—even the sounds of her own moans that merged with the howling wind and the pelting wash of rain.

He left soon after—much too soon, but the sky, so heavily grayed with thunderclouds, was deceiving. It was close to morning, though there was no hint of sunrise when he slipped back into his still-damp clothes and stole away. Susanna watched him go, fighting the feeling of abandonment, of dark forboding that suddenly overcame her.

The entire sky was obscured by a blanket of murky gray that periodically vented its wrath in bursts of torrential rain, then eased back to a persistent drizzle. The wagons moved slowly. The livestock was restless and wild-eyed. The horses shied at imaginings, and even the stolid oxen would raise their heads in the yoke as though listening, and roll back the whites of their eyes at something only they could hear. The sheep running up before the wagon were matted and muddy, their discontented baa-ing falling back like curses upon their drivers.

At first the women rode in the wagons and Susanna sat silently with Prudence and Maryann. Maryann's pale eyes had a look of malice and mischief, and Susanna could not bear it for long. She left and went out to pace beside the grain wagon by herself.

Soon there were other women out, walking beside their household wagons. The alkali flats, ill-accustomed to water, were interspersed with areas of fine-grained sands, which formed a sloppy, dangerous terrain. The oxen had all they could do to haul wagons without the added strain of human cargo. So it was that Maryann came to walk uninvited behind Susanna at the grain wagon. Susanna was carefully ignoring her and did not see the other girl's pace increase until she was beside her, during the stormiest bout of rain. Not until she felt the swift block of the wiry body against her, shoving her down so quickly that her own screams were too slow—were not heeded by the wagon driver before the rear wheel of a grain carrier had rolled with a sickening rumble across her chest.

There was a great hue and cry as wagons halted and people came running up from behind. Susanna stayed conscious long enough to be helped to her feet and to see the thin figure of Maryann Shuttleworth retreating unnoticed. Then the sounds grew more distant. Darkness descended like a curtain.

Susanna awoke to find her wet, muddy garments stripped from her. She was washed and cleanly garbed in a strange nightdress and lying on a soft, comfortable wagon couch. She started to turn her body, but her ribs protested with a deep painful throbbing. A woman had been sitting, half-dozing by the foot of the bed. Susanna did not know her well. She was Brigham Young's wife Miriam.

Her family waited news that she was well. Was there anything she needed? She had fainted. Yes, Brigham had had her carried to their wagon so that she, Miriam, could tend.

Susanna was dizzy. At least one of her ribs was undoubtedly broken—likely more than one. There was a big purple bruise over part of her right breast. She did not attempt to raise the first question in her mind. *Where was Maryann Shuttleworth?* Her mind worked to remember. The rain had been thundering down— the sky was very dark. Had anyone seen the incident? Certainly Maryann wouldn't confess!

Brigham Young had had something of the same thoughts when he was informed of the "accident." One person had remarked seeing Maryann close to the grain wagon. No one raised questions or had seen Susanna actually fall. If Maryann were to be implicated, it was Susanna herself who would accuse.

So he had generously offered the nursing services of his faithful wife and taken charge of Sister Susanna. He would ask her when she was well enough. She would tell him what had happened.

Susanna herself harkened back. What was it Maryann had said, if she, Susanna, should accuse her? But that didn't matter now. Another question, much more basic, composed itself. What had prompted Maryann to attack her just now, The elder was visiting her seldom. Did Maryann know about Susanna's "other" visitor? *Did she know about Jed Taylor?*

Despairingly she recalled little details—Maryann's tent was only yards away from hers. Maryann slept lightly—she had been awake when the elder bedded Susanna late at night in the winter cabin. If Maryann knew, what might she not tell if Susanna accused her of this deed? Suddenly it was not her own pain, but fear for her lover that wracked like a knife at her vitals. These men dealt harshly with outsiders. What

would they do to a Gentile who dared debauch a
Mormon woman—a Mormon wife?

Susanna tried to rise from the couch, but failed, defeated by the grinding pain. Oh, God! she could not
even speak to him! She was trapped and guarded by
the kind ministrations of her hostess and nurse. And
she was too weak to get away. Beads of sweat stuck
out on her forehead. She bit her lip and let her body
sink back upon the bedding. She would say nothing
of Maryann. Perhaps after all, the girl knew nothing.

She heard good Brother Woodruff wish her well
from outside the wagon. Susanna's freak accident and
more freakish survival was, he affirmed, yet another
miracle of God.

Yes, it was a miracle that she lived—that or incredible luck. Had the bottom of that particular stretch
been alkali and not sand—sand wetted by the providential rains, which made it soft and silty—she would
have been broken in two between the heavy wheel and
the hard earth. Instead she had sunk into the soft,
yielding ooze, pressed down and bruised, but still in
one piece.

Miriam Young reentered, bearing greetings. Elder
Shuttleworth was very glad to hear she was awake and
hoped she rested comfortably and well. And Maryann
Shuttleworth brought respects. She waited outside.

Susanna stared at her disbelieving. *Maryann outside?* She nodded her head. Yes, she would see the
girl. Better to know, better always to know. And she
would not dare to harm Susanna here.

The thin second wife, the would-be murderess, was
clearly not at ease. She fidgeted standing before Susanna, who was propped up on the couch and facing
her squarely, with at least an outward calm. Susanna
was not forced to ask the question.

"I know about you," Maryann said, at last meeting
Susanna's eyes. "About you and Clint Beauchamp."

Her voice was tense, drawn like a strung wire. "I come to tell you—I'll help you get away with him. If you'll only go—I'll—I'll do anything I can to help you. And I won't tell no one if you'll only go away!"

Her words took on a ragged edge, lowered to a whisper. "I didn't really want—to kill you," she cried hoarsely. "I just wanted you away from *him*. I don't care about your other man—go away with him!"

It seemed almost too neat—too incredible to Susanna—that Maryann Shuttleworth should be pleading with her to do exactly what was already planned. Clearly it was no good denying the affair. Yet it wouldn't do to trust her too much—just humor her enough to keep her silent. After all, there was still the incident of this afternoon.

"I must think on what you have told me," Susanna said, feigning weariness to be rid of her guest. "But for the time being I will say nothing of what you did this afternoon so long as you take counsel to hold your own tongue."

Maryann's face relaxed visibly, but whether with relief or sly triumph Susanna could not tell for certain. "I'd like to rest now," she said pointedly and breathed a sigh as Maryann departed.

Susanna's mind worked against its own distraction, trying to sort a plan from the chaos of these new developments. She had to get to Jed! Or if not to Jed, then Hoppy. But how to manage it, injured as she was and trapped in this wagon?

Her desperate plans all failed. She managed to have Hoppy called to the wagon, on the pretext of obtaining from him a medicinal salve known among his people. Of course, Sister Miriam was most happy to oblige with the request. And of course, for the sake of propriety, Sister Miriam remained unobtrusively in attendance, smiling with a beaming innocent countenance, her hands busy at their knitting. Hoppy did bring a jar of some rare ointment, red in color with a smell like strong cloves. And wasn't that kind of him, her hostess remarked. He really was a gentlemanly little man. But Susanna's mind was all taken up with the one word Hoppy had managed to mouth at her in answer to her singular frantic gesture. *Soon,* his lips had silently mimed.

It could not be too soon for Susanna.

The rain had given over to sullen overcast heat that filtered from the sun through the still-gray cloud cover. Even inside the wagon and inactive, Susanna's garments clung stickily to her skin. Outside great hordes of flies pestered the horses and stolid oxen. The air was heavy.

It seemed to Susanna that she lay in limbo while all around her the forces of danger were convening. Afraid for her lover, fearing her own return to the Shuttleworth wagon—if the elder lay with her, she would feed new fires to the already almost-fatal wrath of Maryann. And out of touch, out of sight of her lover—ignorant of his plans for their escape.

It had to be soon! She could feel within herself more than desire—the necessity that they must leave soon.

Her ribs were bound in tight linen bandages which afforded her some relief and at last permitted her to move about. On the fifth day, she descended the wagon and made a slow tour of the camp—getting air, she told Miriam Young. Actually she was searching for Hoppy or Jed Taylor, but neither was to be found. She had not expected Jed, and she learned later that the card games that had drawn Hoppy to the society of the wagons had been discontinued since the incident with Clem Hogans. He had continued to visit in the evenings until just two nights ago. Since then no one had seen him about. He was sticking like a burr to Clint Beauchamp somewhere up ahead of the wagon train.

The Mormon camp was buzzing with excitement that

night. They had as their guest a frontiersman—a mountain man, as familiar with the wild western territory as the pilgrims were with the insides of their own wagons. His name was Jim Bridger—Old Gabe he was sometimes called—and not a man jack in the company could resist finding a seat in the circle to see and hear this almost legend speak of the land that they hoped to settle.

Susanna had expressed a wish to join the listeners, hoping fervently to find the one face she sought among the crowd. Brigham lifted her down from the wagon as though she were a china doll and made a comfortable space for her close by the campfire.

Jim Bridger watched the little beauty being so carefully seated near him and grinned to himself with a womanizer's appreciation of Brigham Young's good taste. He borrowed a guitar from one of the younger men and said that the fame of his hosts had proceeded them into this land. If they would grant him leave, he would offer them a song he had heard recently. Even Brigham Young, who was its foil and hero, laughed to hear it, embellished as it was by the vibrating basso of Jim Bridger's booming voice.

> *Brigham Young was a Mormon bold,*
> *And a leader of the roaring rams,*
> *And a shepherd with a heap of pretty little sheep,*
> *And a nice fold of pretty little lambs,*
> *And he'l llive with his five and his forty wives*
> *In a city of the great Salt Lake*
> *Where they woo and coo as pretty doves do,*
> *And cackle like ducks to a drake.*

Brigham Young only mentioned mildly that the number of his wives was somewhat exaggerated, but he refused to say by how many.

Susanna searched with anxious eyes among the many

faces, but the man she looked for was nowhere to be seen. Nor had Hoppy come, and in spite of the fresh warm night and the first clear sight of stars in many days, Susanna felt a chill take her like the ague. She suffered through Jim Bridger's entertainment—tales of whiskey-loving Indians and their antics around his trading post, fur-trapper stories and ribald saloon yarns, watered down to respect the womenfolk. He spoke of the Mexican War being played out in the West, and lent his opinion to everything with the superb arrogance of a man who has conquered mountains and who views the workings down below with a godlike nonchalance.

They wanted to settle in the Salt Lake Valley? He scratched at the thick bush of his beard. It might do. It might do very well, except that the nights there were cold and might be hard on young corn.

"It ain't easy livin' we're looking for," one of the older men remarked. " 'Cause we've been where the grain grew sweet and tall, and we've seen it burned to the ground before the harvest.

"We'll take a hard land to settle," said another, "so long as it ain't in the United States!"

One by one, the Mormons began to tell the storyteller their own hard stories of religious war, of death and pillage, of constant exodus.

"We seek a home that will be ours forever," said Brigham Young, speaking for them all. "A place where we must answer to none but God, and where men and their governments will not make war against us."

Jim Bridger answered in words that deeply moved the assembly. This land, he told them, this wild and empty land they traveled, was not what governments would make it, but what men would make it. It would belong to the settlers, to those who would build and farm and mine—who would bring their wives and children, and whose children would grow on the land and with the land. They needn't fear governments, he said, with an added glint in his eye. The mountains did not like little pettifogging officials with their clerky manners and their baby-cheeked faces. And beyond the mountains was more land and then more mountains, all the way to the western edge of the continent.

In the lull of conversation, Susanna excused herself, and Brigham Young escorted her back to the wagon. His hands lingered just a moment at her waist as he lifted her, but he made no rude advances. Susanna watched his broad figure depart and knew she had a great deal to thank him for. She had told him nothing to implicate Maryann in her accident, but still he had, in confidence and without questions, offered her his wagon and the care of his kind wife. It was this man's authority alone that kept her apart and safe from the elder and Maryann.

Her husband had nodded briefly to her at the assembly, but he made no effort to join her. Nor had he once, since the accident, visited her in the Young wagon, though he had sent proper little wishes for her recovery. *If I were a lame horse, he'd probably shoot me,* she thought dispassionately, having by her injuries lost her singular use to him. Of that she was glad—it was both bitter triumph and relief—and with luck, she hoped she would never again have to lie beneath him.

Yet there was no word from her lover. Susanna's misgivings and anxieties were growing as the absence lengthened. Neither he nor Hoppy had been near the camp for days. Twice she had caught sight of them at a distance—the tall man on the tall, golden horse, and the broad-bottomed wagon and its driver rumbling close behind over the rocky ground. She ached to see him so far out of reach, without the strength to steal away to him, to simply walk to him however far he was, as she had that other time.

Her thoughts departed from logic, refusing to admit

What was it Jed used to call them—*the Three Weavers?* He had said that the last of the three had scissors. When she cut the thread, the person would die.

Was that what happened to Jed? Did some old witch with scissors cut the thread and make him die?

There was nothing more substantial to rail against— nothing real. The sun was real. And the wagons. The ache in her side when she walked—that was real. Like her existence, whether she willed it or no.

She snapped somewhat out of her lethargy when Brigham Young was suddenly taken ill with mountain fever, which began as a blinding headache and quickly followed with swollen joints, back pains, and high raging fevers. Susanna was glad to stay on and aid Miriam with the nursing, laying on cool cloths to ease Brigham's burning forehead and keeping the water which he drank in great quantities near at hand.

By some gargantuan effort, he remained lucid, even during the worst bouts of the delirium-inducing fever. He sent an advance party of trusted men to search out a pass through the mountains. "I have a feeling we are very near the place we seek," he told them before they departed. This wretched sickness did nothing to impair his authority, and Susanna marveled much that he could exert such force of will over his body's failings.

He was a sometimes petulant invalid, scowling and swearing at his pains and weakness, but Susanna's presence seemed to soothe him, and more than once he patted her hand and told her what comfort and ease she brought him with her tender care. "My two ministering angels," he called Miriam and Susanna, and Susanna in turn took a quiet pleasure in tending this man who of all the Mormons had shown her kindness in his way and tried to help her.

She had been too much obsessed with grief at her lover's death to think much on the future. Aside from her nursing duties, the days passed on unremarked and unconsidered, a process of sun and moon that did not draw Susanna into reverie at their passage. She had not considered the extent of her change of fortune until the afternoon that Prudence Shuttleworth stopped outside the Young wagon.

She had brought a loaf of fresh-baked bread for Brother Brigham. And a question from Elder Shuttleworth; *when would Susanna be returning?*

The shock and dismay on Susanna's face stood well beyond any efforts to conceal it. Prudence was moved and reached forward an awkward hand to pat her shoulder. "I don't need an answer now, my girl," she said gently. "I'll just tell him Brigham's still ailing and you're helping out."

Prudence in her own way understood a great deal more than she would say. It was none of the girl's fault, but her presence was a hazard to peace in the Shuttleworth household. Maryann hated her so and was nothing but a jealous misery when she was around. Prudence could see as well as any the significance of Susanna's dwelling with Brigham Young, whatever the arrangement; and with a peculiar farsightedness thought the inquiry of her return might have been just as well left unmade. But that was nothing she could tell her husband. He was a man and Brigham Young was a man; she could only hope there wouldn't come a peck of trouble over Sister Susanna.

Brigham was recovering and sitting up inside the wagon. His heavy brows puckered in a curious frown when Susanna told him of the elder's message. The girl seemed disheartened. "Do you like being here with us, sister?" he asked thoughtfully. Startled, she answered yes. He seemed to muse upon that for a time in silence, but asked her nothing further.

His mind had been dwelling much of late on Sister Susanna. Twice her image had appeared to him in his meditations, and this he took to be a sign from God.

He found himself thinking back to the early days of the prophet, how Joseph Smith had spoken to his elders calling for their wives in his early inspiration of celestial marriage. Reverend Shuttleworth was a loyal man, a man of the faith. Then Brigham realized what he must do.

At a time when both women were out, he sent word for the elder to attend him. Shuttleworth was prompt, as though the summons had been expected, and he reassured Brigham from the start with his smiling acquiescence. He said, "Of course, if she pleases you," and "What, after all, is the importance of earthly union compared with the glory of eternal marriage?" And he said it all in the same reasonable tone until Young expressed himself immeasurably relieved by the elder's keen understanding of the entire affair. All that remained was to speak with Susanna herself.

Shuttleworth left in a perfectly satisfied frame of mind. He himself was not in the least disturbed. Why should he not agree—considering he had nothing to lose. And Brigham Young—though he did not know it yet—had nothing at all to gain.

Miles and miles away, beyond Reed's Cutoff and past Last Creek Canyon, Orson Pratt and Erastus Snow were struggling to the summit of a steep and treacherous hill. What lay before them was a grand and awesome valley, fortified on all sides by sentinel mountains. Toward the center of the land, running far and mightily to the north and western boundaries, were the heavy blue waters of the Great Salt Lake.

Within four weeks, some two hundred acres had been broken up and planted, and the young corn was standing ankle high. An effluent stream that flowed out of Utah Lake they named the Jordan, and from it they drew water for irrigation. The Eastern women who had wept to find no trees in their new home were hauling timber and transplanting saplings from seven miles distant to the rich and now adequately watered land. On what a month ago had been flat, dry wasteland, now there was grass and the beginnings of gardens. Thirty adobes—dried brick dwellings plastered with salt desert clay—gleamed whitely in the hot sun. Work on the temple had begun.

Susanna's coming marriage would be the first performed in the new Zion.

Elder Shuttleworth had called her back to his household as soon as Brigham was well. A matter of propriety, he said. It was two weeks now, and Susanna's original fears had faded. She slept alone and undisturbed in the adobe, in a half-partitioned room which even afforded a little privacy.

There was little enough to prepare for the coming marriage, and Susanna spent most of her days helping Prudence, planting the garden, feeding chickens in the sunny yard, watching the lordly and territorial rooster making his presence felt among the hens. Maryann was ill at ease and avoided her. The elder himself scarcely acknowledged her presence in his home, but busied himself with the building and farming of his allotment. Susanna stayed out of his way as much as she could.

Shadrach, too, she gave wide berth. She had become suspicious of Hoppy, who was now much in company with the younger Shuttleworth. She did not understand why the Oriental stayed on, of the camp but not of the Mormons or their city; lingering but neither settling nor moving out.

Jed Taylor was dead. What was Hoppy's business here?

The fact that he knew her heart made her afraid, and his very presence called up such an anguish of memories that she could scarcely give him nod when they chanced to meet.

Remembering how friendly the two of them used to

be, Shadrach puzzled at the apparent coolness, and he jokingly asked Hoppy if he'd ever had a go with Sister Susanna. The little man's black eyes had drawn hoods and he just said no in that calm, deadly voice that reminded Shad of the night Clem Hogans was cut. And Shadrach, being a fairly intelligent youth with a strong instinct for survival, didn't mention anything more about Susanna.

The rest of the settlement was not under the same restraint, and *they* mentioned Susanna's name constantly. Her proposed marriage to Brigham Young was the keenest item of gossip to come their way since it was rumored that Sister Willoughby was initiating some of the younger men in the rites of manhood. No announcement had been made in the beginning, owing to Brigham's unerring foresight. He reckoned correctly that the news would filter of its own accord at a time when the Saints would be quite busy building their new city.

Maryann and Prudence knew at the start, as did Miriam Young, and very soon so did everybody else. And they managed to find time, between planting and building and tending and praying, to form their separate opinions. The women clucked their tongues en masse; as Brigham said, like a chicken farm gone mad. The prophet Joseph Smith himself was the only man ever to wed a living elder's wife, and even with such a precedent, the matrons jabbered like outraged poultry. If Brigham was to marry again, they opined, was it not more fitting he marry one of the widows who needed support rather than to marry for pleasure—and another man's wife at that!

The men were almost as bad, muttering what *they* would do if Brigham wanted to marry a wife of *theirs*, and though no man had ever managed to talk Brigham down, Elder Shuttleworth endured a wealth of superfluous advice on the matter and much commiseration.

He was fast gaining a reputation for remarkable good nature on the subject. When confronted without courteous means of escape, he had taken to smiling at the would-be consoler and agreeing with whatever advice was offered.

But for the most part Shuttleworth kept himself busy and removed from the gossip centered on his household. His property extended to the foot of the high Oquirrhs where he was building a small wooden shed across the field from the main house and barn. He intended to slaughter the young pigs before winter and wanted good quarters for dressing and hanging the meat. This shed was cool, shaded by the mountains just behind; meanwhile it served to store odd bits of machinery and seldom-used equipment.

Shadrach worked mostly on the main barn and spent his spare time trapping beaver. And every man gave one day's work in ten for the temple, which even in its beginning stages held promise of a monumental beauty; a source of inspiration and pride, spawned of sand and clay and faith in the God who had led His servants here.

Susanna woke early that morning, still in a dreamlike consciousness, musing. Her face was sleepy-soft, and her pale blond hair lay in silky disarray upon the pillow. The breath of morning came in from the still-unwindowed space in the wall—the air was lazy and warm, and only the crickets were awake outside.

A year ago it was summer in Liverpool; a cooler summer than here, and Susanna a so-much-younger girl. In a year she had walked a distance that would have carried her across England a dozen times. She had buried her best friend. She had journeyed and been wedded and had stolen away like a thief of time to lie all night in her lover's arms. Tomorrow, with no lawful husband laid to rest, she would be a woman twice a wife.

Only Brigham Young, forty-six-year-old patriarch of his people, could have managed such a feat. Susanna thought of him now, when he had explained to her how it was he could marry her within the sanctity of the church, how she could stay with him if she liked, that the choice was hers.

He was a good man. A stern commander of sorts among his flock, but a gentle man with his women. And he alone had the power to keep her from Elder Shuttleworth and Maryann.

She told him yes.

It was not passion. But passion was not a consideration. Her passion lay buried in an unmarked grave many miles behind her.

Her new husband-to-be had kissed her mouth for the first time; a kiss that was both sweet and undemanding, almost shy. She did not feel as she had with Jed Taylor. But if she did not grow weak and languid with desire, she did feel a stirring warmth and gentle affection for this broad-shouldered man with the chestnut hair.

I shall try to be a good wife to him, she resolved. *And if it is not quite love, still he shall suffer no lack for it.* There might be children, and if she lived long enough, even grandchildren. The pilgrimage ended here.

Yet it was odd to feel so much the objects of events, the product of random chance and other people's wills. Her thoughts dwelt a moment on Jed Taylor. How strange to think that of all these many miles and events, only one brief walk in the middle of the night had been solely her choice and her decision. *Yet I would have come all this way for that alone,* she thought. *For that one night.*

The house was stirring. Prudence called for her to rise and come to breakfast.

Sometime later in the early afternoon, Elder Shuttleworth found Susanna in the far wheat field and asked her to fetch down a rope rigging from the barn to where he was at work in the shed.

It was Shadrach's day to work on the temple, and no one was about in the big barn, but Susanna found the item quickly enough and carried it back to the far end of the Shuttleworth property.

The small shed door was barred shut, and Susanna called out to the elder. There was no answer, but she knew the back end of the shed was open, with space for a not-yet-constructed double door.

A narrow path led to the rear of the building, beyond which was the step rise that began the bordering ring of mountains. Susanna took two steps into the cool quiet of the shed. She heard a quick soft rustle in the straw behind her. She had not turned fully around before a hard blunt weapon struck the side of her head and felled her where she stood.

Consciousness returned to her in degrees, beginning with a dull throbbing in her head. Dimly she heard a dry chipping sound—*chp, chp, chp*—which slowly became more distinct. *But she couldn't see!* A cloth pressed against her eyes, forcing them shut. Her mouth was stuffed and gagged; she could not move her body. Panic-stricken, she tried to twist herself free of whatever was restraining her, but to no avail. She moaned deep in her throat.

The blindfold was removed.

Her feet were bound to the wooden posts, stretched so that her thighs ached protesting the strain. Her skirts had been thrown up negligently to her waist, and her arms were pulled high above her head and fastened to a hook at the base of the further wall. She could see the figure of her husband looming above her in gigantic disproportion as she lay fastened to the ground. Looking up she saw his face, his dull yellowed teeth showing a smile broader than she had ever seen him smile. And in one horrible instant she saw it all: he was mad, and his madness doomed her.

There was a sharp bowie knife in his hand. And in the other he held a long wooden stake, some half a yard in length. One end had been whittled to a fine point and a ridge had been gouged around the base. Wanting only not to see, her eyes followed of their own accord as the elder braced the stake against a wooden post, slipping a piece of rope first around the ridge and then around the post so that the point of the stake protruded upward some twelve inches. A hoist and pulley such as those used to lift carcasses was set in the ceiling just above the stake. And hanging from the hoist—inexplicably—was a single broad wooden ox yoke, suspended like a two-legged spider in the gloomy shed.

She would learn what it meant. They had plenty of time, and he *wanted* her to know. Let her know exactly what would be done with her, and then let her wait, knowing. Knowing just how she would die.

". . . like the others died, sister." His gray eyes seemed to glow with some hideous inward light. "The Lord had tried his servant with repeated trials. But I am the instrument of the Lord and I obey!"

He stared down at the terrified girl and smiled, like some beneficent butcher readying the lamb. "Satan's puppets are comely," he said softly, "but inside they rot; they stink of sin and corruption. They house the devil inside them and they yield and follow the devil, forgetting duty and righteousness until the Lord calls to His servant and marks them, that they are beyond redemption in the living flesh, that they must suffer, that they must die!"

With every last ounce of strength she owned, Susanna lunged against her bonds, pulling and twisting, working her hands against the rawhide cords, tearing at the gag with her teeth. If she could only scream! Surely someone would hear, someone would save her!

Her torturer watched while she struggled, until the bonds had bitten into her flesh, until her wrists and feet were chafed and bloody and she lay nervously quiet and beaten, the full realization washing over her in waves of horror. There was no escape. The muffled cries could not alert anyone at a distance. And no one wandered this far. There was nothing here but the private little shed, her death cell, and the mountains behind.

The voice changed, became conversational. "You thought I didn't know, didn't you, whore-who-was-my-wife? Just like the others, thinking I could be fooled, that the old man could be fooled so easily. Priscilla, too, and her I trusted until I saw with my own eyes how she met her paramour—a stupid stripling—up on the bluff. And I watched them! They never knew how many times I watched them in their lust, heaving and rutting like animals—and she bred like an animal. I knew, you see, I knew she would have pawned off the whelp as mine. And I stopped it then. No one knew, no one ever knew. But it was too quick. One push and it was done. Still, it put an end to it—to her and her wickedness."

He talked on and on as though at last his words had audience, to hear, to credit his greatness—his most rare accomplishments, these heinous crimes of blood. After all these years the dam had burst, and now he stood to take his bow.

"Sary Lynn was different now. I had to be clever. How wanton she was, shameless—flaunting it at me, flaunting her wickedness while she flaunted her body, and still I was generous to the slut. I left my seed in her. I sealed us for eternity and I prayed for her salvation afterwards, sinner though she was. It stays hot inside a female," he reflected insidiously, "Their lust lingers—even after she was dead she was hot and open.

"You will be too. Even hotter, with the blood . . ."

Susanna felt rather than saw the toe of his boot nudging at her body, unprotected except for a thin undergarment. Her legs were bound wide apart; she could do nothing to evade him. His eyes stared with concentrated interest at the tip of his boot and its frail target. His face was lit yellow in the slanting rays of the sun, and his eyes glittered, glittered like pit fires staring down at her.

For Susanna, it was like a dream spun out of control, past the time any dreamer would have wakened with loud cries to pierce the illusion, to rescue sanity from utter madness. But Susanna could not cry aloud any more than she could dissipate the nightmare or dissolve the gloating figure of her tormentor.

"I've had plenty of time to plan for you, my dainty slut," the voice droned on. "It wasn't enough for you that I got rid of your lover." She stared up at him, dumbfounded. "Yes, I arranged it," he told her proudly. "But it wasn't enough for you. No, you would play whore again. You turned your wanton eyes on Brigham Young and played the seductress—yes, and now you will see what you will reap!"

He was in a state of fiendish excitement, but he explained everything—he told her how in another time she would have been branded with a hot iron, branded with the letter A.

"I have made a study of these matters. I know . . . the Turks were more sophisticated. They planned that the punishment be meted fittingly. 'Where is the sin?' they would ask." He prodded meaningfully with his boot.

Then his hands were at her hair and grabbing a fistful of curls to yank her head up from the floor. "See there!" he cried, gesturing wildly to the sharpened stake, the strange contraption of hoist and yoke. "There I can bind your ankles to the yoke. That should make you accessible enough. And think, as I lower you, think

on your sins, that you may die at least in a state of repentance. I'll guide you over your last paramour, I'll
see you properly mounted. I shall help you to the harvest of your sins!"

Susanna saw exactly what he meant to do. Screams
tore from her parched throat again and again. Her
head shook wildly, and she screamed against all hope,
for only rasping sounds escaped the muffling of the
gag. Her feet kicked up sawdust from the floor and her
arms flailed against the cruel bindings until they were
numb and could move no more. If only she were still
unconscious—beyond pain, beyond horror. She prayed
for deliverance, for quick death.

But she had grown quiet again. The elder was
chuckling softly and lowering the yoke to the floor
where he could unhitch it.

A light footfall sounded outside. An instant later, a
small, slight figure appeared in the doorway, then
sprang inside between Susanna and the elder.

Shuttleworth was quick. He grabbed the knife from
its place and swung to face the intruder. "You've come
where you have no business!" he snarled.

He knew better than to close with this opponent. He
did not charge. He took one step back, set his aim,
and let the bowie fly.

Hoppy twisted away, but the steel was faster—it
caught him in the shoulder. For a moment it hung in
his flesh, then clattered to the ground as he leaped up,
his own knife driving deep and true at the elder's
throat.

It was enough. Blood started in a crimson stream,
and a low, gurgling sounded horribly from the wound
itself.

The same knife, still sticky with blood, cut through
Susanna's bonds and Hoppy pulled her to her feet
from the shed. Her limbs were agonizing and numb,
her throat and mouth parched from the gag. But he

made her run without respite until they were at his wagon, hitched and waiting, until she was seated and the horse was whipped to a trot that took them to a blind mountain pass.

The afternoon sun was setting on the eve of her wedding day. But the city of the Saints, Brigham Young's new Zion, was at her back.

BOOK III
The Journey Home

15

Susanna's voice was cracked and hoarse, barely reaching above a whisper. "Where are you taking me?" she asked the silent, secret little man. He didn't answer, or he hadn't heard. His eyes were fixed on the narrow path before them. It was steeply walled on either side by high stone ridges, and the horse's hooves echoed hollowly on the trail. He cracked the long whip over the flank of the bony gelding, urging it to a swifter gait.

Susanna began to cry in choking whimpers, mindlessly, like a child. She clenched her small hands into fists and pounded on Hoppy's arm. "Where are you taking me?" she repeated, trying to force more sound from her dry constricted throat.

He turned toward her in surprise, his mind so intent on his business that he had all but forgotten her. "I'm taking you to the captain."

Taking her to the captain? "He's dead!" she screamed. Her voice was stronger now. The rocky walls enclosing them called back her words in muffled echo —*dead, dead, dead.* Jed Taylor was dead. Elder Shuttleworth had arranged it. The elder wanted to kill her, too, but Hoppy killed him instead. Now Hoppy was taking her away, in the wake of death, and blood, and horror.

But what did he want with her? He said he was taking her to the captain, but Jed Taylor was dead. Her stricken mind played havoc with his words. Was he going to kill her too? Was that what he meant?

She began to scream and struck at him with her hands, aiming at his face, his eyes. He pulled sharp on the reins and dropped them, grabbing for her arms. Then he shook her until her head hung limp with dizziness. "Captain Taylor is alive," he said, speaking slowly and distinctly. "He's not dead, he's alive." He loosened his grip on her. She was quiet now, but shivering. She did not respond to his words. Her face wore a blank look, as though staring hard at nothing, and her lips were faintly tinged with blue. He pulled a horse blanket from inside the wagon and wrapped it around her. She stayed silent and unmoving. He picked up the reins and chivvied up the horse. On top of the problem of flight, he was worried about the woman. He clucked and cracked the whip. They had to move.

Four miles passed in silence. The sky was already darkening when Hoppy altered their direction slightly to the east, then up another steep and narrow trail, scarcely broad enough to accept the wagon. The timber stood tall and thick ahead of them, and a swift-running mountain stream crossed at their feet. The horse made a great show of splashing through and managed to stumble on a rock. Hoppy cursed.

Up ahead the sound of a stallion's neigh trumpeted in the thinning air. Susanna roused from her stupor. She had heard along with everyone else how William Tanner, a ruffian who had joined the Saints one jump ahead of a Missouri sheriff, had stolen Brushfire during the battle with the renegades, after Beauchamp had been shot from the saddle. Toby Williams had seen him mount the stallion. But what she just heard sounded very like Jed Taylor's horse.

She had granted no credence to Hoppy's words, but now her ears strained at the silence for the sound to come again. The trail broadened suddenly to reveal a high plateau where the same stream they had passed earlier crossed back and broadened out. A stand of aspens shivered in the early evening breeze. They came to a small clearing where a tent was pitched, and beside it a tall man stood waiting, grinning broadly at the sight of her. The same blue eyes, the face clean-shaven as it was a century ago, the same broad, firm hands reaching for her, lifting her from the wagon. *Alive!*

He held her close against him and bent his head to bury his face in her hair. "I didn't expect you so soon," he told her, "but I'm glad you're here."

So prosaic a greeting was the last thing she expected. "I saw them bury you!" she cried.

"You saw them bury William Tanner, who had the gall to try and steal my horse," he corrected.

The terror and despair of the past weeks flooded Susanna's consciousness. She looked from Taylor to Hoppy in astonishment and disbelief. "All this time," she said slowly, as though still trying to comprehend. "All this time you've been alive.

"Oh, how could you! How could you have left me like that—left me thinking you were dead!—you devil, you beast—you unfeeling criminal!" She pounded her fists in fury at his chest. She wanted to wound him. She wanted to make him bleed. "I was to be married tomorrow—I was going to marry Brigham Young!"

He caught her hands. "Easy now, little vixen," he said. He grinned sheepishly. "I'm glad you used the past tense at least. I don't think you'll be marrying Brigham Young now.

"Though I noticed you didn't mourn me overly long." He put on a pained look and laid his hand over his breast. "My heart fair broke when Hoppy brought me *that* little piece of news. And not so much as an invitation!

"It's a good thing I'm a man of a practical frame of mind. I'd as soon steal you from two husbands as one."

She eyed him incredulously. "You think it's a joke," she said. Her voice rose to a high pitch, discordant, jangling. *"So now you need steal me from none!"* she shrieked. "You didn't have to steal me at all—you could have let me die. Perhaps I would rise again like you—you fiend!" She began sobbing again, pushing his arms away from her.

For the first time, he saw she was in earnest. His own smile vanished abruptly. She was trembling and sobbing wildly, like a mad thing. He looked to Hoppy. "For God's sake, what happened?"

His face turned grim as Hoppy related the incidents leading to their arrival. Susanna was quieting, held fast in his arms. "I didn't look to Shuttleworth for that kind of madness," he said in a voice taut with fury. "But I should have known! Leverton was right all along, and I was blind."

"I'm only sorry you got him instead of me," he told Hoppy. "I'm sorry he didn't die slowly. I've learned a few tricks from the Sioux that would have enlightened the Reverend Shuttleworth."

He cradled Susanna's face to his chest, his hands gentle, caressing. "Poor little lamb," he murmured softly. "It's all right now. You're safe with me; no one's going to hurt you now."

His eyes regarded the dying sun. "We'll have to move out tonight," he said frowning. "They may have found the body already. We don't have much time. And I don't intend to be trapped up here with nothing but a box canyon at our backs." He looked down at Susanna, who still trembled in his arms. "We'll bundle her up and lay her in the wagon. It's the best we can do for now."

Susanna slept fitfully on a makeshift couch while the men broke camp and loaded, but she woke crying at the first turn of the wheel. "Hand her up to me," Taylor said, edging his mount next to the wagon. She was quieter with his arm secure at her waist and the warmth of his body at her back. With his other hand, he reined his horse around the first turning, past the stand of aspen and down the narrow pass.

The way down was more treacherous in the failing light, but both horses knew the path. By the time they reached the main trail, it was dark. Taylor conferred with Hoppy briefly before they continued. There was a game trail three miles south, marked by a stand of juniper. It was wide enough only for a single rider, but they could conceal the wagon and lead the horses up. A distance that by day would have been covered in fifteen minutes took them fully two hours of painfully feeling their way and squinting to find landmarks by a narrow crescent of moonlight.

Susanna was wide awake by the time they dismounted and moved to hide the wagon. From there they went on foot, Hoppy and Taylor leading the horses over an uneven path half-choked with underbrush. Branches invisible in the darkness whipped at their faces, but they struggled on another half-mile to the clearing.

"There'll be poor fare for supper," Taylor remarked. "No fires tonight."

Hoppy nodded silently, and the two men set to work, tethering the horses and pitching tents. A chilly wind had started up and whistled through the timber. The slender moon had risen, and a wolf bayed on some distant bluff. A small herd of elk who had come downwind from the heights froze for a long moment, discovering intruders on their mountain, and fled the way they'd come.

Taylor drew a sack from his saddlebag. He pulled out several strips of hard dry beef, and handed some to Susanna. "Good buffalo meat," he said smiling wryly. "Eat, squaw."

She was much better now. There was color in her cheeks. Her eyes were bright. She made a face at him and bit tentatively into the tough stringy beef. He grinned at her. "You'll break your teeth trying to chew it. Just stick it in your mouth until it softens up." He demonstrated, popping a wadded ball of meat into his mouth. "Like this."

He found a store of half-crushed wild grapes that he had gathered and forgotten. Hoppy produced a supply of hard biscuits baked a month before. For a time the three of them squatted on the ground in easy camaraderie, chewing slowly on the salted beef and listening to the night sounds—the calls of a lone hoot owl and the chitterings of small furred creatures hiding in the grass.

They were safe enough, for the night at least. After a while, Taylor pulled out his bedroll and tossed it carelessly at the entrance of his tent. "We could hole up here a few days if we have to," he said. "There's water another quarter mile up the trail. But we're running behind as it is, and we'll be pushing harder if we wait. We should try to get a start before dawn."

Hoppy grunted his agreement and left to seek his own couch. Taylor returned to Susanna, a smile playing about his lips. "Early to bed, little bird," he said softly. "And since you've come without bedding of your own, I guess you'll just have to share mine."

Susanna felt suddenly shy. Time hung between them —all the time that she had believed him dead—and that time no one had touched her. The time was clos-

ing. Any moment he would cross the little space between them, and she waited, bashful but wanting,
knowing *he* would touch her, he would make her naked
and bring his own nakedness close to her. She remembered his body, his caresses, and she blushed, remembering. Now he was next to her. His hands were at
her waist, rising to cover her breasts. He groaned and
pulled her sharp against him, pressing their bodies together as though to make one body. Then he caught
her hand and pulled her to the tent.

No light penetrated the canvas walls. Susanna
reached blindly, groping for him. The darkness made
her bolder; her own hands searched and wandered, discovered and uncovered. She was giddy with wanting
him. Her lips joined in the search, laying a trail of
kisses over his neck, his chin, his eyes.

He tugged at her clothes. "Take them off!" he whispered urgently. "All of them."

Their clothes lay discarded in a heap, and now flesh
strained against bare flesh, impatient, eager. Still she
cried out when he entered her, as though it were the
first time. It had been so long—so long since she had
known such bliss coupled with such hunger. There
was an almost frightening sweetness in wanting a man
so much—so much her belly ached with the wanting.

He was fierce with her now. She felt him bite at
her breasts. His hands tightened on her thighs, forced
them even further apart. Her own teeth bit at him.
She went for his mouth, bit his lips, but she was only
urging him on. She wanted him even more fiercely,
she wanted bruises. It was a battle to glory, and no
one could lose.

It was still dark when he woke her. He was already
dressed, and his boots were damp from the chilly dew
that clung to the grasses. Susanna half-opened her eyes
at his urging, then burrowed deeper into the blanket

of warm rabbit furs where the rest of her sleep was hiding.

"Oh, no, lazybones!" Taylor cried, forestalling her. His hands followed her under the covers and yanked out an arm. Then skillfully and efficiently, he began to separate fur from flesh until she was all uncovered and shivering in her nakedness.

"It's even colder outside, dressed as you are," he said grinning. "Shall I just pull the tent out from under you, or will you come quietly?"

It was strange to be up and about in the eerie stillness of predawn. A dull pink dome of light, harbinger of the sun, sat low on the eastern horizon. But toward the west the night held sway, the stars still brilliant against a backdrop of dark velvet sky.

Hoppy was already leading out the horses, who snorted and pawed at the ground. Jed was breaking branches from thick sturdy evergreens, and gathering them in a pile.

"What are those for?" Susanna asked.

"Cover our trail," he answered briefly. "There's softer ground down below, and I'm not eager to have the Daughters of Zion blowing their skirts at our backs.

"Wiggle your feet now!" he ordered, glancing toward the east. "It'll be getting light in half an hour, and I want to be gone!"

They led the horses back down the steep narrow trail in a dim half-light, gray with mist. The ground was rocky, and Susanna was newly grateful for the heavy ugly toughness of Shadrach's old boots. They came to the stand of juniper and Hoppy harnessed the horse while Taylor scouted the trail ahead.

"Patches of sand for a mile or so," he announced when he returned. He tethered his mount to the back of the wagon and picked up a few long branches, swishing them like a broom across the path. "You want to help with the sweeping, lady?" he asked Susanna.

Altogether it was a bizarre sight—the clumsy false-bottomed wagon, loaded with guns, rolling awkwardly along the roughest ground and narrowest, least-used trails, the noble-looking bay stallion, prancing like royalty behind, and in their wake a couple walking backward, swishing pine brooms across the turf.

South and west. South and west. By midmorning, crossing the first high ridges, Taylor was mounted on the bay and Susanna rode in the wagon. Beyond was another wall of mountains, standing higher, steeper, and more foreboding than anything Susanna had ever seen.

"You won't see the likes of that in England, Susanna," Taylor said, riding up beside the wagon. "Nor in the East here. That's all tame country. But this now —this is another sort."

"Don't they make you feel small?" she asked breathlessly.

He laughed. "They make me think when I get to the top I'll be the biggest man in the world!

"I *was* at the top of one once. On a dare. Took three days of climbing—no place to ride up past the timberline, just clawing my way mostly. And the nights— you'd be like to freeze to death, even now. It's all wind and no cover anywhere unless you're lucky enough to find some boulder you can pull down over your head. And snow—snow that's been there for a thousand years.

"But it's like being a god to stand there and face the wind with the country lying all out below you. You can see all the way to the coast, past the desert, past the valleys, past everything. And going down, there are streams cut into the mountains. The water's deep and clear and fresher than anything I've ever tasted. You can get drunk on high mountain waters. I'd swear it.

"No, a man's a giant in the mountains. He's taller, stronger—he just naturally has to be. It's what's *beyond* the mountains that worries me."

"What's that?"

He answered in a single word that summed up all that he most dreaded in the journey. *"Desert!"*

Desert so hot a man could scarcely breathe the air. Days that set your skin cooking and nights that froze your blood. Scorpions and rattlers and dry sagebrush. Dry waterholes and bad water. He had crossed this desert once before. He almost died there.

The last horse fell with Monty on him. Taylor raised his rifle and took care of the horse, and Monty crawled down in the sand and screamed for Taylor to shoot him, too. Screamed without a voice. Their tongues were so swollen by then their mouths hung half-open.

They soaked their clothes in their own urine just to stay a little cooler—he could still remember the ammonia stench—and they dug in the ground for water. With their bare hands, their fingernails, digging, scratching like animals and then waiting for the hole to fill with water. They lapped it like animals. They built mountains of sand for shade, hiding from the sun and chasing shadows, walking out at night until they dropped. And never enough water.

Monty didn't make it. He went out of his head, started crawling out at midday, heading back across the ground they'd already covered, toward something he was seeing that wasn't there. There was no way to stop him. Nobody had the strength. Except Jenkins, who finally lifted the muzzle of his .38 and put a merciful bullet through Monty's head.

Yet that same land could be so beautiful. Stars were closer, sharper, and more brilliant on a desert night than anywhere else in the world. And desert sunsets

rivaled anything he had seen in the South Seas. They
were swinging well south of the worst of it by his own
calculations. With luck they'd make an easy crossing.
With luck Susanna would see only the wild, unearthly
desert beauty and not its horror.

He eyed her covertly. She'd crossed alkali with the
Mormons traveling into the Great Basin. Walked most
of it, from what he'd seen. And she'd come through
worse than desert—he thought of Shuttleworth and
cursed inwardly. A lot of people—Mel Wayne included—would count him twenty kinds of fool for
bringing a woman on this journey. But they didn't
know Susanna.

Besides, there was no other way to keep her. And
that he was determined to do.

Between the first ridge of mountains and the next
was a steep, narrow vale, lush and grassy, freshened
by wash-off from the slopes on either side. They could
see it now stretched below them, a thin ribbon of
green running some twenty miles north to south. Cottonwood grew thick on the fertile soil, and scattered
fruit trees. Even willows, clinging to the lower reaches,
set their roots down by the stream bed and over secret
underground springs. Close by a narrow gorge, a herd
of fat deer, some twenty in number, were cropping
lazily on the grass.

Taylor grinned at his companions and smacked his
lips. "I've a sudden hankering for a thick, juicy venison
steak. Seems I can almost *taste* it . . ."

By late afternoon, there *was* a haunch of venison
roasting on a makeshift spit while the rest of the meat
hung from the branch of a sturdy alder. Hoppy was
tending the fire, and Taylor had taken Susanna to
gather crab apples and wild peaches.

It was the last easy ground they'd be seeing for some
time, and Taylor wanted to enjoy it. He stretched out

on his back under a spreading willow, with the soft moss as a cushion and the leafy green branches swaying lazily just out of reach.

Helping himself to a choice peach, he called for Susanna to join him, trying the taste of her kisses mingling with the juices of the peach. "I've got another hankering," he said mischievously, popping a bit of peach into her mouth.

She drew away a little, warned by the look he gave her. "And what might that be?"

"To see you naked in the sun!"

He grabbed for her, but she was too quick. Giggling, she slipped from the shelter of the hanging willow with her lover in hot pursuit. Over the pebbles of the gurgling stream and down a grassy incline they ran. Susanna glanced behind her, breathless and laughing, to see Jed closing swiftly. She tried to slip past and run the other way, but he swerved to meet her and caught her fast in his arms.

He dragged her back to the willow and pulled her under the green curtain of its leafy branches. "So, my little bird would fly," he said softly, pinning her down on the springy turf. He plucked at the buttons of her blouse. "Now be tame, little bird."

He bared her breasts and paused long enough to encircle each one with kisses. "The Shoshoko," he said, casually stripping the blouse from her shoulders, "believe that a man who looks at a wholly naked woman will go blind." He began undoing her skirt.

"Their women wear aprons woven of sagebrush that cover them front and back—" His hands slipped under her skirt and pulled down.

"—very scratchy."

He took time to look at her, his keen blue eyes openly appraising, seeming to intrude upon her body. She could *feel* his gaze like some palpable touch exciting her. "Not being a Shoshoko," he was saying softly, "I do not expect I shall go blind."

He followed his eyes with his hands, tracing the narrow shafts of sunlight that moved across her legs. She trembled and his mouth kissed where his hands had been. She tried to close her legs against him, close him out.

"*Let me see,*" he whispered. He touched down with his fingers, gently insisting.

She felt his hands part her thighs, and the warm sun invaded the tender private flesh, laid all open now, so vulnerable with the daylight cast upon it. And his eyes caressed her, his hands explored, his lips made her wanton, so that she cried out in suffering need and pulled at his clothing. At last he too was naked, moving like a shadow over her.

He shut out the sun, but his eyes were bright, intent upon her still. Even as he possessed her, as her own eyes narrowed, blind with passion, he watched her face and hovered over her like a hawk above its prey. He watched her lips, swollen with his kisses, part and breathe faster. And he moved in time to her breathing until they were both caught in the same quickening web, both swaying to the same primal rhythm, both touched by the same magic wand.

Even after their passion was spent, their bodies seemed fused in one piece—a nest of tangled limbs, loath to unlock and separate, loath to part and stand and admit the hour is gone.

But already the sun was spending the last of its gold light. The air was turning chill, and from a grove of cottonwoods, a whippoorwill began his evening song, pausing between each warbling roundelay to wait for answer. Jed Taylor stood and squinted his eyes at the western mountains, rimmed with fire at their snowy peaks.

For the moment, the woman was forgotten. He was

seeing instead the edge of a continent hidden behind those mountains.

But before the coast, and beyond the mountains—four days, he calculated. Five at the most.

Beyond the mountains is the desert.

He harkened back to the here and now—the valley, the moist luxuriant earth, the woman with her soft skin, her dewy nakedness. At the camp a feast of venison awaited them. It was the time of ease, the time for pleasure.

It was not the time to think of deserts.

16

THE MAGIC STAYED with them in those early days of the journey, and the wilderness made music all around them—choruses of crickets, the chitterings of squirrels and chipmunks, the trills and warbling of songbirds. Even in the midday heat of the lower sinks and arroyos, they could hear the shrill incessant drone of the cicadas. They passed stands of virgin forest—giant trees, venerable in their antiquity, which had seen the woodland spawn and die a thousand times until very little moved them. They were lordly trees whose tops were sometimes lost above the clouds, and Susanna could not fault their condescending attitudes.

And for her, above all else, there was the man. He was the thread that bound the happy fabric of her days —the chilly mornings, padding barefoot beside him through the dewy grass. The hot, strong coffee in a cup the three of them shared, squatting on the ground near the cookfire. Mounted before him on the high-stepping stallion in the afternoons.

They explored caves cut out of the mountains. He told her the names of flowers and trees.

He told her of the land on the northern shore, where the cliffs of the mountains rise out of the sea. He described the fertile, sunny valleys of the south, with their fruit orchards and rich farmlands, the sand beaches of the coast and the deep, sheltered harbors with their great merchant ships.

The recent horror of her husband's plot, her near marriage to the Mormon leader, seemed already part of the distant past. She knew now that Davy and James Leverton were waiting them in Los Angels, and her thoughts were eagerly westward seeking. Nothing of the past could mar the gladness of these days—a gladness that seemed to her invincible. Only later she would wonder—with that anguish of bewilderment that still remarked her youth—why happiness must be so brief, why fortune so deceitful, that even as our joys seem boundless and forever, it is a lie. They are even at that moment slipping from us.

He told her he had business in the land of the Californios, but he didn't tell her what it was, or that he planned to leave her in the city of Los Angeles while that business was conducted.

The next evening, he again tracked deer, but brought back only the heart and liver. For her, he said, the heart. His hands were covered with blood from the butchering of the deer, and in some strange fit of passion, Susanna licked the blood from his fingers, delicately, like a cat, tasting the blood of the kill. She excited the hunter; she promised to be delicious prey; she lured him to attack like some she-beast in mating, coy and wanton, teasing until he would stalk her, until he would entrap and take her with a savage joy.

On the afternoon of the third day, Taylor met five Paiute braves stalking elk in the mountain fastness. They were tall, handsome youths with hard bronzed muscles, who moved softly with a shy animal grace and hunted game with arrows, knives, and snares. The Paiute were not a warlike people. They lived in remote and scattered villages, where guns were still looked on as devil's magic, referred to as the "firesticks-that-kill-from-far."

Their dark eyes regarded Susanna with an almost reverent awe. Few white women had ever passed this particular stretch of mountains. And never one with golden hair.

As a gesture of friendship, Taylor gifted them with a pouch of fragrant tobacco, and they in turn, learning that he was crossing to the west, directed him to a little-known pass that saved them a full day's travel.

Now the mountains were behind them, and the ground they covered was low and dry, a prelude to the arid wastes of the Mohave. Some distance away on a bluff that commands a sweeping view of the lower regions, two riders appeared, travel-worn and dusty.

Shadrach was bone-weary. He spat disgustedly in the dirt and drew a long swig from his canteen before raising Brigham's borrowed spyglass to his eye and scanning the terrain below.

He traced back suddenly and refocused the glass, his weariness forgotten. "I've got the wagon sighted!" he cried to his partner. "And both them—no, *three*." He peered through the eyepiece again, then lowered it, a look of consternation spreading across his face. "It's Beauchamp!" he exclaimed in an unbelieving whisper.

"It can't be," Clem Hogans said impatiently, reaching for the spyglass. "You got him that night. Toby Williams saw him fall and Tanner rode out on his horse. For chrissakes, we *buried* Beauchamp weeks ago!"

"It's Beauchamp," Shadrach said flatly. "That's his horse, and it sure ain't Tanner riding him. The beard's gone, but you can see for yourself. He's even wearing the same hat—the one he picked up at Fort Laramie."

Now Hogans surveyed through the scope's glass eye. "There was only you and me and Tanner knew the raid was set up," Shadrach said more quietly. "Tanner took the rifles off my father to bribe the renegades."

Hogans fell to cursing at what he saw. His face went

red with fury. "I get my guts shot up by that stinking coyote who's supposed to be dead, and there he is riding easy as sugar on his fancy horse with your daddy's widow right a'front of him."

"The same horse Tanner rode out on," Shadrach said meaningfully.

"Then the body—"

Shadrach nodded. "Remember now that body didn't have no head to speak of, and they was about the same size.

"I ain't sorry about Tanner—he was running out on us as soon as he saw the chance to grab that horse. But that sneaking polecat down there"— Shadrach's eyes gleamed with vengeance-seeking.—"him and that two-faced wagon driver, they're gonna pay!"

"It was the Chinaman got your paw," Hogans reminded him. "And you was buddies with him, which is more than I could understand you being. My hand still don't work right after the cutting I got from that yellow-skinned rat." He started to turn his horse. "Let's get after them!"

Shadrach checked again through the glass. "They're at least a day's ride ahead of us, and they'll be in the desert before we can catch up. I'm going back to get a pack mule and supplies. It could be a long trek."

He glanced at Hogans, who had sullenly halted his mount. "You can camp below till I get back here," he suggested. "Or ride with me partway. Hell, they only told you to keep clear of the settlement."

"I reckon I'll just head on out," Hogans said in a bitter tone. "But lemme tell you—Stout had no right to call down on my head like he done. It was 'cause Letitia's his sister's kid. He's been down on me since Winter Quarters and that Pawnee raid. They've all been down on me. Me and Russ Emery. Blaming us cause we was the only ones caught." He glanced side-long at Shadrach and added slyly, "Didn't nobody ever tell, it was *your* idea to haul off with the Pawnee brat—"

Shadrach ignored the thrust. He wheeled his horse until it stood head-to-flank with the other. "You sure you want to head out by yourself?" he asked at last.

Hogans nodded, wondering if Shad could be thinking the same as he was, that more than revenge was up ahead. There were the spoils. The sweet-running stud horse—worth gold to a man who had it to spend. He was a rich man's fancy, a horse like that. And the woman—the woman that any man would fancy, but few would have a chance at. And he, Clem Hogans, might have her. Helpless in the desert with two corpses, and himself, alive. Revenge might be very sweet.

He grinned suddenly at Shadrach and saluted. "Ride hard when you start out," he suggested. "Maybe you'll catch up with me!"

He kicked his horse to a weary trot and nursed his grievances and his hopes all the way down the mountain slope. Life for Clem Hogans had lately been a series of miseries and catastrophes, the most recent of which was the reason he was going forward instead of back to the settlement with Shadrach. Because he had "forced his attentions" on Letitia, Hosea Stout's only niece—

Hell, weren't like Letty never had it before, he thought peevishly. *She wasn't no more virgin than the Shuttleworth sow.*

But it was enough that Stout had sworn to gun him down, that the court, the Apostles, his own people had turned him out and locked the gate.

He wouldn't look back. He set his sights on the distant caravan, on the booty that would be his. He told himself his luck was due to change.

Three days in the desert. Three days of clinging to the harsh, ugly ridges of salt and alkali that afforded the only cover. Three days in a land that is never kind to strangers. Hogans cursed the sun, the heat, the gritty sand. His luck hadn't changed.

In the relative cool of morning, he turned his mount to the softer, easier ground below the ridge. The horse spooked at something in the path, sidestepped nervously, and refused to go on.

Hogans, squinting at the ground, saw no disturbance, and he lost what little patience he possessed. Snapping the reins, he shouted "Giddap!" and dug hard with his spurs. Snorting and blowing, the horse planted his forelegs in the dirt and pitched back, tossing his rider almost square on top of the dozing, quietly coiled rattler that lay half-buried in the sand.

The rattler, waking in an even worse temper than Clem Hogans, struck for the nearest target. The wide jaws unhinged and locked over Hogans's thigh, while a well of venom poured through the hollow fangs.

It did not come clear to Hogans all at once. The snakebite was certain enough, but he'd seen men bitten by snakes before. He looked for his bowie to cut the wound, but the knife was in his saddlebag. The snake had slithered off, no doubt to some more peaceful sunning spot, and Hogans was alone. But he didn't realize yet his panicked horse was heading back to the Mormon city. And, like most of the misfortunes in Clem Hogans's life, death came as a surprise.

By midday even the buzzards knew, dressed in their dark feathers and hovering in circles, as patient as dark-robed priests at a deathbed, or undertakers. Waiting.

Hogans saw them. He'd been trying to pray, but his mind could only think of curses. He was seeing double, already parts of his face were numb. He saw the birds in double images, but he knew what they were, and he hated them. He began to curse aloud, trying the taste of the invectives, drawing comfort from the sound of his own voice. He cursed the birds and God and the desert. He cursed the rattlesnake and the horse. He felt a chill start in his veins. It was getting colder.

Two of the boldest birds had descended, lowering their feet like landing gear and running a few paces over the ground before they could stop their own momentum. Hogans's eyesight was failing. He could just make them out, pecking the sand with the utmost unconcern, made brave because he couldn't move. Puffing out their feathers.

He still had his pistol. It cost him the last of his strength to bring it up and aim for the dark, shadowy creatures, but his hatred for the birds was the last thing left to him. It took both hands to cock the hammer, but he managed it three times before the gun slipped from his nerveless fingers. He didn't know the birds had taken flight before the first shot sounded.

They returned when he had stopped moving, and the largest of the flock strutted forth to peck the first delicacy. Ugly as they were, they were kings in their own way—to the victor goes the spoils.

Susanna loved the desert at midday, a lazy time, because Jed wouldn't have them travel in the noonday sun. They moved up to the coolest, highest ground they could reach, and imitated the desert creatures themselves, who barely stirred at all.

The rolling hills of sand and their desolate ridges of salt had an eerie stillness. Like a photograph under water, the heat shimmered; the objects remained fixed. The objects themselves were stark and meager—tall dagger trees with crimped bark, and creosote bushes, low-running sage and thistle. And over it all, dominant in its terrible brightness, was the glaring, burning sun on the burning sand.

Jed regarded the sun as a cunning enemy and acted accordingly. That was the reason that earlier he had covered his hands with grease from the wagon axle and smeared it across his face—especially over his eyes and forehead. He did the same for Susanna and laughed at the results, calling her his little blackface.

Hoppy had dozed off under the wagon. Jed was kneeling by some scrub. He called to her.

"Look here," he said. Susanna saw two spiders facing each other in the shadow of the spiny junco bush. They were large, formidable creatures, each possessed of thick dark-gray bodies and long whiplike tails.

"Are they going to fight?" she asked wonderingly.

"Watch and see," he said. "It's rare to come across it. But don't stand too close—they let off a fine stink if you bother them."

The smaller of the spiders was trotting back and forth in a small semi-circle around the larger, and it paused at times to rise up on its back legs and wave its sensitive front feelers. The second remained in place, but swayed slightly on its spindly shanks and waved back encouragingly. Inspired by its audience, drunk with its own success, the first began to turn little circles leaving thin spiral tracks in the sand.

"Why she's dancing!" Susanna cried.

"I think that's the boy," Taylor said, smiling. "He's smaller than she is. Poor little chap, she's got him mesmerized."

As though on cue, the dancer began a delicate zig-zag path to the courted one, and with timorous, mincing steps approached her. Together they rose on their back legs and joined their long front sensors in an unmistakable embrace. Their thin whip tails swished back and forth and they shuffled like waltzing partners, until finally the smaller one climbed right up over his mate and swung his body around.

Taylor's eyes met Susanna's in a conspirator's glance.

"Let's give them a little privacy, shall we? I'll fill you in on the details later on."

"Would you dance like that for me?" she asked him softly.

He caught her look—the teasing, taunting female look—a bit predatory and homage-seeking, like the great female spider. "I've danced like that already," he told her, "while you've played a Mormon wife. But I don't think it'll answer." He pulled her toward him; his arms bound her in a circle. "You've acquired bad habits and disrespect while I've been dancing round you.

"You need a firm hand," he said judiciously, like a schoolmaster. "And constant guidance." He was guiding her toward the supply tent.

They stopped for a moment, full in the sunlight, and Taylor loosed the arm from around her while the other held her firm. His free hand touched briefly at the curve of her cheek, descended to her breast, her waist, and traveled down the folds of her skirt. He pressed the palm of his hand between her legs, caressing through the fabric of her gown. "A firm hand," he said smiling, watching her green eyes glow like twin emeralds.

In a moment he would have pulled her to the tent, but at that instant the muffled crack of a pistol shot sounded in the distance.

They both froze and waited, listening. Another shot, from the same direction, and after a longer interval, a third.

Susanna looked anxiously to the man beside her. "What could it be?" she asked.

Taylor looked grave. "Somebody not too far behind us with a gun. Probably a white man. It would take a lot to tempt an Indian into these parts." He shot a long glance backward over the land they had covered. "We're traveling north of the main trail. It's possible whoever's back there is following us." He looked up at the high hot sun and frowned. "Anyway, it's too close to ignore."

Hoppy had already risen from his bed under the wagon and was dragging the saddles from the supply tent. Taylor started toward the brush where the horses were tethered. "Get my gun belt!" he called back to Susanna.

The thick leather single-holstered belt lay in haphazard companionship with the clothing and miscellany of Taylor's duffel. Fully half the contents spilled to the floor as Susanna rummaged for the heavy gray pistol which was wrapped in a flannel shirt. Jed kept a rifle close at hand in the desert, but he didn't usually wear the gun.

Another stash of possessions slipped to the floor from the same location in the shirt—two small slips of colored paper winging like butterflies, a sheaf of official-looking documents, cards and notes and a stray sock.

Susanna left things as they fell and hurried out. The men were already mounted. And Taylor, no longer resembling the lazy-eyed teasing lover of moments before, was barking last-minute orders. Keep the rifle in hand, he told her. Stay close to the tent and wagon.

Susanna scarcely heard, concious only that he was riding out. He seemed so far removed from her, sitting astride the tall bay stallion. And he and Hoppy both had turned and gone before she could even speak, before she could even enjoin them to be careful. She watched until they crossed behind a narrow ridge and disappeared from sight.

It felt strange to be alone in the camp. The sun was past its zenith, but stayed strong enough to make the air an oven. The whole dry basin in which Susanna stood was low and flat and insignificant, like a shallow bowl of earth against an infinite sky. Jed was right. The mountains were friendly, companionable. But not the desert. The desert made you feel small, like an ant climbing tiny anthills, with the sky like a giant curtain ripped away.

Listless in the heat, Susanna made for the relative cool of the supply tent. But for the alarm of the pistol shots, Jed would have been with her now, finishing in all likelihood what he had started—or she had started—out in the sun. She knelt on the floor of the tent and began picking up the spilled contents of his traveling bag.

The colored bits of paper were theater stubs—two of them, she noted with a twinge of jealousy. His captain's papers were folded neatly, and her fingers traced his name on the outside. There was a receipt from a tailor for "two gentleman's white shirts," and an elegant menu, printed in gold and all in French from some restaurant in New Orleans. The last odd sheet appeared to be part of a letter, written on plain white stationery in a heavy male scrawl. Susanna hesitated guiltily, but curiosity overcame virtue, and she began to read. The page started in the middle of a sentence:

> . . . *with the Mormons as far as you can.*
> *Don't tarry in Los Angeles. Miguel will*
> *make the arrangements. Leave a message*
> *at Madame Florrie's with the bartender.*
>   *Weather reports all say the heat*
> *Wave is moving south. Get rid of the*
> *burdens and have a nice vacation. Stick*
> *to the shade.*
>   *Louisa is no longer the gay mad sweetheart*
> *of New Orleans. I believe she has gone into*
> *hiding, pining no doubt for your manly charms.*
> *I should think after all these years you'd*
> *get married and make an honest woman of her* . . ."

She stopped reading. Her hands folded the paper neatly, automatically, and she stared for a long time at the innocent-looking little note, which gave no warning, not a hint of what it held for her.

He meant to leave her in Los Angeles. That came suddenly clear. *And the woman Louisa. He'd never spoken of anything beyond Los Angeles. But she had assumed—he said he loved her. She had assumed . . .*

She had assumed too much. She should not have read the note. If only she had never read the note! But what would that have meant? A little more time to listen to his lies, made honey-sweet with kisses and endearments? Lies, all lies.

Or perhaps *not* lies. He had warned her long ago. She had forgotten, but now her mind recalled the scene, recalled his words, clipped and cutting. "When I go," he had said, "and where I'm going, there'll be no place for you!"

Someone already held that place. A woman named Louisa.

So he would dispose of her kindly in Los Angeles, leave her with friends. Why should it surprise her after all? He liked her in his bed—and there was little female competition in the desert. But how she would stack up against "the gay mad sweetheart of New Orleans"—that was another matter. Of course, Susanna was all right for now. For now.

But she had thought it was forever.

She carefully replaced the note and the other items as they had been. Her face was pale, but she was dry-eyed and alert. She knew she couldn't ask Jed or accuse him, not without reference to the letter. He and Hoppy had been gone only half an hour. But she could imagine him riding in, beaming at her with those warm, deceitful eyes, touching her with those hands that would wave goodbye at the journey's end.

No, she could not bear it. She was holding her emotions so firmly in check, but she knew them for what they were. And she could not bear for him to touch her now.

The flap of the tent blew open, and the hot desert sunlight poured inside. The solution was so simple that she almost laughed. She would forestall him; she would beat him to it.

She would be the one to leave.

Outside the wind was rising, blowing sand and whistling through the cat-claws and desert willows.

She was trying to remember something. A character in Mr. Shakespeare's play said it—Prince Hamlet it was. He said he could be bounded in a nutshell and count himself a king of infinite space.

Infinite space. That was what she'd been trying to remember. That was this desert, this borderless dish of earth. Yet it would bound her just as surely as a nutshell, and she could be lost just as easily as a grain of sand.

How long would it take? The sun was still hot— perhaps by tomorrow? She was very calm, but her hands moved quickly to the preparations, plucked off her bonnet and used the strings to bind a rag to the gunstock of the rifle. She might have only a little time to get away, but he had taught her well.

She knew how to travel and leave no trail.

The campsite was already riddled with footprints, and Susanna kept to the most heavily trafficked ground.

Her steps grew hesitant as she neared the junco bush. The spiders were still there, their bodies parallel and connected, the male above the female. Their round, uncurious eyes were motionless—they seemed frozen together in some eternal spider embrace.

Susanna turned away. Her head was bare to the hot sun, and the wind was wailing now, like the moans of ancient widows before the pyre. But she wasn't afraid anymore—she had lost all fear. With deliberate steps she began to back away from it all—the spiders, the junco bush, the tent and wagon. And she swept the trail behind her as she went.

17

IT TOOK HIM four hours to find her. One hour of riding ever-broadening circles around the camp before he could even spot a trail. Jed's mind did not conceive that she had left the camp willingly; obviously someone—probably whoever had been traveling with Clem Hogans—had spirited her away. Kidnapped her.

The scant single tracks confounded him. Men's boots. Susanna was still wearing Shadrach's boots. He circled once more to assure himself it was the only recent trail.

If it *was* Susanna she was alone, and walking in the sun—a thing which he expressly forbade, avoided at all costs. Traveling in the desert meant riding, and sitting as still as possible even then. It took all one's energy just to breathe the desert air.

Then he found her bonnet, its ties caught on a clump of ragweed. He groaned aloud. It was already close to three hours, and he fought to control an inward panic that was seizing him. He was beginning to fear what he might find.

The tracks were scanty; she was traveling hard ridges. At every turning he expected to find her. His own vista was a labyrinth, and he craned his neck at each new sight of dip and basin, hoping it would be the last turning, that he would see her there.

His horse halted suddenly of its own accord and pricked its ears forward. In a wild hope, Jed slacked the reins. The great stallion began to move again, veering somewhat south of where they had been heading. Just fifty yards away, Susanna lay, half-kneeling in the sand, her head bowed. Shouting her name, Jed leaped down from the saddle. He started running.

She raised her head. Her face was swollen with sunburn.

She raised the rifle.

"Susanna!" he cried, sharply now.

She didn't speak. Perhaps she couldn't. And her eyelids were swollen half-shut, but she waved the rifle barrel meaningfully.

"Put it down, Susanna!" He took another step toward her—

The shock of the explosion set him reeling back. A good deal later, he would remark that he was lucky, catching the shot high in the shoulder as he did. He was certain she had been aiming for his head.

Susanna herself would never remember the incident at all.

But for now, Jed wasn't wasting any more time trying to convince her. Recovering from the blast, he closed on her quickly and swung a hard right to her jaw. Then, catching her around her waist with his one good arm, he dragged her limp form back to the horse and flung her across the saddle.

She raved in a fever for three days. They had to strap her down in the wagon with the tarp over her to keep off the sun as they traveled. She could eat nothing, and she used what little strength she had in her delirium to battle off Taylor's ministrations. He bathed her hot dry skin during rest stops, and when she tried to push away the cloth, he grimly bound her hands and poured a quantity of water all over her, laying the cloths on top to retain the moisture. Hoppy held her head while he poured more water down her throat. She sputtered and choked and fought, but she swallowed more than half of it. He cut open cactus and pressed the cool inner fruit against her face and arms and neck. And more quantities of water. Water to renew the dry, wasting flesh, water to restore the sluggish blood. Water to bring back life.

Jed blessed his hard-learned desert caution. He had insisted from the first that every available vessel should carry water, even beyond their needs. They had filled up at the last waterhole a day before. There was plenty.

Water would cool the fever, would bring her back to reason. And to this end three nights and days he kept his vigil, tending her constantly and tirelessly, oblivious to any concept of exhaustion, beyond any thought of failure. He would not even consider that she might die.

And it was a long way back from wherever she had been. Back from the gray clouds over her consciousness and the frightening dreams, peopled with demons and scarecrows. Back from the grisly gates of death itself. Once she fancied that she was drowning—she felt water all around her—and she fought. But gradually, gradually, the thick banks of fog receded, and she recognized the moist cool relief against her burning skin. She began to drink.

She was almost well by the time they were approaching Cajon Pass, beyond which lay the land of milk and honey, the well-watered fertile ease of orange groves and hospitality. Taylor carried her down from the wagon to sit on the mossy beginnings of grassland, to listen to the nightbirds and crickets and watch the moon.

He had caught enough sense in her ravings to understand why she had run away. Yet though she was by now perfectly able to speak, she was sullen and spoke little, no doubt nursing her imagined grievances and woes. Now it was time for an accounting.

"You read Mel's letter," he said flatly.

She started a little, and then it was as though she had heard nothing. She didn't answer.

"If you weren't just recovering from your little escapade," he continued evenly, "I'd whale the curiosity out of you right now, and leave you the better for it."

At this she turned to glare at him. She rose to return to the wagon seat, but he stood before her and barred her way.

"You really think that I would go through all I have, just to drop you off and head back to New Orleans. That's what you thought, wasn't it?"

She tried to shrug off the hands that detained her, but he held her firm. He began to shake her and repeated the words, demanding answer. "Wasn't it?"

"Yes!" The word tore from her throat like a fragmented shriek. "And I don't care anymore, d'ye hear me?" she cried. *"I don't care!"*

He dropped his hands from her sides. "I've had no intentions," he said softly, "of going back to New Orleans."

His fingers cupped her chin. "And if it's true the lady doesn't care, why is the lady crying?"

They stayed a long time together while the slender moon winnowed its way across the dark. They talked in whispers and held each other in a precious rediscovered kind of peace, as though they were just learning about each other, or like friends long separated who finally meet again. "We'll have to go to sleep soon," he said at last, when their embraces threatened to become fiery, "before I decide you're healthy enough for more than sleeping."

"Jed—?" Susanna's voice was hesitant.

"What is it?"

Susanna plucked at a few blades of grass. She didn't raise her head. "Why are we going to Los Angeles?" she asked finally. "What is it you're going to do?"

Taylor frowned. He did not answer immediately, but came to kneel beside her in the grass, and when he spoke, it was not directly answering the question.

"This is a strange land you've come to, Susanna," he began thoughtfully. "It's attracted more great men away from their homelands than any other country in the world. They pay it court and sacrifice to it, as if it's a goddess to be worshiped. Maybe even when it's wrong."

He was searching for words to express what until now he had only vaguely felt and sensed. "I've always felt that governments came with the land," he said slowly, "and that when I found the land I wanted, I would abide by the government that land belonged to . . ."

"Have you found the land?" Susanna asked him.

He nodded eagerly. "The northern coast I told you about. Where the coastline is high and rocky. There's good land just over that ridge of coastal mountains. Little valleys with sweet grassland and lots of rain. And a man could build a house on top of a mountain and watch the ships go sailing up the coast."

"But your business," she reminded him.

"You might say my business is to earn the land I've chosen. It won't take long to do. And then I'll be back to collect you, my pretty baggage."

He put his fingers to her lips to stop further questions. "Exactly what it is I cannot tell you, Susanna. But there are some things you must take on faith."

His fingers traced her sun-ravaged face, where the blisters had begun to peel away, exposing the tender new skin underneath. "You were lucky for that axle grease," he remarked, "or the burns would have scarred you badly.

"And do you know, my unbelieving little one, that even were you scarred, or lamed, or become something less than lovely, I would still want you with me. You doubt so easily, Susanna. And you must finally choose to trust me, or call it a bad bargain and have done with it."

He kissed her lips softly, almost chastely. "Now to bed, little one. We'll give those burns a chance to heal."

The San Gabriel Mission, gleaming whitely in the sun, sheltered the travelers for a night. The squat Mexican padres were its caretakers, shuffling quietly about in their long flowing cassocks, and they extended their unassuming welcome to all who came within their gates. Susanna relaxed in the shade of the courtyard walls and gorged herself on fresh oranges while Jed visited with other guests of the mission—familiar faces from years before, men who had stayed and settled in the western hills and valleys.

And then it was on to Los Angeles. Nothing Jed had told her quite prepared Susanna for the bustling crowds and dizzying contrasts of the young western city. Charming whitewashed adobe houses with red-tiled roofs nestled sleepily just beyond the beach in a semicircle reaching to the shore. Heavy-flowered wisteria vines clung to the awnings and window ledges, and mingled their heady perfume with sweet languid magnolia and bright-colored bougainvillea.

Yet the main street itself brawled and bustled with cowboys and mountain traders, elbowing side by side with fashionable ladies carrying parasols out for a morning promenade. The saloons were filled with gamblers and businessmen, drunkards and expensive whores. There was so much color, so much activity—if you wanted to trade hides for groceries, if you wanted to buy a ranch, if you sought justice for some grievance or were a widow looking for a man, Los Angeles was the place you went, the center of everything, the hub of the Far West.

They had little trouble finding James Leverton's hotel, an impressive affair fully five stories high and overlooking the busy harbor. James Leverton had not changed. The room he shared with Davy was littered with the ubiquitous books, and a cheery oversized teapot shrilled its steamy offerings to the company.

But Davy! Davy had shot up in the time she had not seen him, and he now topped Susanna by half a head. He was a young man now, with broad shoulders and a voice that was more at ease in the lower ranges. But he had the same bright boyish eyes and infectious grin that she remembered. They hugged each other with delight, and Leverton embraced her warmly. "I had rather hoped you would be coming along with this rogue, my dear," he said warmly.

The single flaw in their reunion was their one missing part. Susanna broke the news of Maidie's death.

They listened to the story with sad attention.

"She was a good lass," Leverton said quietly. "A fine, dear lass. God will take note of that, even as we know it."

He turned to Jed. "Did you stop over at the mission?" he asked. "Tom Mellinson was asking for you."

Jed smiled briefly and nodded. "I saw him and John Sutter, too. John seemed kind of tense though."

"He has a right to be. Rumor's been passing around they've found gold up there in the river. Nobody knows for sure, and certainly there have been rumors before, but Sutter is afraid there will be a stampede of men with gold fever running all over his land. He has good reason to be tense.

"There's even a legend—an Indian legend," Leverton said, his eyes twinkling as they did when he began a story. "They say that once the Apache found a cave through which a river flowed. And inside this cave was a great pillar of gold being slowly melted by the rushing waters. The waters that flowed into the cave carried nothing but silt and river sludge. But the waters that flowed *from* the cave carried gold."

He smiled. "The legend is getting a good workout these days. Everybody seems to know an Indian whose ancestor had seen the cave that made the waters gold."

Jed laughed. "Poor John Sutter. I had a feeling Tom was hinting at hiring guns for the mill. Now I know why. There's nothing like the rumor of gold to turn a sane man crazy—and most of the men hereabouts are a little crazy to start with."

The talk turned to other things. Of Shuttleworth Susanna said little, only that he was dead. Leverton expressed himself delighted with the prospect of her company while Jed was away. Nothing more was said of Taylor's imminent departure, but he left for Madame Florrie's soon after.

And Susanna went shopping.

Shops—shops selling everything from finely crafted English saddles to buckskin and moccasins. Cheeses and sweet cakes and butcher shops with huge quarters of red beef hanging in the windows. And shoes! Ladies' shoes at last, shoes made to fit her own dainty feet. Susanna almost wept with joy to pull off for good and all Shadrach's old worn boots. Jed had given her money—gold—that seemed to her more than she could ever spend. And she bought shoes. In happy extravagance, she bought dainty shoes of shiny black leather and slippers. She bought sturdy laced walking shoes and green shoes to match a new dress. In all, she bought twelve pairs, and she had to hire a boy to help her carry the purchases to the wagon.

Halfway down the street she could see Brushfire tethered to the rail in front of Madame Florrie's. The horse was exciting a lot of attention, for the Californios were worshipers of fine horseflesh. One of the cowpokes called to a well-dressed gentleman just exiting a tailor shop. "Here's a challenge for your Peregrine, Mr. Attaby!" the cowboy called out.

The man so addressed swerved toward the crowd gathered around the tall bay stallion. They cleared the way for him and for a few moments, he just stood, thoughtfully evaluating what he saw. Then he sent a boy inside the bar to inquire for the owner of the horse. The boy returned shortly with Jed behind him.

Forgetting the wagon and her purchases, Susanna pushed in closer. She saw the man called Mr. Attaby stand forward and introduce himself to Jed. The two men shook hands, and then the talk passed quickly to horses in general and Brushfire in particular.

"Does his running match his looks?" the man inquired casually, running his knowledgeable eyes over the slim racing lines of the stallion.

"I'd say his looks don't do his running justice," Taylor answered without modesty.

"Might you be wanting to sell him?"

Taylor grinned and shook his head. "Not a chance."

"I have a mare stabled over at the smithy's," Attaby said. "She's my prize runner." His eyes still assessed the golden stallion. "Would you care to wager on a race? I'll have her brought round if you like," he offered equitably. "Before you say."

Taylor's blue eyes were dancing brightly in anticipation of a race. "Bring her on anytime," he said easily. "I'll match Brushfire against any horse in California!"

Racing was a favorite sport, and men began running to clear the street. Attaby himself went to fetch his mare and warm her up before the trial. Being a gentleman, he would not discuss stakes before Taylor had seen his competition.

Peregrine *was* a beauty, and clearly deserved her local fame. Perhaps a hand shorter than Brushfire, she was dove-gray, with a hide as smooth and supple as deerskin. Taylor looked at her admiringly while the growing throng compared the two superb animals.

"She's a might shorter in the withers—" said one.

"But look at the chest," another countered. Wagers were laid with pistol-cracking rapidity. One grizzled old-timer chewed on his lower lip and finally set the scheme. "Even odds," he decided at last.

They had marked off a length something over a mile, which began outside the saloon and would end just past the gate of the Cavanaugh farm. Attaby looked from his opponent's tack to his own flat English racing saddle. "I ought to give you a handicap by rights," he told Taylor.

"I've a bit of weight on you," Taylor admitted. In addition to the beautiful light saddle, Attaby, who obviously intended to ride the mare himself, was some pounds shy of Taylor's own body weight. "If you'll allow it even, I'll go bareback," he said.

Ears pricked and whispers buzzed. *He was going to ride that big horse like an Indian. No saddle.* The old man chewed his lip again and reaffirmed his first opinion. *Even odds.*

"You have my admiration, Mr. Taylor," Attaby raised his fingers to the brim of his round derby in a kind of salute. "And now the wager, sir—" he said gaily.

Taylor smiled suddenly. "Where are you from, sir?" he asked.

"Virginia, *sir*," answered the other.

It had been many years, but Jed could still remember the rolling green hills and honeysuckle that was Virginia. And the voices of its people—those suave gentle voices, softly drawling their polished good manners that sounded as easy and natural as bird songs.

"Why did you leave Virginia, Mr. Attaby?" he now inquired, drawn by some odd curiosity. He saw

now that Attaby was the natural Virginia gentleman—
almost too civilized for this raw country.

"A slight quarrel with my neighbors," he said briefly.
An ironic little smile touched his lips. "They did not
approve my marriage."

"How is it that your neighbors must approve your
marriage?" Jed asked, genuinely puzzled. A few men
standing near enough to hear the conversation nudged
at each other's ribs and winked.

"Not in California, Mr. Taylor," the other remarked.
His expression altered subtly. "But in Virginia, yes!"

Sensing he had hit a sore spot, Taylor shifted attention back to the matter at hand. "The wager," he
recalled.

"What do you say to a hundred in gold, Mr. Taylor?"

"Very good." Taylor brushed at his horse's coat,
damp where the saddle had been. "Shall we find a
keeper for the bets?"

The slender Virginian smiled. "I'll trust you for it,
Mr. Taylor."

"I'll trust *you* for it, Mr. Attaby," Jed retorted.

Everyone agreed it was a splendid race. Both men
were superbly mounted, and the horses broke clean at
the start with Attaby's gray leading by a nose and Attaby riding smooth as syrup on her back. Brushfire
held her at the neck and then began to stretch his
distance-eating long-legged paces while Taylor clung
like a burr low on his back. It was over in less than
two minutes, both riders red-faced and exuberant, despite the loss to Mr. Attaby of a hundred dollars in
gold.

"I'll give you a note for my banker in the morning,"
he said as they walked out their sweating mounts. "Now
what did you say was the price of that horse?"

"About the same price as your gray filly there,"
Taylor answered, "plus a few dollars."

"I have another at my ranch, a four-year-old almost as good," Attaby mentioned thoughtfully. "But I haven't seen a stud horse to compare with my two mares. Until today." He gazed speculatively at the stallion.

"Would you be amenable to a proposition, Mr. Taylor?"

"I'm listening."

"Would you consider *leasing* the services of your stallion to benefit two charming well-bred females of my acquaintance? The dun will be coming into her time soon. It'll be a bit longer with my Peregrine. I'd offer you the dun's foal if they both take."

"My pick of the two," Taylor bargained. "If they both take."

"Leave me the colt if we get only one," Attaby countered.

"Done!" said Taylor, grinning all over himself. It was a good bargain.

"Come to dinner tonight," Attaby invited. "My wife and I"—again came that faint ironic note in his voice —"my wife and I entertain only the very best people."

"Formal?" Taylor asked, grimacing at his dusty leggings.

"In California?" his companion laughed. "You may wear a loincloth if you like."

Susanna, who had worked her way first through the crowds and then down the exit path of the two riders, now approached, smiling at Jed and shaking her head. He looked no older than Davy, all flushed and grinning from the sport. Jed made the introductions and Attaby bowed gallantly and doffed his hat.

"Mistress Hungerford, a fair rose of England, are you not?"

She blushed and nodded. "I am charmed," he said. "Please do us the honor and come tonight—both of you. Mr. Taylor and I have some plans to discuss, and I know my wife would be glad of your company."

Well before sundown, Susanna and Jed, double-mounted on Brushfire, made their way to the eastern outskirts of the city where James Beauregard Attaby had built his hacienda, Southern style. The house itself was a sprawling two-story affair with a long, sweeping veranda of whitewashed oak. There were no great columns in the front, but it was as close to Virginia as adobe and Spanish tiles could achieve.

Jed had mentioned something to Susanna of Attaby's peculiar allusions to his marriage, but when they were introduced to Melissa, it became apparent even to Susanna, who knew less of the South than Jed, why the James Attabys had left Virginia for the free land of the far west.

Melissa Attaby was black.

She acknowledged her guests with a gracious smile, smoothing over that first moment of discomfiture and surprise with an unassailable dignity that combined with a forthright humor, now employed to put them all at ease.

"I see Jim didn't tell you," she said easily. "That means he must have decided you could stand the shock."

Jed Taylor stopped before her and stooped to kiss her hand. The dinner was as superb as was promised. Afterward, Jed and Jim Attaby made for the stables while Melissa Attaby showed Susanna the house and garden. Outside a young boy about six years old was riding a fat calico pony.

"Beau!" Melissa called out. "Come in and meet our guest."

The child slid from his mount, dusted his breeches, and ran inside, bobbing his head to Susanna in an imitation of his father's bow. He had his mother's great dark eyes and his father's aquiline features. His smile was wide and warm, and his skin was the color of honey, golden brown, shining smooth and young.

"Can I take Molly through the pasture gate?" he asked his mother.

Melissa smiled. "Another hour before your bath. But all right, go on with you now."

"He's a beautiful child," Susanna told her hostess as the boy made his exit.

"Yes, beautiful," Melissa commented soberly. "Beautiful and doomed."

"There never should have been a child, not from us, but I never could talk over Jim—he wanted it. And Lord knows I love our little Beau, rascal that he is—you've seen him at his best. Not stealing peaches from the neighbor's orchard or running through the chicken coop scaring the hens half to death so they don't lay for three days."

Melissa poured two glasses of sherry and handed one to Susanna. "Go on, child," she said. "This won't make you drunk."

They sat in comfortable, overstuffed armchairs and sipped their drinks, gazing outside to where the back parlor opened onto a beautiful sweep of formal garden, carefully cultivated for the sweet, heavy scent of magnolias that now delighted them, the huge showy blossoms, almost incandescent in the twilight, the particular placement of tree and walk and lawn, with open spaces for the sky. "It's like a fairy-tale picture!" Susanna exclaimed.

Her hostess beamed with pleasure. "Guess it's *my* fairy tale you're looking at, honey. I'm glad you like it."

"You did the garden—the planting, *everything?*"

"Right from seeds and saplings, mostly. I get a sweet thrill, pure and simple, watching things grow. Guess there's two things I watch and had a part in making, and that's that garden yonder and that boy Beau. And it's a lot to be watching, between the two. It'll do for *my* lifetime."

"And the next—?" asked Susanna.

8

HE NEXT DAY Jed had ridden out with Hoppy and
vo swarthy escorts: Miguel, a weasly small man with
ly avaricious eyes, and a one-eyed bearded monster
alled El Lobo—The Wolf.

Jed had needed only to see Miguel's eyes pass over
rushfire to decide on him. He took up Attaby's offer
nd left the stallion happily companioned by the gentle
ares in a lush green pasture. Jim Attaby was more
han happy to make him a loan of a sturdy old roan
elding—a horse such as the cowboys love—plug-
gly, Roman-nosed, surefooted, long on endurance. A
orse that would serve well without inciting envy.

Susanna watched the procession, the three men
ounted, and Hoppy driving the wagon, until they
uld be seen no more. About three weeks, he had said.
ooner if he was able.

Susanna began to wait the time as soon as he was
ut of sight, telling herself that each hour that passed
ought him closer to returning.

While he was gone. While he was gone, events per-
lated in Los Angeles as never before in the wild
story of the town. While he was gone, the rumor of
ld became a reality. Suddenly the streets were filled
overflowing with fortune seekers and prospectors,
ncy ladies selling their wares, and gamblers come like

"I don't know about that," Melissa said darkly.
"Guess that's why I say Beau, he's doomed. And it
frightens my heart to think on it."

"Jim—he believes in that, in the future. And maybe
that's why he wanted Beau so bad. I tried—Lord
knows the things I tried to tell him. There's waters
can't be crossed in this country. Waters that don't min-
gle for good, 'cause you can't fight everybody. Jim and
me—we were all right 'cause we've got the strength
to fight and the sense to leave when there's no way
of winning.

"But our little boy—what kind of place is *he* gonna
have, our Beau? White children'll have a time with
him. And nigger kids—I know what *they'll* call him.
Lordy, Lordy, won't be no peace there either. He's
going to school next year, and how do you tell a
little boy six years old what he's gonna find out there?
No, I leave future-thinking to the old man, 'cause he
really believes it'll be all right, and that Beau'll be
all right. And if faith is what'll do it, Mr. James Attaby will see it done."

Melissa sighed heavily and glanced apologetically to
her guest. "I'm sorry for talking your ear off like this
—" Her eyes drew up to the ceiling and across the
grand parlor. "This place feels so big and empty sometimes, and we sure don't have a lot of company."

"I thought your husband said you entertained people," Susanna said, trying to recall.

Melissa laughed. "That's another one of his jokes.
He probably said we only entertained the *best* people
—he meant *us*. We entertain each other.

"But *he's* the best joke of all," she said, shaking her
head as though after all this time she still couldn't
credit it. "I was five years old when white men took
us for slaves. Got the men in the village drinking on
sugarcane rum, took us all. And there was nothing our
own after that, not even our bodies.

"And then it's a white man making me free. Now that's the real joke—his best joke—that man out there, that Mr. Attaby."

The men came in from the stables and cut the conversation short. Attaby had suggested that Jed leave Brushfire to board while he traveled on his errand, but Taylor was undecided.

"How do you stay shy of horse thieves?" he asked his host.

Attaby smiled modestly. "My horses are known around these parts. Anyone would have to drive them a long ways from here before they could unload them. The stables are locked at night, and two boys bunk out in the loft.

"But whether it's now or on your return," he said, "we have a bargain, yes?"

"You have my word."

They made their farewells. Jed told Attaby he'd let him know about the stallion.

It was late when they arrived back at the hotel, and all the rooms were dark. Inside their own room, they felt their way, disdaining lamps.

The drapes were drawn, and Jed pulled them back to let the starlight in.

"Here's the bed," whispered Susanna, patting the sheets.

"Feather pillows, too," said Taylor, plumping them with a sigh of satisfaction. "The delights of civilization."

Susanna was yawning luxuriously, stretching her body like a cat.

"Not tired, are you?" Jed remarked, approaching her. His hands traveled up her arm, and Susanna felt her own excitement leap in response to his touch. His fingers traced across her shoulders, under her chin, over her face.

"The burns are pretty well healed," he noted softly.

Her eyes grew wide and caught the glow light. He was going to make love to her. He w ing her toward the bed.

"What have you done with the pillows?" s glancing toward the double bed. He had lef its head. The other he had tossed to the cent mattress.

He was standing over her now, his lips see bare flesh. He chuckled softly against her ear. you to be comfortable," he said.

vultures to glean the pickings other men pulled from the ground.

Word was traveling east and north and south. Never had there been such an influx of so many people in such a hurry. Whole wagon trains from the East pulled up every day. Some came by ship, others on mules and burros. They crossed mountains and desert and oceans, all seeking the pot of gold, and the road to California was their rainbow.

Davy was a great favorite with the sailors, and he spent most of his days down by the docks, watching the great ships put to port. Some days Susanna joined him, but as often as not, she was employed at her own project—that of conspiring a match between James Leverton and Mrs. Jennifer Higgins, proprietress of the Higgins Hotel and widow of Mr. Augustus Higgins of the same establishment. She and her daughter Lydia presently managed the grand five-story hotel by themselves.

After several months, they still addressed each other as "Mr. Leverton" and "Mrs. Higgins," but Susanna had noticed an unusual warmth in the scholar's aspect when "dear Mrs. Higgins" sat with them at tea. At times Susanna would arrange to be called away, as though privacy might draw matters to a speedier conclusion.

But thus far Mr. Leverton's most passionate act of courtship had been a disastrous three-day attempt to bring some order to his books. "Dear Mrs. Higgins," a neat, tidy soul, had on more than one occasion bemoaned that such a fine mind as Mr. Leverton's should allow such wanton disorder among his library. So it was that with neither catalog nor bookshelves, Mr. Leverton undertook the ordeal of organization.

He began with an ever-multiplying series of lists, meant to index and cross-index the culprits by author, title, and subject. These were divided into fiction and nonfiction, which were in turn redivided and subdivided by century and origin of country into novels, stories, biographies, poetry, sciences, etc.

He ended by misplacing a precious volume of Dryden—a first edition—which set them all frantically searching through the ordered and disordered stacks for two-and-a-half of the three days, at which time it was finally unearthed where it had cleverly sneaked between the back of the sofa and the wall. By that time Mr. Leverton's "fine mind" was bleary with the strain of the search, and in no condition to continue the original project.

Susanna was gratified to note that the Great Hunt for the Book had brought Mrs. Higgins clucking with sympathy and offering her services to aid in the search. And it was she who discovered its hideaway.

On the feast day of San Sebastian, the streets outside were alive with preparations for the fiesta, and the air was filled with shouts and songs. Susanna had joined Davy and James Leverton for breakfast when a loud knock sounded on the door. Susanna rose to answer, but she had scarcely opened the door when she was pushed back inside the room and three men stormed through the entry. Two of the men she had never seen before.

The third was Shadrach Shuttleworth.

Leverton, seeing Susanna's face and the threatening aspect of these men, tried to reach his gun—the .38 caliber pistol which Colonel Wayne had insisted he learn to use and keep with him. Little good it did now—it was in the drawer of the narrow desk. Shadrach saw him sidle toward the desk and shouted to his companion, who turned quickly and brought the butt of his gun down hard across the scholar's skull. Susanna screamed and James Leverton sank to the floor.

Outside the crowd had grown louder. The fiesta was

just beginning, and the streets overflowed with people. But no one would hear above the din. Now pistols were trained in a businesslike manner on Davy and Susanna.

"What do we do with the kid?" one of them asked.

"Bring him, too," Shadrach said. "I ain't taking any chances. The old man'll keep long enough. We can leave him." He leered at Susanna. "You're picking them older and younger, ain't you now?" he said, passing his eyes from Leverton to Davy. "Well, if you want to keep each other in one piece, the two of you'll walk down with us nice and easy, and making no fuss.

" 'Cause the first of you that does"—he lifted the barrel of his revolver—"the other'll get it. So you two friends just keep a lookout for each other, and you'll be just fine."

When Mrs. Higgins came in from shopping, she noticed the door to Mr. Leverton's room was ajar. Peeking inside to say hello, she gasped at what she saw. The room lay in a violent disorder, not inspired by books. And James Leverton was lying prone on the hard wooden floor.

"Lydia!" she cried for her daughter. "Lydia!" The girl came running, and together the two women dragged him from the room and into their private chambers.

Such a kind man, Mrs. Higgins thought, outraged. *So pleasant and polite—who would have grievance enough to hurt him? Well, no more harm would come to him.* She, Jennifer Higgins, would see to that.

She and her daughter propped him up on a daybed in the back room and sent for the doctor, who pronounced the wound a concussion and urged that he be kept quiet. "I've given him something to make him sleep," he said before he departed.

But who were his enemies? Mrs. Higgins caught the doctor's arm. She pressed a bill into his hand. "Say nothing of your visit," she said.

Leverton regained consciousness only briefly before the drug began to draw him down into sleep. Mrs. Higgins stood over him, a blurry shadow of concern. He tried to speak. "Susanna!" he said feebly—"Susanna and Davy!"

"There, there," soothed the lady. "We'll call them back." She looked to her daughter. "They must be down by the docks, or at the fiesta. Go, Lydia. Be careful, but see if you can find them. Ask the sailors of the *Snowy Myrtle,* the Atkinson's ship. If they don't know, we probably won't find them until the end of the fiesta." She turned to reassure dear Mr. Leverton, but he was fast asleep.

It was only a few hours later in the afternoon when Mrs. Higgins answered the bell to greet a stranger in her lobby. He was dressed, she thought, like an Easterner, and when he asked for Mr. Leverton, she became wary and excited.

"He's gone," she said briefly. "Checked out." She hoped he would go away.

"Did he leave a forwarding address?" the man asked politely. "Some way to receive his messages?"

Mrs. Higgins grew even more alarmed. This man talked the same precise English as Mr. Leverton. Her overwrought imagination conjured desperate thoughts. *Did Mr. Leverton have enemies in his country, in England? Had he been fleeing some great trouble when he came here?*

She glanced at the stranger again. He didn't look like a ruffian. But she couldn't be sure. No one had visited Mr. Leverton except Susanna and her friends since he had been staying there. If she told him he could leave a message, he would want to know the forwarding address. Better to say nothing.

"He didn't leave any forwarding address," she said firmly. "I'm sorry."

The stranger touched his hat and departed.

He had already been to the Mormon settlement on the Great Salt Lake where he was informed of his daughter's strange and untimely departure, either captive or compatriot of the murderers of her husband. And the day before her proposed marriage to Brigham Young, to boot.

The only Shuttleworth son and the second wife had left on the trail of the killers. Shadrach Shuttleworth had seen them heading west across the desert. They didn't know if Susanna was still with the treacherous Chinaman and the scout Beauchamp. They could tell him nothing more.

Los Angeles had been a likely choice, and he had determined to see if his old teacher Leverton, who had mentioned a friendship with his daughter, had heard any more news. Now it would seem Leverton had disappeared as well.

But Jonathan Hungerford was not a man easily dissuaded from his purpose. There were men he knew in every town who do little else but watch the street, drink beer, and pass the time and local news with friends and strangers. If the scout and Chinaman had taken his daughter here, he would find word of it. He headed down the street to the saloons.

He did not return to the Higgins Hotel, and it was a typical irony of the current service of the mails that the letter, sent months before from England to appraise James Leverton of his plans, arrived three days after he himself.

Susanna and Davy were taken several miles south of the city, along the same route Jed Taylor had gone with his Mexican escort. The camp was well hidden, enclosed by thickly forested hills a safe distance from the main road. There were four people in the camp, beside the hostages: Shadrach Shuttleworth, "Doc" Winer, and Otto Lansky, the three who had abducted them.

And Maryann Shuttleworth.

She came running down from the hill behind the camp when she saw them approaching. She was dressed in men's clothing—a pair of boys' jeans that fit snug across her thin flanks, and a plaid shirt, much-faded, that might have been Shadrach's. The pale blue eyes, lighting on Susanna, marked their victim with a fury that would not be lightly appeased. Maryann Shuttleworth was out for blood.

There was an early quarrel between the second widow of the Elder Shuttleworth and the only son. Both were venegance-seeking, but with a difference. Maryann had her hatred of the woman, Shadrach his desire.

"We'll need her," Shadrach was insisting, "She's the only thing we've got to tempt Beauchamp. After we've got him and the Chinaman, you can do as you like."

"Let her watch," Maryann said. She approached very close to where they'd bound Susanna to a tree. "I'd like you to watch while your lover dies.

"Then it will be *your* turn." She lifted a long sharp bowie knife, turning it so that Susanna must look at it. "I'm better with it now," she said with false sweetness.

Davy had been bound a short distance away, but no one paid him much attention. Susanna was the prize. Otto Lansky also took his turn to look at her, bound and mute. Otto was a hulking brute of a man, but he had a penchant for small women. Doc Winer contented himself with his view from several feet away. He, too, liked looking at Susanna—she fed his visions.

"Doc" Winer was a local reprobate, more out of weakness than of choice. At one time in the East he had studied medicine, but he had left for the lure of the West, as had so many others. He had come to California to seek his fortune and had found opium instead. Skinny, waxen-faced, he still possessed enough of nerves and energy to be useful, and so he had proven himself to Shadrach and Maryann. He knew the territory. He had led them to hire Otto, who supplied whatever brawn was needed without the complications of a mind to go with it.

Maryann reluctantly left off tormenting Susanna and stood up, resheathing her bowie. "Don't feel bad, Maryann," Shadrach drawled. "You can have your fun after I've had mine." He stood up and dusted off his leggings.

"You're disgusting," Maryann said tonelessly. "But go ahead. I'm off to town for supplies."

Susanna, who had kept silent out of futility, began to scream in fear at Shadrach's approach. "For heaven's sake, keep her quiet!" Maryann shouted. "We're not that far from the main trail!"

Doc Winer, who had witnessed the exchange in his own state of opiated content, now roused himself with a welcome offer. "I'll calm the princess," he offered magnanimously. "Better for you than knocking her out."

He walked over to his own cache and withdrew a precious bottle. *She won't need much,* he thought to himself, as though to justify his own generosity.

Shadrach had clamped his broad hand over Susanna's mouth. "Well, bring it quick if it'll quiet her down. What is it, anyway?" he asked curiously as Winer came near. "The same stuff you drink?"

The other nodded. "The nectar of the gods," he said, smiling a sweet, almost mindless smile. "Phantasms and visions of paradise. Liquid treasure. Laudanum."

Susanna was whimpering behind Shadrach's hand, trying to bite. Otto appeared, drawn by his own interest and his own lust, to help hold her down. They dosed her like an animal. Shadrach pulled back her head and closed off her nostrils, forcing her mouth open for breathing. Otto kept her from moving while Doc Winer carefully counted the potent drops of smoky resinous liquid that dripped from the vial to her open mouth.

They waited some minutes until her struggles became less frantic. "You can let her go now," Winer said at last. "She won't be running away."

The laudanum was like a waking dream, a dizzying liquescent change of vision. At first Susanna felt nausea. She had to lie down. Her limbs seemed weighted, dispossessed; yet her head was light, as though it might suddenly float away. She dimly protested their uses of her, but it was no more than the bleating of a lamb or the weeping of a child in sleep.

Shadrach had edged Otto away. "When I'm done," he growled at the other. "Wait your turn." He turned to Winer, feeling generous with his booty. "What about you, Doc?"

But Doc Winer had taken the opportunity for another dose himself. "No, she's for you, the little golden princess," he said softly. "For me"—he gestured at the bottle—"this is enough for me." He closed his eyes.

Susanna's consciousness had altered, and the feeling of nausea had passed. Her body was clothed in the wings of a thousand thousand butterflies, and they were flying from her flesh, leaving her naked. Soft butterfly wings—she could feel them fluttering their departures. But her lover was there and he had a thousand hands, five thousand fingers to caress her. She felt his tongue's laving her body and his legs between her legs and she was penetrated in a hundred places, and there was no pain, just a floating gauzy pleasure.

Yet far away she heard a whimpering, someone with her voice whimpering through her mouth and the voice

was crying *Please stop!* and *Please, no more!,* begging
release from the assault, crying it was too much and
she was bleeding, bleeding, that they were strangers
spearing her, making her bleed.

Then they put more of the stuff down her throat
and she slipped back into the first sweet dream, looking through gossamer as thin and delicate as spider-
webs, which gradually changed and darkened into
opaque crystals before her eyes, until there was nothing at all.

It was late afternoon when Maryann returned. Shadrach and Otto were contentedly dozing after the satia-
tion of their exercise. Doc Winer was dreaming his
multicolored visions. "There's no word of the woman
and boy missing," Maryann informed them with satisfaction. "Beauchamp and the Chinaman headed south.
People figured the other two went with them." She
swept a cursory glance around the camp. "What'd you
do with the boy?"

Shadrach's eyes opened, startled. He looked quickly
to the tree where the boy had been bound. He sprang
up and ran, shouting for Otto and Winer. "Where's
the kid?"

Maryann looked grim. She examined the cords with
disgust. "Cut," she declared. "You telling me not one
of you loggerheads thought to search him?"

Shadrach looked chagrined. "He's just a kid," he
said.

Maryann regarded him angrily. "A kid with a
mouth," she retorted. "What about her?" she asked,
gesturing toward Susanna, bound again in her original
position with a blanket thrown carelessly over her.

At this Shadrach grinned. "She ain't got nothing on
her," he said with lewd emphasis. "Nothing at all."

The three of them—Maryann, Shadrach, and Otto—
searched the area around the camp, but found nothing.
Doc Winer was nodding sleepily in the last rays of

sun. "No tracks on the main trail," Shadrach reported. "He must be staying to the woods."

"Probably heading back to Los Angeles," Maryann reasoned. "We can't spare Otto in case Beauchamp shows up. We'll send Doc back to town in the morning, and let him watch for the kid."

Doc Winer was duly dispatched the next morning, with Maryann insisting he stay alert enough to see Davy if indeed the boy was heading for town. As guarantee, she demanded he leave his supply of laudanum in camp.

Shadrach laughed. "You think that'll stop him? He knows every Eastern ship that comes to port. He pimps for the sailors in trade."

"It's the best we can do," Maryann said angrily. "You got a better solution?"

"Nope," said Shadrach. He picked up the vial, held it casually to the sunlight, and ambled off to where Susanna was bound.

"Where are you going with that?" Maryann asked.

Shadrach grinned. "May as well put it to some use while we're waiting!"

The men in the saloon all remembered the stranger with the swift-running bay. Yes, and a pretty yellow-haired lady with him, and the Chinaman, Hoppy. Well, they had pulled out. He'd left the bay with Attaby, though. One of the grubstakers had seen the wagon headed south.

The woman? Probably with them. They hadn't seen her lately. Probably riding in the wagon. And there were two other men. Looked like Mex.

So Jonathan Hungerford had hired a horse and ridden south where he expected to find two murderers and his daughter.

He found Jed Taylor getting drunk in a dark narrow-spaced cantina in San Diego. Three men drank

with him—Mexicans, apparently. In one corner of
the room the Chinaman sat, silent and concentrated
upon a hand of cards. The man opposite him was similarly occupied. The game was pinochle.

Jed Taylor was dog-tired. He'd been with Garcia
for three days, and the man seemed in no hurry to
get down to business. The war was not going well for
them. They were not anxious to port the guns to cen-
tral Mexico where the fighting was now in progress.
So they delayed and entertained him with *pulque* and
tequila, discussed future business and other business
unrelated to his errand. The business of *putas*, eh, and
they would poke him in the ribs and gesture expan-
sively with their hands, as though sculpturing a woman
in the air.

He hadn't shaved or had a bath in two days, and
he looked almost as swarthy and ill-kempt as his companions. He was hung over and still drinking, forced
to curb his impatience to get on. So far they had welcomed him. So far they seemed to trust him. And he
continued to be the boon companion, buying drinks,
buying rounds, buying bottles. And drinking the drinks,
the rounds, the bottles others bought.

"Beauchamp!" The voice carried crisp and clear,
totally out of place and time. Taylor swung his seat
around. "Who wants him?" he said.

The man who had called from the doorway of the
cantina came forward to the table, and Taylor rose,
albeit swaying slightly, to his feet. For a long moment,
each man took the other's measure. Taylor's eyes went
quickly over the stranger's well-dressed form and
straight bearing. There was something familiar. He settled upon the man's eyes—green as beryl—and he
knew now what seemed familiar, though he knew he
had never met the man before.

"My daughter, Beauchamp," the man said.

"Mr. Hungerford," Taylor said, bowing slightly with

the briefest inclining of his head. "Your daughter no doubt is anxious to see you. How long has it been— almost nineteen years?" His tone was laced with sarcasm. "I understand you have never seen her.

"She is very beautiful, your daughter," he said softly, almost to himself. Then his lips curled slightly in the parody of a smile, and he gestured about the room in which they stood. "But alas, she is not here."

"You are an adventurer, Mr. Beauchamp," Hungerford said calmly. "A murderer, probably, and no doubt other things of which I am not aware. But in any case you are not fit company for my daughter."

At times two men may meet whose very similarities of nature and personality make them adversaries; such was now the case. As a younger man, Hungerford had wrested himself a place and land in America by his own shrewd dealing. Part of the land he owned had been played for in a poker game, little different from the way Jed Taylor had won his stallion.

But ten years separated them, and now Hungerford was acting the outraged father. Taylor sought to conceal his own misgivings. It was for this man that Susanna had first braved the long journey to America. *For a man,* he thought disgustedly, *who has waited nineteen years to be a father to his child.*

"Your daughter is mine, Hungerford," he said softly.

The other man turned stiffly on his heel. "We'll see about that!" he replied.

He had already known when he entered the cantina that the men had come alone, that there had been no woman with them. Obviously he had her secreted somewhere. But Jonathan Hungerford, recently ascended Earl of Wye, was a determined man, and undismayed. Because he remembered another thing which he had paid little mind when first he had heard it. But now he saw it as a weapon.

Beauchamp had something else he valued that was

not with him. The Mormons had remarked on it. It was by that possession the men in Los Angeles remembered him.

"That sweet-running stud horse," they had recalled. "He left him with Attaby, 'fraid the Mex would steal him, and he was probably right. Don't take no chances with a horse like that."

His plans were laid. It needed only his beating Beauchamp back to Los Angeles, back to this Attaby, guardian of Beauchamp's treasure.

And from the looks of Beauchamp, it wouldn't be too hard getting to Los Angeles before him.

Beauchamp did not seem in a hurry to return for his prize.

19

THE MEN JONATHAN HUNGERFORD finally hired to help him break into Attaby's stables were not men to inspire confidence, not even in their employer. He had been surprised to find that the man Attaby was well liked by the Californios, and not one of the locals was willing to ride against him. Had it not been for the recent influx of strangers into Los Angeles—many of whom were not particular as to how they earned a grubstake—Jonathan Hungerford might have ridden out alone. As it was, he rode uneasily. His men were the dregs of the town. He didn't like to turn his back to them.

So he told them only what they had to know. He wanted the horse; they were to help him get it. They would be well paid.

He went to the local gunsmith and purchased side-arms.

They descended on the Attaby estate stealthily that same night, only to find the stable locked and barred from the inside. Hungerford's face was grim and set. He led his riders up to the big house itself.

Here the doors were unbolted—the Attabys did not fear strangers in their house, and the owner was easily located reading in the library. Three of Hungerford's brutes cornered him, and Hungerford made his demand: entry to the stables. He wanted the bay stud horse. Nothing of Attaby's would be disturbed.

Attaby was unarmed. He twisted his body to face the man that held him from behind and examined the man's features with clear, undaunted eyes. A stranger. Attaby spat in his face. The stranger swung a fist to Attaby's jaw, but the Virginian merely staggered back, righted himself, and repeated the act. The other man reached for his gun.

"Leave him alone," Hungerford said.

Alerted by the commotion, Melissa came flying down the stairs. She carried a rifle. Three men immediately drew pistols. One held a gun to Attaby's head. "Drop it, or he's dead." One of the other men swung around and trained his gun on her.

Melicca scanned the room, dismayed to find she recognized no one. The gold rush had drawn thousands of strangers, outlaws, and cutthroats from all over.

She lowered the rifle, but did not relinquish it. "What d'you want?" she demanded. "What d'you want in my house?" She snarled like a great dark panther, defending both territory and mate.

One of the men laughed unpleasantly. His eyes raked over her with a malicious boldness. "Kind of uppity for a nigger gal," he said.

Attaby started up and leaped for his throat. "That's my *wife!*" he shrieked. The other man raised his rifle stock and slammed it down across his shoulders.

Melissa raced to the scene of battle and began kicking at the man with the rifle. "Get on, now! Trash!" she cried. The man turned quickly and would have struck her, but Hungerford turned his gun on the would-be assailant and audibly cocked the hammer. "I said that's enough," he said in a quiet deadly voice. "Now get up."

He turned now to the woman. "I want the bay stud horse you're keeping. Nothing else. Your property will be safe."

Attaby protested. "Melissa, I told him I'd keep that horse safe!" But she had turned to Hungerford.

"I'll give you the damn horse, then. Him"—she gestured toward her husband—"him you leave now. You hear me—white trash! You ain't fit to shine his shoes—you leave him be!"

She returned to the house—alone—a short time later. She paid no attention to her husband's mutterings, but directed herself to finding basin and ointment for his wounds and bruises. "The honor of Virginians," she muttered. "Muttonhead!"

"I don't like it," Maryann was complaining.

"Don't like *what?*" Shadrach questioned wearily.

"Doc's been in Los Angeles a week. No sign of the kid. No sign of the old man. How do we know they ain't all together with Beauchamp and laying a fix on us?"

"That's what we've got Otto looking out for," Shadrach said impatiently. He was tired of Maryann's endless complaints. And it was getting harder and harder to keep her away from their pretty hostage. Just yesterday he had seen her sitting by Susanna, gesturing with the bowie as though marking an animal for slaughter. Shadrach had to keep a sharp eye or he was sure he would return at some point to find the heifer with her throat cut.

To make matters worse, Doc's supply of the drug had been used up. She'd screamed like a banshee yesterday when he had approached. Today he'd have to tie her down. And he'd use a gag, like they had with the little Pawnee. If only Maryann would stop her infernal bitchery.

Maryann saw him heading off and guessed his purpose. "Don't you ever have enough?" she said.

"Just 'cause it don't interest *you*, Maryann," he retorted. "No reason to waste it."

The effects of the drug had worn off, and Susanna found herself fully cognizant of being held in the camp of the enemy. The last thing she remembered before Doc had administered the laudanum was the sight of Maryann—Maryann with the look of bloodlust in her eyes. Maryann, with the knife, the fall under the wagon. The opium gave her nightmares and Maryann was there. And then Shadrach behind her, Shadrach, grabbing her, tormenting her, fingering her and using her, and all the while she cried out in her dreams, searching, calling for the other man, the man who was her lover. And she never reached him. In her nightmares he always stayed a shadow she could not reach.

Now that the drug had worn off, it was strangely easier. Though she knew where she was, among her enemies, she knew the worst they could do was kill her. And somehow she could face that with a calm borne of having borne so much. She did not want to die, but she had borne so much, she did not fear it. Death would not be so hard.

Susanna's death was foremost in Maryann's consciousness and close to her heart. She acted it out in soliloquy every day. Since her husband's death, it was her only lust, her one desire. She could see her retribution near at hand; she did not really see that she could lose.

But her original fears about the missing boy were quite correct. Davy had *not* headed back for Los Angeles. And Taylor, made uneasy by the unexpected appearance of Susanna's father, had explained his hurry in words Garcia could understand. Garcia had grinned, showing a flash of very white teeth against the darkness of his skin. "If the foreign papa would give you trouble, there are simply ways, amigo, no, that trouble can be . . . removed." Taylor had laughed and shaken his head. He would deal with it in his own way. But for now he must hurry, lest the bird be caught back in the nest.

Garcia, he understood now, had wanted to wait for the exchange of rifles and Mexican silver until the guns coming down from Canada had arrived. Jed was relieved that there was no other reason, and that Mel's second supply of arms had been accepted. A scout from the Canada gun wagons had arrived the day before, and now it was not difficult to convince Garcia there would be nothing lost in completing the first exchange and relaxing in the sunny village until the second shipment.

Well satisfied, he rode out with Hoppy late that afternoon. Hoppy intended to take ship from Los Angeles back to New Orleans, to report to Wayne. Taylor was intent only on reaching Los Angeles and Susanna as quickly as possible.

Now it can start, he thought contentedly. He felt ripe for a time of ease. Take Susanna and Brushfire—Davy, too, if he had a mind to go—head up to those high, rugged hills in the north, see about laying over in the valley. Do some trapping, maybe even a little farming. Come spring, he'd come back to see Attaby, see about his claim on the foaling. He smiled to himself at thoughts he would not have ventured to say aloud.

It's high time, he was thinking. *A man can play loose just so long, sipping nectar like a butterfly, but then he has to start to build.* Leverton was right about that. A year ago how he would have laughed at the thoughts he was having now—thoughts of settling, thoughts—why should he deny it?—even thoughts of children. And he wasn't laughing at them now, he was smiling. Smiling because he was taking to the idea.

But no more than a mile farther along the trail, a figure separated itself from the woodland on the right and came running toward him, calling his name.

Davy had managed to get a lift with a peddler's wagon, but the driver could only take him part of the way. Since then he had fared as best he could, keeping always to the forested areas, unseen from the trail, but always watching for the man he needed desperately to find.

Now he spilled the whole story, as much as he knew, of the strangers who had broken into Leverton's hotel room, who had taken him and Susanna prisoner. He hesitated when it came to describing the men's activities with their fair captive, and he watched Taylor's face darken with a fury the like of which he had never seen. He mounted Davy behind him on the sturdy roan, and the three of them set forth at a gallop.

It was for Hoppy to stem Taylor's eagerness for battle, when Davy at last pointed to the almost-hidden path that led to the Shuttleworth camp. "She is in more danger if they know we are here," he told his hot-tempered companion. "You take more risk, more chance to lose what you want to keep safe."

So they camped that night, fireless and well concealed, plotting for the morning.

One man on lookout. Taylor was pleased. And the man was clumsy, easily seen on the bare face of the ridge. He looked at Hoppy, and the little man nodded, briefly touching the knife at his side. The man on watch would sound no alarm. Hoppy would see to it.

According to Davy, there were three others. Taylor had already identified Shadrach and Maryann Shuttleworth. The third would not be much danger—Taylor had seen opium eaters in the Orient. If Hoppy could take care of the lookout, the odds were in their favor.

But still they had to wait, as the brawny watchman returned to the camp, first for a pouch of what was probably tobacco, then for an early midday meal. Taylor was nervous and edgy. Finally Hoppy began a stealthy ascent that would bring him around and above his target. But at just about that time Jed Taylor heard Susanna screaming.

Shadrach had come to her with three lengths of rope, a piece of cloth, and the obvious intention of trying out his latest idea of entertainment. And Susanna, fully clearheaded, shrieked at his approach and struggled against the bonds that held her to the tree. Shadrach once more checking the vial whose contents had rendered her so docile, found it absolutely empty and threw it down in disgust. It shattered against a stone.

Taylor had no intention of holding back further. He began his descent to the camp itself, with Davy following behind.

Everything broke at once. Whether Hoppy had slipped and alerted Lansky, or whether the man was just too big to kill with one blow, there was a bellow from the ridge above the camp and the lumbering giant began running, bleeding and half-stumbling down the path to give the alarm. Maryann shouted to Shadrach, and he, forgetting Susanna for the time, ran for his rifle.

Susanna's heart was thudding with fear and hope. She saw the sun glinting off the shattered remains of the glass vial, and she crawled frantically toward the splinters of glass. Hurriedly, desperately, oblivious to the sharp edges that were cutting into her fingers, she worked the glass over her bonds, feeling them fray and finally give. She ran to the tent where she knew Shadrach kept an extra rifle. By now she could hear shouting and gunshots just beyond the stand of birch where the horses and mule were tethered. She grabbed for the rifle and crept forward.

More gunshots. Just ahead she caught a glimpse of Shadrach and Maryann, both kneeling close to the ground. She heard Jed shout something to Davy—shouting for him to get down. But the warning came too late. Shadrach rose and quickly pulled off a shot. Davy fell.

And now it was Jed, scrambling across the rocks to the boy, grabbing him and pulling him back behind the jutting boulders. Susanna watched him half-standing, saw him make the shot that finished Shadrach Shuttleworth, and Maryann! Maryann raising her own gun, drawing an easy bead on Jed as he paused in that instant making his go for Shadrach. Another explosion joined the general thunder, another cloud of gunsmoke, and Maryann fell forward, propelled by the rifle blast. Susanna stared down the barrel of her rifle, scarcely realizing what she had done.

Then Jed was coming, whole and safe, scrambling down the rocky slope. Hoppy had finished the work he'd started with Otto Lansky. Davy had been shot in the leg, but it was a flesh wound. It would heal.

Jed embraced her, and her fingers traced down the lines of his face like the fingers of the blind—searching, remembering, reassuring themselves once and for all. It was true and flesh. He was really there.

They remained in camp for two days while Susanna and Hoppy tended Davy's leg. Rather than explain the extra animals, Taylor had loosed the two Shuttleworth horses and the mule. Using a shovel he'd found in Shadrach's supplies, he and Hoppy managed to bury the three bodies. Their belongings he left untouched. Travelers, chance comers, would see to their disposal. How soon would all the traces of them be gone? And who would remark their passing?

"What are you thinking about?" Susanna asked him softly.

"My own mortality," he answered, smiling wryly. "But we have better things to think about."

He reached for her, and her flesh was alive to his

touch, responsive, exciting. Their coupling was an affirmation, as natural as the mossy grass, the very earth that cradled them. She was so soft, so yielding; yet she reached for him only that he might take her more completely.

A breeze blew gently over their bodies, cooling them, easing the heat of their passion. The evening air was balmy, freshening, peaceful. But it had grown late. At last they gathered their things and entered the tent.

"We're leaving tomorrow?" Susanna asked before they slept.

"Yes."

"Where will we go?" She could see his eyes, warm and softly glowing from the faint light of the stars shining in from the night sky.

"To Los Angeles first," he said. "Get Davy tended, pick up Brushfire if he's done the mares. Get Hoppy on a ship for New Orleans."

"You're not going back there?"

"Didn't I tell you?" His voice was edged with impatience. He was wondering to himself at the thing he had *not* told her—his meeting with her father. Cursing inwardly, he justified his omission. Enough of men and circumstances had separated them. He had a nagging anxious desire to escape the presence, the paternal righteousness of Jonathan Hungerford.

Her fingers traced odd little patterns on the floor of the tent. "And after Los Angeles—?"

"Then north," he told her, the words pronounced with decision, certainty.

"To the land?" she asked, not needing to define it further.

"To the land." he said. The land in the north was far, far enough and wide enough that a man—a man and a woman—could be lost in it. What was it he feared? The early Susanna, stowing away to America to find her father? But she was a child then, he thought angrily. Hungerford would not approve him, but Susanna was not a child. He stole a quick glance at her, her sweet delicate features already relaxed in sleep. Was it the face of a child, or a woman? He searched her face a moment longer, as though he might find the answer there, but he could read nothing. Nothing save the same loveliness which had first drawn him. After a time he gave it up. He wanted an early start in the morning.

The next day dawned fair and bright, and they broke camp before the sun had risen beyond the low hills to the east. Susanna sat before Jed on the roan, and Davy rode with Hoppy on the same well-traveled nag that had started with them from New Orleans.

By late afternoon, they were only an hour outside of Los Angeles. The trail here narrowed, hemmed in by squat stone hills on either side. From somewhere beyond their vision came the trumpeting call of a stallion—a startling familiar bugle, sounding where it had no place to be. Taylor halted his mount. Hoppy did likewise. There was a sharp turning just ahead, where the trail followed the irregular coast. Between the hills they could see the ocean, lapping hungrily at the western sands. Hoppy made a motion to dismount and climb to the hills to see where the stallion was, but Taylor stayed him.

He gestured that they should go on.

Around the next turning, centered on the narrow trail, stood Brushfire. Two lead ropes hung from the halter rings, held by men at opposite sides of the path, effectively holding the stallion where he was. Taylor looked and was not surprised to see the third man, still mounted, who stayed very near the stallion.

The man waited until Taylor and his party were scarcely fifty yards away. Taylor didn't have to be any closer. He recognized the man. He saw the man raise his rifle and put it close to the stallion's head.

"Beauchamp!" he called.

They stopped the horses. Susanna was startled, even bewildered, hearing the familiar alias pronounced by an unfamiliar voice. She looked to Jed for an answer, but he said nothing. His face was hard and set like a gambler who sees his bets are called.

The foreigner spoke again, calmly, but with a voice that carried easily across the distance between them. "Send the woman, Beauchamp!" the voice called. "Or I'll fire!" The rifle was held bare inches from the stallion's head. The horse danced and pawed the ground nervously, held by the double tether to his position in the center of the road.

Taylor laughed suddenly, loudly, and Susanna felt herself being lowered to the ground. "I'm sending the woman," he shouted back to the man with the rifle.

Susanna stared at him in utter disbelief. "Jed, you can't—!" she cried. "What do you mean? What are you doing?"

He looked at her, his eyes so intense she almost had to look away. Then the look vanished, became casual, commonplace. He smiled. "I don't think you'll be hurt," he said judiciously. "I'll be back for you Susanna."

"Beauchamp—!" the words cut again across the air. "I'm losing patience. Send the woman!"

"I'll be back for you, Susanna. Remember." That same intensity in his eyes, as though he were searching, or demanding something of which she was ignorant, something she did not understand. He turned her around and half-pushed her forward. "Go on, now," he told her. "Walk!"

Slowly, her vision blinded by tears, she crossed the prescribed distance, with no idea where or to whom she was being sent, conscious only that he had sent her, the man she had trusted had sent her in exchange for the other prize, like the spoils of war, between men, one prize for another. And he—Jed—had sent her in exchange.

"Release those tethers!" she heard her lover cry, when she was very near the men who held the stallion. At a word from the leader, they dropped the ropes. Taylor whistled once, loud and shrilly. The stallion snorted and shook himself. Finding no bonds, he trotted obediently to his master.

20

HE HAD GREEN eyes, like hers. His hair, too, was fair, though streaked with the beginnings of gray. He held himself erect. He was very polite.

Her father.

All of her dreams, woven of fancy, had not prepared her for this meeting, the bizarre tableau against which they played their parts. Her father! Now she understood that Jed could send her over, not fearing for her safety. But she could not think what to say. What had she imagined? That it would be as though they had always understood each other, always known each other? The paternal embrace, the long, long years of absence whistling down the wind?

She was tongue-tied. She felt stupid. At last she inquired politely after his estates in Hampshire.

He, too, was relieved to have a topic. The years were gone more quickly than he'd realized, and this was not what he had expected. He had expected a child— *his* child—somewhat grown in the years he had spent in America, but a child nonetheless. Then the trail had led across a country, through murder and intrigue and finally to this—this windblown, disheveled female, unquestionably his daughter. But not his child.

So he was more than happy to describe for her the

rolling, soft green hills of Hampshire, the garden of England, and more particularly, his own estates of Wye.

"Your life will be very different there, Susanna," he was saying. "Civilized. The East of this country is not so bad. They're catching up, taking the best from Europe and making it their own. But this West—no place for a woman. I intend to see you properly settled. Of course there are the—unfortunate circumstances of your birth. But a good dowry can go a long way to making up for that, I can assure you. You needn't worry."

Susanna, listening with half an ear, caught the drift of his words, and her eyes widened in amazement. Dowry? Marriage? She *had* been married. She had almost been married *twice!* And neither time to the man she wanted.

"But Jed—" she began.

"If you mean Beauchamp," her father said. "Forget him. He's no fit match for you. He's a scoundrel and a rogue. Didn't you see him send you off in trade for a horse?" He paused for emphasis. "*A horse!* Do you see how he values you?"

"He knew I was safe," Susanna cried in his defense. "He's coming back for me!"

"By now he's probably whoring in the taverns of Los Angeles," Hungerford told her. "Where he belongs."

He gentled his tone, and his eyes, so like her own, regarded her earnestly. "You must school yourself to put all this behind you, Susanna. A few months from now, when you're back at home in England, all this will be no more than a bad dream."

"But he loves me. He's coming back for me. I know it!"

Her father's words were hard again. "You can only be disappointed, putting your faith in such a man. I tell you he's gone by now. As it is, he's lucky I didn't shoot him for making my daughter his whore. Has he asked to marry you?"

"Did you marry my mother?" The words were out before she could stop them, and she drew back from her own attack, fearful, feeling as though she tread forbidden ground.

But she needn't have feared. His answer came softly, musingly, in a tone she hadn't heard before. "I was younger than you are now, Susanna, when I knew your mother. Things were handled by other people, and I was sent away. I was always told that you and she were well provided for. And for most of those years, the years that you were growing up, I was an ocean away, in this country.

"Had I been older, had I been my own man—" the voice hesitated in painful honesty. "I cannot say. There's no way to tell. And at any rate, it's far too late to tell. I am married now. You have a brother, younger than you. You'll meet him when we return to England. And your mother is dead—"

"Dead?" Susanna repeated. "You say my mother is dead?"

"I thought you knew!" her father said. "I heard it from a man named Bernhisel, there in the Mormon city. She died on board ship." His hand reached for hers in the first intimate gesture since they had met. "My dear child, I'm sorry, deeply sorry. I would have told you more gently had I known."

"That's all right. That's all right," Susanna reassured him. How long had it been since she had thought of her mother? Months perhaps. Other things had taken all her concern. And all the time, her mother had been dead. "It's all right for me," she said again. "I guess it doesn't change much. It's rather sad, but it doesn't really change things, I guess . . ." Her voice trailed off in wondering.

She stood and formally begged pardon. "I'd like to rest for a while, if you don't mind—"

"Of course," he said quickly. He had instructed his riders to pitch a separate tent for his daughter. "As to this man—Beauchamp, or Taylor—trust me, Susanna. I know more of these matters than you."

Susanna did not answer. She needed to be alone. Alone to think. Her father had spoken of trust. And Jed, too—hadn't Jed spoken of trust? Yet he had given her back, given her away to her father, in trade, like a token, an item of exchange.

Has he asked to marry you? her father had said. And she had not answered. Instead she had attacked him. But Jed never did ask her. He said, "I love you," but he'd never asked to marry her.

She did not even know if he would return.

Outside it was growing dark. The moon was rising. From the dark silhouette of scrub brush, a lone whippoorwill uttered his plaintive call, but no one answered. For a long time Susanna listened, to the crickets, to the night breeze whistling across the grass, to the lonely whippoorwill. And then she heard something else . . .

She felt wild laughter starting in her throat. Even before she heard the words, she recognized the song. She knew the singer.

Her father was wrong! Jed *was* coming back. Jed was coming back and he was singing Susanna's song, singing the song for her. The same silly nonsense words she had listened to on the ship and around the campfires, during the Mormon festivities. Now she could hear the words:

> *It rained all night the day I left,*
> *The weather it was dry,*
> *The sun so hot I froze to death,*
> *Susanna don't you cry.*

The singer was approaching and Susanna hurried from the tent. Her father was there, too. She stopped in mid-step.

Her father was carrying a gun.

The singing stopped abruptly, and Jed Taylor emerged from the shadows into the light of the watch-fire. "I'm unarmed, Hungerford," he said, casually stepping closer to the tents.

"Stop where you are," Hungerford said angrily. "Armed or not, Beauchamp, you're not welcome here."

"I've come for what belongs to me, Hungerford," Taylor said evenly. "Then I'll be on my way."

"My daughter knows where she belongs, and it's not with the likes of you."

Susanna had run to a place between the two men. Jed took another step toward her. Her father raised his pistol. "One more step and you're a dead man," he said with finality.

"Father, you can't!" Susanna cried. She stepped in front of the gun.

"Move aside, Susanna," her father ordered.

Move aside. What would they do—decide with guns where she belonged? Move aside while her life was decided, perhaps by the death of one of these men?

She raised anguished eyes to the other man. "Jed, *please!*"

Taylor looked at her, saw the indecision in her eyes. He saw what he had feared from the beginning—that he might lose this bet, lose this prize, this woman he had chosen for his own.

He smiled suddenly, a cool, mocking smile, and bowed to Hungerford, who regarded him with grudging admiration even while he steadied the gun in his hand. The man had guts if nothing else.

"No need to shoot me, Hungerford," he said casually. "I'm going." His eyes turned to Susanna, and his gaze lingered like a brief caress. "I told you I'd come back for you, Susanna," he said softly. "And I have. Now it's up to you."

He turned his back and he was walking away, calmly, leisurely starting through the woods that led to the main trail, where Hoppy waited with the horses, where he would mount and ride out. He was leaving.

"Jed—!" Susanna cried. He couldn't leave. *Not without her!* He couldn't leave.

"Jed—wait!"

She saw her father, standing near the tent. He had put up the gun. She ran to him and briefly touched his hand. "I have to go," she said. "It's too late. Please understand, I don't blame you, it's just too late. Too late for a father."

Jed was already out of sight and she was running, running and calling his name, calling for him to wait for her.

Home. Not England. Somewhere on the northern coast, perhaps. Some raw land in the West of this America.

He was in view now. He had stopped. He was waiting for her, a broad smile on his face, his arms outstretched to welcome her. That was her place—there, close in the circle of his arms. Wherever this man was —that was home.

PART TWO

1

It was an elegant carriage, set on high wooden wheels, with varnished running boards and a bright red body. But it was built for the smooth, even grading of city pavements, and it appeared out of place as it bounced and rolled precariously over the rocky turns and steep ruts of the California wagon road. Inside, the two passengers, mother and son, alternated sporadic conversation and companionable silences born of long journeying. The road had not been easy. No roads were easy in 1863, least of all those in the South.

And New Orleans, dark jewel of the Mississippi, was a closed and conquered city.

Still, Louisa thought with satisfaction, they had managed to get out. With the greedy militia as crooked as Butler himself, all things were possible—for a price. They sold the saddle horses at the first town and traveled by rail and stage. There were fewer patrols the farther west they went, and those they met Louisa dealt with, using charm when possible and bribery when necessary. Finally, though, as public transportation grew from unreliable to almost nonexistent, they bought their own. They had been lucky to hire this driver, too. Louisa's servant rode with him. The carriage would suit them well enough in San Francisco. By mutual consent, they did not speak of the war. They spoke of

yesterday and tomorrow. They spoke of years ago and
now, today. But they did not speak of four weeks ago,
when Mumford—poor bad-luck gambler Mumford—
was hanged in the public square for wearing a scrap
of the fallen blue flag in the buttonhole of his suit.

". . . still don't understand, *maman*, why you insist
on the visit before even our settling in the city."

Louisa focused her attentions on her son, petulant
from the confinement of the journey. But it was too soon
yet for the truth. "A man," she said briefly. "An old
friend I haven't seen in many years. But I'd like you to
meet him . . . "

She answered herself more honestly. *Why do I insist?* Because for sixteen long years I have been silent.
For sixteen years I have held this secret; but before I
die, I want to see Jed again, just once. I want to see
Jed and his son together. My son. My son and Jed's.

"An old flame, *maman?*" the boy teased. "In this
God-forsaken land?"

"This God-forsaken land might be good for you.
You could do with a bit of hardening." She tried to
compose herself to look disapprovingly at her son, and,
as usual, she failed. Beauty can defend all manner of
sin, and in Jules beauty bordered on vice. His dark eyes
sparkled with sly humor. "I'm hard enough, *maman*,"
he answered. "Ask Labella."

"Ask Labella," she mocked. "Ask Jeanette or Barbara—do you think your exploits are a secret to me?
But that's not all there is to being a man, my spoiled
pet. That incident at the academy—" He was laughing. "You're a shameless wretch, and you'll go to hell.
A nun? You could find no other outlet for your—
energies?"

"A *young* nun," he corrected, smiling broadly to
show strong, even teeth. "Her spirit was married to
God, but her body, I assure you, has not risen to the
Father."

"You'll come to a bad end," she reproached him.

"So long as I enjoy getting there," he answered unperturbed. He smiled, secure in her indulgence, and stretched himself luxuriously like a cat. His fingers toyed idly with the trimming of lace on his sleeves.

"And you're an incorrigible fop," she said. But she could not be hard with him, and even her criticism came forth like a caress. He was her very bones, her dearest vice.

"You enjoy showing me off too much to do anything but encourage my fashion." The boy was piqued. He could not bear even her teasing disapproval. When he scowled, his eyebrows knit together across his forehead. *Just like Jed,* she thought. *Strange, and they've never even seen each other. Just like Jed.*

She marveled at the passage of time. She had not laid eyes on Jed Taylor in sixteen years. Yet she could see him so plainly in her mind—she saw him daily, did she not, in their child, this *young man* sitting next to her. How could it be? Sometimes the time had seemed so long, but just now it was as though she had picked up a piece of needlework for an infant's gown and turned around to find him grown. Already seeking out the gayest companions and the easiest women. Already probing and exploring in the pockets of willing girls the potent mysteries of his own lust.

But he was here still. From the first he had been hers. And if fortune favors me, I shall have him till I die, because it won't be very long.

Poor Doctor Tom had done his best, trying first to be firm and severe, then pleading. But for the time I have left, I shall not end it like an old woman, trading life for a living death, blanketed with shawls and quiet pastimes. For what? A few meager years? While my one great indulgence—my son—would fly like a new-winged bird and never look back.

The style of the South was dead. The silks had be-

come flags, and the flags were falling. The castles were
burning. In a little time she could see it would be no
more than a fairy tale. And New Orleans, that most
magical queen of cities, was dying, too. Butler was
making her bleed, and others would finish the job by
suffocating her, stilling the voices of her citizens, sending the brave to prison, or to the hangman. How ironic
that sometimes death is on time. She would be spared
witnessing the shattering changes in the South. And for
Jules, there would be a new life in a new place. The
West was a new mecca where anything was possible.
Jules would fit into it. He was young enough.

She eyed her son covertly. *My blackguard,* she
thought. *My devil child.* The thick waves of his hair,
black and glossy as raven wings, fell in sweeps about
his head. His mouth was almost too beautiful to be a
man's, but the jaw below it was set and firm, the bones
of a face masculine but elegant.

It was only for him that she could play the *char-
mante* till dawn in fashionable salons. For him, she
still would fast dance the polka and the waltz, though
her body gave more pain than pleasure now. For him
she was still the most gay, the most *bon vivant.* Only
the best and richest—that is left to the old *belle dame,*
she would say—old wines and her young man.

Such a life took its toll. And of course, she was
forty-five. A widow. For herself, an odd balancing, was
it not, that her blood, so hot and so demanding when
she was young, had cooled quickly in the intervening
years. So swift and subtle in its leaving, she had scarcely
noticed its passing.

No, her pulse did not quicken so easily anymore, and
her breath did not shorten in that soft, panting hunger.
The heated frenzy of the act itself had become just
faintly repugnant to her, now that her blood no longer
leaped in answer to the touch, the softly whispered
word, the hard male intrusion.

Even for Jed it was the memory of great passion that stirred her, rather than present desire. No, her one remaining passion was maternal and sat beside her. With that she was content. Criticizing the landscape, she thought, bemusedly watching the young man's face turned toward the carriage window. *He is more my child than Jed's*, she thought. *A child of cities.*

High above their heads and atop a splintery crag, a lone rider squinted against the sun at their approach. The slight figure of a young girl perched casually on the bare back of her rangy mount and watched the dust that rose from the horses' hooves.

They had to be coming to visit. The wagon road ended at the main house. She wheeled the big dun mare abruptly and cantered down the rocky shale. The mare's shod feet lit sparks on the winding trail.

She was well ahead of the carriage turning into the gate. Dismounting, she whooped like an Indian and called to her mother in the kitchen.

"There's a carriage coming up the drive!" she hollered. Tethering her mount and calling to one of the wranglers, she ducked beneath the middle rail of the fence, dusted off her pants, and trotted up to the house.

"Melissa isn't due for two weeks," Susanna told her daughter. "You certain they're not prospectors?"

"You didn't see the carriage, Mother!" the girl said excitedly. It's light and slick and they have a team of chestnuts—but they're not Attaby horses. I'd know if they were. It's a fancy carriage. I wonder who's inside. Mother, can't you guess?"

"We're not expecting anyone, Lorelei. No, I can't imagine." She hastened to untie her apron. "But, it will be nice to have company . . ."

She looked at her daughter in dismay. "Well, do you expect to greet our visitors decked out like an Indian? Upstairs with you, and wash up quickly—you've been at the strawberry patch again, and half your face is red. Comb the burrs from your hair. Dear heaven, you're worse than a field horse!"

Lorelei made a face and started for the stairs.

"—and a *skirt,* Lorelei!" her mother called after her.

Susanna peeked through the parlor curtains. The carriage was still out of sight, but she could hear the defined and rhythmic tattoo of the horses growing louder.

Now she could see it; the polished brass rings of the harness catching the late afternoon sun, the high-stepping horses taking the turn at a stylish trot. They halted at the gate and Ed, their second foreman, ran to open it, taking the opportunity to survey the horses with a practiced eye and steal a curious glance at the passengers inside.

A servant knocked at the front door, and bobbing her head in a curtsy to Susanna, extended her mistress's card.

Susanna quickly scanned the elegant script, printed in gold on the white glossy paper. Louisa Dolarier Hutchinson. The address, New Orleans. *Louisa!* Susanna read it again, consternation spreading in hot blushes over her face.

She straightened up suddenly, bracing herself to meet the challenge and forced her voice to speak calmly, evenly. "My *husband* is not at home," she said, with only the barest emphasis. "Does Mrs. Hutchinson wish to see me?"

Sensing something extraordinary, the little maid turned back to her mistress. Louisa carefully pinned back her veil. She showed her son no trace of disappointment, no surprise. "Wait at the carriage, Jules. I shan't be long." With a rustle of her taffeta skirts, she descended the carriage.

For a brief moment, both women stood face to face, each taking the other's measure; one thinking: *this is the woman who came before*—the other: *this is the one who came after*. Susanna remembered even more: a note, a misunderstanding, a name—this woman's name —for which she had lost faith in her lover and almost died. She did not call for Ed to unhitch the team of horses, nor to Elsa to kill an extra chicken for dinner. But she would not ignore simple courtesy. She opened the front door and stepped aside to permit her guest to enter.

"Come in," she said quietly.

They sat on matching wing chairs in the parlor, a strange pair, the dark-haired woman and the silvery blonde. Susanna brought out a crystal decanter with two glasses. "Sherry, Mrs. Hutchinson?" she asked.

"Please."

Louisa sipped at the amber beverage and lowered the glass. *Strange,* she thought to herself. *Ten years ago I would have liked to rake my nails across that delicate pink and white face. Ten years ago I would have been a tiger of jealousy, yet here I sit like a lady, feeling very little.*

"You know who I am, Mrs. Taylor?" she asked gently.

"You were Jed's—lady friend," Susanna said softly.

"A long time ago," Louisa said. She rose and paced the brief length of the room, then turned in a swish of skirts to face her hostess. "But, I was hoping to see him today. Will he be away long? I haven't seen him in sixteen years."

"Probably as long as there's a war on, Mrs. Hutchison," Susanna replied. "The last I knew he was close to Atlanta."

"Was he with Johnston?" Louisa asked. She knew several men with General Johnston's troops.

"He was with Admiral Farragut until three months ago. He's with the Twenty-fourth battalion, California. With General Grant," Susanna informed her, "The *Union* Army."

That hit Louisa hardest of all. She still shivered remembering that night Farragut's fleet passed from Charlotte. She understood enough of politics to see the underlying causes. She understood enough of the military to know that the South could only lose. But none of that negated the knowledge that along with the politics and the mechanics of war, her way of life was dying. And Jed was helping to destroy it.

To Susanna, bearer of these tidings, she said only, "I see."

Susanna broke the uncomfortable lull in the conversation. "If you could tell me why you'd like to see Jed—I do receive word now and then—"

Louisa looked at the woman Jed had married trying to read inside her mind, trying to decide. Without a word, she went to the door and called outside to her son.

Despondent and feeling badly used and neglected, Jules had been sitting on the carriage's running board and looking at the outlying mountains with curiosity.

"This is my son, Jules, Mrs. Taylor," Louisa said.

Jules smiled charmingly from his height well above the pretty blond lady and bowed. Susanna, looking up into that face—that too-familiar stranger's face—gasped audibly. Her hands fluttered to her breast. "My God!" she spoke low, almost moaning.

Malice had not been Louisa's intent, and even had it been so, she would have been moved to pity for the woman who blanched like a horrified ghost at the face of her son, and now looked so pained, as though her heart was breaking.

Alarmed and confused, Jules lapsed into French. "*Mais, je regrette, madame. S'il vous plaît. Mon Dieu, q'est-ce qu'il ce passe, maman? Qu'est-ce que j'ai fait?* —What have I done?"

Susanna recovered with a gargantuan effort, tried to pass off her response as a weakness. "It's nothing. I'm all right," she said quickly. "There's a pain sometimes overtakes me . . . "

"I'll help Mrs. Taylor, Jules. I'll be out directly," Louisa said, taking charge and dismissing her son.

The young man bowed again, gracefully like a big cat. *Like his father.* "Forgive me, madame," he said, all smiles again, white teeth in the handsome dark face. "I confess it is not a reaction I usually inspire."

He left.

"I'm sorry as well," Louisa said to the woman, still shaking badly, as though chilled. "I did not know it would so upset you."

"Did he—did Jed know about the boy?"

Louisa looked almost haughty, a still remarkably handsome, still proud woman. "No. I would not have used the child that way."

"Does your son know?" She could not say *his son.*

"I was married before he was born," she said quietly, offering no further explanation.

"And your husband—"

"Dead, these past six years."

"I think you understand now, Mrs. Taylor," she continued, "why I would like to see Jed—why I want Jules to meet him."

Susanna raised a stricken face to the unwelcome guest. "Why now?" she insisted. "Why now, after all these years—when the boy knows nothing, when he thinks he has a father. For God's sake, why now?"

Louisa leaned back in the chair. She picked up the goblet of cut crystal and spun the glass watching the play of light make rainbows on the shimmering surface. "I have a bad heart, Mrs. Taylor. According to my doctor, I have probably not a great deal more time to enjoy this exalted world." She waved away Susanna's confused distress. "Please, not on my account. You need not worry about me. Or money. Jules has plenty, more than even he can spend.

"He also has a father," she said meaningfully. "I would like—I was hoping they could meet."

Her slender fingers, ringed with jewels, brought forth a slip of paper on which she quickly scrawled an address in San Francisco. "I shan't inconvenience you further—if you would only give him this—the Beauvilles are friends of mine, they will know where to find me. If Jed wishes, he can contact me through them. We'll go on to Sacramento tonight. And then to San Francisco."

Susanna found the paper pressed into her hand. She recoiled slightly at the other woman's touch, but managed to stand and face her. Louisa withdrew the pin from her hat and let the netting fall to veil her face. From behind that camouflage, she viewed Jed Taylor's wife a moment longer. Susanna met her gaze unflinchingly. Her green eyes were now as veiled as the face of this woman who had come so casually to destroy the peace of her world and was now departing in the same manner, like an innocent visitor. This uninvited guest.

"Good day, Mrs. Taylor," Louisa said, in a voice still soft, still calm and unaffected.

"Good day," Susanna said.

Jules was waiting at the carriage, but Louisa did not look at him. She stepped quickly to her seat, put on her gloves though the day was warm, and waved out to the driver.

"Back to the coast road," she instructed. "South to Sacramento."

The driver shrugged and clucked to the horses. He was not familiar with the country, but he thought Sacramento farther than an evening's journey, at least it seemed so on the map. Still he did not want to question the lady who had hired him. Something strange had gone on at the big white house, and he had felt a kind

of tension, like coiled springs, as she brushed past
him. Still, he just drove on. He didn't want to ask the
lady any questions.

Jules had no such compunction. "Well, *maman*," he
said as soon as she had settled. "Will you enlighten me
on that little bit of drama just enacted?"

Louisa shot a quick glance at her son. He gave her
a superior urbane smile, as though he'd found her out
in some naughtiness, some past indiscretion. *He hadn't
guessed. He didn't know.*

"Blessings on innocence," she thought gratefully.
"For all his gadding about, he does not suspect the
truth." Were he a few years older, he might have seen
it all—might have seen them all quite clearly in their
respective parts. The sweet blond wife, the dark-
haired mistress, the pervasive presence of the absent
male, and himself the connection between them all—
the mystery child, the changeling.

But of course, he had no reason to suspect. He had a
father—as far as he knew.

*Perhaps I should have let John take more of a hand
in raising him,* she thought. *But he was too old, and
too gentle himself to assert his own authority.*

And I wanted him to myself, she amended honestly.
John knew that too, I think.   ....

"Come, *maman,* you shall not escape so easily. Explain yourself. And tell me about that little blond lady."

She was brought back abruptly. At least now she
could smile easily; the knotted-up tension in her body
had relaxed. "It was before you were born, you young
puppy," she said severely. "And you are too much of
a gossip to know your mother's secrets."

"Oh, la, how she guards her past!" he teased. But
he probed no further. Instead he began to sing:

> *Ah! Celeste, ah! Celeste,*
> *mo bel bijou,*

> *mo l'aimai to com cochon*
> *l'aimai la bou*

His mother, lost in her own thoughts, seemed not to hear him. He continued singing, a little louder:

> *Si to 'tai lo bou, zami.*
> *mo 'tai cochon, zami.*
> *mo 'tai raboure dan toi, zami.*
> *a fo'ce l'amai toi.*

He had her attention now. "Ah, you are a trial, Jules. Do you think I have sent you to the best schools to pick up that Cajun patois? To sing low tavern songs in that corrupted tongue?"

He grinned wickedly, delighted to have roused her. "Would you prefer it in English, *maman?*" Before she could answer, he began again:

> *Ah, Celeste, ah! Celeste,*
> *my pretty jewel,*
> *I love you as a pig loves mud.*

"It's vulgar, you oafish monkey—"

"—it's a love song," he countered, "and how is love vulgar? Now let me sing it through."

> *If you were mud, my friend, sweet friend*
> *I a pig, my friend,*
> *I would wallow in you, my friend, sweet friend,*
> *because I love you so.*

"Oh, it's impossible in any language, and so are you!"

"Madame, you are a snob," he said. "It is tragic and romantic. Now shut your great red mouth and hear the rest—

If you were a bird, my friend, sweet friend
and I had a gun, my friend,
I would kill you my friend, sweet friend, sweet bird,
because I love you so.

"Barbaric, too," Louisa said dryly. "Ah, Jules, my pretty jewel," she mocked, "you put the best talents to the worst use of anyone I know. And, unhappily, I know a great many wastrels."

"Well, I've done with it now. I can't remember any more," he said to comfort her.

This was how he loved her best—vain and gay and mocking. Sometimes now she seemed to be—withdrawn from him, pensive in a way that disturbed him. And so he would woo and tease her back, like now, until she was again his spirited playmate, his droll, sharp-witted *maman*.

Appeased now, he lay back on his seat, and let his eyes grow dreamy. In a few moments he was asleep.

Louisa pulled a few strands of errant black hair from his eyes, and smoothed his face with her fingers, rasping slightly from the beginnings of beard. This was her pleasure—the soft play of his thick dark lashes on his cheek, the even rise and fall of his breathing, the greedy sensual pleasure he took, even in sleep. Her thoughts began to drift again. She remembered Susanna's face when she had seen Jules.

I didn't mean to cause her such pain. I'm becoming selfish, I suppose, in my old age. Who knows what trouble this might bring.

And he sleeps on, knowing nothing of this. Believing with all the innocence of those who have not yet found their mothers to be liars, that a man named John Hutchison, who died six years ago, was his father.

What a strange *mariagé de convenance* that had been. They were old friends—indeed, he was one of the two or three intimates who had known the true circumstances of Jules's birth. And he had offered—offered her on any terms she chose—the loan of his good name, his house, his board. He was a sometimes lover, always friend, and it had taken her years of that sedate and sometimes sweet wedded life to finally realize that he had offered to marry her because he loved her with an understated, unassuming fidelity of devotion that surprised her more than anything else except perhaps how much and how often she missed him since his death. How used to his body next to her she had become, though their trysts had ended long before his death. *I miss the old bones,* she would think, *the "good night, my dear." The fastidious morning toilet and impeccable manners of a man who had been nothing but a gentleman all his life. Right to the morning that he didn't wake.*

And some morning soon I will be that one—if I'm lucky and get out easily, just closing my eyes and starting a long dream. It is only the young, she mused, *who delight in the romance of violent death. For myself I hope an easy sleep.* Sometimes her body felt so weary and the efforts of daily living a chore only.

The boy was waking. He always woke so strangely—in a single gesture, like an animal. His eyes would simply open, clear-sighted and aware, as an animal might wake from sleep in a single gesture to assure its own safety. That no enemy had emerged on stealthy feet while he was sleeping. His whole body lengthened and stretched to loosen his muscles. Then he sighed, saying mockingly, "Will we ever see civilization again?"

"Eventually," his mother answered dryly.

He looked out the window again, vainly searching for some sight that might amuse him.

"Jules," Louisa said suddenly. "I want to be buried in New Orleans, in the Hutchison family crypt. Promise me—promise me if anything happens, you'll see to it."

The boy looked at his mother in amazement. "Why you indulgent old cow," he said, masking his dread in pique. "You're not half an age to die. How dare you go dreaming your own funeral. *Mon Dieu,* you'll outlive everyone, you're such a stubborn thing. You're being morbid and terrible, and I'll not have it!" He wanted her to draw back the very words she had uttered, but for once he failed to change her mood.

Her face was unusually gentle and serene. "All the same, promise me," she insisted.

"Well, all right," he said sulkily, "anything to quiet you. But see that you don't rely on me to keep any promises. You know how unreliable I am."

"I'll hold you to your promise," she warned him. "I'll haunt you. I'll become a grasshopper in your soup. So remember."

Lorelei had seen their guests from her bedroom window upstairs. She had witnessed the odd little march of the maid back and forth from carriage to porch. Then the mistress had emerged, clad in a stylish gown of gold taffeta double-bordered in creamy lace. Its hem was drawn up to let the elaborate edging of the petticoat show the same lace as the borders. She pressed her face against the windowpane and watched the woman ascend to the porch and disappear from view.

Then she saw the boy.

He looked a bit older than she. He was very tall, his figure slender and perfectly fitted in black velvet breeches and a burgundy coat, cut broad at the shoulders and tight at the waist. Around his neck was tied a silk foulard, the same wine color as his coat. His hair was as black as an Indian's.

"Oh, why doesn't he look up!" she thought impatiently. She wanted to see his face. She thought of calling him or whistling, but she was suddenly too shy.

Oblivious to the spy at the second-floor window,

Jules slackened his pace and stopped in front of a flower bed, burgeoning with the deep blue gentians Lorelei loved. She had brought them from the lower woodland. They were her favorites and she had nursed and worried over them until they had taken.

Now at last she could see his face, brooding and intent upon the flowers. He had snapped one of the flowers from its stem and held it to his nose. She saw him peer curiously at the funnel-shaped blossom, then poke his finger inside, catching the yellow pollen on his hands. With the same odd deliberateness, he began to rip the petals from the body of the flower, dropping them negligently to the ground until only the tiny disk of the base remained. That, too, was discarded.

Lorelei found herself holding her breath as the last of the flower was discarded. She suddenly realized she was standing half-naked at the window. Excitedly, she turned from the window and peeled off the ragged pants and sweat-stained calico shirt she had been wearing. She splashed water from the basin over her face and throat and rummaged impatiently through her wardrobe for a seldom-used chemise and her single pair of high-heeled sandals. Unplaited, her hair fell in one heavy mass to the middle of her back, and she brushed it 'till sparks crackled against the brush.

She was adjusting the neckline of her blouse to leave her shoulders bare when she heard the sound of departing horses. Racing to the window, she stared at the carriage, already small and well down the drive and felt a choking disappointment. She had been robbed.

She made for the stairs and descended in a flurry, unmindful of her bare feet and unfastened skirt.

"Where are they going, Mother?" she cried. "Aren't they coming back? Why did they leave so quickly?"

"They were going on to Sacramento tonight," Susanna said with forced casualness.

"But they'll never make that distance!"

"I know," Susanna said shortly.

"Then why didn't you ask them to stay? I could have shown the boy around. We haven't had company in ages. Nobody comes anymore."

"There's a war on, Lorelei," her mother said wearily.

"There's no war in California!" I don't understand why Daddy and Davy had to go anyway. It's only in the East they're fighting—"

"We've discussed all this before, Lorelei. It's a matter of principle."

"Who were they, Mother—the lady and the boy?"

"No one important," she replied guardedly. "They got off the coastal road somehow. Their driver thought it was a shortcut."

"From where? Where were they coming from? You said they were going to Sacramento, but that's south of here."

"I don't know," Susanna replied sharply with the last of her patience. "I don't ask strangers their business. Let's hear no more about it."

Sulky with disappointment, Lorelei eyed her mother angrily. *She could have asked them to stay.* What pretty clothes the lady wore! And the boy—the boy was a creature of much interest, snatched away before he could be enjoyed. Her mother—really, her mother was growing quite impossible.

She turned angrily in a swish of skirts and started for the door.

"Where are you going, Lorelei?" her mother asked.

"—for a ride!" came the terse reply.

"You can't go dressed like that! Change your skirt —put on some shoes—"

But the front door only slammed in answer. Then the girl was gone. Shaking her head, Susanna did not pursue the issue. It was a relief, really, to be alone. To give in to the pain that had come as fresh as today when she had looked into the face of Louisa's son. *Jed's son*. It was as though a scab had been brutishly ripped from a wound and salt pressed in. A wound that had never healed.

We mark and measure our lives by certain particular things—by moments of decision, times of love, and those incidents that indelibly mark us, incidents of life and death. This would be another marker in Susanna's personal perception. Like the year Lorelei was born. The year Jed took her to the mountains.

The year Benji died.

Without willing it, her footsteps had carried her out into the field behind the house, where purple fireweed blanketed the earth like a soft carpet. On a little rise, the earth had been cleared and other flowers planted —shooting stars and red maids, cream cups and yellow orchids, like guardians around the single marble stone that marked another son.

Jonathan Benjamin Taylor. Such a big name for such a little thing. And a single year: 1852. Because that was all there was.

The second child should have been easier than the first. And Lorelei had been such an easy birth, so quick. Susanna's body had stretched so naturally to help the baby out. At Benji's time that body should have been practiced, ripe. It should have been an easy birth . . .

But it wasn't. It was almost three days. After nine months, the unborn have as much character as the others. And Benji was fighting to find his way out. She had felt his futile kicks—he was set wrong, and it was so long, so long that she thought he would never be born, that she would die before he would find the passage out.

Then the miracle of his birth. Oh, it had taken a long time to heal up, but that didn't matter. He was worth it. A sweet baby, sunny natured, like those days. He was a summer child.

It was a warm evening, just like this one, she'd tucked him in. He had practiced his new smile on her and curled his tiny hand around her fingers. And the morning after was just like any other fine morning. Except that her baby was dead.

The doctor had shrugged his shoulders. Crib death, he called it. Nothing to be done. It seemed to happen without cause. Nothing to be done.

Just bury him. Just clear a little piece of land, build a tiny coffin. Just bury the dead and mourn.

And Jed had been with her all that time. But a father does not grieve the same as a mother, and they were separate beings in separate mourning, for a child who had been longer in his mother's womb than outside of it.

And the nights when she had cried herself out, and Jed would finally sleep beside her, her breasts ached, swollen with milk that oozed like blood between the sheets where she lay because there was no tiny rosebud mouth to drink.

She was still young; there would be other babies. And so the months had passed. Month after month, the blood came down like a mockery, each time a failed hope, until, while Jed was away, she had taken the carriage and traveled to a special doctor in Monterey who told her there would be no more babies. Not ever.

Something had gone out of her then, and left a hollowness in its place. She pulled a few weeds from among the flowers and straightened up. Time to put supper on. Her hands went to her apron pockets and found the address which Louisa had pressed upon her. She stared down at the paper for a moment. Then, with bitter resolution, she began to shred the note, erasing the unwelcome news of the afternoon, hoping only that Louisa Dolarier Hutchison would die soon, and that her son would lose himself in the world outside her life.

The wind rose slightly from the mountains and carried the bits of paper from her loosened fingers. Against the wall of the house, the dimpled blue petals of the morning glories folded themselves against the growing dark.

2

LORELEI KNEW THAT both her mother and Mrs. Attaby were lying when she asked about Beau, and she was not above a little eavesdropping to learn the truth. So far, two weeks into Melissa's visit, she had heard only talk of the war, of the men, of when the men might return. Lorelei knew Beau would not be among the soldiers. Hadn't he said as much three years ago, when the war was only a question mark and a point of speculation—in California especially, no more than issues for politicking?

She thought Davy would know, but the last time he'd been back, and she had put the question to him, he had denied knowing anything. He was lying, too. She always knew when Davy was lying, because he wasn't good at it—he always blushed. Usually she could get him to tell her anything—even those things her parents didn't think she should know—how her mother had been married to a bad man when she was young, and how Jed Taylor had rescued her from kidnappers after her husband died. She thought it was all terribly romantic and Davy told the stories so well —of course she never let on that she knew anything of the past, and that made it even more exciting.

But about Beau she could learn nothing. Davy became guarded when she'd accused him of not telling her what he knew. And when she'd persisted, he'd threatened to throw her in the horse trough if she didn't stop.

And he had, the big ox!

She'd been furious. Sputtering and dripping, with the water running in rivers down her back and over her face, she had employed every cuss word ever used around a bunkhouse full of cowboys.

"Just because you're bigger than me!" she'd accused him.

And he'd just laughed, just threw back his head and hollered so loud he'd drawn spectators to witness her embarrassing position, standing up to her knees in water. A couple of the cowpokes had applauded, which served only to make her madder. But it was hard to stay mad at Davy.

She missed him. She missed him almost as much as she missed her father, and that was a lot. But she knew they would be back to stay as soon as the war was over. Beau was another story—he hadn't been to visit since before the war. She knew there was some terrible mystery about Beau, something so terrible even Davy wouldn't tell her.

And as luck would have it, just when she was ready to retire from leaning over the upstairs banister and hiding behind the acacia bushes, as she happened to be passing the screened window that looked out on the porch where Melissa and her mother sat, she heard his name. It was her mother talking.

"Any news yet of Beau?" Susanna said.

Still and silent, Lorelei froze like a statue by the window and she held her breath. Her turquoise eyes, bright as agates, watched unblinkingly. Both women were seated in the wicker chairs; both had their backs to her.

"If it's news we've had, I wish we'd heard nothing a-tall," Melissa said heavily. "We've always been real

close, Susanna, and I guess trouble's not a secret between friends."

Her voice lowered and Lorelei strained to hear the
words . . . ". . . holdup in Virginia City . . . Whitey
Loomis and . . . description . . . maybe Beau."

Her mother's voice came clearer. "But they're not
certain it's Beau. He's just a boy, Melissa."

"He's twenty-one, Susanna. He's twenty-one and
he's been gone three years. And he wasn't a boy when
he left. When he left he was bloodied up and bitter
and God, I don't know what he is now! Only it's like
death with him being gone and not knowing where he
is, not knowing even *what* he is—if he's turned mean
with being bitter or what."

"Beau never had a touch of meanness in him, Melissa. He was raised with all the love in the world—"

"That's not enough!" Melissa cried. "When he was
a child it was enough. But nobody stays a child, Susanna. Beau had no people. Nobody but Jim and me.
A boy grows up, he looks to find out where he belongs
in the world, he's needing more than his mammy and
daddy—"

Her voice began to break, but she collected herself
and went on. "Funny thing, in the South you always
knew who you were, of course, even if you were
nothin' but a cracker. If you were white, you were
white. If you were black, you were a nigger.

"That'll change. In time, that'll change, and it's only
right. But it'll take more than this war to change it,
Susanna. Mark me, this war may make slaves free,
but it won't turn niggers white.

"Family of free colored folks moved down by us
last year," she said. "I was thinking it'd be nice to
get acquainted, brought over some fresh-baked bread
for the family."

There was an unaccustomed choler in her tone. "I
might have been a three-headed chicken. No, worse,

some bad-luck voodoo charm. They'd heard all about me—the nigger what married a white man cause a black man wouldn't suit. Putting on airs in the big house and sending her boy to white schools. No, they wouldn't be a-mixing with the likes of us.

"It's not just the white folks, Susanna. There's bad blood on both sides. But where does that leave Beau?— with nobody a-tall." Through the screen Lorelei could just make out Melissa's hands, clenched into fists at her sides. "Oh, in a better world maybe everybody'd be his people. I think that's what Jim was dreaming of. But not in our time, honey. And it won't come soon enough for my Beau."

"Don't you believe that, Melissa!" Susanna said. "If Jed and I aren't your friends, what are we? Davy Cavanaugh and Lorelei, too. All our hands up here. And John Sutter's been close to you all. The Danburys down in San Diego, Jenny Leverton and her Lydia— lots of folks you don't even think, because you're feeling low.

"And Beau? Beau's a strong boy, Melissa. He'll turn out all right. Any young man has to find himself, and some go by the stony road. You don't even know for sure he's joined those outlaws—"

"But *three years*, Susanna!" The words were almost a moan. "Three years and not a word. Not knowing is he hurt or lonely. Not knowing if he'll ever be coming home."

"When the war is over, Melissa," Susanna said. "When the war is over and Jim's back on the ranch, you'll find him. Jed and Davy'll help, and Beau'll be back. If he doesn't come back before."

Melissa shook her head. "I get a feeling of doom come on me, Susanna. And I've got nowhere to put it up. Jim hasn't been back in nine months. And Beau, three years now. And sometimes I'm feeling like there's some big dark shadow heading toward me, like a storm you know is coming. And I can just as like put my arms up to stop the thundercloud as break out from under it."

"Well, there'll be no doom on this visit, Melissa Attaby," Susanna said firmly. "There'll be riding—on Taylor nags. And picnics in the hills, and if we want to play at farming, we can help the boys cut wheat in a few days."

"Lord, no, child," Melissa laughed. "Not these old bones. Leave that to the young folk—them with broad backs and little minds."

Susanna was relieved to hear her laughing. *It's not natural being without our men,* she thought. *It makes us strange and worrisome.* Not that there wasn't plenty to worry over. There was more than enough without seeing omens and dire portents in the color of a sunset or the shape of a storm cloud coming. Her gaze shifted to the east where a black wall of ridges began the sharp ascent of the Sierras. Behind them, and reaching high above, the white peaks kept their everlasting winter, where few things lived and no trees ever grew.

As if she caught the vision through Susanna's eyes, Melissa remarked, "If God was a stonecutter, he'd have carved those mountains."

"Still wild country," Susanna said. "And the mountains never change. It's hard to believe there's a war going on, living up here with the mountains standing the way they've always stood. I don't know—maybe it's a false security—I just feel as though it's safe here, with the mountains keeping guard."

Inside the house, Lorelei was hugging herself with excitement. She'd found out Beau's secret. But she could go her mother and Mrs. Attaby one better.

She knew where Beau was.

Some three weeks ago she'd ridden out into the mountains to spend a few days at the trappers' cabin as she did every year at this time. Davy and her father had built it in the earliest years, before the ranch had begun paying its way. They spent most of the winters in those first years trapping beaver and otter and sold them in the port cities. "Cash on the paw," her dad would say.

The cabin was set in a clearing just beyond a deep clear mountain lake—Indian Lake they called it, though the Navajo and Chinooks that had sometime occupied the high sweeping forestland had long since been driven out. During the early part of the gold rush, prospectors had run over the land like locusts, spoiling the hunting all around. The last of the Indians had gone—some to the sleepier south, some to the far northern vastness of the continent.

The prospectors had found no gold. They moved on to other streams and other hills, and the animals had returned. The little cabin remained, its door unlocked, the hospitality of the wilderness extended to any fur trader or occasional prospector who happened by.

No one had used the cabin, and Lorelei had stowed her gear inside and set about the task of cleaning and oiling the traps. She and Davy still worked the line for a few weeks every winter, gathering pelts and hunting game for their own use in the cold mountain winters.

It was her favorite place—the grassy clearing carpeted in the summer with wildflowers, and in the winter with virgin snow. The land around was riddled with game trails, and Lorelei knew most of them, as well as the caves that sometimes housed the massive grizzly and the high eyries of the hawks and eagles.

She had been hiking through the forest, along last year's traplines and scouting for signs of fox and marten when she heard the shot, which echoed across the steep stone walls and frightened the chittering birds to silence. Carefully, clinging to the low-lying scrub,

Lorelei had climbed a steep, direct route to the summit of the ridge and peered across the edge.

Some forty feet below her perch, a man stood over a fallen deer. When he moved aside, Lorelei knew a shock of deep outrage. His kill was a young doe whose swollen udders marked two deaths for one. No responsible hunter would make such a kill. She did not make her presence known, but watched him for a time, bleeding and gutting the animal with a practiced hand and wrapping the chosen meat in a leather hide. He wore a large-brimmed sombrero which effectively hid his face, but once he pulled it off to wipe his brow, and Lorelei stared at him in amazement.

The hair on his head was pure white and sparse; the pink of his scalp showed through. She could make out the edges of a scraggly moustache drooping down on each side of his mouth. His skin appeared different than any person's she'd ever seen—it was so thin that the blood vessels were visible beneath it. And she knew only vaguely what he was—that is, until this afternoon when she had heard Melissa talking and the little bits of vague knowledge came together like a finished puzzle.

The man she saw was an albino, and there was only one such man known in all of California. His name was Whitey Loomis.

Lorelei had not followed him any distance, but she had seen him mount his horse and ride northeast up an ancient trail. Several miles farther, that trail led up to a strange series of interconnected caverns cut into the mountains. She had been there with Davy, only once some years before. The path was overgrown in parts and hard to follow. It was a long hike from the cabin. Game didn't use the trail because there was nothing to attract them, and the caverns were eerie, empty places. Bats lived in the inner chambers—she and Davy had startled several to flight. And, aside from a meager pile of very old bones that lay scattered in one cavern, or "room" of the stone city, there was nothing to excite interest.

Except that it was big enough to hide an army and so far out of the way that only chance could discover it.

And, unless she had calculated very wrong, if Beau were with Whitey Loomis, he was probably no more than thirty miles from the Taylor ranch.

Fleetingly it crossed her mind that she might tell Mrs. Attaby and her mother what she had seen. But the idea was quickly dismissed. People learned to keep their own counsel, growing up as she had. Perhaps the silent mountains taught them—those vast stone titans of primeval birth which endured but never spoke. And, of course, she didn't *know* that Beau was there. She might be mistaken about everything. It wouldn't do to grieve Mrs. Attaby with her speculations.

It would take more than a week to ride out to the caves and back, and the harvesting would take every hand available. They were short of help as it was. After the harvest, she decided, and before the snow. Davy was supposed to return for several weeks—they had his letter yesterday. Davy could be trusted. She would enlist his aid.

The women had stopped talking. They were coming into the house. Feeling a twinge of guilt at her deceit, Lorelei greeted them as though she had just now come downstairs.

"Ed was asking about your running Sandalwood today," Susanna told her daughter. "But if you ride now, be back in time for supper."

Lorelei nodded eagerly and raced upstairs for her boots. Her body felt cramped from the awkward stillness imposed by her spying activities. Sandalwood was a husky high-spirited colt, just brought in from the pasture that season. He'd take a lot of running.

Susanna watched her daughter from the kitchen window. Lorelei headed for the corral at a dead run, her single long braid flying out behind her, her booted feet kicking up dust and gravel. "My wild Indian maid," she told Melissa dryly.

"She's growing up some, isn't she?" Melissa said. "Growing up real pretty, too, with those long legs and bright eyes."

"She's growing up like a mustang though," Susanna said. "Headstrong and hot-tempered. I worry about her, especially with Jed gone. He can always get her to listen, but I can't seem to get a handle on her. She's not like me. Never has been. She rides and runs and trains those horses like any of the cowhands, and often as not, she's off in the mountains till past sunset. I've tried teaching her to sew, and she balks like an old mule. And cooking?—Oh, Lord, Elsa and I both gave up long ago. Sat down to one of her dinners . . ."

"Well, I wouldn't be worrying my head about that, honey," Melissa said. "She'll be cooking up a storm once she finds out there's somebody she wants to cook for."

"More likely she'll be out hunting the meat and leave her man to roast it."

"She starting with the boys yet?"

"Not yet, but it's coming. And she's only fourteen. She still runs with the hands like one of them, but the time's coming when they're going to start noticing she's not. And that's going to be one battle I'll leave to Jed.

"It always amazes me to see her so knowing of the ways of beasts and so ignorant of the ways of people. She knows when a colt's due for training and when the mare should be set to the stallion. But try and tell her a girl has to put up her hair and start wearing dresses, and she can't see a speck of reason in it! I've got to get Jed to talk to her when he comes back. Maybe he can make her understand."

"Any word when he's coming back?"

Susanna sighed and shook her head. "Young Tommy Colby brought word three months ago—he was one of the boys in the California battalion, the group Jed trained. Lost his right hand, so he's out of it. I think his folks are just glad to get him back.

"Anyway, Jed was alive and well when he left. The batallion had received a commendation from Grant directly—Tommy spent most of his visit talking about *that,* and Jed'll be back when he gets orders for new recruits, whenever that may be."

Melissa reached for her friend's hand in a sudden gesture of sympathy. Both of them were worried and uncertain. Both were just marking time until their men came home.

"Oh, Melissa, you're a gem," Susanna said gratefully. "It's such a relief just to say it—how worried I am. It seems so isolated now! I never felt it before— Jed was never away for so long.

"Sometimes I get so angry—angry at all of them. Half our hands signed up to go, the local boys—some of them too young to go, and lying about it. And we hear all the high talk about principle and honor, but it's more than that, Melissa. *They want to go!* Let them make speeches with high-sounding words, and rattle the drums, and haul up the flags, and they'll leave their folks and their home and their land and *run!"*

"I know," Melissa said, soberly. "Even if it's the devil they're running to."

"I can't say these things to anyone else," Susanna went on. Her voice trembled with distress. "Lorelei—" she smiled faintly. "Lorelei knows her daddy's invincible, so she doesn't worry. And, Lord knows, I'm grateful she's spared that—terrible uncertainty. But I can't tell myself no bullet made will down my man—I've seen him shot!

"Forgive me, Melissa. You know, I'm about to say, 'why don't you please stay awhile longer?' and I'm going to drive you away faster with this fretting and complaining."

"Oh, no, child," Melissa said soothingly. "I tell you, I've done more'n my share of trouble-wailing this trip, and you've been kindness itself. I'd dearly love to stay, at least long enough to see Davy. Haven't seen the scamp these last two years. But I've got to get back to the ranch. I don't have but two men I trust working the place, and I don't expect to see the old man before spring. Somebody's got to keep a proprietary eye—"

"Since when has your place needed that kind of watching?" Susanna asked suspiciously. "Come to think of it, I recall hearing some rumors about Santa Barbara some months back. I didn't think much of it. I heard it was a small party of rebel deserters raiding the farms for food and provisions. It didn't sound like anything the vigilantes couldn't control."

"Well, it's not exactly raiding in Los Angeles," Melissa said. "You know a lot of the hard-luck miners that drifted down our way were Southerners. They've been trying to organize"—she smiled wryly with a hint of malice in her eye—"they've been working toward a secession movement."

Susanna's eyes widened in astonishment, "Here in California?"

Melissa giggled. "Honey, you should see your face. Oh, yes. Here in California. Of course, most of the Californians couldn't care less. They figure the East should settle its own problems. Down in Los Angeles, a group come a-calling themselves the Knights of the Golden Circle and asked in the town for a list of influential families. Well, you met Sheriff Donleavy— loves a joke, he does. And he put the Attaby name at the top of the list without bothering to tell those good folks that Jim was away fighting for the Yankees and that his wife was"—she lowered her head and made a mock curtsy—"a lady of color.

"So the Knights of the Golden Circle paid Mrs. Attaby a formal call—only they didn't look like knights to me. Matter of fact, they minded me of the kind of people I'd just as soon forget. And so I told them real polite-like that if they didn't want to be picking buck-shot out of their eyeballs, they'd best secede off my property! And I had Mr. Attaby's big ole double-barreled shotgun snug in my hand when I said it."

Susanna clapped her hands, delighted. "Melissa At-taby, you are the rashest and pluckiest female I know. So, you drove the Confederacy from the Attaby lands, and you have to get back to guard against reprisals." Her voice became serious again. "Are they dangerous, Melissa?"

"Oh, I don't think so. There were ten men all told. The head man was a politician-type. They tend to get violent mostly with speechmaking. And the others—just sheep, Susanna. So dumb that if they stepped in a tin tub, they'd drown.

"I did leave Jacob Donleavy word before I left. I told him any rustling on Attaby property while I was away, there'd be a bounty on his hide."

"I guess I just feel like I ought to be home." She shrugged apologetically. "There's that unaccounted part of my household"—she referred to Beau—"you never know.

"But, before I go, I'm going to set work on a project I've got in mind." Her face brightened and she leaned toward Susanna with a conspirator's air. "I'm going to sew a fine dress for Lorelei Taylor."

The remaining week of Melissa's visit was rapidly consumed by the project of Lorelei's dress. Most sur-prising of all was Lorelei's own enthusiasm, once the fabric had been picked and the pattern approved. She suffered through the fittings with unaccustomed patience, and the household of women—Susanna, Melissa, and Elsa—fussed and pinned and basted like collective fairy godmothers dressing Cinderella for the ball.

"I can't get over it!" Susanna confided to her friend. "Melissa, you must have brought some magic with you. That girl hasn't held still so long since she was an infant sleeping in her crib."

She might have been less gratified to know the real source of her daughter's interest in a proper lady's wardrobe; that Lorelei's inspiration came from their visitors of a month before—the ones who hadn't stayed —the stylish city lady in the taffeta gown, and her beautiful dark-eyed son.

But day by day, the dress took shape in the soft mauve-colored silk that was their final choice. The glorious full skirt swirled down from a velvet cummerbund that wrapped caressingly around the slender waist and its hem was cut daringly at mid-calf. The neckline was square and cut lower than Susanna liked, but both Lorelei and Melissa gainsaid her. The bodice was embroidered with pale sprigs of pink flowers, as was the border at the hem and the edges of the broad romantic leg-of-mutton sleeves.

They used the left over velvet of the waist sash for hair ribbons, which they wove like garlands into two thick braids. They pinned the braids in a circle around her head where it formed a crown of black and purple.

Elsa stood in the kitchen doorway, and her mouth gaped in a big round O. Melissa touched the edges of the dress the way she would touch the earliest buds on her favorite tree. "My, oh, my," she murmured under her breath, "My, oh, my!"

And Susanna, who stood a few yards away, to catch the full effect, found her memory drawn back a long long way in time and space to when she was a young girl in a new green dress and her red-haired friend had watched the transformation.

Now her daughter's eyes—those blue eyes ringed with her own green like leaves against flower petals— were seeking hers, and the question was the very same.

"How do I look?" she asked breathlessly excited, young, vain, and self-conscious. And Susanna, hugging her daughter close, could make no better answer than Maidie had those many years before. "Like a princess," she said softly. "Like a princess in a fairy tale."

Discreetly, the women left the room, so that Lorelei could acquaint herself with the image in the mirror in privacy.

"I think you're going to have a belle on your hands, Mother Taylor," Melissa told her friend. "She'll be chasing boys away with a stick."

"Just so long as she doesn't beat them to death," Susanna joked wryly. "But doesn't she look like an angel! You were right about the color, Melissa. It just catches that dusky pink in her face. She's been getting sun riding in the hills."

"Wait till those cowpokes of yours catch sight of her. She'll swing their heads around a fair turn."

"There'll be square-dancing on Saturday night, for the harvesters," Susanna said thoughtfully. "Why don't you stay a few more days?"

"I've already stayed longer than I planned," Melissa answered. "No, honey, I've got to get on first thing tomorrow."

Susanna gave in. The house was growing dark. She moved to light some lanterns and the candles in the parlor.

"Getting dark already," Melissa observed. "We're in for a bad winter. Saw some wooly bears today. Hair thick as squirrel fur."

"What is a wooly bear?" Susanna asked ingenuously.

"Girl, you mean to tell me you folks pretending to

be farming and you don't know about wooly bears?"
Her face showed genuine surprise. "Well, you just
get us one of them lanterns and we'll see if we can't
scare up a few."

The night air was crisp and cool and the bright
half-moon streamed over the pastureland. Melissa found
the wooly bears—fat heavy furred little caterpillars—
moving sluggishly over the rich pasture grass that grew
up by the rail fence. From a near meadow, a stallion
neighed a brief shrill trumpet, and across the main
pasture, another answered with a long thundering roar.

"That's Ravenspur across the field," Susanna said.
"Let's walk this way and see old Brushfire."

The stallion was standing still and alert in the open
grassland. The edge of his coat caught the full glow of
the moonlight, setting it sharp and golden against the
night. His neck was arched and his ears pricked forward following the approach of the two women. Susanna whistled once, shrilly, the way Jed did, and the still
creature suddenly came to life. He pawed once at the
grass and shook his head, then trotted expectantly
toward the fence.

Susanna straightened his forelock and pulled play-
fully at his ears to make him nod his head. "Coup,
coup, my beauty," she murmured. He snuffled about her
face and neck and licked the salt taste from her fingers.

"Still looks good, doesn't he," Melissa said. "And
gentle as a lamb."

"Yes, he's aging gracefully, Brushfire is," Susanna
remarked. "Jed retired him from stud these last three
years," she smiled. "Said he'd worked hard enough
pleasing the ladies. Time to conserve energy for his
old age."

"Does he still run?"

"Oh, he's like a colt on frosty mornings, kicking up
his heels and chasing tumbleweeds across the grass. Not
like that Ravenspur." She shuddered slightly. "First

animal I ever disliked. But that horse is just plain mean
—as though he had some long-time grudge on everything that moves. He even tears at the mares—scarred
up Lorelei's Butterfly last year. Lorelei said she never
wanted another horse of hers bred to him, and I don't
blame her. Jed's been working on crossing his line with
one of Brushfire's fillies, but it takes time, and meanwhile Ravenspur's the most valuable stud we've got. But
he's a monster."

"Well, he's sure breeding fine," Melissa said judiciously. "Jim started training that little black filly we
got last year, and the boys are bringing her along while
he's away—she got the makings of a first-class runner."

Susanna gave Brushfire a final pat and remarked, "As
long as she doesn't inherit his temper." She drew her
sweater closer around her. "It's getting chilly," she
said suddenly. "Shall we go inside?"

Upstairs in the bedroom, still clad in the marvelous
dress, Lorelei carefully drew the curtains shut and returned to the seldom-used cheval glass for a final viewing. The image that stared back at her was thoughtful
now—why did the dress make such a difference?

As though to find an answer, she began undoing the
fastenings—the cummerbund first and then the row
of little buttons on the back. Released from her shoulders, the dress fell to her feet, leaving the starched
white petticoats and lace-trimmed chemise. These too
she removed. Then the long-legged pantalets with their
little satin panels.

Now she was naked, but the mystery remained. Impatiently her fingers tugged at the hair ribbons and
released the braids, so that her hair fell in one great
mass about her face. *She didn't look the same.* Or was
it simply that she didn't look often. Usually not more
than to assure herself that her face was clean. Her
young breasts lifted from her chest like muffins newly
risen—white, so white against her tan—and tender as

new things are. She brushed her hands across them and the nipples tightened perceptively, sending out little prickles of excitement. Her hands moved down over her flat belly and the gentle rise of the mount with its dark beginnings of hair. Her legs were long and straight, but they were losing their coltish lankiness.

Feeling strangely unsettled, she paced the length of her room, back and forth, returning always to that naked female in the mirror, pausing to look, to frown and chew her knuckles. She realized that the dress was daring—but not daring like putting a horse to a fence or climbing the face of a mountain. The dress displayed the body—invited attention. *Dared attention.* And Lorelei was perplexed. She didn't want the dress to bring irrevocable changes. She thought she might just try it on. She could show it to her father. Or Davy, perhaps.

She shook her head, seeking to refute what her nakedness had taught her, trying to blame the rosy purple silk, the stiff-skirted flounces and ribboned hair.

But standing once again before her image, unadorned, unquestionably female, she faced the root of the matter. "It isn't the dress. *It's me!*"

Melissa left as planned early the next morning, and for the next week there was little time to dwell on frills and ribbons. Susanna canned and pickled and stored the garden crops and the fruit. Lorelei helped bring in the small herd of cattle for the marking and branding of late calves. The pigs marked for slaughter were butchered and hung, and the harvesters' children sat crosslegged in noisy circles shucking peas and corn. They burned the husks in the evening, building large bonfires, and the Taylor women brought out foaming mugs of ale for the men and lemonade for the children.

The first Saturday harvest dance came, but Lorelei made no move to put on her new dress for the occasion. To be sure, she danced with the harvesters and cowboys, and she was pretty in spite of herself, with her blue-green eyes glittering and her face flushed rosy from the rapid spins and turns. Susanna wisely did not press the issue. She watched her daughter with a little secret smile. There was a change, and she wondered if she was the only one to see it—something subtle in the carriage, the slightest undulation of the hips, the walk a trifle slower than before. The dress would come in its own good time, she thought. It was already on its way. Because Lorelei was walking and sitting and dancing in her old blue jeans and denim skirt just as though she were wearing a ballroom gown.

The second week began the big field labor—harvesting the grain. Between the broads row that Ed Crandall cut with a team of horses, men worked with scythes, downing the tall golden grain with great sweeps of the blades—*swish, swish,* and the wheat bowed down. *Swish,* then the rows of barley. The crop was not large compared with the grain fields of the Midwest, but it fed their stock through the heavy winter, and it was the single most important object of the harvest. It had to be taken in quickly because of the hailstorms that could destroy the entire field in a single day.

Susanna kept a constant vigil over the sky and clouds and sun. So far it looked like a perfect harvest.

Wagons and riders had been coming and going all day, so little notice was taken when another Taylor mount turned into the yard and its rider dismounted. Only Elsa, guarding her row of fresh-baked pies from grasping little fingers, saw who it was and gave a little cry.

"Shhhhh!" Davy put his fingers to his lips. "Where are the ladies?"

Elsa grinned and pointed toward the grain fields. Davy nodded and started over, taking a deep breath of the clean mountain air as he walked. It was good to be back, even for a little while.

He saw Susanna first and managed to stay concealed until he could reach her from behind and cover her eyes with his big hands.

She tugged at his hands and spun around. "Davy!" She hugged him tight. "Just when I've been thinking I've been deserted for the harvest, and I'm settling into my weather-worrying—oh, but it's good to see you. Glad you're home, Davy."

She turned brightly and called to her daughter. "Lorelei, Davy's home," and the girl came loping toward them to find herself also embraced in the general family reunion. Only Susanna sensed Lorelei's momentary reticence—the new female consciousness inhibiting the usual bear hugs and unabashed effusive kisses. Davy plowed right over the reserves and swept Lorelei into the standard greeting until she was giggling and struggling to escape.

"Let me go, you ape!" she squealed. He was holding her fast with one negligent arm and grinning innocently. "I've caught a young piglet. Listen to it squeal!"

His look altered to one of mock severity. "Have you been behaving yourself?" he asked in his schoolmaster voice. He was egging her on. "Have you been a *good little girl*, or do I have to tan your bottom like I did when you were seven?"

At that she planted a well-aimed kick to his knee. He dropped his arm. She scrambled out of reach and put her thumb to her nose, waving the other fingers derisively. Then, just as suddenly, she stopped and glared at him. *He's treating me like a child*, she thought angrily. *And I'm acting like one.* Mustering her injured dignity, she straightened her clothing, and with vague excuses about work at hand, stalked off toward the fields.

"Well, what's gotten into her?" Dave asked, amused.

"Growing pains," Susanna answered, smiling briefly. Davy shrugged.

That evening at supper, Lorelei put on the mauve silk dress, This time, Davy did not shrug. He gulped as though the roast beef which he was in the process of swallowing had suddenly grown thorns. Susanna affected not to notice anything out of the ordinary. Lorelei was trying hard to do the same. But there was a suspended silence in the air—a waiting for his reaction.

If Davy felt it, he gave no sign. He swallowed the roast beef, turned his eyes back to the table, and when Lorelei was seated, asked her to pass the mashed potatoes.

For a short time, Lorelei endured it. But well before dessert, she had lost all pretensions of casual femininity. She clattered her fork over the empty plate, and, catching his upraised eyes, she demanded sharply, "Well, what do you think of it?"

His brown eyes crinkled at the corners. He waved with his fork, pausing between mouthfuls of corn, and answered. "The dress? It's pretty." He returned to his dinner.

"Is that all you can say—or mumble?" Lorelei asked tartly.

Davy retained his good nature unperturbed. "Ask me when I'm not so hungry."

Now Lorelei stood up, infuriated, hands on her hips, all traces of the coy sophisticate blown to the winds. "I'll do that, Davy Cavanaugh—sometime when you're not too hungry!" She stomped away from the table.

"Lore—?"

She stopped and turned. "What is it?" she said curtly.

He looked her over lazily, from the dress and dainty ankles to the ribbon in her hair. "It appears to me you've got some growing up to do before that dress fits you proper."

The slipper that she threw with deadly purpose he caught in his hand, and she refused him the satisfaction of a second failed attempt. Muttering vague warnings of dire retribution, she made her way upstairs, stumbling slightly.

Now Davy turned to Susanna. "Since when is Lorelei wearing dresses like that?" he asked, a slight frown crossing his face.

"Since now," Susanna answered calmly. "It's her own choice."

"Well, she's too young to be choosing like that. It makes her look"—his voice hesitated—"it makes her look—older than she is. She's a child. She's what?—thirteen?"

"She's almost fifteen," Susanna corrected gently, watching Davy's discomfiture with a certain glee. *So, Lorelei's new dress has not been without effect.*

She leaned over the table to slice Elsa's blackberry pie. "Dessert, Davy?" she offered.

"Later, thanks," he said. "I think I'll take a walk outside."

The night wind was whistling down the mountains, tunneling through the stone passages and out into the valley with drawn-out sighs and high-pitched wailing. Davy breathed deeply and listened. The Indians believed that spirits spoke in the wind and said wise things. Sometimes, when he listened, he would, without hearing words, feel a kind of peace settling over him— not an empty easiness, but a profound affirmation that was his own silent answer to the wind. The forests and mountains were right; the Indians were right. And the taste of the air was sweet.

But tonight the feeling eluded him. Tonight he wasn't thinking of the mountains or the forest, but of the way, when he had first hugged Lorelei today, her breasts had pressed against his jacket—he could feel where the roundness formed and peaked. And it disturbed him because it was *Lorelei*—it was Susanna's daughter. He swore softly to himself. *He had bottle-fed the little imp!*

He rounded the corral where the workhorses were kept ready for the morning. His thoughts were becoming more rational now. It was easy to see the pattern of things. *I've been gone almost a year,* he told himself. *Of course things are changing.* Pretty soon there'd be pimply-faced boys running all over the ranch like a swarm of bees smelling honey. He just wasn't used to the idea.

The way she'd looked in that dress—Lorelei! Lorelei the disheveled tomboy, the leggy hoyden with her braid always coming undone, looking like—he frowned again —looking like she wasn't a child at all.

The dress did not appear again at supper, and after half a day of holding herself aloof, Lorelei was over her annoyance and acting as she always had.

For a week the days were all usurped by labor, but they were golden days, bright with sunshine glowing on the grain. The men worked stripped to the waist, for the labor kept them warm and the sun nourished them. The women walked bent slightly forward, their aprons heavy with apples or corn.

The last harvest dance went on well into the night, with Ed Crandall as caller and Martin Jaeger on the fiddle. Davy pulled out his mouth organ, wedged it between his lips like a set of buck teeth, and accompanied them to "Wait for the Wagon" and "Darling Nellie Gray." Gay dancing songs were all they played. Susanna had insisted, and Davy agreed. He had heard enough of war songs—war hymns and war marches—and they weren't songs to dance to. They weren't songs of the harvest—unless you counted death as the reaper.

That was what he wanted to forget. He'd walked out of the field at Gettysburg, with the ground littered with bodies, and he heard the sickening *squish* of blood against his boots. And the hideous death rattles sounding like a chorus of snakes, and the cries of pain that made death a mercy.

There is no war here, he thought, and he smiled and jigged and swung his partners, fiercely glad to be dancing instead of marching. Glad to be cutting down wheat instead of men.

The next day only the rooster rose at dawn. Everyone was on holiday, and a good part of it was spent sleeping off the late-night residue of the night before. Davy woke about noon, drowsy from dreams of soft bosoms and flower petals merging strangely with the sound of a woodpecker hard at work. He rolled over and realized that the woodpecker was knocking at the bedroom door and calling his name.

"Davy, wake up, you lazy oaf!" It was Lorelei.

"What d'ya want?" he mumbled through the door.

"We're going to the cabin today. And if we don't get started soon, we won't make it before dark!"

Still half-asleep, Davy reached for his clothes. "Do I smell coffee?" he asked hopefully.

"A full pot."

They rode single file on the lower trail, where the late-summer undergrowth narrowed the open space. Along the higher ground, the trees were already bare except for the pines and spruces which never shed their coats. The wind swept through the dense needles and glanced off the naked wood whispering thoughts of snow. But the gusts had quieted by late afternoon, and the cabin and lake, sheltered all around by the higher hills, glowed in the gold light of Indian summer.

Lorelei threw off her shoes, rolled up her pant legs, and danced along the water's edge. "I think it's warm enough for a swim," she called. Davy was inside the cabin.

He came out a few moments later in an old pair of jeans, but Lorelei had disappeared. Calling her name, he trotted down the grassy beach and waded into the shallow water just before a steep drop in the sandy bottom.

He missed the billow of water that warned of a girl-sized predator below. It was easy to knock him backward from his risky balance on the lake's bottom. By the time he sputtered to the surface, she was yards away, giggling like a hysterical chipmunk. He went after her.

She crossed fifty yards, just out of reach, then turned and rolled under him. He grabbed for her ankle and missed, and the race was on again.

Around them, tall hemlocks guarding the western bank sent long, dark reflections into the lake. The gold light had turned to orange and was dying. The twilight hush was starting in the woodland, but the watery chase went on and a few fish broke water and splashed through applauding.

Davy caught her in the shallow water. She was trying the same trick, but she misjudged the depth. He was ready for her. He had a handful of streaming black hair and one arm hard in his grasp, and he dunked her a little for good measure before pulling her up beside him. It had grown quite dark and the moon had not yet risen. The full, wet length of her was against him before he realized she was naked.

Her nipples tightened from the chill clear depths, and her breasts were like ice against his chest. The rise and fall of their breathing drew their bodies closer and then apart. The night was silent; there was nothing but the pine boughs and the lake. Davy could feel her thighs with the dampness of the swim clinging to them. She wasn't Lorelei, Susanna's little girl. She was some naiad risen from the lake with her hair like weaving streams of water grass. Beneath the cool of the lake, her flesh was warm.

His hands discovered her. His fingers traced the outline of her lips and parted them gently from the corners. And he tasted the upper and the lower and he searched out the warmth of her mouth until it grew slack and moist against his own. He felt his own demanding flesh strain against the denim while his hands chafed lightly along her back, up and down. The kissing went on and Davy wanted more—suddenly wanted much more than kisses.

Little waves were lapping at their ankles and a keen brisk wind was starting up. Deprived of the sun, the air was cooling rapidly, and Davy was thinking about the cabin. About the warm shelter of the cabin and Lorelei.

"Lore!" She clung to him, half-swooning. He began to shake her. She was warm. Her face was thrown back to reveal the lovely line of her jaw, her neck. Her eyes were closed. The water from the lake had formed into little beads on her face, like misplaced tears.

"Lore!" *He couldn't do this.* He pulled her hands from around his neck and pushed her away, so that she stumbled back a step toward the shore.

He pointed to the cabin and waved her up, but he refused to meet her eyes, which were bewildered and accusing. "Get some clothes on!" he said hoarsely, and the effort of speaking grated against his throat. His words sounded ugly and harsh in his own ears. *Lorelei.*

She was half-kneeling at the very edge of the lake, staring out at him steadily. Her eyes were shadowed as dark as dark as the hemlock bark. There was bitterness, and, in the depths of those eyes, shame.

But when she stood, there was no embarrassment in the strong, beautiful lines of her body. The full moon had risen behind a bank of clouds with a pale yellow light. She stood poised with the frozen stillness of an animal just before it runs. Then she turned and vanished up the slope to the cabin.

Davy followed some ten minutes later. By then he was shivering from the nippy air on his wet skin. Lorelei was dressed. She had banked the fire and now crouched beside the hearth. Davy pulled out a change of clothes, some linen, and a bedroll.

A grim silence hung between them. Davy shuffled uncomfortably in the doorway. "I think we'd better head back tomorrow," he said at last. "At least I will."

His hand was on the latch. Now he opened the door. "Where are you going?" she asked.

His tanned, good-natured face was set and stony. "I'll sleep outside," he said.

He stayed outside only part of the night before the freakish weather drove him in. Some hours before dawn, a light snow fell and woke him from his fitful sleep. He shook his bedroll and quietly opened the cabin door. Lighting no lanterns, he moved stealthily across the floor to the second cot and gratefully sank down. Lorelei did not stir. She was sleeping, or pretending to.

At least the snow gave them an excuse for their early return to the ranch. They had not taken hard-weather supplies—ski parkas and heavy mittens, axes, snowshoes—and it was dangerous not to be prepared. Besides, Davy had suddenly recalled another soldier on leave, one whom he had promised to visit. And Lorelei was anxious to try Sandalwood on the flat track before the heavy snows.

And Susanna, looking from one averted face to the other, knew there was less than a scrap of truth in all that they said. But she knew she would learn no more by asking, and she saved herself the effort.

If anything really wrong had happened, Davy would have told me.

Lorelei was very busy that day, working Sandalwood on the training track. So busy she didn't even notice Davy setting his gear at the back of his saddle. His big sorrel gelding was already past the gate and cantering toward the road when she did see him. Sandlewood half-reared—her hands tightened suddenly on the reins, and she brought him down. She sat her mount quietly watching until there was nothing more to see. The snow had melted from the night before. The track was clear and fast. She suddenly remembered that she hadn't told Davy about Beau and Whitey Loomis—and that the way up the old trail was too treacherous in the snow season. It would wait till spring. It would wait.

She backed the rangy colt to the starting post and held him, feeling his muscles coiled for the spring. She crouched over his neck, set her weight in her legs, and turned to Ed Crandall, who leaned against the rail. Her voice snapped out in the cold air and she braced herself like her mount preparing to run it to oblivion—the fever, the anger, the waiting.

"Clock him!" she said. And they were off.

3

DAVY KEPT DUE south on the winding mid-valley road. The way was deeply rutted where the land had flooded, and in other places little more than a path. Ten years ago this same road had carried thousands of prospectors like a surging army over the hills where they scattered like rice at a wedding.

Then the vein had petered out, and the gold-seekers had gone with it. Towns that had begun with the influx of men and big money—towns that had boasted grand hotels and fancy stores—were ghost towns. There were a hundred such along this route. And others like Darleytown, Amberville, Canton, that were reduced to a minuscule population eking out a living in the hills and growing their own produce in patchy gardens.

Davy's regiment was due to re-form in San Jose for the trip back east. But that was two weeks away. And the last thing to die in a dying town is the saloon.

He toured the ruin of the Golden Eagle in Darleytown, got drunk in Amberville, and spent the night on the barroom floor. In Canton at the Café D'Oro, he picked a fight and was escorted from the premises. He had a five-day growth of beard and he was chewing his own moustache when he skirted around Sacramento. Now he was closer to San Jose. Closer to the war.

Davy woke up cold sober next to a slightly overdone lady of the town named Tillie, whose scent, called Perfume of a Thousand Bayonets, did not serve to adequately cover the odor of her unwashed flesh—the swimming breasts and soft, fat thighs that wiggled lewdly beneath her negligee.

He made gallant apologies for her trouble, got a drink, and made his way outside into the startling midday sunshine.

He found the public baths and soaked for an hour in a real bathtub with porcelain glazing and great clawed feet. For two dollars, a barber scraped off a week's worth of whiskers and trimmed his moustache. He found a barge to take him and his horse across the bay to San Jose, and he told himself he'd been on a proper drunk. That was what he'd wanted—not to go back to the ranch and not to go back to his regiment. A spree to wash the war out of his stomach. To wash out Lorelei, who had changed too fast, slyly, while he was away.

Then on his last night in San Jose, he saw the girl.

She was standing outside the cantina—a young girl, dark-skinned, barefoot, standing rather stiffly against the wall. And Davy knew there were only two reasons for her to be there. Either she was waiting for her father, who was inside the cantina drinking, or she was plying her youth in the most ancient trade of women outside the shelter of the saloon. She was too young to be allowed inside.

He passed by her twice. Still he could not guess. It could be settled in a single question, and it was: she was not waiting for her father.

He took her to his hotel and unplaited her hair which was bound in two neat braids and tied with strips of white linen. He was glad that she was not fair, and that her eyes were brown and unconfusing, straightforward and knowing—not like those other eyes. She was young, but not innocent, and there was nothing he would do to her that had not been done before. That thought eased his conscience even while the nubile body, brown as a berry and smooth, almost hairless, cradled his lust.

It was dawn before he'd finished with her, and he gave her twice her modest fee. She had eased him, and he was grateful. He had a handle on himself; he would not be spinning off in confusion again because some little girl was growing up.

Winter took early hold of the Northwest that year, and Jed Taylor did not return. Grant was holding an army 100,000 strong in the northern hills of Virginia, and he wanted every man. Susanna and Lorelei did get a note around Christmas—apologetic but confident and full of high spirits. Surely in the spring, it said. By late spring the war would be over.

He came back in the early spring, when the fields were still drenched from the melted snow, and only the sturdy crocuses were in bloom. The war was not over.

He had sent no notice of his coming. Susanna had been tending the ground by Benji's grave when she heard footsteps in the still, frosty grass and turned. Then she was flying over the distance that was all that stood between them. She felt his coat, his arms, his face. He wrapped them both inside his long blue cloak. Unaccountably, tears were streaming down her face and she was holding him tightly. "It's been so long— why didn't you let me know?" she cried against his ear. "So long, So long."

He wrapped her tighter and closer against him. They stayed that way for a long time, until the time apart had slipped away from them and the time together could begin. Arm in arm they went back to the house.

Lorelei came running in all breathless, calling, and

laughing. He caught her at a full run and lifted her off the ground, spinning her before he set her down.

"Break out some brandy," he told his daughter. She hurried off and returned with a dusty bottle and a tray with glasses. She eyed him questioningly and he nodded, pouring three glasses.

"I came back with Jim Attaby," he began quietly.

The tone of his voice warned Susanna. "Is he—all right?" she asked.

He nodded.

"Beau?"

He shook his head. There was no easy way to say it. "Melissa's dead, Susanna."

Her face went deathly pale. It was several moments before she could say anything at all. "But how? How could it happen, Jed? She visited just last summer— she seemed fine. What happened?"

Her husband's face was lined and grim. "Their house was fired. She was inside. I—I don't know much more. It happened ten days ago. They buried her before Jim could get back—they had to. You know how warm it is down there . . ."

Susanna scarcely heard. She had a picture of Melissa in her mind—Melissa sitting out on the porch and talking about a big dark shadow. What had she said?— *like a storm. Like a storm you know is coming.*

And it was true. That was the horror of the memory —that it was true.

Lorelei was remembering, too—the overheard discussion. When she had been trying to learn the truth about Beau.

If what she suspected was true, Beau might not even be aware of the tragedy. It was on the tip of her tongue to ask, but Susanna did it for her.

"Any news of the boy?" she asked.

Jed shook his head. "Nobody would know where to look or send word. He's an outlaw."

Susanna looked quickly to Lorelei and then to Jed. "It's no secret, Susanna. His picture is on wanted posters in every town big enough to have a post office." He glanced at his daughter, who did not seem surprised.

"I knew," she said quietly, but she didn't say how. And no one at that moment thought to question.

"I invited Jim to stay up here awhile. He was— pretty broken up." That was putting it delicately; devastated was more accurate.

"Of course he's welcome," Susanna said.

"He—didn't think he should come right away. He hasn't decided about the ranch." *And he didn't want to impose his grief.* Stiff-necked, honorable Jim. The sounds that came from his hotel room that last night. Jim Attaby, gentleman and soldier. Weeping.

Damn the war. Damn the war!

"Jed, don't go back!"

Susanna was sitting on the bed. She was half-wrapped in the cotton sheet in a state of charming disarray. Jed could see her reflected in the mirror that stood above the oaken dresser.

"I've got two weeks, sweetheart," he said patiently. "I'm picking up the new regiment in San Francisco. Colonel Halston is meeting me."

He saw her face crumple like a child's, and she buried her head in the sheet.

"Susanna!" He drew her close to him and laid soft kisses on her brow, her eyes, her wet cheeks. "What is it, Susanna? Tell me."

But she could not tell him. Could not say that she had bad dreams, that she felt Melissa's doom passed on to her, felt it closing in around her. Could not explain the terror, now that he was here, for when he would leave her again. *Damn the war!*

And the secret she held from him—of the visitors

who had not stayed, the boy who was his son. Was she a monster to deprive him? And yet she could not speak it.

They peopled her dreams that night in a cruel, bizarre circus. Melissa stood off to one side and shook her head, back and forth, like a broken doll. The boy was there, pointing his finger, accusing her. And the other woman, dressed in her gold-colored gown, who lifted a glass of sherry and shattered it in her hand so the blood ran down her fingers with the spilled wine. A tall, thin man with yellow eyes entered from a hidden door and he leered at her. He passed to Louisa Hutchison and took from her the shattered splinters of glass and caught the wine and blood in his hands and came toward Susanna. He held his offering before him and he laughed and laughed and Susanna began to scream —it was Shuttleworth coming to destroy her. She looked for Jed, but he wasn't there . . .

"Susanna!" He *was* there, right beside her, holding her, soothing her again until she'd quieted, until she slept again. He was reminded of the days and weeks after Benji died. The tears, the near-hysteria. "It's all right," he whispered soothingly. But he wasn't sure.

He rode over the ranch the next morning, and Lorelei, mounted on Sandalwood, rode with him. Susanna watched them both from the parlor window. Father and daughter, so alike, both sitting tall and easy on their mounts, their dark heads matched in color. Even their horses loping stride for stride.

But no son.

Susanna turned away from the window. She had flowers to sow on Benji's little plot—early marigolds for sunshine, and sweet-scented hyacinth, snapdragons, single-flowered trillium. It was still early for planting, but she worked as though driven, digging in cold wet earth.

Jed and Lorelei had dismounted to walk through the

small herd of brood mares. They looked sleek and plump and placid. Butterfly was there, and a sturdy handsome black colt trotted confidently beside her.

A grin started on Jed's lean face and spread until he was beaming. "That may be our boy!" He said excitedly. "You were holding out on me!" he accused his daughter.

She laughed, delighted with his pleasure. "I wanted you to see." She looked back over to her horses. The colt was chasing the silk of its tail, spinning on long matchstick legs. "He's a strong little devil, too. I've seen him run."

Jed was looking him over with an expert eye. "Ravenspur's breeding true color. The seventh black—"

"He ought to be good for something, that black-hearted cur," Lorelei said feelingly. "I'm glad we got the colt this time. I wouldn't have put Butterfly to him again.

"He's a savage, all right," Jed said easily, "but what a magnificent monster he is. He tried to kill me after he threw me off—just turned around and came back on me like a mad black bull. But he was most charged piece of horseflesh I've ever had between my legs. And his blood running with Brushfire"—his eyes glowed looking toward the little black foal—"we'll have ourselves a horse that'll outrun his own shadow."

Lorelei smiled at her father's enthusiasm and commented dryly, "Let's wait till he gets off his mother's milk before we run him in too many races.

"Do you remember that last race, Lory-girl?" he said suddenly. "When we won that big black devil?"

She nodded. It was the last grand festa any of them had attended. The last great fair before the war.

There were banners streaming for miles along the fairgrounds, and the biggest crowd to descend on Los Angeles in a decade. Horsemen came from the East and Mexico and from Canada. Old Sawtooth, Harley

Griffith, was there, chewing on a fat cigar and ogling the young women the way he did every year. He'd made one of the richest strikes in California—when the streams had been giving up nuggets like rockbed pebbles —But he'd never won with horses, and Jed Taylor was a long-time thorn of jealousy in his side.

Jed was running for the purse, and the pressure was on. The winter had been unusually bad that year, beginning with a gut-ripping nor'easter that had cost him several head of stock—more than he could afford. For the first time in years, he'd had to buy grain to see him through, and it was purchased with borrowed money. The purse wouldn't clear all debts, but it would hold the creditors at bay. Brushfire had won the race the past four years. He was getting old, but he was still the strongest runner in the lot. He'd beaten two of his own colts the year before.

"I got me a range horse this year," Griffith was saying, stroking on his whiskers. "From Australia." He glance slyly at Jed. "You up for a wager, Taylor?"

I heard you got yourself a locomotive down there, Harley," Jed replied grinning. A bet with Griffith was just about sure money. "Let's see him." It took two men to bring the stallion to the paddock with the great horse fighting every bit of the way—a huge deep-chested beast with a back like iron and a muzzle that could fit inside a teacup. "Where did that come from?" Jed asked in disbelief.

Griffith beamed all over himself and almost bit through his cigar. "A breeder down there lost track of him out in open pasture. The dam came in bloody, and they figured the colt probably dropped somewheres. Then, about three years later, come this thieving stud leading off his mares. They rounded him up, did a real quick breaking, and I bought him first time I laid eyes on him."

Overbred. That was his only fault. His legs just a

mite thin, bred down to the bone. But heavy muscles in his haunches for a lightning start. Overbred. Brushfire's legs were stronger. In his prime, Brushfire could stand to a horse like that, but Brushfire was an old man. This race, win or lose, was his last.

A nervous beast. He pawed up the turf and Jed saw the whites of his eyes roll back at his handlers. But he could outrun Brushfire. An angry horse. Manhater by his looks.

"Who're you putting up on him?" Jed asked casually.

"My man, Appleton," Griffith said.

That was the wager then. Appleton was a good man; he tried hard for his boss. But could Appleton bring that horse past a grandstand of screaming spectators?

"What'll tempt you to put him up?" Jed asked brusquely. Just looking at the stallion made him see a line of horses—this black fire-horse and his gold mares—a string of perfect racers.

"Well, now," Griffith began, "You've got so many things to tempt me." He puffed deeply on his cigar. His voice became insidious, wheedling. "You got yourself a real pretty wife."

Such wagers sometimes occurred—usually the objects were fair ladies of the town, or, occasionally, mistresses. Jed was wearing his six-gun—it was necessary at the fair—and the palm of his hand now rested casually on its butt. "You'd best be careful of your joking, Harley," he drawled, smiling affably all the while. "Somebody might think you were serious. *Somebody might shoot you thinking you were serious.*"

Griffith wore a gun, too. For show. He took a half-step back and kept a smile pasted on his face, thinking all the while how he hated this man. "Don't mean nothing, Jed," he said placatingly. "You know I like to job yer balls now and again.

"Put Brushfire and a thousand," he offered equitably, "I'm not a man to say no to a wager."

"Brushfire and a thousand!" Jed choked. "You're still joking. Granted he's pretty, but where's his record? *How many races has he won, Harley? How many times have you run him?*"

Griffith shrugged, "Brushfire's getting old, Jed. This here Ravenspur's a four-year-old. Ten years of racing in him. How much longer can Brushfire run?"

He had struck home. He knew it. He switched to another maneuver.

"Now, I'm not downing your horse none. But let's sweeten the pot. I'll put up cash, Taylor, and we'll call the horses even plus the hard stuff. What do you say to ten thousand?"

"I keep horses, Griffith," Jed answered coldly. "Not money."

"I'll make it twenty, Taylor. *Put up your ranch.*"

Jed had never told a soul what had been riding on that race. Not Susanna. Not even Davy.

It was a long race. Almost two miles. And, all the way, it was Ravenspur and Brushfire, Brushfire and Ravenspur, as though they were the only two horses in the race. Brushfire had been behind the black at the rail when he went over and the women were all screaming at the sound of splintering wood. He laid right through the fence and Jake Appleton broke his back. Brushfire had almost gone down. The black had gone stark mad, it looked like—over the fence and into the field. And Brushfire had come in alone, but running hard just the same—running his heart out just as though the black monster had been at his heels.

It was the celebration that Lorelei remembered. "You got drunk as a lord after that race," she reminded her father. "You turned your hat upside-down and filled it with champagne, tried to get Brushfire to drink it."

"And you had your first champagne that night,"

Jed retorted. "Threw up your dinner and we put you to bed."

"I was a kid then."

"Yup," Jed agreed. "All legs and pigtails." He felt a flood of warmth and pride as he looked at this almost-woman, his daughter. Her remarkable sea-colored eyes were sharp and keen. The coltishness that he recalled was gone, and her body had filled out in that wonderful female way. She was confident and strong, and she was growing even more beautiful. "Your mother and I must have been good stock," he told her softly. She looked at him questioningly.

He turned her by the shoulders to face him and his eyes smiled down into hers. "We've bred a champion," he said. She basked in his praise, and, side by side, they paced back over the pastureland to where their horses were tethered by the rails.

"Any trouble while I was away?" Jed asked, trying to make the question sound casual, indifferent.

"No more than usual," she answered slowly. "We lost a couple of calves over the winter, but the rest came along fine. Horses are fat—"

He had to be more direct. "Lorelei, did anything happen to upset your mother?"

"No, nothing!" she said, surprised. "Leastways not that I—" She frowned. There *was* something. "She acted a little funny over the—grave, you know. She cleared the snow off—kept it clear all winter, and we must have had six feet all told. I tried to talk her out of it, but she insisted. That's the only thing . . .

"We've both been missing you. That's the main part. Davy came back, but he only stayed till the end of the harvest." She spoke the last in a rush, not wanting to dwell on Davy's hurried departure.

"Your mother hurt more than any of us, losing Benji," he said, almost to himself. "Well, I'll speak with her later."

He returned to the house early while Lorelei was working a yearling. He was not surprised to find Susanna out in back, stooped over that small muddy and singular rise of the earth. He plucked the trowel from her hand and brushed dirt from her fingers. "It's too early for gardening, Susanna," he said quietly. "Come inside."

She held back a little, like a child caught in mischief, but he took her upstairs into their bedroom and carefully closed the door. The silence weighed between them. Silence and the little patch of ground with its stone marker.

"This has to stop, Susanna," he said tensely. "This wallowing in yesterday." She bent her head, saying nothing, and he remembered the agony of those early days of mourning. Her silences that he could not break through. The fear that he could not reach her.

He pulled her over to the window. He was rough, desperate, angry, determined. He pointed toward the track and beyond to the pastures. "What do you see out there?" he demanded. "Tell me what you see."

Her voice came hesitantly, rasping over her dry throat. "The horses," she said, "and cattle. Lorelei on the track with the chestnut filly."

He spun her around to face him. *"Living things,* Susanna." Her eyes were glazed with tears, but he was beyond kindness. He shook her until he felt her fighting back, felt her focused and aware. "Living things," he repeated. "We have cows calving and new horses. We have a daughter, woman—a *living* daughter. *Benji is dead."*

She began crying softly, but to Jed it was a welcome sound following the deathly silence. Like a fresh rain falling. Healing tears. He sat her on the bed and stroked the golden curls back from her forehead. "Benji's death was a sad thing, a tragic thing. For all of us. But I won't

have you bury your heart with the dead, Susanna.
You're alive! Do you understand?"

She nodded mutely, her green eyes wide and glowing
softly, wonderingly. He rose from her side and closed
the curtains at the window, then in the semidark he
pulled free the ribbons at her waist.

She issued the mildest of protests and he stopped her
mouth with a kiss, which continued while his hands
played among her garments and beneath. "Your wedding vows, madam," he whispered against her ear.
"Your duty." He lay her back among the cushions.
"And your husband, my pet, is very much alive."

Lorelei postponed her mission to seek Beau Attaby
in the hills until after her father had left the ranch. They
had waited so long for him to come home that she
couldn't bear to miss the little time there was. Things
were so much brighter since he had returned. Her
mother was warm and happy again, reaching like a
flower to sunshine. The early rains and melted snow
had soaked freshened the earth. The only bad part was
watching him ride out again.

Already the men were breaking the ground with
plows, but they wouldn't need her for that. The first
green shoots would be up by the time she returned.

She scouted the overlying hills and arroyos that lay
about the caves, and for two days she lit no fires. She
knew there were men about. Two she had seen, leading
their horses up the steep and treacherous entrance to
the multi-caverned rise. But they posted no lookouts.
Evidently they considered their fortress well disguised.

No sign of Beau. But Lorelei did not consider making
herself known—not with the memory of Whitey Loomis
standing over the fallen doe still fresh in her mind.

On the afternoon of the third day, her hunter's patience was rewarded. Three horses struck their echoing
hoofbeats up the ancient trail and emerged five paces

from where she crouched in a blind of thick-leaved brush. Her heart hammered against her ribs as she recognized the first of the riders—the wide-brimmed hat was dusty and the hands that had bloodied the doe wore gloves, but it was unmistakably Whitey Loomis.

The second rider appeared a moment later. It was Beau.

She waited until all three had passed her by a hundred yards. Then, cupping her fingers to her mouth, she blew a clear, sharp bird call. She waited, then repeated it twice again. She didn't know if Beau would still remember. The call had been a signal between them —the start of secret midnight mischief when they were children visiting at each other's houses.

There was no answer, but she settled herself doggedly in the brush. She would try again at twilight before returning to her camp. If that didn't work, she'd have to think of something else.

By late afternoon, she was getting cramped and hungry. She pulled out a bit of dried beef, chewing the stringy stuff slowly and longing for the hot camp meal a cookfire would produce.

The call came back to her like a postponed echo, once and then twice again, driving off all thoughts of food. She waited. It came once more. There was no mistaking it. She stayed low in the bushes and sent back an answer. Two minutes later, she could just see him, peering into the brush. She stood like a jack-in-the-box and waved him over.

His eyes widened in surprise. "Lorelei!" he cried. His words rough, trembling, "I couldn't believe it when I heard the call. Then, I thought it might be Davy. God, I haven't—" He hugged her tightly then set her back on her feet. "You look swell, Lore. All grown up."

"I'm sixteen," the girl told him. "Beau, I—"

"But you've got to tell me how you found the place," he said, a trace of worry in his voice. "No one's ever been up this far. Not since we've been using it." He looked carefully around him.

"No one's here," Lorelei reassured him. "Beau, have you—have you heard anything about your folks?"

His face changed. "I know about my mother," he said flatly.

"I—that's why I came," she said, confused. At first she thought Beau much the same as she remembered, but now she could see—differences. He didn't look so different—slightly built like his father, brown hair curling close and tight against his head—it used to give him an angelic air.

But there were new hard lines around his mouth, and a grimness that belied his youth. Beau was twenty-two years old, and Lorelei was startled to realize that he looked closer to thirty.

"I was outside San Pasqual when it happened," he explained. "With Whitey and Tinker. I came after the funeral."

"Did you see your father?"

His expression became wooden. "I saw him," he replied tightly. He could still close his eyes and see the old man—old man. A gray old man, estranged and full of malice. Could still hear the damning words that were greeting and parting all at once.

"You broke your mother's heart," the voice said. *"Smirched all honor and your parentage. She was right —you should have never been born."*

"What happened, Beau?"

"I don't want to talk about it, Lore. I—" He looked at her earnest face, those clear, bright eyes, gemlike in the sun, lighting up both blue and green, and he smiled, a rarity that lit his face and made him more like the boy she'd known. "Well, it's real nice that you came. Real nice . . ."

"Beau, are you ever coming back? Your dad must be so lonely—"

'But he was shaking his head. "Nothing to go back to, Lorelei," he said and there was a dreadful finality in his words. Lorelei looked at his face and felt an overwhelming sadness take possession of her. She could not guess what had happened—or what these last four years had been to him. She knew only that Beau's face was like a shuttered room, and she sensed vaguely that no one was inside with him. He was alone.

"Why did you go away, Beau?" the girl asked softly. "The folks would never say."

He shook off other more recent thoughts. "Doesn't that seem a long time ago . . . I loved a fair lady," he began. "Several shades *too fair.* She had a large father and several large brothers, and they betook themselves one night to show me the error of my ways. There would be no—I repeat, no half-nigger in their white-white family." Lorelei felt her stomach turn over. Melissa's words to her mother came clear—*they beat him up*—"Bloodied and bitter," she said.

"What about the girl?" she asked.

"I don't blame Amy, Lore," he answered. "Least not anymore, I don't. She was a shy girl, gentle. I don't think she could have stood the fight—not with her own family." He tugged on Lorelei's black hair. "Not a hellion like you."

"Funny, isn't it. If it had been the two of us, it might have been okay. But you were a skinny little pipsqueak back then—and now—hell, I buy my women now. My courting days are over. That's one thing nice about a whore—the only color she cares about is gold."

"You gave up easy, Beau."

"Easy?" he said. "Easy, little girl? See, what you don't understand about us Attabys—we don't go abegging, not for love or friendship—"

"Stop it, Beau Attaby! Just you don't go talking down your mouth at me. You've never gone abegging with me or mine." She started to turn away.

He grabbed her hand. "Lore, I'm sorry. I didn't mean it to sound that way. I'm real glad you came. Don't go off like that." He put his hand to his forehead, frowning, unhappy. "I almost forgot who you are. It's been that long. You camped far?"

She shook her head. "Just beyond the next hill, across the whitewater. But I've got to go back tomorrow."

"I can't exactly show you around," he said ruefully. "It ain't no boarding school."

"That doesn't matter. I could come back again sometime . . ."

He seemed to consider this. "Lorelei, if there's ever anything I can do for you—if you need money or you got trouble—you come back here."

"—but I can't do anything for you. Is that it?"

"This ain't no game, Lorelei." He glanced up at the sun, barely visible above the hills. "I've got to get along—they'll be wondering."

"But the call, Lore. Remember the call. You can try it. If I'm here, I'll send it back. Give me a few hours before you give up. Dont' forget. If you ever need—"

"I'll remember," she said softly. He was already headed through the brush to the caverns. Her camp lay in the opposite direction. *I'll remember.*

4

SUSANNA HEARD THE stallion's clamoring all the way up in the main house. "Damn that beast," she thought. The sound made her shudder in her bones, and it had been almost continuous these past two days.

The heat had them all edgy—horses, cattle, people. Ed Crandall, who had lived his whole life in these mountains, remembered nothing like it in fifty-odd summers. For ten days there had been no relief. The dawns were cloudless, the rose rapidly turning yellow, white-yellow in the steady climbing of the sun. By midmorning, a crackling southern wind would start that made the dry leaves rustle like a fancy lady's petticoat. The water level in the troughs went down inches overnight, and by midday the remainder was gone. Even wild birds were coming down to drink, and their fine, tall willow had gone sere and brown like a petrified old woman with scorched hair.

Then yesterday a few clouds had gathered—just thin high wisps of gray at first; but by midafternoon the sky was a murky mud-yellow and the sun had disappeared. It should have rained, but instead the cloud cover seemed to bank the heat, to render it, if possible, even more oppressive. Today there had been no dawn.

She thought she heard a knocking on the front door. Strange how the closed-in sky seemed to deaden the normal sounds. Ed Crandall stood outside, his friendly grizzled face furrowed with worry.

"Begging your pardon, Miz Taylor," he began, "I wanted to remind you to shutter the house tonight." He looked at the sky. "Looks like the twilight already, and here it is just past noon. But it's fixing to blow, ma'am. Shoulda done last night—"

As though in answer, a streak of lightning cut across the massive dark. Moments later came the hollow boom of distant thunder.

"Do you think it'll be soon?" Susanna asked anxiously. "I can start now."

"Dry lightning," the foreman said. "I confess I've never seen the like—but I'd have to say no, I don't think it'll be that soon."

Like an echo of the thunder, the stallion once again vented his spleen upon the universe.

"There goes Ravenspur again," the foreman observed. "He's got the storm on his mind, all right."

"What about the stock? Will they be all right?"

"We're bringing in the cows and the brood mares with foals. Lorelei's out at the back pasture now with Tommy." A wry little smile lit his face. "Sheltering the women and children, like. The others'll be all right. Pigs are laying quiet up to their eyeballs in mud. Smart critters, pigs."

"Maybe that's where we ought to be," Susanna commented dryly. "Well, I'll see to the house, Ed." She half-turned back to the house, then changed her mind and went out into the yard.

It was quiet. Eerie quiet. And still hot. Not a chicken had left the shelter of the coop to brave the somber semidark. There was no wind—not even the barest breeze—and the entire sky seemed to be holding its breath.

The evening brought no change. They ate supper by lantern light. Susanna picked listlessly at her food and retired early. She could just hear the wind starting up as she drifted off to sleep.

The wooden shutters clapped against the window frames and there was a howling like a pack of wolves, shrill and whining. Someone was knocking—banging on her door. She heard men's cries over the roar of the thunder. It seemed that she hardly slept, but the wall clock showed it was past two. Something was very wrong.

By the time she dressed and reached the door, no one was there. She could hear raised voices downstairs, the clatter of boots on the wooden floors.

She caught sight of Ed Crandall hurrying outside. He was carrying a rifle.

"What is it?" she cried. The rains had started up and the screen door was loose, slamming open and shut as the winds pushed.

"It's the horses!" he answered, shouting to be heard above the din. He caught the door and secured it. He was breathing hard, and rain was pouring down his slicker in rivers. "Ravenspur it was. The willow fell and toppled the rails and he jumped clear—"

Susanna grabbed at his sleeve. "Why the rifle?" she demanded.

"It's Brushfire," he said hesitantly. "That's where Ravenspur—where he headed. He's down, Miz Taylor. Best to end it."

Susanna turned on him, as furious as the wind. "And you were just going to *shoot him?* Just shoot that stallion without so much as a by-your-leave? That's Brushfire you're talking about, not some old Dobbin!"

He adverted her eyes, and his voice broke with misery. "He's dying slow as it is, ma'am."

She couldn't doubt him, but she took the rifle from his hand. "If it needs doing," she said in a stricken voice, a voice that already knew the answer, "then I guess I'm the one. Next to Jed, he knows me best."

The rains had begun, but Susanna paid no heed. Her thoughts were all a jumble of memories, meeting at one convergent point—her destination. It was the horse that had been the foundation of this very ranch, this very land. The horse her own father had stolen to try her lover's faith. The horse which had carried them into the fastness of these mountains before there was a road or a field or a wooden house.

She left Crandall at the gate. The dark form, unnaturally recumbent, lay just ahead.

"Brushfire!"

She saw him raise his head at the sound of her voice. Then it fell back. He was down on his side, and when she approached, she could smell the blood mingled with earth and rain. He flinched and trembled when she touched his shoulder, then let out his breath in a long, shuddering sigh. She knelt beside him in the grass.

"It's all done, old boy," she said. "Old warrior horse, it's done. You've had your fillies and the races and the glory, Brushfire. You've had your time." She kept her voice soothing, continuous, and her hands caressed the dark, velvety nose, the bristly old whiskers that had grayed. A horse is such a big beast to go down. Like a monument. Brushfire. Big gentle old thing. "It's time, old chap, old friend." Her right hand felt under her slicker for the rifle and drew it out, keeping the barrel down to keep the workings dry.

The rain poured down, turning the pasture to mud and mire. It bent the heavy blades of grass to the ground curling under themselves like moss. Susanna set the rifle against his head. Her tears, unchecked, were falling just as fast and heavy as the rain. Brushfire's ears pricked forward, and she had to check her grip upon the gun. He was trying to nuzzle her.

"Down, old chappie," she said softly. "Ease back, old boy." Obediently the great head lay back. His nos-

trils flared and snuffled as he breathed. Her left hand
scratched him under the jaw, where he liked it. Then
she brought her hand away to steady the rifle and with
the other, squeezed the trigger until the report sent her
staggering back. The little burst of smoke cleared away.
The stallion was dead.

Ed Crandall had waited with two of the cowboys by
the fence. At the sound of the rifle, they came forward. Oblivious to the pounding rain and the sodden
ground beneath her, Susanna knelt by the stallion's
head. The wind whistled suddenly and rose to a high-
pitched wailing. It snapped at the oilskins the men
were wearing. Ed pulled Susanna from the ground.
"We've got to get back to the main house. It's no place
to be, Miz Taylor." He had to shout to be heard
above the rain and wind. And as if to give his warning
merit, a long, jagged shaft of lightning lit the sky with
a yellow glare.

Susanna shrugged off the foreman's hands and stood
firmly against the wind. "Tommy!," she shouted. "Go
to the barn and bring down a tarp—a big one." She
turned to Crandall again. "I want a trench dug in the
morning."

"Ground'll be a swamp tomorrow," the man protested. "The beast is dead—"

"*I want that trench dug!*" she repeated in clear tones
of command. "They can work on higher ground. But
I want that horse buried by sundown tomorrow."

She spoke as though she knew the sun would shine
tomorrow. She handed him the rifle and walked back
through the mud and the rain. She scarcely saw Lorelei riding in with three of the cowboys—it had taken
all four of them to rope and subdue the black. She
seemed unaware of the lightning that flashed great
lines of jagged gold and lit the edges of her wet hair.
What she felt or thought would not bear saying. But
an ineffable weariness dogged her footsteps and a hol-

lowness lay at the pit of her belly that did not come from hunger.

The sun shone the next day, and Brushfire was buried. The telegram came two days after. It was brief and neatly typed on a single sheet of paper—the cold, rote military propriety with all the stops in place that began *We regret to inform you* and commended the colonel's bravery after giving her the time and place and circumstances of her husband's death.

Susanna stayed downstairs in the parlor, with her head cradled in her hands. Sunlight streamed in through the big bay window. Roses were wilting in a vase. *Cows calving and new horses. Living things, Susanna. And living things die. Damn the war!*

She heard Lorelei coming down the stairs and saw her pass, her face red and swollen with weeping, but controlled now and grim. Susanna made no move to stop her, though she saw what her daughter carried and could guess the object. She did not rise until she heard the shotgun blast. Then she went directly to the pasture where the cowboys were already in a hubbub and Ed Crandall looked to be tearing his hair out.

Lorelei ducked back between the fence rails and walked straight on past the foreman and gaping cowboys. She stopped before her mother without apology, and for one rare moment, the two were in perfect accord. It mattered to neither of them that the Taylor ranch had no main stud. Ravenspur was shot dead and no one mourned. Susanna slipped her arm around her daughter's narrow waist and together they walked back across the field.

"Well, *maman,* how do you like it?"

Louisa sat and played an indulgent audience to her beautiful son, who strutted up and down the Persian runner like a misplaced peacock. "Well, I've seen the frock coat and trousers before," she began dryly. "The cravat is not new, and you're practicing your footwork. Shall I be passing judgment on a new pair of boots, Jules?"

"If you would lift your queenly nose from that letter for longer than it takes to sneeze, madame, you could see—" The young man struck a pose of elegant disdain, but in a moment he was impatiently drumming the tip of the cane upon the carpet.

"Ah, a walking stick!" she exclaimed with a great show of emotion. "Now, may I go on with my reading, which you have for the third time interrupted?"

"Maman!"

She laughed and pinched the glasses from her nose. "Jules, I know I shall not get a moment's peace nor leisure to read my correspondence until you are duly admired. Pray, puff up your feathers and strut once more with your new toy.

"I think it very handsome," he said, a trifle miffed. He caressed the ebony shaft with a connoisseur's delight. "And, look, it has a gold head stamped round with a charming fleur-de-lis. It's my magic wand, *maman*. I stroll thusly through the streets"— he demonstrated—"for an evening of theater, a visit to a fashionable salon, and women swoon in my wake—maids and matrons, nymphs and wide-bosomed Junos—"

"Fools and fat whores," his mother said. "And as for theater, if you would go on occasion to see the play, you would spare me much embarrassment. Sometimes I think you only act to vex me—what you did in the box last week with your plump little doxy could have well been left for a more appropriate time and place—and with the Beauvilles as our guests, no less! I don't know how I shall face Jeanne when I see her—"

"Jeanne loved every moment of it," he said laughing. "She's something of a voyeur you know, our

Jeanne. She told me during the intermission, were she only a century or two younger, Claudia would have some competition—"

"Scandalous," his mother said mildly. "And of course you provoke it. Were you not beautiful, you would be a bore, my dear. It is your singular saving grace."

"And the only reason you put up with me, you old cow," he murmured, coming to stand behind her. "And what news of the old city? What has Emile sent?"

"Three new journals—all politics. It seems even the divided sides are dividing. And he sends you his best—which is more than you deserve, ingrate. You never even wrote a thank-you note for the books."

"I haven't read them yet—how can I write a thank-you when I don't know the content. And Emile never sends anything spicy. Nonetheless I shall see to it tonight to thank him for the *fascinating* things. They make fine paperweights, at least."

"Were it not for Emile, you would no doubt invest your fortune in Sydney town mansions and become the chief procurer for the city."

"Tut tut, madame," he said soothingly. "There's little chance of that. What I catch I keep, as long as it amuses me."

"Well, hand me my cards before you go, so that I may amuse myself."

"Are you sure you won't change your mind and come along? I don't know how I shall sit through Annabelle's music recital without you. It's bad enough that the girl has arms like drumsticks, without her employing them to beat up on an innocent piano."

"I'll not come along," Louisa said, "and if the Fontaines could overhear you, you would have been spared the invitation." Her voice was stern. "Jules, do guard that vicious tongue of yours—I swear, you're worse than a woman—and try to act with propriety for once.

You know if you don't mend your ways no decent woman will have you."

"What would I want with a decent woman, *maman?*" he retorted. "Fear not, good women all love wicked men. We have, do you know, a *terrible fascination* for them. They delight in the contrast and manage to feel righteous by comparison—a chance to wallow in the mud and escape the aftersmell . . ."

"Oh, do take your wretched self outside, Jules. I can't bear you."

He handed her the cards and kissed her cheek. "I love you too, *maman.* Au 'voir."

He left the house in sudden silence. It was growing dark, and outside, the diners and revelers were just emerging. Louisa sat awhile listening to the night sounds of the city, the turning of carriage wheels and the *clop clop* of the horses' hooves on the cobblestone streets. Here in the French Quarter, at this particular time of night, she could close her eyes and imagine herself back in New Orleans, in the house on Rue Toulouse. San Francisco could never claim her. She hadn't changed from her first opinion—*brass and tinsel,* she'd written to Emile. *The smell of cows and dust, and the streets not lined with gold but with much more prosaic stuff that I shall spare description of.*

At least Jules seemed content. She smiled to herself. Give him a saloon, a gambling hall with suitable devices to risk his money, sufficient fawning women to tempt his palate, and he was thoroughly at home.

But it was getting harder and harder to keep up. Her chest pained her often now, and increasingly she found herself resorting to the white powdery medicine which calmed the pains but made her very drowsy. She worried that Jules was beginning to notice, so she sent him out alone most evenings and conserved her strength for once-a-week excursions.

If I live to see this war end, I shall go home, she

promised herself. *I shall surround myself with the old furniture and familiar faces—whatever has survived. The war is three years old. Grant will have his victory if he marches knee-deep in bodies to achieve it. It must end soon, because soon even the Union will run out of cannon fodder.*

She thought of Jed, from whom they'd had no word, though more than a year had passed since their strained visit to Taylor ranch. War years were not like other years. *But, if he can wait until after the war to see his son, then let him come to New Orleans. I shall grow fat eating bonbons and lying around all day on my couch. And my visitors shall come to me.*

Smiling a little at her fancies, she picked up the deck of cards and began to deal. She felt lucky tonight.

Then the doorbell in the front hall began to chime. Little Marianne, Minette's successor, ran to answer it, and came upstairs a moment later. Her eyes were big and she spoke in a whisper, as though they were still in New Orleans.

"A soldier, Madame!" she exclaimed. "A *Yankee* soldier!"

Louisa felt her heart thudding dangerously against her ribs. She caught at the edge of the secretary and willed herself calm. Marianne didn't know Jed.

"Did he give his name, Marianne?" she asked breathlessly.

"Monsieur Lieutenant General Melvyn Wayne, madame," the girl answered, hoping that the so-important-looking man had only friendly business with her mistress. Marianne remembered the Yankee uniforms in New Orleans. A girl she had known in service had spit on one. The girl had been raped.

But her mistress was laughing! "Please, madame," Marianne begged. "There's some joke?"

"Only to me," Louisa answered. "Have no fear,

Marianne, this Yankee will not eat you. You may show him upstairs."

The little maid ushered the visitor into the parlor and discreetly closed the door behind her. She wanted no part of Yankee business.

"I hope I haven't intruded, Louisa," Mel began.

"Only a boring evening of my own company," Louisa said, extending her hand. "And you are indeed an unexpected pleasure—*general*." The last was a delicate compliment, and Wayne smiled. "You look as wonderful as ever," he said gallantly. "I could have gone back from Sacramento, but I couldn't resist coming here. Francine knew where you were."

"Can I fix a room for you, Mel?"

"I have a train to catch at ten for San Jose," he replied. "I came through New Orleans on my way. It made me think of you—" He held his cap in his hands and shifted uncomfortably on his feet.

"Take off your fine jacket and sit down, Mel. You're among friends." He doffed the waistcoat gratefully as though the gold braid were heavy on his shoulders. "And how did you find our fair city?"

He shook his head sadly. "You were wise to come here Louisa. There are changes—you wouldn't care for them."

She sat down at her little secretary and motioned him to a chair. Mel Wayne had left New Orleans at the outset of the war to serve elsewhere. It was his city, too. "There's whiskey in the bottom cupboard," she told him. "And no more sad questions.

"I was playing solitaire when you came in. Would you care to try a double hand?"

He was pouring himself a whiskey. "I'll pass," he said. "But I'll watch your game."

She set up the deck and turned the first card. "Nothing," she sighed. "And, I felt so lucky!" Her hands were quick and deft on the cards.

"No poker hands anymore, Louisa?" he asked.

"Only the most innocent of old ladies' games," she said. "I'm becoming tame in my old age—I shall leave it to my son to take the risks."

"Will I have a chance to meet him?"

"I'm afraid not—unless he insults his kind hosts and they throw him out. A pity you've never met Jules—" She spoke tongue-in-cheek, all the while wondering what Mel Wayne's reaction to her son might be. Would he see what she saw so clearly? He and Jed were friends of long standing.

The next card was the ace of spades. She set it up, delighted. "Now, that's more like it," she exclaimed. She turned to her guest. "Tell me what brought you out here, Mel."

"That's a sad question," he told her. "We're breaking the rules already. I came out for a funeral. An old flame of yours, Louisa, before you married John—"

Louisa felt a dryness in her throat. Her body was suddenly rigid, and her mind was crying sharp denials. *No, it's not, don't let it be!*

"—Jed Taylor—remember, Louisa?"

She managed to nod, not trusting herself to speak.

"He had a ranch up north of Sacramento—you remember that bay horse he set so much store by?"

Again she nodded. If she only had to nod she would be all right, she would not lose control . . . *would not . . .*

"Strange story—the horse died the same night as Jed. Got into a battle with their new stud. His wife—his *widow* told me. He got married a little while after you and John—remember, he sent best wishes for your happiness—"

She remembered very well. How she hated him then —big with his child—to receive secondhand felicitations, followed by news of his marriage. What stiff-necked pride she had owned, vowing never to tell him. *And isn't honor always the pawn,* she thought, *I just sacrificed it too late.*

But I never thought he would die. Not him. Too vital, too full-blooded and full of animal savvy. Not Jed.

She cleared her throat once and then again. "How—how did he die?" she asked in a whisper.

Mel's eyes did not meet hers. "Got his head blown off by a musket ball," he said gruffly, adding, as if in defense, "No pretty ways to die in a war."

"No," she agreed, catching her breath. "Of course not." *I'm going to begin sobbing any moment—any moment,* she thought, But she held on.

She lost the game of solitaire, and after Mel had another whiskey (she had one, too) and they exchanged other more innocent pleasantries, he left for his train.

She managed to put the lights out in the parlor, but found she hadn't the strength or the will to leave. She sank to a chair in the corner and let go the iron will that had sustained her this last hour. Anger mingled with grief. Her thoughts were in a turmoil—she had never thought it. In spite of the war, Grant's casual sacrifices, she had never thought of that.

Jules will never see him—oh, wretched man! She had not understood until just now how great a place Jed held with her. Even though she had not seen him in all these years, that he and Jules should meet—that one day she would present him with his son—she had never doubted. And now it would never happen. She began to weep.

That was how Jules found her, still sitting in the darkened room, moaning softly as though singing to herself. Marianne had heard her mistress weeping earlier, but she had not dared to enter. She could only tell Jules of the Yankee officer who had come before.

"Maman," his voice was desperate. He had never seen her like this. *"Maman,* who came here? What did he do to you, *maman?"*

"Oh, Jules," she said, droning mindlessly, "your father is dead. Poor Jules."

"My father has been dead for seven years! Please, *maman,* tell me what is wrong."

"No, Jules, not your father," she caught her breath. "Your father was a Union officer in this hideous war." How wearily the words came forth. "Your father had a ranch in the northern hills.

"Your father's name was Jed Taylor, Jules, and your father is dead."

There was no secret to be kept anymore, though she wondered vaguely why she was telling him all this. Poor Jules—his face was blanched white, but whether from shock at her disclosure or fear for her sanity she could not tell. Poor Jules.

"Can it be true?" he said. "But how, *maman?* All this time—if so, why didn't you tell me?"

She couldn't think clearly anymore. It occurred to her she had done wrong. "Forgive me," she said softly. "Forgive your *maman,* Jules. It was the price of honor at the time. Or so I thought . . ."

He watched with shock and horror as his mother seemed to wither before his eyes—to become an old woman, broken, apologetic.

She arose stiffly from the chair, and spoke like a stranger, in an old woman's voice. "Give me your arm, my Jules, and help me to my room, I'm very tired—"

5

LORELEI CROUCHED IN the brush and sent the call into the air, full and clear and sweet. A moment between, then twice again. She had her fingers crossed. Beau might well not even be there.

Ten minutes later, the call was returned. Her luck was holding. He was coming, searching eagerly through the brush. Almost the very same place where they had last met, when she had come to tell him the sad news he had already heard. Now the arrow had spun round to her. It was her turn.

She stood. "Over here, Beau."

"Lorelei," he smiled eagerly, embraced her. "I didn't know if you'd ever come back after the last time—"

"It isn't just for a visit, Beau." She pulled the hat from her head. "I've come to stay—for a while at least."

His brown eyes widened gaping at her. "My God! What have you done to your hair? Have you gone loco?"

"I'm not loco," she declared hotly. "I've left the ranch, Beau. And I mean to ride with you and the others."

"You ran away," he said accusingly.

"Left," she argued. "And I'm not going back, Beau. I stayed through the harvest, but I'm not going back. My father's dead."

Beau looked up sharply. "Lore, I'm sorry," he said, his voice gentle now. "How'd it happen?"

"He was with Grant at Cold Harbor," she said briefly. Seven thousand men had died within an hour. Her father was one of them.

"But, why are you *here,* Lore? You can't mean to stay." He puzzled over her worriedly, she could outdo a boar hog for tenacity.

"I just had to leave, Beau. My mother was arguing about sending me to England, complaining of my not being lady like and what was going to become of me, and I couldn't stand it anymore."

He watched her face carefully, reading it as he had when she was a child. "You're not telling me all of it," he accused.

She bit at her lower lip and shoved her hands into the pockets of her jeans. "I got to feeling—it's funny, you know—I got to feeling like I spent my whole life waiting for Daddy to come home. It was always like that —he'd run down to fairs and races with the horses. Traveled long ways sometimes. And I guess I didn't think much more of the war than that.

"Only this time"—she stuck out her chin in defiance of the tears she felt rising—"this time—he won't be coming back. He *is* back—what they left of him, and buried. Dead. And I can't stay there anymore. I can't! Because it's like I'm still waiting, do you see. My mother—doesn't say anything hardly, and I think she's worse with it than anybody. But we don't do each other any good. Somehow it just made things worse—"

Beau moved to hold her, "Oh, little girl, little girl," he said.

She drew herself away. *"No little girl,* Beau. And I can't be waiting anymore, I want—I want to *be,* Beau. I don't want to wait." She paced restlessly back and forth.

"Well, this is no place to start, Lorelei," he said

harshly. "And if you think I'm going to let you play bandits and posse, you're still a little girl." He ran his hand over the brief shock of black hair. "Your mama would weep to see what you done to your hair, girl."

She shook him off and faced him squarely. Her voice was low and calm. "I can pass as a boy, Beau. I ride as well as you—"

"And you're small enough on top, I guess," he said judiciously, to get her mad. "And, what about six-guns, Lore?"

"I'm a better shot than you with a rifle," she said crossly. "Beau, you're gonna help me." She looked casually over at the caverns. "It's a nice secret place, Beau. You don't want anyone to know about it—"

"Lorelei, I know you wouldn't do anything like that."

"Don't take the chance, Beau," she said softly. "Help me."

He shook his head, but he knew himself beaten. "You don't know what it's like, Lore," he said desperately. "You even winter in a cold stone cave—what it's like to sleep on? Running, Lore! People hating you—*you don't know what it's like!*"

After six months, she knew. After six months—the late fall and the whole of winter—she could pass through the bowels of the hollow mountain with the blind certainy of a mole. She knew every snakelike twist in the narrow tunnels—the places that opened into great stone rooms and the places you had to duck.

She told them her name was Lenny Smith, and no one questioned her. They didn't call her that anyway. Whitey Loomis had given her another name.

When Beau had brought her in, Whitey had been the one—the chief—who would pass judgment on her. She could still remember the stare of those unnatural pinkish eyes, squinting against the sun despite the shade of his broad hat. He had pulled at the ends of his white moustache. "Don look like much to me," he said.

"Skinny dude—looks like I could lift him with one hand—"

And it was true. He could—and he had done so, banding his arm across her chest and ribs, while Lorelei held her breath, terrified that he would feel her breasts beneath the binding strip of linen. She was wearing a thick coarse jacket of sheepskin, and he had not noticed. He just leaned on her like a casual victor, certain of his prowess.

He was only a little *too* sure. The others were laughing and yipping—all but Beau, who watched the proceedings nervously. Lorelei got her chance when he lifted her off the ground. She twisted one hand free and brought her knife up from its sheath, flipping it into her other hand. Her elbows whipped back hard. She heard Whitey grunt and stumble back.

She was free and there was a knife in her hand.

"I don't like being handled," she said bluntly, keeping her voice low.

Whitey grunted. It was that simple. And so she was Skinny among the men. The skinny dude.

There were eight all told, and they often worked in pairs and teams. For small jobs, as often as not, it was only Whitey and one or two others. Always Whitey. Lorelei was partnered with Beau, since he had brought her in, and she was grateful to have escaped—so far at least—doing a job with Whitey alone.

Whitey was smart and slick and he could move over ground like a rattlesnake. He hated daylight because his eyes were peculiarly sensitive to the sun, but his eyes were weak, and once she'd seen him shimmy up the face of a cliff in the dark night just by feel when a bridge washed out and they'd been trapped below. It was after a job—the first time she'd seen Whitey at his "game." She and Beau and Whitey had stopped a merchant in his private coach, heading south from Sacramento. It was well planned, well timed, as Whitey's jobs always were, and they took him off a winding deserted stretch of road, ten miles away from the nearest town. It had been near dusk, and they'd had cover from the thick stand of pine towering up the hillside.

The merchant was fat, well dressed, prosperous. He carried gold to purchase goods from the Eastern ships in San Francisco. Whitey took the gold, checked the coach, and sent the driver on.

The merchant was uncomfortable and angry, watching his carriage pass out of sight at a gallop. But he wasn't particularly frightened. Whitey had his money. But there was more.

The outlaw leader casually reached inside his victim's coat and produced, as though by magic, a fob watch and gold chain. His colorless lips drew back in a snarl. He looked at the merchant and said, "Strip!"

Now the merchant was sweating—a fact which Whitey took pleasure in observing and relating to his compatriots. Lorelei was embarrassed watching the revelation of vulnerable gross obesity—the sunken chest and the big white belly round as a pregnant woman. *And the hidden purse, suspended on a thin waistcord tucked down inside his pants.* Whitey smiled when he saw it. He tore it free and tossed it carefully to Beau, who was on horseback and eager to be off. Beau already knew the game.

Lorelei was mounted, too, holding the reins of Whitey's nag. "Now you just stand right there, fat man, and don't move," she heard Whitey say, and the merchant obeyed. She saw Whitey pull a stub-barreled shotgun from his saddlebag and listened incredulously as he glanced up to her and whispered under his breath. "You watch real good now, Skinny. I'll show you how to gut a pig!" Then he turned around and blasted the fat, naked merchant full in the midsection. Pieces of flesh were scattered several feet around. Only then did Whitey mount his beast and give the word to ride.

They held up in the caves for most of the winter, seldom venturing forth except for game and supplies. Lorelei kept the secret of her sex well guarded—they all thought her an unbearded boy—and when privacy became difficult, she stayed dirty—especially her face which was fair and rosy and too feminine. She wore grime like a mask. She slouched. She was not social. Beau was the only one with whom she dared a conversation.

Now it was spring and Whitey was laying plans—a kind of itinerary of possible jobs. There seemed to be no limit to his sources and resources—men like the driver of the merchant's coach, and others, less visible.

"He's wily, all right," Lorelei told Beau. "But he turns my stomach." Six months had toughened her to many things, but not to Whitey Loomis. "There's something *wrong* about him, Beau."

"He hates a lot," Beau said. "That's what you feel bothering you. I reckon Whitey hates more than anybody I ever knew—even hates his own men. He does love to torment—I remember when he shot up that fat man in front of you. He knew how you'd react. You were smart not to show it much, or it might have been worse."

"You know what's strange, Beau," she said musingly. "Remember that white hart up in the timberland when we were kids?"

He nodded. "God, yes. I saw it twice. Once with Davy when we were out fishing. And once with you—that was the first time."

"Yeah, funny what a magical thing it was—all graceful—glowy white. It always came like a surprise present. Just seeing it. Hunters used to come up, but nobody ever shot that deer. They's just put up their rifles and stare. And I was thinking how that deer and Whitey could be the same odd thing. That white hart was an albino, too."

"Whitey's a man, Lore," Beau said shortly. "It's not the same."

"No," she said viciously. "The deer was beautiful—it made you glad just because it was there. Whitey's ugly and evil—he scares me, Beau." This last confession came forth with difficulty. It was not her habit to admit weakness.

"Whitey scares everybody, Lore," Beau answered. He scratched his head and frowned. "He doesn't answer to anybody's rules. He doesn't figure the same as other folks.

"But I'll tell you this, Lore," he added to ease her. "You—I don't think this is the thing for you—but you can make it. I've seen you working, and some of it's been tight. You're fast and you're sure and you don't break."

She had the steel nerves and lightning reflexes that the work required for survival. And she was still new enough to feed on the excitement.

She shrugged at his compliment, but she was pleased. "Whitey want to do a bank job," she told him, to change the subject. "He said sometime next month."

Their object lay in the tiny village of San Rafael, tucked away on the quiet side of the great bay, across the water from San Francisco. The bank was an unprepossessing one-story adobe, and there was little in the town to suggest purses worthy of Whitey's elaborate plan. But unless Whitey's informants erred—and they seldom did—that tiny bank in the sleepy village was playing host to a large fortune in bullion—a responsibility of which Whitey Loomis was most anxious to relieve them.

It was the largest group Lorelei had ever seen working. There were seven. Only Laderman was left in the camp, nursing a bullet wound from the last job. She and

Beau crouched on the roofs of buildings adjacent to the bank. Another team was on the roofs across the street, all of them armed with rifles. Behind them, in a narrow cul-de-sac, Kitteridge waited with the horses. Tinker was with Whitey just below.

It was dusk—Whitey's favorite time—and as Lorelei watched, another man emerged from the saloon across the street and casually joined the two loitering in front of the general store. This was Whitey's informant. He was a dark, wiry little man with unkempt whiskers and a shifty way of gazing around. Lorelei was certain he had seen her, hugging low to the roof, though he gave no sign. In a quiet, sauntering group of three, the men moved away, heading to where the manager of the bank was undoubtedly supping with his family.

They returned some twenty minutes later, still a party of three, but the informant had been replaced by another man—evidently the one they sought. To the casual observer, there seemed nothing unusual or amiss. But Lorelei of course would notice that the big, pale man in the dark sombrero was walking very closely behind the bank manager.

The three men disappeared inside the bank, and Beau and Lorelei, acting on cue, immediately crawled to the rear of their respective buildings and leaped down. The men of the opposite buildings would remain to watch the front.

It was running as smooth as a well-oiled machine. No noise, no blood. Even Whitey would hold off killing in the middle of a town. The back door of the bank was opened by T. J. Rafferty himself. Whitey was right behind him.

Hand to hand, out the door and into the saddlebags, the bullion passed, just one stop out of the mines in heavy, precious bars. Lorelei found herself grinning at Beau. This was by far the biggest haul she'd seen, and it was coming so easy, like picking ticks off a dog.

Mr. T. J. Rafferty wasn't smiling. He was the bank's president as well as its manager, and what was being so handily passed down the line of outlaws and out the back door was the biggest load to enter his bank since the town had begun.

"Tie him up," Whitey said, and threw Tinker several loops of cord. Rafferty thought longingly and furiously of the gun in his desk drawer but his hands were bound behind his back, his mouth was gagged, and his feet were tied together.

Then he remembered his penknife.

It wasn't doing him much good while the gold was changing hands, and he had to wait until he was certain that Tinker would not be back. Then he began to twist and wiggle to free the knife from his waistcoat pocket. He'd never thought of it as a weapon; he used it to pare his nails.

Working with desperate haste, he sawed at his bonds. He could hear them mounting just outside the door, and his rage and frustration increased. With his hands free, the rest came off quickly. He stumbled forward and grabbed the gun from the drawer, then ran outside.

The horses were turned for flight. Whitey and Tinker were up in front, farthest away. Rafferty, who scarcely knew the workings of firearms, pointed the gun into the melee of fleeting men and horses and fired. He got off three quick shots before Kitteridge turned and gunned him down. One of the shots caught Lorelei's gelding in the foreleg. It shattered the bone and the horse went down.

Lorelei found herself spinning out of the saddle and, in agonizing slow motion, she saw the ground rising to meet her. She hadn't caught her breath when the back legs of her mount rose above her and rapidly descended. She screamed as a flailing hoof struck her ribs. Another glanced across her temple. Her head twisted sideways. Beau was coming toward her at a gallop, and she thought herself being lifted. Then she was floating. The day was turning dark.

There were drums beating and a band was playing. It was the day of the big race. The day she was to kill the black horse. The black horse that killed her father. She was trying to tell him not to ride, but she couldn't make herself heard over the band.

She opened her eyes. There was a band—or several of them. And shouting and cheering outside the window. *Where was she?* The room was totally unfamiliar. She was in a real bed, the first she'd known in months. She struggled up to a sitting position, wincing at the sudden pain. A wave of dizziness forced her head back to the pillow. A feather pillow. The sheets were soft and smooth and cool. *Wherever it was, it wasn't jail.*

Under the covers, her hands encountered her own body, and that made her start. She had hidden her sex for so long, the touch of her own skin was strange to her. Strange—and frightening. No one must know. They musn't guess she was—

She heard giggling outside the door of the room, and a full-throated matronly voice scolding and hushing. A moment later the door opened, and a woman stepped inside. Lorelei grasped the edges of the sheets and pulled them up to her neck.

"There's no need to be hiding yourself from me, dearie," the woman said cheerily. "And didn't I undress you and tend you myself, and haven't I seen the likes of what you got to show a thousand times! So just you lie easy."

"Who are you?" she asked.

"You kin call me Ma Belle," the woman said. She smiled showing uneven yellowed teeth. "Everybody does. When I was a lass now, it was Bella. But that was before your time.

"We're just a little busy now, what with the celebration and all, but don't you fret yourself at little noises. I told young Beau I'd take the right kind of care, me girl. He knows I don't run those houses of lost children."

Lorelei fought the grogginess, desperate to comprehend this turn of events. A friend of Beau's. A woman who looked like some farmer's wife, plump and country-bred. A celebration. The bands.

"Is there a festival?" she asked. She needed to know something concrete. What house was she in? What city?

"Why, and how could I be forgetting how long it is you've been asleep?" the woman exclaimed. "And you don't know the news that's rocking the whole land. Aye, and farther than that—the war's done, my girl. The war's over. And the town's gone stark mad, dearie. The pubs is standing rounds to all their customers and I have to say I'm as soft as any—I've let each of me girls a turn with their favorite gentleman. All, in the spirit of patriotism, it is."

"Then your girls—"

"Angels of the evening, dearie, every one. But don't get on a-fretting now. As I said before, I don't make converts to the life. There's enough girls out there as is willing to bargain for a fair price to fair bargain. Besides," she added more honestly, "somebody'd steal you for a keeper before I'd get my investment back. You're so new you shine." The old bawd could almost believe she was looking at a virgin maid. "How old are you, dearie?"

"Twenty-one," Lorelei lied easily, and of course the woman knew it was a lie. "Did Beau—did he say anything else?"

"Oh, me, he left you a note, the boy did. I have it in my bag." She reached into a voluminous satchel that hung on a strap over her shoulder. "He's a right good customer, your friend, speaking straight of mind, you know," she said conversationally, all the while groping blindly in her bag. "Always treats the girls fair and decent, not like some others in that gang. Mind you, I'd not be talking as I am, except that he led me to believe that the two of you didn't—"

"We don't," Lorelei said coldly. *My God, what else had Beau told this woman?*

"Well, don't you worry yourself a mite, Ma Belle's gonna get things arranged for you. I've spoken to Mr. Gerald Todd already, and I'll introduce you as soon as you're well. Of course, there's your money, dearie, and you're in no present need to work, but if you want to live high in this town, it's a dear price. Your fortune won't see you forever."

"Fortune?"

Her hostess rambled on, oblivious. "Ah, here's the letter now. Right in me corset all the time. I promised to keep it tight." She chuckled and handed it to the anxious girl. Lorelei opened it and read—

I reckoned as how that kick from the horse might have knocked some of the dumbness out of you. At least the game is up for you here. Everybody heard you screaming under that horse, and they know you ain't no man or boy. Whitey would as like to kill you as have you a woman knowing what you know, so, for God's sake, stay low!

If you're still of a mind to go your own way, Ma will get you some work—legal. She knows everybody in San Francisco, and I made her promise. I left your share with Ma. Looks to be about seven thousand. Gold. If I can, I'll check back on you. But I don't think it'll be soon.

Beau

Most of the questions were answered, but something stood out in her mind—*her share*. Her share had been in the saddlebag of the fallen gelding. They were running. Shots had been fired. Beau couldn't have rceovered the gold.

His share. He'd left his share with her. Her quick mind was rapidly assimilating this new turn of events. His money she'd damn well keep for him. The note mentioned work. So be it. She shook her head to clear it. Her ears still rang.

"Beau said something about employment—" she said to her hostess. A *madam!* She was dressed so plainly in a dark plaid housedress with a proper little collar of white lace. Her sparse curly iron-gray hair peeked out beneath her cap. A madam!

Ma Belle clucked and eased Lorelei back down on the pillow. "You'd better not plan on working today, dearie," she said, "or the next, or the next. Beau said you were a tough little gal, and I well believe it. But the least you've got is a couple a cracked ribs, and your head's got a lump as big as a goose egg. Get yourself rested proper, and we'll see about Mr. Todd."

"Who's Mr. Todd?" Lorelei asked.

Ma Belle's sharp eyes widened in genuine surprise. "Upon my word!" she exclaimed. "And you really don't know? Well, my dear, Mr. Todd runs the 'change here —San Francisco Stock Exchange. Mining stocks— Savage and Ophir. Gould and Curry—Comstock! Surely you've heard of that!"

Lorelei nodded vaguely. Her hostess appeared relieved. "Well, Mr. Todd is Billy Ralston's right hand, you might say. And they hire young girls—nothing questionable, all strictly correct—to sell shares at the 'change. Put you in a way to make a comfortable living just in commissions, plus whatever you might pick up—" She left the phrase dangling and went on.

"I'm sure Mr. Todd will take you on." She looked at the girl appreciatively. Even pale and ill, this was a looker. It would have been hard to tell under the

scrapes and blood she'd come in with. But cleaning her
up now, it was like polishing a gem. Lord you could
scarcely tell she was a girl at first. "Your hair's a mite
short," she said judiciously, "but that's all the fashion
now. Trim it up and in a week of growing you'll have a
proper French bob. Though I'm partial to long hair myself, each to his own, I always say. You could get one
of those funny little pancake hats to go with it—*berets,*
they call 'em. From Paree."

Lorelei stifled a yawn and listened with half an ear
to the rambling discourse on fashion and style. The
bands had begun again. They were closer now, and
Lorelei yearned toward the sound—bright, gay marches
and the high-strung excitement of a parade.

Delicately, she placed her palm to her temple. "I'm
a little sleepy," she said apologetically.

"Oh, and me going on with my steam-engine mouth.
I'll leave you now, my dear. You rest easy. Here, I'll
close up the shutters—"

She had no sooner closed the door, than Lorelei had
flung back the covers, tiptoed to the window. She un-
latched the shutters and drew the lace curtain aside a
little, then peered down into the street below.

The mid-afternoon daylight startled her. She must
have been out since last night! Oh, and the band was
just below her now—how impressive were the uniforms.
Behind them another group marched in disciplined
precision. These were the San Francisco Vigilantes—
she recognized them from pictures she had seen. Ten
years before, they had been the only uncorrupted justice
in the territory, and they were still a much-respected
troop.

A young man at the nearest end of the line glanced
up at the second-story window and caught her eye. He
raised his hand to the shiny black visor of his cap and
flashed a smile. She found herself waving back, and the
troop marched on. She giggled, wondering what the

young man would have thought if he knew she was naked.

But there was so much to see! Across the street and playing in opposition to the band, an organ grinder worked while his partner, a well-dressed brown monkey, begged coins from the passersby. Unformed men were everywhere, and handsomely garbed ladies in bright spring dresses of light silk and muslin. A man had his head buried inside a square device mounted on three heavy legs. He was making pictures of the event. Carriages had been barred from the street, but mounted horsemen milled about—cowboys clad in work-worn denims lent a familiar note. Not so the dandies in their velvet breeches, the silk-hatted businessmen, the ladies with their dainty parasols.

Lorelei was enchanted. The entire city was like a great fair—greater than any she had ever seen. When she had been at home, they has almost made the trip so many times, but something always interfered. Her mother never seemed to take to the prospect of San Francisco, though they often traveled an equal distance to other places.

She turned from the window and spun about, doing a little dance in time to the street music. She felt so free —so gay. Except for the bandage wound about her ribs, she was naked. Clean and naked, her breasts unbound. She had not realized till this moment what strain, what constant guarded tension had been her lot in the outlaw camp. But now she hugged herself, reveling in the sweet sensation of her own flesh. She ran to the window again. Another band was approaching, playing "Wait for the Wagon." Lorelei did a little jig holding out an imaginary skirt, curtsying to an imaginary partner. A wave of dizziness struck her, and she clutched at the windowsill, but it did nothing to quell her high spirits, her rediscovery of herself. Across the room, she could see her own lithe form reeflcted in the full-length mirror. Below her, the city was aglitter with celebration. She flopped backward into the soft feather-bed and waved her arms in angel wings. She was going to love it here.

In another part of town, the French section, which outsiders called Keskedee, Jules Hutchison took no pleasure from the sound of the marching bands. *"Damn them and their victories!"* he exclaimed to no one in particular, and he resumed his pacing back and forth across the drawing room. Things nearer pressed upon him—his mother upstairs, closeted with the doctor. The alarm that summoned him from his pleasure couch of the afternoon—a charming lady whose husband left her too much alone.

What did it matter—the war or the women? Mari-anne entered softly, with brandy on a tray, and he whirled on her, "For Chrissakes, if he's not down in five minutes, I shall drag him out by his whiskers! What can he be doing to her?"

"Please, Monsieur Jules, have a care," she whispered. "It will do madame no good, no good at all if you be-come—distracted."

He poured himself a generous drink and downed it. Five minutes passed, and then another five. Another drink. He heard shuffling on the floor above and hur-ried to the staircase. The doctor was coming down.

Dr. Walker was a balding, usually genial man in his mid-fifties, whose single physical distinction was a pair of thick muttonchop whiskers of which he was inor-dinately proud. At the moment, however, he was not feeling genial, and he did not, as was his custom, stroke and smooth the thick brush of his moustache as he sat in the richly upholstered armchair and faced his pa-tient's son. Dr. Walker was a good and knowledgable physician, and such a duty as now faced him was never pleasant.

"Your mother," he began carefully feeling for the words," has had an attack, Jules. A relatively mild attack—"

"Of what nature?" the young man asked, his dark eyes focused unsparingly on the man in front of him.

"Why, her heart," the doctor replied. "Your mother has been ill for a very long time. Do you mean to say you didn't know?"

Jules half-moaned and shook his head. But he could think of things—little things—*he should have known!* He should have guessed. Of course, she had been different since the night she told him about his father— his real father. She went out less. She seemed to have less energy. But he could still bring her out of what he took for melancholy, her sometimes malaise. But not ill. Not his *maman!* Not she!

"You say it was a mild attack?" He clung to the beneficent word. *Mild.*

"Well, yes," the doctor said with difficulty. "She's resting now, and she will recover—after a fashion."

"What do you mean, *after a fashion?*"

"She is suffering a partial paralysis on her left side, and this will gradually disappear. But you must understand that her heart is very weak." He repeated it for emphasis. "Very weak. She must not strain herself in any manner. She must not be upset.

"From this attack, I do not fear for her, Jules. *It is the next . . .*"

Misery stood out in the boy's handsome face. His voice was hoarse. "Why should there be another?" The question pleaded for some ease, some hope.

The doctor had begun to wish, as he so often did in these circumstances, that he had chosen some other profession, that he could be excused from being the bearer of unwelcome tidings, the harbinger of doom. He fidgeted slightly, but only slightly. He wanted to spare the boy, but that was just an idle wish.

"Her heart is tired, Jules. It wants to rest. She may go quietly. Or there may be another attack, more violent than this. But it will happen."

"When?" he could scarcely utter the word.

"With care, perhaps a year. But I must be honest: it could be anytime."

"She'll get care," the boy said.

The doctor had rounds to make. He took his leave, descending the steps of the house with heavy footsteps. The boy had upset him—the dark eyes which had become vacant, the face so pale. Stricken, and Dr. Walker had no cure for that either. He made his way through the crowded festival streets like a somber note jangling out of tempo with the happy marching bands.

6

THE LARSON FUNERAL Parlor, established in 1856 by
Mortimer Larson, sat just off the Rue Dumaine on a
street of private dwellings. It had previously been the
home of Douglas and Althea Larson—a hardware merchant and his wife—until the fever had taken them
both in a single summer, and their son, a mortician
fresh from his apprenticeship, had foreseen a boom in
business and decided that the lower stories would convert nicely to a showcase of his services.

The hitching posts of the street were headed with
gargoyles, for the Creoles were fond of monsters, and
Jules glared at their iron faces as he walked. The shell
of the city—its streets and buildings—appeared relatively unchanged. Here and their the houses evidenced
signs of disrepair—rust on the wrought-iron banister,
a broken window boarded up rather than repaired—the
early signs of dereliction referred to as genteel poverty.
Strangers dwelt in the well-kept houses—smug victors
nesting in their spoils. Jules absorbed the subtle changes
along with the late-morning heat which was both familiar and oppressive. A churning restlessness possessed
him, a distaste for his cursed errand that brought him
to this place.

Mr. Larson answered the young man's knock. He
was a natty little man dressed appropriately in drab

colors. His eyes were red-rimmed, his thin mouth puckered. He had the dismal look of perpetual mourning suited to his profession.

Jules hated him on sight.

Mr. Larson was well used to the antics of the recently bereaved. He knew and understood the hysteria, the residual guilt, the anguished eulogizing and public weeping of his clients; he had pockets full of clean white handkerchiefs awaiting the emotional moment. But he was not prepared for the cold young man who stalked through the narrow rooms of the funeral parlor like a caged beast and abruptly demanded to see the caskets.

The proprietor tried to maintain his role. He smiled with a slight wrinkle of his lips in an expression meant to appear both benign and sorrowing. "You are burying your dear dead departed—?"

There was no answer forthcoming, though Jules was at his elbow. Larson indulged himself in private pique, but somehow could not bring himself to ask again. He shuffled nervously toward the display room, pausing at the doorway to let Jules enter first. He was very proud of the layout of the room, designed to draw the client's eye to the more expensive models which caught sunlight from the eastern window. The less exalted caskets lined the walls on tiered benches, with the best of the second string displayed in the highest tiers, as though to be nearer to heaven.

With a sale at hand, the little man began to itemize the features of each model, praising the aged and wood superior varnish, the special fittings of the various caskets in the droning voice of sober righteousness. Again it was as though he was not heard. Jules paced between the rows of caskets, paused before one or the other, peering inside with a brooding distaste for the entire procedure.

The young man was exasperating, though obviously

a man of means. Mr. Larson did not miss that his suit
was of fine woven cashmere or that his cane was topped
with gold. He cleared his throat meaningfully, determined to gain acknowledgment.

"—I'll take this."

Larson's face brightened at his patron's choice—it
was one of their costliest pieces. "You have an eye for
quality, young man," he said beaming. "Solid oak with
special brass handles imported from—"

He was cut off rudely. "I'll send for it this afternoon,"
Jules stated.

The little man's hands fluttered nervously. "Oh, but
that's impossible, dear sir. We must have two days to
assemble the order. Our woodworker is already—"

"You have one right here," Jules said pointedly.

"But that's for display," Larson said desperately. "I
assure you we will process with all speed—" Larson felt
himself sputtering. His client was advancing on him,
holding before his face a fistful of dollars, so close that
he could see the clenched blue veins of the hand. He
was uncertain whether he was being threatened or
bribed. It was evident that the solid oak casket with its
imported brass fittings would be leaving the funeral
parlor that afternoon.

"How much is it?" It was not a question but a command.

"T-two hundred dollars."

Jules glanced at the box again. "I want it lined in
purple velvet," he said absently.

"It's not included with the casket," the man said
quickly. "Velvet's frightfully expensive now—I'll have
to add it to the bill."

Jules peeled off several bills and thrust it forward, as
though he would avoid the slightest contact with the
death dealer. "Will that cover it?" he asked icily.

The little man looked down at the money in his
hands. Three hundred dollars. "It's more than enough.

If you'll wait here a moment, I can give you a receipt . . ."

"Just see that it's ready at four o'clock, Larson," Jules said. "I'll be sending a man." He looked down at the little man and saw a carrion feeder, an officious little body-counter. His mobile features formed something that should have been a smile, but was no smile. It was the grimace of something not quite human and the timid undertaker, looking up at the lips drawn over the strong white teeth, shivered in his soul, as if death were a young man come calling at his shop.

He pulled a clean white handkerchief from his pocket and wiped away the sweat that drenched his brow and beaded above his lips.

Jules continued walking after he left the funeral parlor looking neither left nor right, but tapping his cane with each rapid step as though the cane were something he chased, some destination always tapping a pace ahead. He had to walk off the distasteful residue of the funeral parlor, the very air of the place that had invaded his clothing and lay like soot upon his skin.

It's because I'm burying her, he thought, angry because his anger might oversway the rest. *The old she-dog, to leave me here in the heat and flies. To witness the waste. To stand and watch while the dirt covers her. Bury her. How dare she? How dare she leave me?*

The street broadened out to a boulevard. It was too public, too open. He turned off to narrow alleys and back streets where sheets and linens hung out on clothes-lines like so many ghosts, flapping feebly in the sluggish air.

He could feel a cramp start in his belly, but he didn't slow his pace. Above all, he didn't want to go back to the house. His cane tapped along the walk like a blind man's stick. It was siesta time; fewer people were abroad. Some children played in a backyard. A dog barked at his heels.

He walked farther, leaving the streets of the saints, and paced the Champs-Elysées, where canal barges took the place of carriages and the dockhands continued working, even through the heat of the day.

He walked for fully two hours, until exhaustion took him and there was no place else to go. He hailed a carriage and gave the address of the house on Rue Toulouse.

He had hired two women to serve food for the visitors tomorrow. They were taking inventory of the larder—he could hear them giggling in the kitchen. He dispatched the one named Yvonne to hire a carter. Then he poured himself a brandy from the cupboard.

"M'sieur, if you please, but brandy is all you have here," the other woman said. She gestured broadly with her arms to encompass the whole of the kitchen and pantry. "The cellar is stocked, yes," she admitted, "but there is no food!"

"I have made a list, m'sieur," she said, offering him the painstakingly scrawled scrap of paper. He carried it out with him when he went to instruct the carter and returned it to her when he came back inside, though he had not so much as glanced at the contents.

"You may purchase these items at the market," he told her. "Have the bills sent to Emile Adante on Rue Dumaine." Emile was a long-standing friend and his mother's executor. They were meeting later in the evening.

He turned to Yvonne. "Go with her and carry the purchases back to the house. I won't need you the rest of the day." He chafed against their presence in the house. The old servants were gone. These were strangers.

But the people he knew depressed him even more.

He had happened on Jennie Duval that morning, as he crossed in front of the Cathedral St. Louis. He didn't see her until she called his name.

Her face and figure had not changed—she had always been angular, a long-faced girl with a pointed chin and sharp brown eyes. But when he last knew her, she had been dressed in the height of fashion—and she had walked imperiously, secure in the Duval fortune that stood behind her. She possessed a caustic and sometimes devastating wit that made her amusing company. Jules used to tease that he spent time with her only in order that his reputation got no blacker than it deserved to be.

But now the haughtiness was gone, along with the finery. She was plainly dressed in clothing that her maid would have scorned, and she seemed ill at ease beyond the first amenities.

She had received his announcement. Yes, she and her mother would be there tomorrow to pay their respects. Her father? Downed at Vicksburg. Half the male population could be placed similarly. Gettysburg, Chickamauga, Fisher's Hill, Cedar Creek.

It was as he was making excuses to move on that she caught his arm and said fiercely, "They're the lucky ones, Jules."

At first he did not comprehend.

"My father," she said. "Your mama. They're the lucky ones. My father died in glory, and your mama went peacefully, you say. But there's no peace for the rest of us, Jules. And no glory either." Her voice was sharp with rancor.

"It's not the poverty," she went on in ragged tones, "it's not going without new dresses and worrying over the food."

"They've left us no dignity! The Union militia insult us on the street and we have no recourse. We're less than niggers—they can vote—and the carpetbaggers

ship them down on barges before election day and get them drunk with liquor. Then they put their arms around them and show them where to scrawl their stinking X's. They can't read or write, but they can elect Yankees.

"Our field niggers! Those dumb brutes that couldn't say no more than 'Yes, missy!' They're strong, Jules—did you ever see them cutting grain with those big, long knives? Out in broad daylight—they talk to us! Big field bucks, Jules—"

Jules pulled her into a corner of the cathedral courtyard. She was talking too loudly, and there were people about. *And she wasn't talking right.*

Her voice rose higher and shriller. "They had a meeting last week in Congo Square—d'you know what one of them said? 'I would not permit any white man to marry my daughter—from my due respect for the colored ladies.' "

Her fingers were still clutching at his sleeve, and Jules felt a sharp pang of something like pity. *She needs a man,* he thought. But he didn't want her. *No more balls, Jennie. No more boys. And yes, no more dignity.*

He wanted to get away from her, but he couldn't leave her on the street. He whistled for a hack and helped her in. He gave the driver some money.

"Go home, Jennie," he said as gently as he could. "I'll see you tomorrow."

"I'll send you a card, Jules," she said. "You'll take supper with us one evening?" Now she spoke with a forced brightness that was even more unnerving than her bitterness. Jules smiled and nodded dumbly and waved his hand, and at the same time determined to settle his affairs and leave New Orleans as soon as that was done.

He laid his plans before Emile that same evening. Their personal possessions were already in San Francisco. The house could be sold complete.

Emile nodded his head as he poured the cognac into the snifters. "If you don't mind selling to Yankees, I can see to it quickly. I would advise you—" he half-smiled, amending himself—*"On the basis of my own prejudices,* I would advise you to keep it awhile longer. This—Reconstruction—can't go on forever. And you're certainly not in need of the proceeds."

He adjusted his spectacles and poured over a mass of papers spread before them on the table. "Your mother took great care with your inheritance, Jules. She invested a portion of her own money in the Confederacy, as did we all. Out of loyalty, I think. But she was shrewd with what she had set aside as your fortune." He lifted a sheaf of stock certificates. "She invested your money in the West," he remarked, "and wisely. They were purchased in your name, and they're as good as gold."

"Did you know she was ill when we left New Orleans?" Jules asked.

The old man regarded him kindly. "I knew," he admitted. "I had to know because she wanted everything settled when she left. But she didn't want you to know. She swore both Tom Miller and me to silence. She said whenever it happened would be time enough."

"How long did you know my mother?" Jules asked suddenly.

"Since she was seventeen and ran away from her folks." The old man's eyes softened, and his smile went a long way back. "They had fixed it in their minds that she was going to marry their neighbor's son, and that's when Louisa Dolarier first came to New Orleans. Because she had her own mind a-fixing it in her own way.

"Ah, Jules, what a coquette your mother was! It was as natural to her as breathing. She charmed every man from the governor to the barkeeps—at least half a dozen duels were fought for her. Always life-hungry—what sparkle she had, what vibrant appetite!"

But Jules was not listening to his friend. He had

asked a leading question and now he could not follow
it. He wanted to grab Emile by the collar and shout,
"And did you know all these years I was a bastard? Did
you know, *mon vieux,* the truth of this *jeune homme de
bonchance?*—this lucky boy? Two fathers—that's the
joke. And both of them dead! Of mothers, only one.
And she is in a box. But that of course is common
knowledge."

He kept silent with some effort, and let Emile run on
with reminiscences that all predated the one question in
his mind—the question he could not bring himself to
ask. So he waited his moment and made his departure,
choking on unsaid words and wondering why it mattered. How could it possibly matter now?

The sun was setting pink and gray when he carefully
closed and locked the heavy walnut doors of the town
house and descended to the streets. A few rainclouds
hastened the darkness, and it began to rain; a fine misty
rain that did nothing to slake the fever in him.

Nothing was the same. The familiar faces were gone
from the streets, old stately homes housed rabble from
the North, carpetbaggers, speculators, and outright
crooks. So he went to those parts of town where nothing
ever changes—towards the saloons and gaming halls,
through Congo Square where the blacks still danced to
the voodoo drums at sunset, past the Cajun whores and
the gypsy village.

A young woman caught at his arm. "Your fortune,
han'some gentleman. Jus' one dollar for your right
hand, and I read fortune, me."

She was young. Her breasts swung free beneath her
blouse and pressed warmly against his arm. She wore a
loose-fitting blouse that left her round dark shoulders
bare. She was dumpy and richly bodied, and Jules considered paying her price, but not for the fortunetelling.
A woman could ease him.

He hesitated just long enough for the girl to draw

him into a narrow ground-floor room. They passed through a curtain of strung wooden beads that marked the entryway, and she seated him at a squat wooden table. A single candle lit the shabby room with its drably curtained windows.

She sat, too, and smiled broadly at her patron. Her lips were very full, her teeth very white against the darkness of her skin. She looked ripe and willing. *Full of cream,* he thought. *Like a chocolate eclair.* She still held his hand a prisoner.

"And what do you see, little dark jewel," he said softly.

She turned his palm upward to the light and pored over it. At the same time her dark hair fell in long, thick tresses, obscuring her face and throwing a weird jagged shadow across his hand. Her grip on his hand loosened, but she did not look up. "I see nothing," she said quietly.

"Nothing?" he said. "Oh, come, my dear." But now she looked at him with a sober, secretive face. "Oh, what is it? Not that cut across my palm. It's nothing—I cut myself with a knife when I was a child. I wasn't born with it."

"You were unlucky then, monsieur." Her face was closed, her dark eyes guarded.

"Don't look so serious, little night flower. I will accept, if I must, that my future is a ballad unsung."

She pushed away his hand and stood. "There is no charge. I am sorry, m'sieur, but I mus' close the shop, you see? I mus' make a call."

He found himself outside again, alone. Unlucky—that much was true—losing the little baggage to some gombo gypsy superstition. But he had a purpose now—he could thank the fortuneteller for that. And he wondered if Julie Elliot would remember him.

Julie Elliott ran the classiest whorehouse in New

Orleans. Mahogany Hall. It had been built for a Spanish grandee over half a century before—a little palace, and inlaid with costly mosaics and built of the rich red wood which gave it its name. Its thirty-two bedrooms had tiled baths and soft woven carpets on the floors. When the Spanish moved out, a speculator bought it for a song. But palaces were out of fashion, and it took the wiles of a natural entrepreneur, which Julie was, to put it to its most natural use.

She installed a bar in the drawing room, populated the house with thirty beautiful women who never stepped out of sheer lounging robes into anything else, and furnished each of the bedrooms with the biggest, stoutest bed that money could buy. Her girls were the best—it was rumored she broke them in herself—and for two years Jules had been one of her most favored patrons.

The house still looked set up for business. The lights were lit. Jules breathed a sigh of relief and turned the bell. The girl who answered the door did not know him. He asked for Julie.

She stepped out from the parlor, where the revelers were warming up and the girls were preening their feathers. A mammoth of a woman, corseted up in iron girdles and winking with jewels like a Christmas tree. She wore a scarlet dress cut low from which her enormous breasts poked forth like huge melons, and it was into this overwhelming embrace that Jules found himself drawn.

"Now let me look at you, bad boy," she said, releasing him. "So long it has been you do not come to visit Jules, and I hear you go to the West. You find gold, yes?" Her eyes roved over his face and figure with familiar license and a broad smile spread across her face. "Ah, as beautiful as ever, you devil. If I didn't keep an eye out, my girls would give you for free."

"But still you don't eat right," she admonished him. She patted the weighty meat of her thighs, and laughed, "Like Julie."

"And you still smoke those Jackson squares," he accused, referring to the squat cigar that burned acridly between her fat bejeweled fingers. "It's time you switched to something more ladylike."

She rolled her eyes and cackled in her husky voice, "Well, I know ladies don't and Julie does. But Julie does most of what ladies don't. That's how come Julie does good business!"

"And how is your *maman?*" she asked.

"She's—resting," Jules replied with some effort. He could not bear to answer the cluckings of sympathy he knew would follow the truth. He could not admit that he was fleeing the handsomely laid new casket in the parlor and the still woman inside. That he had come precisely to escape the night in the house and the vigil over the dead.

"So come in to Julie's little party," she said, taking his arm. "Not for you to stand out in the doorway."

Like a great hen, she tucked her charge beneath her ample feathers and escorted him inside. The parlor was brightly lit with massive chandeliers, and the walls were hung with silk. Women were perched everywhere—on divans and loveseats, posing in corners, draped over heavily upholstered chairs. One girl, giggling and squealing protests, had been upended over an armchair. Her lounging robe was raised above her waist, and one of the gallants made a great show of examining the merchandise.

"Oh, that Leonine!" a girl nearby complained. "Always showing off."

"She always shows her best side," another said dryly.

"You're just jealous, Elena, because you have such a skinny bottom!"

Jules stood to one side and enjoyed the spectacle.

Some dozen men were in attendance—none of them, Jules found to his relief, familiar faces.

Big Julie was still at his elbow. "I'll get for you my pretty Marietta," she told him. She gestured lewdly and grinned. "A mouth like wet strawberries—you'll like her."

She lumbered her way across the floor and into a circle of people, and emerged a moment later with her charge—a tall girl with flaming red hair and bold bright eyes, who looked across at Jules and licked her lips.

"She thinks to eat you in one bite, this one," Julie warned, "but me, I think it's a good match. You watch out for the claws now, yes?"

Jules kept the girl till dawn, and the claws never came unsheathed. She was as good as Julie promised— talented, supple, smooth as butter. He prolonged the play and kept the lights burning. But when he finally entered her, he put them out. He wanted to bury her secrets in her body—he didn't want his face giving him away, for he could feel the girl was new and the patrons were all strangers. But the room, the bed, the very act were all too well remembered, and led him to the memory of the rest—the parlor where the ghost was waiting, where always before she would be sitting at the desk, as likely as not spreading out a game of solitaire and swearing at her cards when he came in.

And "Jules!" she would say, "you hexed my cards again, you gypsy scoundrel. Spending your sweat at a gallop on the mattresses at Julie's." She would stop his denial with a shaking of her fingers. "Don't bother me with innocent tales. When you are an old man, you'll have the leisure to reconstruct your history with honor and good deeds." And they would laugh together and take a glass of sherry, toasting one another as the best of companions, and he would bring regards from Julie and the girls and regale her with the antics of the flesh-pot's patrons.

The body beside him was vague, like a memory. Only the ghost was real. The girl could not ease him, though he emptied himself in her willing body like a drunk retching up his liquor. It did no good. Escape was temporary, and in the pale streaks of the southern dawn, he was again walking Burgundy Street to the turnoff on Rue Toulouse. He entered the house with a guilty air, and, lighting no lights, stepped quickly past the parlor without going in, and continued directly to his room where he slept fitfully until noon.

About three o'clock, the guests began arriving, bringing their gifts of fruit and little sweet cakes. Jules felt suffocated entertaining them in the parlor where his mother lay like a wooden doll, displaying her death to the visitors. He drank himself full to take the grating edge off the sound of their voices and cursed the custom and propriety that brought them there. Adele Fornee, his mother's friend, had grown fat since he'd seen her last. She seized his sleeve and held on like a bulldog.

"Oh, Jules, she looks magnificent, your *maman*," the old lady simpered. "And purple always was her favorite color—it sets her skin off beautifully. Ah, may I look half so well—"

And all the while the old hag was congratulating herself it was not she, lying there waxen and so lovely still, but reduced to a mute centerpiece, an object of conversation.

Jennie was there as well, subdued from her outbursts the day before, and Jules breathed more easily. Her mother—a pale, colorless woman whom no one ever noticed—made the initial amenities and betook herself to a chair where she proceeded to fade into the wallpaper.

But others made more demands on the host. Falsely gay or falsely sympathetic, they pressed in upon him; he felt trapped. The women especially clung to him, the matrons fawning grotesquely under the guise of

comfort—the younger women trying out their rusty
charms, jabbering nervously, because Jules had known
them, before the war, and things were so different now.
They did bad imitations of the old charm, and it was
sham—sad, empty, fake.

Jules was glad he had arranged a private burial—
just the Reverend Joe Fisk and the sexton. It was Joe
Fisk who had last made Louisa laugh, though it was
only his words quoted in a New Orleans journal. Jules
remembered hearing her calling him into the sitting
room in San Francisco. The paper had quoted the closing of a sermon given by Fisk just after the convention
that abolished the South's state governments and
barred all leaders of the Confederacy from voting and
holding office, and it was the end of the service that
closed the convention.

The Reverend Joseph Fisk stood forth and gestured
the pious assemblage to join with him. "Bless President Andrew Johnson of these United States. Enable
him to pause in his career of vice and folly. May he
cease from doing evil and learn to do right."

She had read the passage aloud to Jules, and she had
laughed, that light, feathery laugh of long-ago days before the pain and drugs had brought silence to the house.
"Joe always did know what side God was on," she told
her son. "And he was always trying to make God see
the error of His ways!"

Of course, Jules had not told Reverend Fisk that.

He felt a hand on his shoulder and turned around to
see Emile, the only guest inside the crowded room
whose sympathy Jules felt as a genuine comfort. Jules
could not remember his mother when she had excited
such desire as Emile had described. But he had known
her to inspire something else—which was also a form

of love—a chivalry, a splendid gallantry, which hall-marked the best of the Southern man, and which as a gentlewoman, had been his mother's due. Jules had no doubt that Emile Adante had loved his mother. Emile could share a portion of his grief. Emile knew that he was leaving tomorrow for San Francisco directly after the funeral.

"It's nearing six o'clock, Jules," the older man said. "I think I must be going soon. I'm taking a party with me."

Jules was grateful. Emile would begin the leavetaking, and the others would follow suit. He was beginning to wonder how long he could deal with the Adeles and Jennies and the other matrons.

Within an hour, the last good-byes had been said, the last hands shaken, the last powdered cheeks and foreheads kissed. The servingwomen were cleaning off the plates and drying the glasses. Jules left them and went upstairs.

Room after room he entered, each time pausing before each window for a final look. Views he remembered from his childhood—of the streets, the neighbor's yard, the inner patio and garden. Then he closed the wooden shutters and the rooms grew dark, one by one, as though the sun were slowly parting from the house.

From the last window in his bedroom which faced west, he could see storm clouds gathering, heavier than the day before. Opening his wardrobe, he withdrew a long black cape which fastened at the collar with a thick gold chain. He flung it over his shoulders and went down the stairs. In the kitchen, he gave the maids their wages and dismissed them. In the parlor he lit two tall candles that stood in silver holders on the mantel. From a stand in the reception hall, he withdrew his walking stick. Then he was outside, walking rapidly without a glance back to the darkened house.

He crossed west to La Douane and then toward the

river and the park that bordered on the levee. But the gates to the park were locked. Pacing along the public boulevard, he watched the ships at anchor in the harbor. The rain had started, and people caught out were scrambling for cover, but Jules remained, watching the bare masts bobbing in the tide. He leaned against a lamp post, and the hard, glowing gaslight caught the sweep of pallid brow, where the skin was drawn tight over the bone. His eyes were shadowed, weighted with the sleeplessness of last night and the night before, and the rain was soaking his hair. But it did not seem to matter.

A crew of men, some eight or nine on leave, drew up to the dock and disembarked with much cursing and laughter, on their way to the brothels and taverns and other delights of port. They eyed Jules curiously and grew more silent as they passed his strange, still figure, standing like a specter in the rain.

"Peculiar chap," one of them whispered.

"This place is full of peculiar," another said judiciously. "Why the last time I was here, I seen an old graybeard out a-walking in nothin' but his nightshirt—imagine that!"

"I'd rather imagine something else a-walkin' about in a nightshirt," his companion said jovially. "And I know where this man is gonna find it."

One of the men paused several times to turn and look back at the tall figure, silhouetted against the sky, except where the street light marked the passages of his face. He sighed once under his breath, shrugged his shoulders and moved on.

In the distance, the thunder roared out of its stormy percussion, but the air stayed warm and a breeze rose slightly from the river, chasing the heaviest of the rain before it. Jules, who had welcomed the tiny drumming of raindrops on his head and face, became restless again and moved on.

His head was giddy from the wine, and his body protested the lack of food. A few doors down, he saw Big Otis Weylander, standing under the awning of the old Queen's Parlor. After a moment's hesitation, he shook the rain from his head and started over.

"Why, Mr. Jules!" Otis's beefy face spread out in a welcoming smile. "Fancy seeing you back in the old place. Well, come right in." He opened the door and stood aside for Jules to enter.

But just as quickly, Jules had changed his mind. "I think I'll pass tonight, Otis," he said. "I'm slumming. Thanks all the same."

"Just arrive back?" the doorman asked.

Jules mumbled something for politeness' sake and turned away quickly to avoid further questions. He was cursed with welcome everywhere. Otis's next question would have been the same as Julie's—"And your *mamon*," he would have said. "And how is your *maman?*" He couldn't go back to Julie's either. He drummed his cane upon the sidewalk and continued down the street.

He had gone some fifteen blocks and passed into the *Vieux Carré* before he became aware of someone following him. The streets were almost deserted now; the workmen had gone home, and evening lights shone through the open windows of the squat stone houses that lined the streets.

Perhaps he was mistaken. He slowed his steps; the other walked more slowly, too. Returning to a normal pace, Jules casually put his hand in his right pocket and closed his fingers on the derringer he carried there. A little farther up the street, the door to a local tavern stood open. The click of echoing heels behind his own followed him five more houses. He turned and entered the saloon. He sat at the bar on a high wooden stool and spun the seat so he could glance toward the street window. The glass was foggy, but someone stood out-side.

Jules ordered cognac and the bartender pulled down a dusty bottle. Few of his customers drank anything but wine and beer, except on payday, and fewer still came so elegantly attired. Jules was out of place. A few of the regulars shuffled nervously and lowered their voices when he first came in. But the young man kept silent and unobtrusive, and after a time, the voices full of gossip and arguments rose to normal pitch. Ironically, Jules had found what he was seeking—a place where no one knew him.

And the figure at the window had disappeared.

Now the weight of the day's events fell on him in full force. But tomorrow he would be on his way. To-morrow he would be on the westbound train. Tomor-row. After he buried her.

He had shuttered the windows. Old Rosa used to say ghosts slept in darkened houses—they haunted only by evening light. " 'Cos if they ain't no folks t' haunt, what's th' good o' gettin' up?" But it was the last night, and the house drew him.

Slouching over his drink, Jules hunched his shoulders and avoided his reflection in the wide bartender's mir-ror. He drank steadily, motioning his orders with an upraised finger and speaking to no one. Vaguely he wondered if he might drink so much that he could not get home. Perhaps if he was very quiet they would let him stay all night. It would be finished tomorrow.

He was setting down his fourth when he felt a hand tentatively touch his elbow. He started up at the in-trusion.

He had already forgotten the man outside.

"I'll buy ye the next if you'll have it."

The man looked to be a bit shorter than Jules, and stockier. His hair was coarse and dark, his skin swarthy.

The gold earring hoop in his left ear marked him for a sailor. A long jagged scar made a wrinkled seam across his right cheek, beginning near the corner of his mouth and ending just below his eye. At first Jules did not understand, and then he had to stifle the urge to laugh. The man was a sailor apparently, with the drawn and hungry look men have coming ashore from a while at sea. The hungry look, the tentative appeal were for Jules. The sailor's eyes glanced over his face and strayed to his mouth with an obvious longing.

He glanced up and the man's scar recalled the little gypsy girl and the old knife wound on his hand. A wry smile crossed his face with the thought that he had inherited another scar, one that stood before him in silent pleading. "I ought to shoot the bugger," he thought. But he nodded casually instead, with the slightest inclining of his head, and dropped his eyes like a coquette.

The next drink was delivered, plus one for his host. The sailor raised his glass.

"To days at sea, fair winds, and nights ashore," he said.

Jules nodded to spare himself answering, and sipped his drink. The sailor did not press him. He had escaped his reveling fellows to return to the levee where he had first seen Jules, but the boy had gone by then. Swallowing his disappointment, the sailor had moved on, and it was only by chance he had found the boy again. The first overture had been accepted. But the sailor felt strangely insecure—out of his depth. This was not common quarry, and the drink might mean nothing. He eyed the young man speculatively. "What's yer name, lad?" he asked.

Jules hesitated a moment and answered, "Louis," thinking of the woman in the box. "Louis," he repeated, satisfied with the sound. He was slightly drunk.

"They call me Jack Thunder," the sailor offered when his companion failed to ask.

Jules mumbled something unintelligible. He didn't want the man to have a name.

"What'd ye say?" the sailor asked.

"I said my father was a seaman," Jules said, uttering the words in spitefully clear enunciation.

"And what do you do?" the sailor was pressing now, anxious to firm the unvoiced connection.

"I'm an actor," Jules replied, as though that effectively closed the conversation. He considered it a most appropriate lie. He returned to his drink.

Feeling the rebuff, the sailor turned back to his own glass, stealing glances at the boy and cursing inwardly. It might all be for nothing. Why had he followed this young man? There were others—willing, available. But not like this one. Beauty lured him, and desire so acute it rose like pain. The sailor finished his drink and rose from his seat. He cleared his throat and worked to make his voice commonplace, unaffected. "You coming?" he said.

Jules turned his head slowly, eyes first, watching the man, watching the jagged scar twitch in the man's cheek. The sailor found himself fidgeting under the calm gaze of those dark eyes and almost abandoned the hunt. He almost wished he'd never begun it.

But Jules swung his long legs around and stood, a slight smile on his face, and followed the sailor outside.

The rain was still falling lightly, in a mist. The sailor had his hands in his pockets, nervously jingling the change. Jules remained silent as though waiting, and uncommitted. Like a flirtatious woman, passive, cruel.

The sailor glanced at him uneasily, but could not bring himself to meet those dark eyes. "I've got forty dollars," he said desperately, feeling a very fool. He'd never paid more than ten.

Something warned him the boy had his own game. He didn't fear a fight. No, something else. He might be skivvied for the drink and told to go to hell. But now the boy had turned his eyes full on the sailor, and the man was amazed to see they were not cold as he had thought at first, but smoldering—as though something burned behind those eyes, like a buried fire. He blinked —it was just the street lights reflected like small glowing candles. It was just that he had such *dark* eyes.

Jules watched and his mouth curved into a smile. The full cupid's bow of that perfect upper lip stretched just a little tighter. "Fine," he said.

The sailor swallowed hard. *He had not expected to win.* The full extent of his lust, doubtful of its fulfillment, now ran to his head like wine and made him giddy. Like an ant setting out to climb a mountain. He would crush those lips. He would devour them. The boy—he would have him!

He licked his own lips, which were dry. They'd go to Harry's first. "I know another place," the sailor said at last.

Outside the saloon, the man took his arm protectively and led him to another bar, situated in the back room of a whorehouse parlor. A tall woman, heavily rouged and tightly girdled in glittering cloth, brawled in a throaty contralto to entertain the company. The hard glow of the gaslight saw through the makeup as the singer raised her head. A thin stubble was revealed along her throat. The customers were all men.

....They knew the man who had brought him and greeted him with enthusiasm. "Well, how ye doing, Jack Thunder!" one said.

Jules found himself, eyed, appraised, approved. Several men looked at him covetously. Like a woman on display.

"And where did you pick *this* up, scoundrel?" A fat-bellied, hairy giant bellowed to the sailor. He meant Jules—the new meat, the novitiate.

A fantasy was taking shape inside his mind. He embraced the female role he'd been given to play and carried it even further into his own disturbed reality. He gave the sailor a name of his own choosing. Jed Taylor. And he was himself the female role, the woman best known, the mother. *I dub thee Jed Taylor. And I—shall be my mother.* Like a cynical bystander, his mind absorbed the part in the joining. *I shall create myself,* he thought, a sardonic observation. His was a mad, demented logic, warped but acute. *The fruit of this union that I create—how appropriate—Merde.* He threw back his fine dark head and swallowed the tears. How appropriate.

It wasn't long in coming. The sailor was anxious. He felt the grinding hunger in his body. He knew a hotel.

Outside, the night air was soft and sullen. Moisture hung suspended in the low weaving fog. But the freshening of the rain did not quite mask the faint odor of dying vegetation and waste, the slow seeping sewers that ran their sluggish way along the curb. Their boots splashed dully through shallow puddles on the pavement, and the gaslight reflected in the dark streets like tiny moons.

The desk clerk and the sailor were well acquainted. The room was small and ugly, the iron bedstead topped by a cruelly misshapen mattress. There were only two candles. The sailor lit them both. He wanted to see.

Usually the sailor was in a hurry. Usually it wasn't even on a bed, but against a rack of storage crates, and the object some street urchin in dirty rags to whom a fiver was riches. Usually he wanted only to make it happen quickly, to ease the tight hunger in his loins. Boys were easy to find if you knew where to look.

But never a boy like this. A young gentleman by all signs, smooth-skinned, clean. With a face like some dark angel—a high, wide sweep of brow, the high, lean cheeks and strong jaw of a man, with the maddening lips of a woman. He could drown himself in a mouth like that.

He pressed his face to the boy's flesh and inhaled deeply the odor of cologne, starch, fresh linen. The shirt was open and the chest beneath it smooth. Silky skin.

"Oh, me boy, I've never had one the likes of you." His words groaned against the boy's flesh.

"Let me kiss you, dearie." It was a lover's plea. "Let me kiss your mouth."

Jules suffered his kisses unmoved, but passive, acquiescent. He let himself be undressed. The sailor closed his arms around Jules and pressed his body against the other. Their genitals touched, the sailor hard and eager, Jules soft and curiously unaffected. His mind was crying, *Jed, Jed,* in a woman's voice, as his mother had called in a dying voice.

The sex was painful, but Jules submitted in silence. He allowed the strange male kisses on his body, the odd scraping of the man's beard against his face, the square callused hands that touched and patted his skin, smoothing him like a restive horse. The pain seemed to ease toward the end, and Jules heard his own soft groans bury themselves in the mattress.

At last the sailor was done. He turned to embrace the dark beauty, but Jules disengaged himself. Politely. As though a stranger had brushed his arm in passing on the street.

"What is it?" the sailor asked. He ached to hold the boy, ached with a need that was inexplicable to him, not composed of the appetites he understood. The boy's isolation hurt him. Something of the boy's beauty.

"I've not hurt 'e, lad," he said worriedly. " 'Ave ye nivver done it wi' a man, then?"

"Oh, that," Jules answered negligently, as though in some incredible way the act just completed were already long forgotten. "It doesn't matter."

Then, incredibly, he laughed and began to dress, encasing his long legs in the fawn breeches, pulling them to his waist with a businesslike air.

Wounded, the sailor said no more, just watched in dumb misery as the young man covered himself, dusted his trousers, put on his boots.

As though suddenly awakened to the sailor's presence and discomfited silence, Jules excused himself with an apologetic shrug. "My mother is waiting, you see. I must get on."

He was halfway to the landing when the sailor ran out after him. "Louis!" he called. He extended four folded dirty bills toward the boy. His scarred face held a tentative wince, as if expecting to be struck.

Unaccountably, the boy laughed again, thanked the sailor, but a hollowness underlay the laughter, a sad, empty mockery. The sailor did not like the sound of it. For the sailor, the sound was almost more than he could bear. Jules thanked him politely, pocketed the bills, and went down the narrow stairs.

The hour was dark except for the parlor where the candles still burned above the mantel. Jules began to sing, softly:

> Ah! Celeste, ah! Celeste,
> mo bel bojou,
> mo l'aimai to com cochon
> l'aimai la bou.

He sang louder. Loud enough that the woman in the parlor could hear if she were listening:

If you were a bird, my friend, sweet friend,
and I a gun, my friend,
I would kill you, my friend, sweet friend,
    sweet bird,
because I love you so.

He was hoping his song would put out the candles
and put the ghosts to sleep, but it did not. His feet
carried him into the quiet parlor which smelled all of
lilacs and tiny lilies, and he called her softly, calling
Maman! in a strangled, terrible whisper that got no
answer.

At last he knelt by the side of the box with its edging
of purple velvet, and let the tears come down.

7

FROM THE WINDOW of her apartment, Lorelei could see the mist rising over the bay. It was the same every morning—the silver water cloud, coming in whispers like the first breath of day, dispersed in sunlight and changing from silver to gold. Up north in the highlands, the leaves would already be showing their autumn colors, but San Francisco seemed to dwell in eternal spring.

She had not been north since she left the outlaw band more than a year before. She had not even left the city in that time, and it was going on two years since she had seen her mother.

Another two months to harvest time, she thought. There would be square dances and bonfires, and a bite in the evening air. She had put off going at first out of caution, left over from her career as a member of Whitey's gang. She didn't know who might speak of a woman bandit, who might identify her. So for a time she had watched and waited, and stayed low to the horizon.

Gradually her wariness passed. She felt safe, and she entered wholeheartedly into her love affair with the wild golden city. She was one of the most popular stockbrokers at the 'change, and as such, she lived well. She was courted and propositioned, swept to suppers and theaters and fashionable teas.

She wasn't ready to go back. She had a strange premonition that when she returned, it would be to stay. Sometimes she missed the mountains fiercely. She thought of her mother, and of Butterfly's black colt, that her father had named Ravensfire before he left the ranch that last time. She remembered the taste of wild strawberries in summer, corn and chicken roasting in the fire. And the mountain winds that shifted and sang through the branches of juniper and spruce. *But not yet. She wasn't ready to go back yet.*

"Aye, you're waiting, dearie," Ma Belle would say, shaking her finger with its long red-painted nail. "You've been keeping the boys at bay, and you're just waiting for one of them to catch you.

"I fear for you, me girl," the old bawd had told her. "You've a romantic heart beneath it all, and that's dangerous. Dealing with men, 'tis better you have craft and cool—else you only get the short end of it—a swollen belly and an empty purse."

Lorelei had laughed. "I'm made for the chase, Ma, and who knows that better than you?"

"But the capture, my pet," the woman admonished. "And not some playing at men's games. No, you don't hide your bosom for this, and guard yourself with zippered trousers." She looked Lorelei over with unerring appraisal.

"I detect the sweet scent of perfume, do I not? And your face ain't painted with dirt. There's gold in your ears and 'round your neck, and you needn't have dressed with that immodest neckline today. You're not at the 'change—"

"And I don't know why I'm here, you embarrassing old bawd, when you're always examining me for a telltale sign of some bedroom tumble."

"You're here," the old woman said genially, "because

Ma Belle knows all your secrets—or most of them, at any rate. And that makes this a comfortable place to set your buns. You can rest easy and slouch like a tomboy, and you listed to my girls jawing slut-talk and you think you know all about it, when you're so innocent you got no idea how dumb you really are. You walk around that overblown saloon like a flower full of honey a-shimmying on a beehive. And you're just having the time of your life, watching all those bees dancing."

"I heard a rumor," she said slyly. " 'Course I don't pay rumors much mind—that the Ralston boy asked to marry with you."

"After I turned down his first offer," Lorelei said coolly. "And I turned down his second as well."

"That's just what I mean to say!" Ma exclaimed. "And do you know, fair maiden, what that family is worth—what his daddy is worth who built this town and still owns a sizable chunk?—including where you work!"

"If you think I'm worried about my job, Ma Belle, I'm not," the girl said loftily. "Billy doesn't pay Mark's fooleries any mind. He's a mincing dandy—pettish boy can't even ride a horse—the smell offends him."

"And so you'll none of 'im, my lady," Ma Belle said spiritedly, "which is just what I mean to say. There's nothing gained in keeping it till it rots now, is there? But you wouldn't trade a maidenhead for a fortune— no, 'he's a mincing dandy,' and you'll keep your virtue, not even stretch it a little for a night of profit.

"There's no fooling an old jade, my Lorelei, so mark me well. You'll give it away in the end, and foolishly, too, no doubt. Some empty-pocketed swindler with broad shoulders and hairy hands, and he'll set a horse well, me darlin' but don't you know he'll have lost the best in a poker game and per'aps he could borrow yours—"

Lorelei was laughing into her tea. "If you think me that thin-witted, it's a wonder I still survive."

"No, perhaps you're not so dumb as that, quite," her hostess admitted, "but I swear I'll see you one day singing and sighing like a lovesick chicken a'lying spread-legged on the block. Love doesn't have no sense in it, my girl, and even less profit. And love's what you'll call it first time you find yourself wiggling and a-humping yer pillow."

The old lady never minced words. *Well, I'm certainly not going to lie under Mark Ralston to please her sense of female business acumen,* she thought. Still, his marriage proposal had pleased her vanity.

She pulled out a sheer satiny dressing gown, just as Nan came in with a tray. A lady's maid had been Lorelei's first acquired luxury. Nan was good-natured and not very clever, but she managed the important things like breakfast and taking messages when her mistress was avoiding suitors.

It was a working day. She reached for the black silk frock and patent heels. For jewels—a simple beryl pin and matching earbobs that winked and glittered the reflection of her eyes. Nothing too provocative. Just enough in the subtle dip of the black neckline against her white skin. Gerald Todd chose his lady sellers largely for their looks, but he expected style to go along with it, and a certain decorum to be observed. Vices were catered to on a grand scale, but woe to the girl who caused a public scene. There were discreet back rooms where a stockholder might entertain his mistress for lunch whether she was a broker or not, and other rooms for those gamblers finding insufficient action in the fluctuations of their investments. But just last month, when Arnold Penny had challenged McPherson over a well-endowed broker named Bernice, in the center of the Exchange, the girl had been dismissed.

Well, so Bernice cussed Todd out and two weeks later

came back to the Exchange as a buyer bearing a bank draft drawn on Arnold Penny's account. Lorelei had taken her order, and the two of them had giggled half the afternoon. Socially acceptable, though Gerald had scowled from his chair in the great hall.

The day was bright and sunny and the 'change was a ten-minute walk from her apartment. She passed the bookshop and the bakery without a glance, but the third shop made her pause and stare, pressing her nose like a child against the glass.

Madame Claire had changed her window, and the mannequin now displayed the pride of the latest European shipment. The art was in the simplicity of design, and Madame Claire's wooden dummy with its stiff mockery of female form could not do it justice.

The cloth was a creamy crepe de chine, held at the shoulder with a single strap of delicate gold-threaded trim. It edged across the bust like a piece of ribbon, while the silk faultlessly molded the form below. The waistband was of the same thin strip of gold, as was the trimming at the hem of the narrow skirt which was slit on the left side all the way to the knee.

But it needed a real body inside it. Lorelei hesitated only a moment, holding her purse as though to weigh it. Madame Claire ran an exclusive dress shop; her prices kept it that way.

The shop was small and outfitted like a parlor, its floors covered with costly Persian carpets, wing chairs upholstered in rich silvery brocade. But Lorelei had no time to sit. Fortunately, the shop was not crowded in the morning hours, and Madame Claire came out of the back room in a froth and bubble of energy.

"Ah, Mademoiselle Lorelei!" she cried. "It is too long that you do not grace my shop."

"I suppose you set up your window just to tempt me," Lorelei said, smiling.

"Oh, yes, the cream—I should have known. Not for

everyone it is made, but for you, I think *yes*." She put
on her spectacles to again examine her client's figure,
a pleasure in itself. Thin broad shoulders, long and
narrow-waisted, perfect legs. "You are lucky," she told
the girl. "Only two copies do I have, and I think it will
be a match *très chic*, you and this dress."

"I barely have time to try it on," Lorelei said.

"So, you come and try it now. If you like, we mark
it for you." She accompanied the girl to the dressing
room and pulled the curtain. She undid the fastenings
to Lorelei's dress and the girl slipped it off.

"Everything," she said. "Under this is only skin,
chérie. For most of us"—she gestured to her own corseted form—"c'est impossible. But not for you."

Blushing slightly, Lorelei pulled off the chemise and
lace drawers as well, and Madame Claire slipped the
ivory silk over her head. A series of four ribbony ties
held the gown together—one at the neck and waist, and
two between down the center back. When she turned in
the mirror she could see her own skin winking sensually
between the ties all the way down to the curve of her
back.

"It is shockingly wicked," she announced to the
proprietress.

"I knew you would love it," Madame Claire replied.

Lorelei emptied her purse at the counter, but left
unregretting. Brad Lowry was taking her to dinner tonight, and she wouldn't need cash till tomorrow. Besides, didn't Madame Claire say it was *her dress*? She
chuckled to herself. *Have to own my own dress, don't
I?* she chewed on her lip thoughtfully, trying to decide
when she would wear it. But the problem wasn't really
when or where, she realized suddenly.

The problem was *for whom*.

That was what the damned dress was made for, with
its four little bows holding it together. Not for the awkward hands of the garment's wearer stretching back-

ward for the ties. Not for Nan's unromantic fingers to undo. *I'll be proving Ma Belle right if I don't watch out.* But there it was. Made for the easy turn of a man's hand—nothing but to pull four little ribbons, and the lady was all undone.

Ma Belle had been incredulous that Lorelei retained her virtue still after a year in the wild town. The girls at the 'change all had their keepers—and weren't they picked from the cream of the city? And they teased her too—Bernice and Genevieve, and plucky little Constance, whose easy tumbling belied her name. But there was something wrong with every man to Lorelei's critical eye—too fat, too foppish, too dull, and she had yet to acquire what most of the girls accepted as natural: a physical attraction to material wealth.

"Aye, me girl, a hundred thousand can make a man look mighty pretty," Ma Belle would say in the tone of a lecturer imparting weighty facts. "Don't you know the young get old as well, and the trim ones grow fat, if they can afford it? A smart girl bears that in mind.

"But you!" she'd exclaim, throwing up her hands. "Waiting for a knight on a white charger, you are. Still full of fairy tales and thinking all particular this and that he'll be, when you'll be blind to whatever it is, if you only think you've found it."

But Ma Belle couldn't think of love as anything but a flesh market, a form of barter superior to any other. "After the first time, a girl just gets and never misses what she's trading," she intoned with other assorted homilies of similar import.

Lorelei could carry a parasol as easily as a rifle now, and she made a sensation in the park riding her blooded mare astride. She played her charme, she flirted sometimes outrageously, but something she held back. She still remembered the night with Davy at the lake—her anger afterward, his rejection. Yet the feelings that had come so naturally then had not come again. She blamed the city, too sophisticated to be natural; she blamed the men, who seemed to view women as something they wore, like a topcoat.

The day seemed to pass slower than usual. Stock trading was slow until a brief rush in the afternoon, that forced her to hurry for her dinner date. She dated Brad Lowry because he was basically shy and lonely and thought himself in love with her.

But tonight the play was overlong and boring, and Brad was his most irritating, insipid, fawning self, beginning almost every utterance with, "I know what you feel for me isn't love," or "I know I'm not much with words," then going on with far too many words about how love grows with time and how just being near her was enough for him. She endured it all until the fifth act, when she felt his thin, damp paw settle itself covertly on her knee. She removed it as though she were picking off a piece of lint. It would be her last supper with Bradford Lowry.

It was late when he finally dropped her off and her farewell was cool and final.

Nan was already asleep, and Lorelei was grateful. More jabbering avoided. She pressed back a yawn, and began idly undoing the buttons of her blouse.

A man's arm shot out from behind her and pressed over her mouth. She had no weapon! Her reflexes, dulled by city living, began to work, and she braced her body to twist free.

"For God's sake, Lore, don't scream!" the intruder whispered urgently. She turned around. Her eyes widened in amazement.

"Beau! Well, you were like to scare me to death." Her eyes went over him quickly, noting the bristly unshaven face, the circle of fatigue under his eyes, the tension in his stance.

"You're on the run," she said flatly. It was a statement, not a question.

"I've got to get away, Lorelei. I wouldn't have set it on you, but there's no one else. I've got to get far this time. If you can help—"

She nodded impatiently. "Of course I'll help." She went to the dresser, picked up a purse and dropped it without opening it. That damned dress. She'd used up the last of her cash.

"We'll have to wait till tomorrow," she said absently. "I've still got your seven thousand from the bank job."

"I've got money right now," Beau said. "And I have to leave tonight. I can't chance it."

"Where'd you get the money?" she asked suspiciously.

"Lore, I got no time for questions!" He was eyeing the door to her apartment anxiously. "You can help me or what? If not, I've got to get a move on—"

"It's bad?" This time it was a question.

"Bad," he said.

"Well, you'd better tell me something while I'm getting dressed." She reached for a pair of riding breeches and shiny leather boots, putting them on under her skirts with an unabashed and businesslike air.

"Wells Fargo man," Beau said quickly. "It was tight, that payroll job—and Whitey decided to take him hostage, get us past the townspeople, keep them from following. He could have let him loose, when we got clear, but you know Whitey—how he loves his games. Turned him loose ten miles out of town—the man thought he was letting him go."

Lorelei nodded. She'd seen this "game" before.

"Well, he shot him in the leg, then the other leg, then in the back."

"He's getting more elaborate," Lorelei said coolly. But inside she felt sick.

"The thing is, they got Whitey."

Lorelei looked up, startled. Somehow, she never thought they'd get Whitey. He was too cunning, too sly.

He could take a turn between two rocks, and you'd swear he'd disappeared before your eyes.

"So—"

"There was only the two of us on that job, Lorelei," he said grimly. She saw the wrath on his face, the tight black anger. "He's saying I shot the Wells Fargo man."

"How could anyone believe that, for heaven's sake, Beau. It's Whitey's specialty."

"Who else but the gang knows that?" he retorted. "You know, Whitey's changed his style in the past year, Lore. He's done a little quiet politicking—got a few 'friends' elected. One of them's assistant to the county sheriff."

Lorelei nodded. That sounded more like Whitey.

"Lore, if they catch me, they'll hang me."

"Beau, they're not going to get you," she said with conviction. She chewed at her lower lip and shot a glance at Beau from under her lashes. He fidgeted. He looked scared. For a moment she could see so clearly the boy who used to play with her. Cowboys and Indians and Beggar-My-Lad. She searched her head for an answer. Beau wasn't safe here. But where would he be truly safe?

"Beau, we're going to get you out of the country." The idea had come, fully formed, and she knew instantly it was the answer, the only real chance.

Although Susanna's father had disapproved of her marriage to Jed, the family in England had re-established contact with Susanna to advise her of her father's death, and on learning of Lorelei's birth, had kept intermittently in touch. "You're going to Hampshire in England, Beau. To my uncle. I'll give you a letter for him."

"Your uncle?"

"Hush up, now, I'm thinking." She felt the old excitement rising in her as the challenge presented itself and she faced it squarely. Her eyes blazed like a cat in the dimly lit room. She snapped her fingers suddenly and eyed Beau speculatively, grinning.

With long-legged strides, she crossed to her wardrobe and began pulling out dresses. She stripped several from their hangers and tossed them onto the couch. The last of these she examined and then carefully, casually ripped the side seams from collar to hem.

"Lorelei, you gone crazy?" Beau stared at her in disbelief. "By tomorrow the posse'll be all over this town, and you're playing with dresses!"

"Shut up, Beau, and start blessing yourself that I'm tall for a girl and you aren't for a boy and these dresses are expensive—they've got side seams." She held up the devastated dress with apparent satisfaction. "Now, this one'll do nicely when we've tacked it together."

"You don't mean to put *me* in that thing—"

She hooted gleefully. "I do indeed, my fond chum. The safest way to get you out is in disguise, and who's going to be looking for a dangerous killer under a woman's skirt?

"And just to make sure you don't mess up your costume, I'm going to get you on a ship myself. There's no ship out of here till morning. What about Los Angeles?"

Beau shook his head miserable. "We were chased up all the way from San Diego."

"Then it's out of the state tonight," she said. "Well, dammit, Beau, strip out of those duds. She wrinkled her nose. "Smells like you've been wearing 'em for a month!"

He grinned sheepishly, relieved at her authority. "You're not far wrong."

"Well, wash up over there. Can't have my lady's maid smelling like a cow barn."

He stripped off his shirt and passed it to Lorelei, who held it by the edge of the collar and carried it at arm's length toward a hamper. "On second thought, maybe

I'll burn it with the garbage." She caught his disgruntled glance. "Or bury it."

"Lorelei, that's all the clothes I've got!"

"*I've* got all the clothes you need, my girl," she said, already setting the tone of the play. "Give me those breeches, too."

Reluctantly, he obeyed, while she thoroughly enjoyed his discomfiture. She was eyeing his shorts. There he drew the line. "No!" he said in outraged finality.

"I guess you can keep them on," she said judiciously. "So long as you don't get it into your head to flirt with the porters."

"Lorelei, this is no joke."

"It's the best joke to come my way since I was playing 'the skinny dude.' And speaking of skinny," she said, tapping his chest, "those flat titties of yours will not pass. We'll just have to rig up a little stuffing to make up for what the Lord didn't give you, honey."

He was at her mercy, and he knew it. "Lorelei, you're the Lord God meanest woman I know!"

"Makes you glad I'm on your side, doesn't it?" she replied. At least he'd stopped fidgeting and that fearful look on his face had ceased. She checked the watch on the mantel, her mind rapidly working out the details of their journey. "There's a St. Louis train leaves at midnight," she said. "Haul out some of that money you've got. I'll go for the tickets while you finish washing. The less you're seen in this town, the better."

He handed her several crumpled bills which she stuffed into her blouse. She pinched his cheek. "There's a razor and soap in the bathroom. Shave close, sweetie."

The railway station was a huge, pretentious affair, built along the lines of a Gothic cathedral. It was quiet inside, except for the cooing and ruffling of roosting pigeons. The ticket seller had his feet up on a desk behind the iron grille and was snoring in obvious content.

He rose sleepily, adjusted his visor and bifocals, and peered over them at the girl.

"Two tickets, St. Louis," she said crisply.

"Well, you're in luck, ma'am. It's running right on schedule." He fumbled through a stack of tickets, talking all the time. "Nice time of year to be going to St. Louis," he said conversationally. "You visiting there?"

Lorelei made a point to pretend she didn't hear and concentrated her attentions on the big black and yellow posters advertising trips and listing timetables. Scanning quickly, she was relieved to note that theirs was the last train out. There as one train due from the South, and that any minute. She ought to get Beau out undetected. The old man would probably have gone back to snoring by the time she departed with her "maid."

The huge railway clock began its slow and ponderous chimes, and the expected train pulled up. "Just five minutes off," the ticket seller said proudly. "Yessir, the railroad really is a miracle wagon."

Only one passenger disembarked from the train. Lorelei, who had glanced over curiously found her eyes riveted on the new arrival. He was tall and except for a white silk shirt, was dressed entirely in black—a fitted suit of finely woven broadcloth. He carried a gold-headed cane with a shaft of polished ebony. His eyes were very dark—under heavy black brows and there was something achingly familiar, something she couldn't quite recall . . . But he was without a doubt the handsomest man she had ever seen.

He passed close by on his way to the street, and Lorelei felt herself trembling. *Stupid!* she thought to herself. He didn't even see her. Turning aside to keep from staring, she concentrated on his elongated shadow, thrown into relief against the huge wall of the station. He nodded briefly to the ticket seller and went outside, tapping his cane in time to his strides so that without looking she could feel the rhythm of his stride as he left, and the tapping grew faint.

"That's poor Mr. Hutchison," the ticket seller said.

Suddenly, Lorelei was all attention. "I'm sorry," she said sweetly. "I didn't hear—"

"Young Mr. Hutchison," the old man repeated obligingly. "I shouldn't say *poor*. Rumor has it he's a well-set-up fellow—financially, that is."

"I say poor," he explained pedantically, "because he's just come from burying his mother. Took her all the way to New Orleans—"

Now she remembered! The boy—the boy with his mother at the ranch. Oh, she'd been angry with her mother for days because they hadn't been invited to stay. Of course it was the same boy, older now.

The ticket seller was still talking. "—very fond of his mother, I understand." Lorelei nodded vaguely. What damned luck to see him again and be on her way elsewhere in a hurry. If only she could find out something more. He couldn't be married, or he wouldn't have been traveling alone. *Hutchison*. Well, she would remember the name.

Beau was in better spirits when she returned with the tickets. As wild and chancy as it seemed, her scheme reassured him. And from figuring himself a dead man, there wasn't anywhere to go but up.

Lorelei looked him over with approval, pulled out a hat, removed the feathers, and plopped it on his head.

"No, something a little uglier," she said thoughtfully, doing an imitation of Madame Claire. "Something with a little less chic." She brought down a paisley scarf and tied it around his head, then burst into irrepressible giggles.

"Least I don't have to worry about competition, Beau. You make one homely-looking female."

He scowled at her, but said nothing, not even when

she slipped the turned-out dress down over his head and attacked the seams with straight pins. Only after she stuck him with one did he remark her resemblance to a puckered-up porcupine.

"I'll have my own back for that," she threatened, mumbling through closed lips. "And for all the time when we were with Whitey." He had teased her unmercifully at times, knowing what no one else knew.

She pulled off the dress and tossed her guest a dressing gown—a frilly lace-trimmed robe of flaming red velvet. She went to rouse Nan, who emerged sleepy-eyed and stupid. The girl gaped at Beau, standing uncomfortably in the corner in her mistress's lounging attire.

"Don't pay him any mind, Nan," Lorelei said easily. She scrawled a note on a piece of stationery and sealed it in an envelope. "Bring this to Gerald Todd at the Stock Exchange," she said, handing it to the girl. "First thing in the morning. *Mr. Gerald Todd.* Ask anyone there." The girl nodded slowly and looked back wide-eyed to Beau.

Lorelei paid no mind, but gave the girl the altered dress and a sewing kit. "Stitch this up quick as you can. You're going to have a couple of weeks off, so be good. I'm going to pack."

"You sure we're safe, her knowing?" Beau asked anxiously as they departed.

"She's loyal," Lorelei answered briefly, "and she's too dumb to be dangerous. I'll be lucky if she remembers to deliver that note when she wakes up tomorrow."

But for all her assurances, Lorelei breathed a sigh of relief when they were on the train and the screeching reversal of the engines told them they were on their way.

"Tickets. Tickets, please. Have your tickets ready, ladies and gentlemen." The conductor looked tired. His run ended at Sacramento, and he barely glanced at the passengers beyond the hands that held the tickets. "Change at Sacramento," he droned, handing back the stubs. "Ten-minute rest."

They boarded the eastern train without incident, and Lorelei found a newsboy. She purchased over a dozen journals.

"What do you want with those?" Beau said. "My company inadequate?"

"San Francisco, Salt Lake, Denver, St. Louis, St. Louis, New Orleans," she recited, picking through the stack. She tossed the first two to Beau. "We'd best know where we're going," she said, "and what we might find when we get there." She picked up the *St. Louis Chronicle*. "I'm looking to see what ships are due out. My father had a friend, a shipper. Worked St. Louis and New Orleans mainly out of Liverpool and London. What was his name, dammit . . . Ackerson—Altman. No. It had a T in it. Atkinson! That was it." She pored over the journals. "I don't even see his name. But there are two ships leaving New Orleans—"

"We gonna have to go all the way down there?" Beau asked. "I was hoping to stay north."

"So was I," Lorelei agreed. "But we'll take what comes." She picked up the journal again. "According to this, things are a little hot down there. Read this—" She handed Beau an article on the recently formed Ku Klux Klan activities. "This one's pro—" She picked up another New Orleans chronicle. "This one—hell, this one's in French!"

"Give it here," Beau said.

"Beau! You've been holding out on me all this time. You can read it?"

He grinned happily. "Never thought it would do me any good. My father insisted. Isn't it funny—he used to talk about sending me to the Continent—" His voice fell slightly, then went on. "Least it's good for something."

He read silently for a few moments. "Lore, you know this is published by *blacks!*"

Lorelei took the news calmly. "You think you're the only nigger can read, my boy? What's it say?"

"Founded just three months ago, the so-called Ku Klux Klan, composed of disgruntled white supremacists in an effort to foil the efforts of Reconstruction, have begun a series of night raids—tactics of terror, burnings, hangings, and shootings. It is believed these men are drawn from the erstwhile privileged class of New Orleans and surrounding environs, slave dealers and plantation owners, previous members of the Confederacy of the United States.

He glanced at Lorelei. "You want more?"

"May as well hear the worst."

"On July twelfth, men believed to be members of the Klan descended on the home of E. Sinclair of Hamilton Row. Mr. Sinclair, enslaved as a field hand previous to the Emancipation, was bodily removed from his house and dragged to the outskirts of the city where white-robed judges behind hoods formed a mockery of a court and alleging that Mr. Sinclair had insulted a white woman with obscene suggestions the previous day, condemned him to death. The sentence was carried out immediately after the so-called trial. Of the numerous bystanders witness to this travesty of justice, those who protested the actions of the Klan were greatly outnumbered and powerless to prevent the tragedy."

Beau tossed the paper onto the seat in front of him. "I don't want to read anymore."

"This one looks like it covers the same stuff. It's a Republican journal. Least I can read it—it's in English."

The night wore on, and the train rumbled east, traveling into dawn. The two travelers gradually slumped lower in their seats and fell into uneasy slumber.

"Could've gotten a pullman—" Beau complained in final muttering before he fell asleep.

"Lucky to get a compartment," Lorelei replied. It was the last they knew until morning.

They awoke to clouds in Virginia City, and stopped just long enough to purchase food in a nearby café. They rolled into the rain and out of it again. There was more heat in the Mormon territory, which cooled as they passed over the mountains. They marked their time in light and dark for five days, dulled by the incessant rocking of their seats and the rumbling cadence of the train.

Past Fort Bridger and Cheyenne, and following the Platte across Nebraska, the seats remained the same. Lorelei knew every lump by heart. Kansas changed little from Nebraska, but beyond Lexington the land was hillier, the night sky not so far away.

They arrived in St. Louis past midnight of the fifth day. What little luggage they had, they carried off with them, stumbling several times before their legs became accustomed to the solid ground.

Beau hadn't shaved that morning, and Lorelei had to stay on guard at a public ladies room while he rapidly set up soap and brush and scraped away the stubble.

"Lore, why can't we cut out the disguise?" he said petulantly. The days of travel had worn on them both. "We're out of the state by a long way."

"I just have a feeling we're safer this way—until you're on the ship," she said. "I'll buy you some duds tomorrow when the shops open. But we've got to see about getting out of here. So far, they only list carriers going to New Orleans and stopping there. Nothing to England at all."

There was no place to make inquiries, so they headed for the docks. "Just stay close and don't say anything," she whispered.

A serene quiet dominated the fresh moist air, and a

breeze stirred in from the river. On one smallish boat, tied to a narrow wharf, three men were working rigging by the light from a string of lanterns hung from the risen anchor chain.

"Do you know any ships bound for England?" Lorelei called down.

The nearest man looked up at her and shielded his eyes against the hard glow of the lanterns. He was a huge man with enormous shoulders and heavy barrel-chested torso that strained against the fabric of his jersey, and he frowned, disturbed at his labor. But she was pretty and looked like a lady of quality. His tone was civil though brusque.

"Don't you know, ma'am, they ain't no ships from St. Lou no more, but that change in New Orleans. There's dredging on the west riverside now, for the new deep-bellied ships. For the meantime you cannot go direct."

"Ain't none leave on Sunday," he informed her, "but you can catch a fare for Monday morning, I'll be bound, a-going to New Orleans."

Lorelei looked at Beau. "We can't wait that long," she whispered. What'll we do between now and then, and I've got to be back—oh, hell—"

She called again to the boatman. "Do you happen to know anyone going down tomorrow?"

"Nay, and I know only trawlers, ma'am, which none of 'em go so far." He scratched his head. "I suppose you could pass by barge if you've a mind. It's no comfort for a lady, but there you are—"

"Too slow. The barge'll take forever." She thanked him for his trouble and turned away.

"Beau, I can't bear this anymore." Lorelei was straining with impatience and her muscles were all cramped and stiff from the interminable train journey. "We're going to get a couple of nags, Beau, and ride!"

She woke the disgruntled hostler at the stables, but for a generous price they were outfitted with horses.

"Sound horses," she demanded. "And looks don't matter."

Within an hour they were saddled and packed with the most portable of their luggage, and they started south following the east bank of the Missouri. They rode twenty miles along the dark, broad road, both eased by the sweet action of the horses, welcoming the activity of the ride. They made camp without a fire and both sank quickly into an exhausted but triumphant sleep.

"This seems familiar," Lorelei remarked, awakening the next morning.

"Except that we usually have coffee," Beau said. "And a hard biscuit at least."

"I'm ahead of you," the girl said, grinning, and pulled forth a small parcel from her bag. Two sandwiches, unimproved by age, but edible, emerged from the wrappings. She passed him one sandwich and a second package.

"What's in here?" he asked.

"Your shaving kit, missy," she answered sweetly.

As they continued south, Lorelei became more and more cautious. She sensed a change in the travelers they passed on the road. Black families seemed to be moving north in ever-increasing numbers, and many had looked with obvious hostility at Lorelei and her "maid." Beau had had to endure more than one caustic reference to his color and service, and he took it ill that Lorelei still insisted on the disguise.

They were just outside of Memphis when she finally gave in. The two rode into town to pick up supplies and an outfit of men's clothing for Beau.

Memphis was a crossroads town, begun as a fort, and settled as a frontier post, then populated by cowboys and southern planters dwelling in uneasy proximity. The war memories of the city were bitter—Memphis had fallen to Grant in the spring of 1862, and the only consolation to its people was that the Union death toll had been considerably higher than that of the defeated.

Lorelei was edgy. Several of the families moving north had been from Memphis.

She left Beau to mind the horses while she entered the general store to make the purchases. Keeping watch outside the storefront window, she saw three men separate themselves from a larger group and saunter over to where Beau, clad in his female garments, sat miserably on the stoop.

"Hold these for me, darlin'," she told the bewildered storekeeper. She had to remember not to run across the street.

"You'all got a problem with my nigger, gentlemen?" she asked in honeyed tones. The men turned to her in pleased surprise and she thanked mercy she had dressed well for this excursion into the unknown city. The customary breeches were replaced by a long burgundy skirt, a sprigged cotton blouse and stylish jacket. Her broad-brimmed hat boasted a jaunty soft-plumed feather that bobbed with every movement of her head.

The men doffed their caps and stiffened to attention before the lady of quality. "No trouble, ma'am, long's she's with you." The man who spoke was tall and lanky and smiled meaningfully at Lorelei. "We got us an official ordinance hereabouts, ma'am, which you might not know, being a stranger. But we had a little trouble yesterweek concerning some shivaree doings—nothing much, a few niggers getting out of hand—but it was all brought under control real quick, like. We just make it a habit to check out strange niggers—buck or wench. Cain't never be too careful in these times. So we was just fixing to ask your gal some questions—"

"Oh, she don't speak," Lorelei said, drawling out the syllables and smiling like a true Southern belle. "She got her tongue cut out long time back. Gal was telling tales, and you know how these niggers gossip. My daddy just figgered he'd tackle the root of the problem.

" 'Course, that was befo' th' *Emancipation*," she added. "But Nellie wouldn't be leaving her folks. She gets her room and board still, and a nickel a week wages, don't you now, Nellie?—and that suits her fine."

"She's been with you for a piece, then?" the tall man asked.

"Oh, since she was a little tyke, born and bred, almost, wasn't you, Nellie?" She turned quite deliberately from her "servant" and sent up sunbeams of warm approval to the leader of the trio. "Makes me feel real good you-all takin' such *care* of folks. 'Course Nellie's all right. My daddy named her himself—after his favorite hunter. A dun mare she was. Yessir, and he raised her up just like he raised that there horse—with a saddle and a riding crop. Didn't he, sugar?" She chucked Beau under the chin, smiling all the time, that same sweet, open smile. Beau was sweating.

"The reason for asking, ma'am," another of them said apologetically, "we been lookin out for a buck nigger coming outa Bonneville—that's about fifteen mile from here. Done robbed a gentleman in that town, and he was traveling with a mue-latto gal. But it don't figger to be none of yourn."

"Well, if that's the case," Lorelei said genially, "we won't be taking up your time further. I thank you-all especially for your concern."

The tall man melted in his boots under the warm glances of those remarkable eyes. " 'T'aint nothing but a pleasure, ma'am, I assure you. If we can be of any further help to you now, you just ask over in the saloon yonder. Send your nigger gal—it ain't no place for a lady. Just ask the barkeep for Tom Willard. Ask just anytime. Anytime at all."

"I thank you most kindly," she answered, keeping

the smile pasted on her face. "Now come along, Nellie-girl," she said.

They picked up the articles of clothing from the storekeeper, added a few supplies and rode out, neither speaking a word. Ten miles passed under their horses' hooves. Lorelei rode half a length ahead, and she turned off onto a forest road that led eventually to a distant farm.

She halted her mount and waited for Beau to pull up beside her. "You're not mad at me, are you, Beau? It was all I could think of."

"You probably saved my skin, sure enough," he said softly. "No, Lore, I ain't mad."

"You want to change your duds?" she said, hoping to raise his spirits.

"Maybe it'd better wait till we get closer to the boat," he answered, offering her an attempt at a smile. He plucked at his padded breasts. "Cute, ain't I?"

They shared a meager lunch still mounted on their horses, and turned back to the carriage road that followed the broad Mississippi all the way to the end.

They had a fire that night—hot bacon and fried potatoes, and coffee to wash it down. Lorelei gratefully doffed her city clothes for a faded pair of breeches and tried to ignore Beau's quiet, which hadn't altered from the incident in Memphis. There he was, squatting by the fire and staring into the flames as though they might tell him something. He didn't sit still, though—he changed posture like a twitching cat, shifting one leg and then another, rocking lightly, and finally burying his head in his arms.

"What is it, Beau?" she said at last.

He raised his head as though startled, but he didn't look at her. She thought he would not answer, that perhaps she shouldn't have asked.

"I'm scared, Lore," he said, and it was no more than

a whisper. "I'm almighty *scared*." She heard the tremor in his voice, saw tears forming in the corners of his eyes. He was trying so hard to hold back, as though the tears were his crime, and pain his punishment. She watched his features contort in some tortured grimace, and then it broke, and the words came in a rush and the tears slipped down unheeded.

"It ain't what happened today. It's funny, but—I'm scared of *going,* Lore! Isn't that the dumbest thing? I'm so scared I feel like my guts are turning over—'cause I don't know where I'm going. I've been living like a dog these past six years, and the way I feel now, I'd rather live like that. Like hell—because it's *my* hell—*it's the hell I know!*"

She knelt down beside him and wrapped him in her arms. "It won't be like that when you get there, Beau." She wiped his tears with her fingers. "Remember how your daddy used to talk about it—the green, green hills and the gentle people? The tall rose bushes in the gardens and the yellow daffodils all getting sunny at once, so a whole field would just spring up yellow?"

"I can't see it, Lore," he cried miserably. "I see the boat, the *maybe* boat, and then it's empty. I'm nowhere!"

"My uncle's got horses, Beau," the girl told him. "Hunters they are—ride 'em over fences chasing foxes through the woods. And I'll send you the money. You'll be *free* there, Beau. Do you understand? Nothing to be afraid of, no lawmen, no cowboys at your back. You go where you please and do what's right for you." The low flames lit his face like footlights in a theater. It was drawn and tired-looking. His eyes were swollen from weeping.

"I know it's scary. And you don't have to go. You know I'll help you stay if that's what you want. But you have to know—"

"There's nothing here," he said quietly. "I've got to

get out—I know it. At least my sense tells me that clear enough. But sense isn't all there is."

She cradled him close to her and stroked his tear-wet face. "It's gonna be fine, Beau," she said softly. "It's gonna be okay. You'll see."

The fire spit and crackled, and Beau burrowed into the warmth she offered. Lorelei had a momentary thought that Beau might want her, but he seemed content to lie close and be soothed. The ground was soft and after a while they stretched out side by side, finding an extra warmth, a certain peacefulness descend with their shared slumber.

Beau seemed easier of mind in the days that followed. The lands were warmer the farther south they journeyed, the forests more lush. Parts of the moist lowlands boasted immense black trees, rooted in swampy primordial majesty full of snakes and ghostly mists.

They arrived in New Orleans, exhausted but triumphant. Beau was dressed again in his natural attire. The devils had been vanquished—his eyes were bright and clear, his hands steady on the reins of his mount. They rode directly to the harbormaster's office. Yes, there was a ship that very morning bound for London.

"Ye must be quick about it though," the harbormaster warned. "She boards in just an hour, and Ray Clamper don't hold up his sailing for nothing."

They looked at each other, hesitating only a moment. Beau's eyes were glowing with excitement, Lorelei nodded her head. The next boat didn't leave till tomorrow. It would be this one. Today. Right now.

After the days and days of travel, it was upon them. They raced to book passage, to buy provisions.

Then suddenly it was time.

"You've got the address?"

He nodded.

"There'll be trains from London, I think."

He nodded again. The line of passengers began to

move, and both of them were swept along. Lorelei followed all the way up the gangplank. Beau put his arm around her waist and drew her close.

"I don't know what to say, Lore. There's so much—" He stroked her hair. "My best buddy, Lore," he whispered. "The very best—"

The people behind them were pushing forward. Lorelei grabbed the rail and pressed herself aside. Beau let her go and began to move again, more rapidly now, and Lorelei had just enough time to scramble free so that she could still see him, pacing in the orderly line that passed between the officers of the ship.

"Beau!" she cried. "Oh, good-bye, Beau. Write your daddy—"

He must have heard because she saw him turn and nod and wave. Then the crowd of strangers pressed in around him and swallowed him up from view.

Lorelei began to work her way back down against the tide of people still pressing to board the ship. It was one of the new big passenger ships, broad-beamed, equipped with a hundred cabins and a huge galley where elegant suppers were served. A comfortable start for Beau, she thought.

The harbormaster had been right—in a remarkably short time, the gangplank was cleared and withdrawn. The huge engines began to bellow and roll. The great horn sounded, and the ship began to glide past tugs and fishing trawlers and on to the open sea.

Lorelei did not wait for it to pass from sight, but made her way from the docks to the stable where they'd left their horses. She'd have to dispose of them before the *St. Louis Belle,* a proper steam-rolling riverboat, left for her home port this afternoon. No time to play tourist in this queen-madam of cities. Gerald Todd was probably practicing sarcastic reprimands directed at brokers who took leave without notice. To Todd, it was equivalent to desertion.

Lorelei cast a final brief look upon the city with its ornate spires and steeples and the handsome carriages turned out along the quay. The dark-eyed youth in the railway station had come from here.

It suits him, she thought in that single glimpse of the exotic city, the flower of the Mississippi. She chuckled to herself. It was more than Gerald Todd drawing her back to San Francisco.

8

Lorelei did not have to search out Jules Hutchison —he came to her. Or rather, he came to the San Francisco Stock Exchange just three days after her return.

Her reappearance at the 'change was marked by a short-lived but potent scene of critical hysteria on the part of Gerald Todd. Dressed in his traditional bowler and pinstriped suit, in flattering imitation of English bankers, Todd raised his hands, his voice, and several eyebrows belonging to patrons standing in the ever-increasing range of his intonations. Lorelei quite expected to see him biting through his tie, but fortunately, she had far too much experience to be upset. When he had fired Bernice Carson, it was done in a single line; quiet, well modulated, succinct.

His voice was slowly climbing toward glass-shattering proportions and pitch when the uniformed guard at the door announced Mrs. Merriwether. Like a whistling teapot denied the flame, Todd's vocal motors shifted gear. Standing obediently at attention during the tirade, Lorelei swore she could see the steam rise from his round little hat and dissipate into the smoky air of the great hall.

Mrs. Merriwether, widow of Francis J. Merriwether, was one of the most astute and quietly successful investors on the 'change. Her late husband had stumbled onto a hole full of silver in Nevada twenty years before, a discovery which gave rise to Merriwether Mines—a small but remarkably stable enterprise. This had in turn loaned capital to a growing line of purchases in other mining ventures. Mrs. Merriwether—who had co-sponsored a series of European recitals with no less a friend than Billy Ralston—who began the first public lending library in San Francisco, and whose polite social engagements included most of the financial and political giants of the time—had the stock, the clout, and the savvy to make her the darling and the tyrant of the Stock Exchange.

And Mrs. Merriwether, regally silver-haired and soft-spoken, was known to heartily abhor loud voices and bad tempers. It was rumored her late husband had not always been a paragon of gentlemanly virtue, but few had ever raised that thought aloud.

Gerald Todd carefully smoothed his tie, practiced a hideous stiff-muscled smile, and nodded to the guard. He glanced at Lorelei, muttered some final *sotto voce* threat of eternal damnation, and dismissed her to her table.

"Oh, la! You got off light," Genevieve exclaimed, pretending business at Lorelei's station. Her red curls, bunched in lovelocks at her forehead, fell forward and bounced as she performed a hilarious pantomime of Gerald Todd, complete with gestures and wide-open mouth. "We think for certain he either fires you or screams you to death!" she confided, and they both began to laugh.

From across the hall, Gerald Todd sent his far-reaching glance of disapproval. Lorelei lowered her eyes demurely to her ledgers. "Old Cat-face is giving us the evil eye," she whispered to Genevieve. "I'd better stay low awhile." The girl nodded and left.

Later, the incident was discussed in more detail. "You really must carry a lucky charm," Constance said.

"He's been saving up speeches for weeks. You could hear him muttering while he was walking around the hall—especially when it was busy—I'm sure he was practicing."

"Mark Ralston was nearly wild when he couldn't find you. He badgered us so much about it, Billy finally barred him from the 'change!"

"Wonderful!" Lorelei said. "If I can just keep him from finding out I'm back, I'll have some peace for a change."

"Mark's not so bad," little Constance said in his defense. "I think he's kind of cute."

"You think anything that shaves is cute," said Genevieve, who had had firsthand experience with young Ralston when she was at the Stock Exchange.

They badgered Lorelei about her sick friend, accused her of nefarious and novel escapades, and volubly complained when none of the delightfully shocking details came to light. Still, there was nothing to be gained by trying to wring the truth out of Lorelei Taylor, who was well known to be tight as a clam when she didn't care to discuss something.

Wednesday began like every other working day, with all of the brokers in attendance on the manager in his "conference room," a small, austere cubbyhole nestled in the western corner of the hall. He read off a list of appointments for each broker with separate accounts, gave Constance the task of bringing old man Donahue up to date on his assets, and then, as the brokers were already filing out, he called in the negligent voice of afterthought, "Oh, yes, someone take care of young Hutchison, two o'clock. He may mortgage some property in New Orleans, if we can tempt him with a profit. Whoever sees him, remember we're pushing Ophir on our long-termers. It's a bargain—they need the money for machinery to work the deeper veins, and they'll be generous to their stockholders—"

Lorelei had stopped dead at the first mention of the name. *"Hutchison?"* she said incredulously. "Did he say Hutchison?" How many young Hutchisons could there be in San Francisco? *Hundreds,* she reflected glumly. *But could it be?*

"Oh, my!" Genevieve said at her elbow. "Jules must be back in circulation. Look to your wits, ladies!"

"Gen!" Lorelei all but pounced on her. "Genevieve, I'll take care of Hutchison!" The eagerness in her voice betrayed her, and Genevieve smiled archly and cocked an eyebrow.

"Ah, so our beautiful Jules has already been at work! It all comes out in the end." She called to Constance and Lorraine. "I think we've discovered our little Lorelei's secret, ladies," she said. The girls gathered round like cats at a saucer of milk.

"What is it?" Constance said.

"Who is it?" cried Lorraine. "Her sick friend recover from his deathbed?"

Genevieve presided, center stage. "Jules Hutchison," she announced with smug and precise enunciation.

"He hasn't been around in ages!" Lorraine noted. "Wasn't his mother ill?"

"She died," said Constance. "I heard it from Toby Meyers."

Lorelei was blushing and trying frantically to voice denials. "For heaven's sake, you bevy of gossip-mongers, I only said I'd see to him!"

"Oh, listen to her. She'll see to him. It's more likely Jules will see to *you,* unless he's changed his style," Genevieve said. The others nodded sagely.

"Don't mind us, Lorelei, we'll let you take his order," Genevieve promised consolingly, winking at her companions. "I wouldn't miss it for the world!"

Lorelei was dismayed at the furor. *All this fuss,* she thought, *for a man I've barely seen twice, and never even met.* She was easily convinced from the girls' conversation, that this was indeed that young Hutchison.

The morning wore on. The lunch break was interminable. Two o'clock crept upon them.

And passed.

It was sometime just short of three that she saw him. He was standing with Gerald Todd near the door that led onto the private gambling parlor. The harsh unflattering light, escaping from the shade of the wall sconces, gave his face the stark bony look of a skull, and Lorelei, with mingled disappointment and relief, thought, *he's not so beautiful as I remembered.*

From the corner of her eye, she could see him approaching her table. Todd had directed him. She turned to face him only when he stood directly before the client's chair, and then she felt her heart leap to her throat and the palms of her hands grow suddenly warm and damp, because her far glimpse had lied. Here, close at hand, was the fact.

The high plane of the cheek, the paleness of the brow suggested not the hard stinginess of bone, but the warmth of ivory, firm but smooth, flawed only by traces of fatigue around the eyes—like a young god stayed too late at the revels. His eyes were as she had remembered—dark and broody, sheltering secret riches in their fluid depths. She was petrified of staring too long. She lowered her eyes.

What had been the clever greetings she'd prepared? Where was the coquettish toss of her head she had so diligently practiced in the powder room at lunch, to show the glitter of earrings on her sweetly scalloped ear? She heard him introduce himself. She motioned him to the chair. Then she began to gather her energies for the challenge of pretending away her agitation in the presence of this man.

She averted her face to hide her blushes and focused her attention on a stray pencil in the middle of the table, its satiny reflection in the varnished rosewood top. Jules could see little more than the top of her head—a gleaming black coronet of braided hair, grown out from her days with the outlaw band.

"A new face at the Exchange," he remarked. She lifted her head. "And a pretty one."

She smiled to hide her confusion and began to relax. She found she could look at him without blushing if she did it in small doses.

"Aquamarine," he said musingly.

"I'm sorry, I didn't hear—"

"Aquamarine," he repeated. "The color of your eyes. It means the waters of the sea, but they are really precious gems. Remarkable eyes."

She swallowed hard and shuffled the papers in front of her. He was flirting with her, and she had forgotten all the moves of the game and how to play it. She stole another glance at him—how amazing—she could see a clear reflection of herself in his dark eyes. She saw the edges of her own hair, the lamplight defining the curve of her cheek, and his eyes were the mirror. More. They approved her—they made her feel pretty. He had never seen her before, but of course she had seen him. It was on the tip of her tongue to tell him—to say, "But I've seen you before!" Wasn't that what she'd planned? "Ah, but we've almost met!" she was going to say, and he would wonder where. That was when she would have tossed her head and smiled and made him guess. Well, it was too late now for opening phrases. She noticed Genevieve peeking over toward her table.

"Your stock investment, Mr. Hutchison," she said calmly, hiding her quivering fingers inside the stack of papers.

"May I ask your recommendation?" he said, catching her tone. But the propriety went no further than his words. His eyes mocked her, *dared* her almost, as though he could read her mind, which had painfully little to do with stock investments.

"Ophir—" the first try was only a whisper. Her throat was suddenly parched. *"Ophir.* We expect a twenty percent increase within twenty-four months. They're working a deeper vein. Production is down only until they hit." The words came forth audibly, but mechanically. She found herself staring at the jeweled stickpin on his tie.

"I can have five thousand by the first of next month," he said. "Dinner?"

"Yes—" she began. "I'll process your order. And yes."

"Eight o'clock. Hazard's. You know it?"

She nodded, feeling a burst of pure happiness possess her. She felt like leaping up to dance on the rosewood table like those Spanish gypsy dancers in the cafés. *And wouldn't Gerald love that!* she thought. *I can just see him jumping around below like an outraged frog and trying to swat me with his little bowler.*

"There sits our happy smiling chicken," came a voice behind her, "ready to leap into the fox's waiting jaws." It was Genevieve, of course.

"Oh, stuff it, Gen!" Lorelei retorted with imperturbable good nature.

"What's the word?"

"Dinner tonight at Hazard's," Lorelei answered with exaggerated calm.

Genevieve whistled appreciatively. "You must have made quite an impression," she sighed. "I guess there has to be a Jules Hutchison once in every girl's life— and in this town, that's just about what it's been. Just one word of advice, Lorelei—take it from a friend." Her voice grew more serious now. "Enjoy him if that's what you want. But don't get yourself in deep. Women are a game with Jules—unless he's changed a great deal in the past year—and you'll do fine as long as you remember that."

"Um," Lorelei said absently, hoping to discourage

more of Genevieve's unwanted wisdom. Her friend shrugged and turned away shaking her head. Lorelei sent a message to Nan at the first opportunity telling her to press the cream silk dress from Madame Claire's.

At least Nan did not object to joining in the spirit of the thing. The dress was pressed when Lorelei came home, and a bath already drawn.

"My gold satin slippers," she said anxiously, "and the new stockings. It'll be cool tonight—the black shawl, Nan, the Spanish wool." Naked in preparation for her bath, she paced the room, keeping an anxious eye on the mantel clock.

The bath relaxed her, and she let herself be lulled by the scented waves that lapped at the edges of her body and made little islands of her breasts. She sat for Nan to wash her back. Nan had never seen her mistress so excited.

"I warrant he must be a handsome fellow," she said.

"He's—like every prince you ever imagined, Nan." She laughed gaily. "Except from what I hear, he's not all good and pure—and you know, I don't care! Don't I sound silly? He's tall, Nan, and his eyes are so so dark—the darkest you can imagine. And—oh, Lord! I've got to hurry! Fetch my robe!"

She powdered herself with the dust of roses and touched perfume to her ears and neck and bosom. Into the robe and out of the robe. Into the dress.

"Oh, Nan, *do* hurry with the bows. But make them perfect!"

Nothing around her slender neck but the gold-trimmed ribbon tie. A bracelet carved of precious white jade worn above the elbow. Gleaming white earrings that matched. Rouge for her lips and cheeks, little though they required it. She winked at her own reflection in the mirror. *Aquamarine,* she thought dreamily, like a handmaiden of Narcissus falling in love with her own image. *Really quite pretty,* she congratulated the mirror. Hadn't she seen her own reflection in his eyes?

"Will you be coming back tonight?" Nan asked shrewdly.

"I don't know," was the thoughtful reply.

"Your wrap, madame?"

"Thank you." She let the shawl slip from her arms, and handed it to the maître d'. The reception hall at Hazard's was lit by small, intimate chandeliers, winking teardrops of crystal suspended from the ceiling on thick brass chains. Her bare shoulders caught the rays of tiny rainbows. The cream silk of her dress glowed hauntingly beautiful against the dark mahogany woodwork, and the maître d' himself was not slow to appreciate the vision.

"Mr. Hutchison's table please."

He bowed with stiff precision. "Very good, madame. This way."

He led her past a crowded table and through the main dining room, into the alcove reserved by Jules Hutchison. In the past, Mr. Hutchison had entertained frequently, but this was the first time in over a year's absence. *He chooses well, the lucky devil,* decided the maître d' glumly. *It's never been me with the likes of her on me arm.* He could feel the turning of heads in her wake as she followed him briskly between the tables. He comforted himself on the tips he would receive from the gentlemen wanting to know her name. They were none of them slow, these gents, when they saw something they wanted.

"Mr. Hutchison is trying his luck at the gaming tables, madame," he said as he seated her. "I'll send him word that you've arrived."

A few moments later he appeared, and at last the evening could begin. Champagne and Olympia oysters. He toasted her and she watched his smile, watched his

lips part over the rim of the glass and she watched his
hands on the fork and great-bladed chef's knife. He
carved the pheasant skillfully and well, wielding the
blade, guiding it through the delicate breast of the bird
so that the succulent meat folded down in perfect slices.
He had long, slender hands, more delicately veined and
paler than the rough hands of the cowpokes she had
known. But they weren't the pudgy clerk's fingers of a
Clyde McPherson or the limp, girlish hand of a Brad
Lowry. Male hands. Sure and subtle and strong.

She thought of the four little ties at the back of her
gown and shivered.

"More wine?"

She nodded and extended her glass. And she watched
him with her jeweled cat's eyes. "You didn't bring your
cane," she said softly.

"I threw it away," he said in abrupt and feeling tones.
He looked up at her, startled. "But that was weeks ago.
How did you—?"

Now it was her turn to be teasing him. "I saw you
in the railway station when you got off the train from
New Orleans—" She could see him frowning, trying to
recall. He'd been exhausted then, depressed. "—But it
wasn't the first time I'd seen you."

Now he really seemed surprised. He smiled charmingly. "I may be forgiven perhaps for missing you once.
But *twice!* I'd be a fool."

"Oh, but you didn't see me!" she said, and proceeded
to confess her long-ago spying activities from the bedroom window of her old room at the ranch, how she
had seen him waiting by the carriage while his mother
was inside and—blushing slightly—how disappointed
she had been when he didn't stay.

He leaned forward, eyes narrowed, focused upon the
story, and upon this girl with the uncommon looks and
the very common name. *The name that should have*

been mine, he thought in anger and in wonder. This girl—unknowing, displaying herself before him—this tall and shapely butterfly fluttering to his net—a sardonic gleam kindled in his eyes. He took her hand across the table and raised it to his lips. Wasn't she melting—eager catlike thing. Purring to have her belly rubbed—

"Shall we take a turn at the gaming tables?" he asked. He needed time to think. "I'd like to show you off."

"If you're sure it will be all right," she answered. Women were not always welcomed in the gambling rooms of Hazard's, and not always accorded the usual respect extended to their sex, partly a result of the prostitutes who so commonly frequented the establishment seeking custom.

He smiled amiably. "Have no fear. I'll get you some chips and you can play. And I'll see that Armand takes care of you well. I'll tell him to treat you"—He spoke with his eyes full on her—those dark eyes full of secrets—"like you are my little sister."

Something in his smile made her momentarily apprehensive—it was the look of a predator. She remembered her airy words of confidence to Ma Belle, and the old harridan's reply—*"Aye, but the capture, dearie—and not some playing at men's games—"*

His hands settled briefly on her shoulders as he helped her from the chair and she felt her flesh yield to his touch with a terrible yearning. Her apprehensions slipped away. She had been waiting—all evening, and before—ever since she had seen him, she had been waiting to feel his hands on her. The wine made her giddy when she stood. She leaned gracefully on his arm, and those who saw them pass to the gaming room all remarked what a handsome couple they made, both dark-haired, tall, and slender, like a well-matched pair.

The tables were a blur of smoke, the hard lights above shone on hard intense faces. Wine stewards eased their way between the players, serving and taking orders. No food was offered in the gambling parlor.

Like a master of ceremonies, Armand eased his rake over the table. "Place your bets, ladies and gentlemen. Place your bets." Jules managed to find two seats and promptly placed three blue chips upon a square which said 16 in red numbers. He was still drinking brandy, but Lorelei, already dizzy from the wine, declined.

The number came up 4 on the black. Jules did no more than shrug, though Lorelei understood by now that each blue chip represented a thousand dollars.

"I'm not lucky," he said lightly. "A gypsy in the old town told me so."

Armand, who heard the remark, glanced over at Lorelei and said, "May we all be so unlucky, you old dog."

Lorelei blushed. "Perhaps I can bring you luck," she said.

He looked at her oddly. "Perhaps."

His mind was not on gambling. His thoughts were scarcely coherent—a riot of images seemed to play around the image of this girl—a montage of his mother, a faceless man, a blond lady who had been so distressed at the sight of him so many years ago. And this invisible girl spying from her bedroom window.

He seemed at last to reach a decision, and a short time later he took her to his house. He pulled down a bottle of wine from a rack in the hall outside the kitchen while she waited in silence beside him. He led her up one flight of stairs and then another. At the top of the landing he turned to her, himself a darker shade against the darkness of the hallway.

"I'm taking you to bed," he said softly.

She was glad the darkness hid her face, the flush and tremors of anticipation, her legs that scarcely would support her now that the waiting was almost done.

He drew her inside to the master bedchamber, with

its high ceilings and dark walls. He lit a single lamp and turned it low so that the light it cast was a gentle one, and the shadows soft.

Skilled hands drew the gold pins from her hair until it fell to her arms and shoulders like a black waterfall. She felt his breath through the fine silk, his lips pressing upon her breasts, while his hands circled to her neck and continued down her back, pausing briefly at each ribbon, until all the ribbons were undone.

Her own breaths came faster when his hands began again, slipping down her shoulders, drawing the fabric from her flesh. Her breasts were naked. His fingers chafed over the nipples until they stiffened to his touch and the girl was moaning softly, wanting it only to continue, wanting more.

He lay her down across the bed and stood before her, watching her wait, watching her with eyes like a hawk upon a dove. He shrugged off his own waistcoat and casually undid his cuffs, his linen shirtfront. Lorelei watched, her beautiful eyes enormous as she waited in wonder at her own desires to touch and to enfold.

He was closer now. He reached to play with clever fingers on her flesh, teasing, drawing out the fires. His palm pressed upon the delicate black curls at the pit of her belly and she arched up to meet the caress, and again, until his fingers caught her fast and he was well over her, pressing into her body. The first thrust brought a wave of hot pain, but Lorelei willed herself to silence and then she felt the pain recede before a stronger rhythm that was primitive, piercing-sweet. She reached to draw him closer and he descended on her like a storm, sweeping her into the maelstrom until she was lost and spent and done.

"Why didn't you tell me?" The blood on the sheets marked her initiation—there was no denying it. *Who*

*in the world would have guessed—a city 'change girl—
a virgin? And of all of them, this girl?*

Her naked flesh curled in upon itself like a splendid
resting cat. Her eyes in this light showed only the blue—
deep indigo, the color of sweet, dark plums. "I didn't
think it would matter to you," she answered softly. She
touched herself gingerly with her fingertips and stared
at the blood with curious wonder. *A wound,* she thought
vaguely, but she felt beautiful and strong.

He watched her in uneasy fascination, and he felt
himself wanting her again. Well, by God, he'd better
take precautions on his own—nothing a virgin would
be thinking about. His thoughts did not make him gentle. He drove hard into her body without preliminaries
and continued hammering at the tender passage; yet as
much as he thrust inward, she yielded up to it. At last
he was drained and finished and lay panting on her
breast.

He turned her about in the big, soft bed so that her
back pressed close against his chest. One arm swept
around to take possession of her breast. "It's not your
fault," he said, half to himself. She stirred softly in his
arms. "What'd you say?"

"Nothing," he said, disturbed by his own response.
"Go to sleep."

The night became morning and many nights followed.
Lorelei grew familiar with the big mahogany bed, the
location of the lamps, the cords to the burgundy drapes.
When the nights grew chilly, he would build a great fire
and they would sit close to it. Sometimes he would take
her on the rug. They went to gay parties with a group
of young rakes and their mistresses—parties that lasted
well into the night. The young men played at cards or
billiards, and everyone drank too much.

"Young Ralston's asked to trade up sometime," he
mentioned casually one night.

"What do you mean, *trade up?*" Lorelei stopped brushing her hair. Whatever it meant, she had a feeling she wouldn't like it.

"You know, he's seeing little Connie now," Jules said, smiling with supreme unconcern. "He was suggesting a change of partners—"

"—and I hope you knew what to tell him, that primping weasel." Her eyes flashed furiously in suspicion. "If you ever told him yes, I'd kill you," she said in a deadly tone. "I'm not to be traded, Jules."

"What a proud witch you are!" he said, setting his tie in an elaborate knot. "You really are quite lovely when you're angry, little spitting kitten." He approached her slowly and purposefully and plucked the hairbrush from her hand. "The party can wait," he said.

His lovemaking was subtle, insidious. Once he bound her hands with a silken cord so that she could not touch him, and sometimes he would hurt her, cruelly, deliberately, even as he aroused her. He had a cruel, soft mouth and strong white teeth that would bite her—bite her until she began to love the pain even as she loved his offhand tenderness. He had only to touch her and she was gone—enflamed and possessed by the cool arousing skillful fingers, the impeccably manicured nails, just long enough to scratch if he was so inclined.

He taught her how to please him—to use her hands and mouth to fan his lust, and she was an apt and eager pupil. She was so vital, so thrillingly aware. It was his gift to her—this knowledge of her own power and the splendor of her womanhood.

He desired her often. He was drawn to her. And yet sometimes he would see her off in the morning and there would be a look about him—she would think, *"There's the end of it. He won't call me again."* Nothing said, just that look and the feeling. A day might pass, or two, and she would turn to see his carriage waiting, or find a message calling her to supper at a friend's.

And the suppers always ended at a gaming table where the air was blue and hazy with smoke and the rounds of brandy came in endless cycles. In the morning her head would ache, and some days she didn't go to the Exchange.

Sometimes they just declared a holiday. They spent an afternoon at Dr. Jordan's Museum on St. Bartholemew's Lane. They saw Three-fingered Jack's mutilated hand and the head of Joaquin Murrietta preserved in jars of *aguardiente* and appropriately labeled. They saw wax dummies of famous criminals and a two-headed chicken. They made love in her apartments with the drapes opened to the sunshine and frolicked while the city labored on.

Everything was Jules. Ma Belle was displeased and took no pains to hide it. She had known Jules since he had come to San Francisco, and until his mother had taken ill, he had been a fairly frequent patron of her establishment. She knew his sexual tastes; she knew his weaknesses. He was right for one of her girls—a professional who could serve the beauty and be paid for it and done with it. But not for a romantic loving heart. Ma Belle knew Lorelei, too—better than the child would ever admit. And it was a gentle soul beneath the tough little tomboy-sophisticate.

"He's not to be trusted," she declared bluntly. "He's a womanizer, girl, and don't you know it's his mama the only woman he's ever held real fondness for."

She could see Lorelei thrust out her chin in that stubborn gesture she had come to know well. "You just don't understand, Ma Belle, and there you are going on like you had the future in your pocket."

"Understand?—my fat round arse, me girl. Don't try to be a-tellin Ma that all is honey and chocolates with you—you look peaked. When was the last time you had a full night's sleep. And if the boy truly cares for you, how come he's not looking out, heh? No, he'll drag you on his sorry rounds till you fall off the carousel—and you, you stupid stubborn lass, you won't give it up until they pry your fingers off the pole!"

"I love him, Ma Belle—"

"Love!" the old woman spat. "And didn't I tell you that'd come. It's not love, my Lorelei. Love is something people grow with—and nourish—love—"

"Well, it'll do for me!" the girl exclaimed haughtily. She left angry that day and it was several weeks before she returned. She thought of his hands reaching for her, his mouth descending to possess her. *He loves me.* She thought of the nights—brandy warmed by the fire, and Jules. *He loves me. I know it.*

But sometimes she wasn't sure.

They had a picnic one afternoon at the far end of the bay. They gorged themselves on the contents of the picnic basket and lay fat and content on the soft white sandy beach. The breeze that drifted in from the water was soft and moist, and Lorelei lay with her head in his lap and burrowed into the warmth of his thighs.

"There'll be snow up north by now," she said dreamily.

She had mentioned the ranch before. Jules never seemed to tire of hearing about the land where she'd grown up. He plied her with questions about her home and family, though he seemed oddly reticent about his own. He seldom spoke of his mother to her, though everyone who knew him said they'd been extremely close. His father, whom others had told her died when Jules was young, he never mentioned at all.

He did not understand himself why he continued. Part certainly was lust and part revenge. And part was some more nebulous thing—something that was only Lorelei. Lorelei with her dark hair and her wonderful eyes. Lorelei—savage, proud, innocent. Lorelei—gone in passion with her black hair spread across his pillow.

Now her black hair lay across his lap and the edges

of the curls were dipped in sand. "Tell me about your father," he said, stroking her hair with gentle hands.

"He was tall," she replied. "And his eyes were blue—dark like deep lake water. He was strong—he could do anything—ride any horse, build anything you could think of—"

She told him many things, but never what he sought to know. At times he sought in Lorelei pieces of himself. The same for the descriptions of her father. *What was he like? What part of him is mine?* But he was never satisfied. He never found an answer.

He continued his soft caresses and worked to make his next question just as casual. "Did he have other women, your father?"

"What an odd question, Jules!" the girl said. "You think all men are cads like you? No, just my mother."

She could not see his fingers poised above her head, fingers that for one blind and furious moment ached to find her throat. *No, damn you, little girl, there wasn't just your mother—there was my mother too. There was my mother and there was me!*

Lorelei may have sensed a change, but Jules was so moody, mercurial. She had tried unsuccessfully to discover what changed him sometimes from glowing smiles to glowering rages. That night, in the big mahogany bed, she felt the rage in him driving into her body, and he hurt her.

"Stop!" she cried. She tried to disengage herself, but he was far too strong. And it wasn't until he'd finished with her that she could speak.

"Jules, what is it?" She searched for the words, hesitating even to say them now, with his dark eyes shining above her. "Sometimes I feel as though you hate me. When you lie on top of me, as though you'd like to crush me, as though you're burying me!—Jules—" Her voice was small and unhappy. "I love you, Jules—why are you like this? You leave me and you come back and back and I don't understand. *I'm trying. Please!* Don't drink so much, Jules. You frighten me when you drink too much."

He didn't answer. His eyes settled briefly on her face and moved down, pausing at her breasts. Then his hand reached out to cover what he saw, and she shivered to see the smile that played about his lips—a taunting mockery of a smile.

"You have small breasts," he said, as though he had just discovered it. He rolled the nipple between his fingers and she dared not move. "Small," he repeated, "but useful." He continued to toy with her breasts.

"Stop it, Jules!"

He brought the other hand into play. "Stop being so emotional, Lorelei," he said with a voice like velvet, smooth and sly. "Besides, you don't want me to stop." The hands began to move with knowing art. "Do you?"

He consumed her—her time, her thoughts. But others thought of her. A week later, Nan announced a visitor waiting downstairs.

"Well, who is it, Nan?" Lorelei said impatiently. She was expecting Jules.

"He didn't give his name," the maid said worriedly. She was such a timid thing, and here was this stranger coming just when her mistress was awaiting her lover. It didn't bode well. Not well at all.

Lorelei shrugged and donned a dressing gown, then made her way downstairs. In the vestry below, Davy Cavanaugh waited, his sheepskin jacket and rugged mountain boots strangely out of place in the tiny reception area.

How long had it been since the crisp cold morning he had ridden out on that sorrel gelding to escape her? He had been down with the fever in a Union hospital and never gotten back for her father's funeral. She had not seen him since well before the war ended. Years.

She extended her hand and knew one sweet moment of female satisfaction to see his eyes widen in distinct admiration. It made up in some small way for that night at the lake. All the same, his presence made her uneasy. It brought her back to the beginning, and she wasn't ready. There was Jules. He would be coming any moment.

"We'll have to meet again later, perhaps tomorrow," she said quickly. "I'm expecting a guest. But sit a little." She motioned him to the parlor.

He perched uncomfortably on the edge of a chair. "We had a letter from Beau," he explained. "He mentioned you. So I wrote and asked him to please say where you were. It took a while to get the answer."

"You were looking for me?"

His eyes avoided her. "Since the war ended. Your mother's been worried about you, Lore."

She tossed her head spiritedly. "Nobody has to worry about me," she said, "I'm doing just fine."

"She's been *lonely*, Lorelei," he said pointedly. "You're all she's got left." His words were a rebuke, and she felt it keenly. Oh, why did he have to come now? Why could he make her feel like crying just by coming here? What right did he have to come here and bother her?

"She's got the ranch," she said in a cold and angry voice. "She's got *you*. She's got her flowers and her graves—"

He took her by the shoulders and shook her hard. *"Lorelei!* Just—shut—up. My God, I don't recognize you!"

Yet he was still the same. Big and broad-shouldered. A blond giant, he had grown to be even taller than her father. The honest brown eyes, the good-natured smile that could come like sunshine on mountaintops. *But he wasn't smiling now.* And she hated him because he didn't approve of her. Because he made her sad, he made her feel ashamed. Dammit, what right had he to make her feel ashamed?

His brown eyes looked angry and puzzled and hurt. "I don't suspect you're wanting to come back. But I'll tell your mother I've seen you and that you're well. He turned and she saw he was preparing to go. "Shall I give her your address?" he asked.

"Of course," she replied tonelessly, choking on her own unhappiness. She hadn't wanted him here, but she didn't want him to go. Oh, not like this—like a stranger. Not Davy!

He was leaving. She was going to call him back. The words were on her lips as the front door opened and Jules appeared. The two men almost collided.

Both men looked startled. Lorelei rushed to the vestry. She made clumsy introductions.

"I was just leaving," Davy said.

"How convenient," Jules commented dryly. The enmity was established as quickly as that. Even their appearances contrasted sharply. Davy, the elder, fair and ruddy and blond. Jules slender, dark, and pale.

Jules slipped an arm around Lorelei and brought his fingers up to casually cup her breast. He cocked an eyebrow in Davy's direction as though to say, "You see how things are, *old family friend.*" Davy saw. He didn't offer to shake Jules's hand. He said good night and left, and Lorelei watched him go. *They hadn't set a time to meet tomorrow.* And now it was too late. She had a mad impulse to run out after him, to leave everything behind her and go back. But Jules was touching her; his hands moved inside her dressing gown, slipping between the fabric and her flesh, and, of course, she didn't go.

"So," he said softly against her ear. "I have some competition."

"It's not like that," she answered sullenly. She hadn't seen him for two days. She was angry that he had caressed her in front of the other man. *As though he owned me,* she thought furiously. Yet inside a voice taunted her! *"Doesn't he?"*

That was the night he took her to the party in Sydney-town.

It began at the El Dorado and continued through the Belle Union, La Chat, and a half dozen others, gathering momentum and celebrants as the evening progressed. First the regulars—Toby Meyers and Lorraine, Mark Ralston with Constance, Gen with Brian McCarthy. Jules's gaming cronies were there, some alone and some with women. A group of young militiamen on holiday joined them at The Lucky Lady. It was one of the young officers, himself alone, who suggested the brothel.

They took over the entire reception floor at Madame Lea's, and the single men were matched for an evening's entertainment by whatever girls were free of clients upstairs. Mark Ralston purchased whiskey and Jules a case of champagne for the assembled company. Lorelei, who had begun the evening with misgivings, kept her glass full and her mind dull.

She lost track of Jules, and after wandering about between sodden couples spilling off the armchairs and gyrating on the carpets, she began searching in earnest. One of the cadets had spread his whore across the sofa and was preparing to mount her. A girl was vomiting quietly in one corner of the room. Lorelei half-stumbled over a sleeping drunk. She felt nauseated. The scene depressed her. *And where was Jules?*

The door to the tearoom was closed. Lorelei heard a man laughing within. She opened the door.

The girl that was with him was still naked—a dark-skinned girl, short and plump with full round breasts that dipped like heavy fruit. Lorelei didn't recognize her—one of Lea's girls. Jules had on his breeches, nothing else. They had evidently finished shortly before.

"Is that my duenna?" Jules called out sarcastically. She could see the white teeth and his vicious smile in the dim light. He sounded very drunk.

"Pardon me for interrupting," she answered in icy tones. "I'm going home."

"Oh, no!" he said. "Don't leave. Party's just beginning." With surprising speed, he reached for her, and pulled her toward the couch. "Just sit!" he said, pushing her down.

"Can't you take a little competition?" he jeered. "Come on. Let me see the two of you fight. You can fight, little Camilla, can't you?" The dark-skinned girl grinned and nodded. She knew what was expected.

Lorelei swore, viewing the two of them with clear disgust. "You're drunk and you're crude—"

Jules sidled up beside her and stroked up and down her arms. In a second he had locked her hands behind her back. He pulled down, forcing an arch in her chest, and with one free hand ripped her blouse from neck to waist. He held her helpless before the other girl.

"This is how you work cockfights in the old town," he informed her. He nodded to the little whore. "Hit her!"

Camilla understood what he wanted. She slapped Lorelei's face, and twice across her naked breasts. Lorelei kicked savagely out at her attacker, and twisted frantically against Jules's hold. But he was prepared for her. He kept her off balance.

Then he let her go. She came at the other girl with flying fists and an animal savagery that knew no rules. She would have liked to pound their faces into bloody pulp. It was no match between her and the whore, and in the end, Jules had to restrain her. He gave Camilla an extra $50 for her blackened eye and swollen face, and she departed, well pleased.

Somewhat sobered, Jules began to make apologies, blaming the liquor and his companions, promising never to do it again. Lorelei stared at him as though she had never seen him before. She felt sickened and dizzy. She started for the door, but it began to move away from her. She reached up a blind hand to stop the motion, but things were turning too fast. They were spinning, and she was going down.

She fainted before she could find the way out.

9

LORELEI GROANED. HER face was pale and waxen; her head throbbed dully with a terrible ache. Nan came in carrying a tray with soft-boiled eggs and toast, which her mistress waved away, nauseated by their very presence. The eggs quickly departed. She sipped hot chocolate, but then her stomach began churning. She thought of the champagne—how could anything with such innocent little bubbles wreak such havoc?

Jules had departed early in the morning, and Nan had brought her excuses to Gerald Todd, who had not been pleased. Lorelei was still furious with Jules, except that she lacked the strength for a proper scene. Her curses were weak, and her whole body pained her. The little whore Camilla—poor a combatant though she was—had landed several blows.

She managed to down a cup of tea and then, covering her head with pillows, she hid herself beneath the covers and wasn't seen again till noon. By then she felt much better, and she was ravenous.

"A steak," she thought, her mouth watering in anticipation. "A thick rare juicy steak, charred on the outside and bloody in the middle." She was dressing to go out when a messenger arrived from Ma Belle, whom she hadn't seen in some weeks. Ma wanted to see her—the boy said it was urgent.

Puzzled, she postponed her feast and satisfied herself with two sad, soggy slices of toast left over from breakfast. She drew on a cloak and hailed a carriage outside, wondering what could be wrong.

"Oh, my dearie, I'm so glad to see you!" Ma exclaimed when she arrived. She quickly dismissed the messenger and shooed two of her girls from the parlor, with strict admonitions not to be setting their ears against the door.

"Well, what is it, Ma?" Lorelei asked when they were alone. She had never seen the old lady so nervous.

"There's a body looking for you, my Lorelei," she said darkly.

"Oh, for heaven's sake—you mean Davy? I just saw him yesterday. It wasn't anything to get upset about—well, maybe for me, but—"

"Wasn't no Davy." The old lady lowered her voice. "'Twas the albino, Lorelei. He come in here big as life. In broad daylight, too, not three hours ago. I don't know how he gets his information, me girl. But he knew Beau left you in my care. He's been looking for Beau and you both—"

"But what could he want with me? I've done him no harm!" Lorelei exclaimed. She felt a chill run down her spine. *Whitey Loomis!* It was like having a snake on her trail.

"Maybe it was Beau in particular—"

What had she heard about Whitey? Of course! There had been a trial recently. Just a small item in the paper. *He must have been released.*

"—but he knows things, Lorelei. He finds things out. He knew Beau come to see you when he was on the run. At least he knew it was a woman, and he seemed sure enough it was you. Angry that you'd fooled him, too. I could feel that."

Lorelei was shaking her head. "I should think he'd be glad not to see either of us, Beau or me. There's a warrant out on Beau—I saw it in the post office. Whitey's lucky as it is. And Whitey doesn't even know what I look like—as a girl, I mean. And he doesn't know my name—does he, Ma?"

She shook her head. "He didn't know it this morning," she said with a certain satisfaction. "And he knew better than to try and flurry an old hen. I stopped letting him around my girls after he beat up Janey so bad, and I still say what goes and doesn't in my house."

Lorelei kissed the old lady's cheek. "You're a wonder, Ma Belle," she said gratefully. "Do you know where he was headed?"

"I hope out of town, but I don't know. I told him you and Beau had both shipped out of the country. I wouldn't count on him believing me, though."

Lorelei nodded. "I'll be careful."

She left soon after, stopping at a side-street café, only to find she didn't want to eat. She went a circuitous path back to her rooms, and entered by the back door. No one followed her. It seemed foolish after all. What could Whitey want with her, even if he found her? But the unease remained.

In the night it grew and became a cloudy anguish, without cause, or with too many causes. Her dreams were crowded with the faces of men—Davy and Whitey, her father and Beau, and Jules. She couldn't sort them out—they melded and changed faces. She wept in her sleep, quietly, a small creature alone in the dark.

She was sick again the next morning, though she managed to go to work. She told Jules she wouldn't go out. *A touch of fever, perhaps,* she thought. It seemed to come in waves, and then disappear. She retired early that night, but she didn't sleep well. Early in the morning, she found her breasts were swollen and too tender to lie upon.

The nausea returned on the third morning, and she counted days. She stared at her body in the mirror in a confusion of emotions. She was certain—it might not be. How did she feel? She didn't know how she felt, except that she cried at nothing, she felt somehow weak, vulnerable. She was nauseous and weepy, and just a little scared.

The ride back to the ranch was long and cold and hard, and Davy took his time, easing his shaggy-haired mount between towns in the brief, cool daylight, resting early at night wherever he could find a room. His saddlebags held few supplies—new leather to make harnesses for spring, some fancy dress goods for Susanna. She hadn't cared much for sewing or dressing up since Jed died. She hadn't cared much for anything, though she tried hard to hide the fact. Ed Crandall and his son, and Davy since he'd returned, had worked to keep things going just as they had when Jed was alive.

It had been a blow to Davy as well—Jed, whom he still thought of as "the captain," who had been first like his father and then his most trusted friend. *Grant's fault,* he still thought angrily. *Just his blasted luck to be serving with a man who could see 10,000 of his own men killed in an afternoon and not twitch.* Now they were talking about putting Grant up for President. *The hero.* Davy drove the thought from his mind—it maddened him. *The heroes were dead.*

Time to start over. Wasn't that what this past year had been? But he hated to be returning from this failed mission now. He thought she would be coming back with him, and he cursed himself for a simple fool. She was on her own—hadn't she made that clear? Or, more significantly, Jules Hutchison had.

The ranch was quiet. It was bitter cold. Snow had fallen two days before, they told him, and turned to

rain. Then just last night, a cold snap had turned everything to ice—it lay like a slippery crust atop the snow
and made outdoor work all but impossible.

Davy handed the reins of his horse to Ed and looked
around. The forested hillsides were held in icy clutches,
evergreen boughs and naked branches alike, all glinting
in the sunlight. He took a deep breath of the pure,
frosty air, as though to brace himself.

"Susanna inside?" he asked.

Ed nodded. "She's been waiting for you to come
back." Ed knew why he'd gone. And he could easily
see, he had returned alone.

Susanna hurried from the kitchen. "In the parlor,
Davy," she said, embracing him briefly. "I've kept the
fire going, and I'll bring us some tea. Isn't it just the
coldest out there?" She rambled nervously, and Davy
thought, *She knows. She doesn't really want to hear it.
She already knows Lorelei isn't coming back.*

They sat in the parlor where the winter darkness was
dispelled by cheerful lamps. It was warm. Comforting.
It was home.

"Did you find her?" Susanna said at last.

That much he could affirm. "And she looked really
fine, Susanna. She sent her best and asked you to write.
I have her address—" His voice trailed off, regretting
he had so little to say. "She's got a fellow there. She
introduced him—"

"She's all right," Susanna said, almost to herself.
"And that's the most important thing." She turned back
to Davy. "What's he like, her boyfriend?" she asked.

Davy shrugged and kept his eyes low. "Well off, I
should think, by the way he was dressed." He worked
to keep his dislike of Jules from betraying him. "He's
young, good-looking, I guess. Lorelei seems to like
him." He almost choked as he said it. "Black hair,
speaks a bit foreign. French maybe."

A knot had begun to form in Susanna's throat. A

ridiculous notion, easy to dispel. "Do you know his name, Davy?" she said, reaching for her tea.

"Hutchison, it was—" She dropped the china cup and it shattered on the floor.

The sins of the family fall on the daughter, the daughter, the daughter.

"Oh, merciful God, no!" Then soft cries. She rocked herself, clutching her fingers to her breasts, begging— forgiveness. *Someone else was there. Davy. Davy didn't understand.*

"Her brother. Jed's son," she said.

"What are you talking about Susanna?" Davy's voice. Davy didn't know. Lorelei didn't know. She had told no one.

"My fault," she said, and she told him. His face turned white. He understood. He remembered Louisa in New Orleans. Jules Hutchison.

Lorelei.

"I'll leave tomorrow," he told Susanna.

"What will you do?" she whispered hoarsely.

"Tell Lorelei—" he said briefly. Before him was the image of Jules Hutchison, the gloating smile of triumph on his lips, his hands so *casually* possessive, intimate.

"—and bring her back!"

Jules was staring at her in horror. She didn't care. She had become protective of this other being growing inside her, even before the doctor had confirmed it.

"We'll get rid of it," he said as soon as he found his voice. He still couldn't grasp the whole of it. He'd tried to be careful.

Not careful enough.

It would have been so easy, so convenient to imagine someone else. *You're a slut—it's someone else. Not I. Not I!* But he couldn't believe his own voice.

"I know some people," he continued. It was all he could think of.

"No!"

He looked at her as though she had become an enemy. A calamity in the flesh. She had. She was. It was no longer folly and play. Some weird unvoiced revenge. It was real. This nightmare in her belly made it real, made the full horror of it manifest.

"I haven't asked you for anything, Jules," she said with dignity. Her hands folded automatically across her lap, as though to keep it safe.

"Well, what do you expect?" he demanded. "I won't marry you—Are you going to raise a nameless bastard—?"

"If necessary!" She used a voice he had never heard before—icy, distant. He had ceased to matter to her now. That was all changed.

"I can go back to the ranch." She smiled mirthlessly. "I won't be the first errant girl returning in disgrace. *But I will have this child.* It's mine! I claim it—even if you don't!"

"I never said that, Lorelei!" He had to be cunning now. He had to keep her calm. *But he couldn't let this happen.*

"It's all happened so fast," he said gently. "I need time to think about it. We both do." He stole a quick glance at her face. It was softening.

"I don't want to fight with you, Jules," she said. Perhaps they could stop now. She could stop feeling that he was attacking her. It was his child, too. He didn't deny it.

He needed time to think.

"We're both overwrought," he said in caressing tones. "I'm going to let you sleep." He kissed her forehead and she clung to him before she let him go.

He sent her roses in the afternoon—crimson red with velvety petals. Nan was unimpressed. "Shoulda been a ring," she muttered to herself. At least her mistress seemed cheered by them. She was eating better, too.

"Men!" the maid thought angrily. She had little first-hand experience, but a great deal of observation to her credit. "Happy times or misery, and mostly misery, it's always a man."

He came again in the evening, subdued and perfectly sober, though it had been an effort. He needed all his wits. And he was calm and gallant. The perfect lover, except for the act itself, and that would be taken for solicitude.

She sat up among the satin cushions like a delighted child, glad that he had returned, hopeful, glowing. A starry-eyed innocent, in spite of all.

"I was thinking of a picnic tomorrow," he suggested. "We could go out to the beach again. It hasn't been too chilly."

She nodded happily. "I can get Nan to fix up a basket. I've been ravenous!" The bloom was on her, and he could not bear to see it—the curving richness of her slender form, the ripening, the milk-smooth sweetness of her complexion. And her jeweled cat's eyes fringed by her dark lashes, half-closed in content.

He had to stop it.

"We can take a carriage," he said, "if you're not up to riding."

"Oh, no! We'll ride," she said, as he'd known she would. "I'm feeling fine. Besides, our son will be a horseman," she said grinning. "Can't start too soon."

If he failed to echo her delight, at least he maintained a neutral look. And he kissed her face, a gentle Judas kiss.

The next morning he purchased a small penknife.

The afternoon was perfect riding weather—cool and sunny. Lorelei raced him across the sands, and afterward, pulled off her shoes and stockings and went wading in the shallow of the bay. When the sun glowed crimson over the water, she packed up the remains of the picnic feast while Jules went to fetch the horses.

A perfect day, she thought as he helped her to the saddle. She didn't want it to end.

"We could take a turn in the park," he said, smoothing her skirt over the saddle. His attention was constant and comforting. *Every detail.* His desperation was masked, his charm so practiced it needed little thought. *Only control. He must stay in control.*

He could see she was flushed and happy.

She was his nemesis. She carried a monster.

They walked the horses to the nearby wood. "Let's run the course, shall we?" he shouted back to her. He spurred his horse forward, daring her to follow. Of course she did, pressing her mount to a full gallop, laughing her answer to his challenge.

He stayed a few lengths ahead. They ducked branches and spun through sharp turns in the course. She was gaining on him as they approached the first jump. He could hear her "Holloa!" just over his shoulder. Jules's mount took it in a mighty stretch. His heart lurched. He could feel her coming up right behind him. He knew when her mount approached, how it extended for the leap and Lorelei would swing up and grip the saddle with her knees, and he heard her scream when the saddle cinch snapped—the cinch he had cut almost through with the small penknife he'd purchased that morning—

Lorelei lay where she had fallen in a crumpled heap by the side of the bridle path.

The monster was gone.

He had succeeded. And Lorelei would be all right, the doctor said. Bruised up a bit, and she'd lost some blood. But she was young and strong. Nothing so resilient as youth.

"She'll have others," the doctor told Jules, thinking to comfort the young man who paced, pale as a ghost, back and forth the brief length of the sitting room. He didn't know they were not married. He didn't know that Jules had killed the thing. That Jules had slain the monster growing in her womb.

It was gone now. But it wasn't over. There were a thousand devils biting at his entrails, holding him fast to the place he occupied when the only thing he wanted to do was flee the girl who lay in the bed upstairs.

She knew.

In that singular instant that he stood over her in the path—when she must have felt, because he could see the undulating tremors wracking her body where the thing was housed—her eyes had opened. And he had seen the knowledge in her face—more positive than an accusation, the look that damned him to hell with one terrible stare.

Then she had lost consciousness, as though it was that moment's hate which sapped her strength. And there was blood.

"You might go up and see her now," Nan told him curtly. He looked up at her, startled by the sound of her voice. Nan felt some of her anger subside to pity. He looked almost as bad as her mistress. "She's awake," she added more gently.

If he could run away, disappear, evaporate. If he could only summon the will to flee! But he ascended the stairs. He was not free of it. He was not free of her. His hand shook on the banister. His mind sang madly as he took another step, *I'm going up to hell, up to hell, up to hell.* Another step.

Her face was ashen. Her eyes were red. She had been crying then. He wondered how long she had been awake. How long she had been conscious and knowing, dwelling on the thing that he had done.

He needn't have feared her curses. She was subdued. The doctor had given her drugs for the pain. Her eyes were dull and vacant. There was an apathy in her posture. She was so pale.

Her actions were all drawn out in time. She seemed to discover him in some gradual dawning of recognition, and her face, her aspect haunted him. A tortured, grieving wraith—his victim. Her lips framed words, dry painful whispers.

"Why?"

He had not slain the monster. It sat on his shoulder while he stood, mute and guilty, before his crime.

"You didn't have to take a part in it. Why did you have to kill it?" Her voice was breaking like splintered wood, yet it continued.

"I didn't ask you for anything. I wouldn't have bothered you—" She was crying now, but he was paralyzed. *As long as he couldn't speak, as long as he didn't move, he was safe. Like a living tree petrified to stone, impervious, he was all right as long as he didn't feel, didn't move, didn't speak.*

Nan was arguing with someone in the hallway downstairs. The voices grew louder. Both Lorelei and Jules could hear them now. Plainly. There were hurried footsteps up the stairs, and a man's voice calling Lorelei.

The bedroom door burst open, and Davy rushed inside. At first he saw only Lorelei. He hurried forward.

Then he saw Jules.

"You can't go on with this, Lorelei. I've come to take you back!" he said forcefully. She only stared at him. Puzzled. Each pair of eyes in the room found two opponents, two other, too-intimate beings. But only Jules felt cornered. Still he didn't move.

"He's your half-brother, Lorelei. His mother and Jed —before you—"

He had come from the ranch almost nonstop to reach her. Downstairs, he hadn't waited on Nan's frantic explanations. He blurted out his revelations and finally stopped because she wasn't even looking at him. She was looking at the other man with a penetrating and multiplying horror.

Jules felt the look like a physical blow. He had not succeeded. He heard her hiss *you knew,* saw her half-rise from the bed. And the monster roared in his ears. He had not succeeded.

The monster was himself.

Davy was the first to see his move. "Look out, Lorelei!" he cried and threw himself over her.

Jules had pulled the little derringer from his coat, but he did not turn it on the others. With a mocking little bow in their direction, he made as though to kiss the gun. He parted his lips around the barrel, and with his beautiful, slender fingers, he pressed the trigger.

10

DAVY SAW TO the sheriff, and the coroner, signed the statement as a witness to the death of Jules Hutchison, who might have been Taylor. *Killed by his own hand,* the statement read.

"Pity 'e done it like he did," the coroner, who knew him only slightly, remarked laconically. "Would'a made a handsome corpse. As 'tis, I guess me boy kin do wi' him well enough. Only the back of his head—"

Davy spoke also with the doctor, who said Lorelei must wait a week to travel. In that week, she did not venture down the stairs, but Nan attended her in her room. She said little when Davy sat with her in the afternoons. Only when he told her they would be leaving for the ranch did she respond, and then it was with violent and teary refusal.

"I can't go back, Davy. I won't see Mother like this!" Her flesh had wasted in the consecutive shocks to body and mind, and she was ghastly pale.

"I can't leave you here, Lorelei," he said. "I won't."

"Then take me up to the mountains, Davy. Take me to the cabin by the lake."

He argued that the trip was dangerous in winter. *But they went out on the traplines every year.* She wasn't well enough. *It was the cabin or nothing.* She had little strength, but her pride sustained her. She would not budge in her decision, and at the last, Davy gave in.

On the day they were to leave, Lorelei sent Nan out while she dressed and packed her few belongings. All of her skirts and fancy dresses she was leaving. All her furniture, the various accumulations of her city life— souvenirs and decorations—strange how little there was to carry with her. She had sold even her riding horse— she was too delicate a beast for a mountain winter. Davy persuaded her they could do with one.

Was he afraid she would run away?

She didn't want to run. She wanted to rest. She slept overmuch of the days, but when she was awake the appalling sadness, the loss would take her and she couldn't stop weeping. How empty she was! How her body had been cheated! And the sleeping was better than the pain.

The blood that still came down between her legs reminded her. How different from the virgin stain of her first night with Jules. Jules who was her lover and the father of her child. Jules who was her brother. Jules who was dead like the never-to-be baby they had started.

It's better this way, Davy had told her. *Far better it should not be born.*

She hated him for that. What did he know? What did a man know of a woman's body quickening with life— the shared blood, the fertile mysteries, the wordless, mindless primitive communication. Every cell and substance of her altered subtlety, crying *life!* Ripped from her. Slaughtered. Stolen.

Her fingers, deft but mechanical, folded a linen pad and slipped it between her legs.

"You almost ready, Lore?" It was Davy calling.

One last look, little more than a glance. She was clad in heavy woolen trousers and a fur-lined cowhide jacket. Ironic that her departure from the city so closely paralleled her entrance. Like then, mounted behind a rider and traveling light. Wounded, like then. Dressed for the mountains in what would pass for male attire.

The city images passed swiftly before her vision—the same bustle, the shops and grand hotels, the brawling crowds. Faces—some glancing her way. No one she knew. The face of a short, dark man watched intently from a saloon window, then let the curtain fall. The sun stood high and bright above the waters of the bay, where the ships were busy loading at the docks.

Nothing would change without her; nothing would stop and wonder at her absence. She had said all her good-byes the night before. The rest she carried with her, very little that remained. No matter. Her own emptiness had weight.

"Can't we go any further, Davy?" she complained a few days into the journey. He insisted they travel slowly, and he watched her like a mother hen for any sign of fatigue. Rest stops were frequent. They didn't camp, and sometimes the price of a room was half a day's travel. But he was obdurate. So it was more than two weeks before they reached the cabin by the lake.

And there it seemed the healing could begin. The snows came often in the first days of their arrival—fresh and clean and white. Days sometimes she walked the trapline path, though they didn't set any down. Sometimes she waited in ambush where the deer, the foxes, the raccoons, each at his own time, came to drink in the broken surfaces of the frozen lake. The deer sipped delicately. The foxes lapped with long pink tongues. The raccoon seemed to hesitate and watch his reflection before he dipped his muzzle.

Davy busied himself cutting wood and hunting small game in the woods. Lorelei cooked up hunter's stews in a great cast iron pot and delighted in keeping it simmering night and day. The flavor altered day by day as the meat changed from rabbit to pintail to venison, cooked with onions and great chunks of potato. The thin crisp mountain air gave them hearty appetites. Lorelei began to take on flesh.

But with the healing came a kind of hunger—the aching void stood out in high relief against the physical recovery.

She wanted Davy to make love to her.

They slept each night in their respective cots. He made no move toward her. He never touched her. Yet he was solicitous—almost tender at times, doing little things to make her comfortable. Like making her a pillow stuffed with duck down. But he didn't share the pillow. He never spoke of Jules of San Francisco.

She stalked him the way she stalked the deer and foxes. At night sometimes she watched him while he slept. The early morning sun would wake him, but the silver cool of moonlight never did. And one night, driven by her unrelenting hunger, she crept into his bed.

The covers were warm from his body. The cot was narrow and he stirred as she stretched out beside him. She was wearing an old flannel shirt and nothing else.

She felt his hand stiffen when she moved it over her body, and he awakened. She called his name softly in the dark, she cried for him to touch her. After a while she felt his hands caressing her, and he was kissing her softly, laying kisses in gentle rows. She arched toward him, aching with the need, the persisten hungers of her cheated womb.

But it was no good.

Davy drew back from her, ashamed, bitter, expecting denunciations of his manhood. But the assault took a different form. The anger, the fury and frustration were there. And pain and old wounds.

"Before I was too young," she accused him, rising from his bed. *"Now I'm too dirty!"*

"Lore, it's not like that!" She was so wrong! How could she be so wrong? She lay back stiffly on her own bed and would not respond. The night passed in silent wakefulness.

In the days that followed, Lorelei became more distant, withdrawn to some singular isolation. Davy remembered the night at the lake, the night Lorelei had referred to, when she was too young.

Or he was too frightened by her youth.

So he had fled, finally back to war, and all the time he was away he was thinking of her, afraid that she would be lost to him before he ever returned. Then Susanna had written to say she'd disappeared. And it had taken him so long to find her. Wounded. Abused. Distrustful.

But this time he wasn't leaving her. He could be patient. This time he wasn't going away from her, and he could wait until she was truly healed of the other wounds.

The sun stayed longer now, and some of the snow was settling. Lorelei's anger gradually dissipated. They went on much as before. But she never reached toward him again. She vowed to herself that she would not. And a little core of bitterness remained, together with the longing she denied.

Their meat supply was running low, and Davy left to hunt early in the morning. Lorelei waited until the sun was beaming through the cabin's single window before she ventured forth for water. The ice was thinnest on the east side of the lake—one swing with the pick pierced through.

It was a peaceful morning, with a moist freshness in the wind that was a prelude to the melting snows. Already a thin layer of water sat upon the lake. In a week or so there would be great fissures in the ice, and gradually they would become floating ice islands, treacherous but beautiful. Then they would shrink and melt and sink back into the lake. She could see where it would begin, some two yards beyond the tallest hemlock, where an underground stream fed the quieter water around it. In past winters, she and Davy sometimes ice-fished in that spot. They could squat securely on ice five inches thick, while just above the hidden spring it rarely froze an inch.

She struggled up to the cabin with two brimming buckets and pressed her shoulder against the door. Tea before anything. Hot steaming tea.

Humming to herself, she filled the kettle and hung it over the fire.

"Now that's real kindly, Skinny, offering your guest a cup of tea—"

She didn't turn around. Her hand was bare inches from the handle of the poker.

"Oh, I wouldn't be considerin' anything drastic, *compadre*," the voice intoned. She heard the business-like metallic *click* as he cocked the pistol. "Just move your hands out real slow."

She hadn't so much as a knife.

"And turn around."

She did as she was told.

He leered at her, his strange pink eyes bright with malice and gloating triumph. "Had to follow you a ways, Skinny," he drawled, "Skippin' outa town like you did, right after your boyfriend did himself in.

"Heard you got a new one to ride out here with," he cackled. "Busy gal, ain't you? Off with the old—?" He pulled out the chair from the little table and sat down, keeping the gun in a comfortable grip in his hand.

Lorelei said nothing.

"You've taken to washing your face, Skinny," he observed affably. "Now, that's real fine. Cleanliness is a virtue, you know." Again came that ugly laugh. "Like honesty."

"What d'you want, Whitey?" she asked.

"Well, speaking of all this funning you been up to, Skinny, let's start with ole Beau. He's even harder to track than you are. And you ain't easy."

"Beau's gone," she told him with satisfaction. "You want to chase him all the way to England?"

"That's what the old bitch tried to tell me," he said musingly, fingering his gun. "She tried to tell me you and Beau both gone 'cross the water and disappeared into the old country.

"But here you are." He spoke the last words with chilling articulation.

"You got the truth about Beau first time, Whitey," Lorelei said evenly. "If you're expecting anything else, you may as well shoot me now and spare us both the trouble. I put Beau on the ship to London myself, better than six months ago."

It occurred to her that none of it mattered. *He's going to kill me anyway. That's what he's really come for.* She had seen the look the moment she had turned around. Like a coyote licking its chops.

"Funny to hear you talking like a woman, Skinny, 'stead of grunting all the time." He grinned at her, displaying a broken front tooth. " 'Nough to give a man ideas."

She shuddered, for the first time realizing that some things could be worse than dying. *"I wouldn't have him around after he beat Janey up so bad."* And Ma Belle catered to some rough trade in Sydneytown.

"I reckon Whitey's got more hate in him than anybody I've ever known." Beau had been with him years longer than she. Had seen years more. *"He even hates his own men . . ."*

And Whitey's men didn't quit him. She'd been the first. She and Beau. Beau was safe in England. And she was—

Not safe.

The kettle was hot. "You want some tea, Whitey?" she said, making a move toward the fire.

"You take another step closer to that poker, old buddy, you ain't gonna have a foot."

She stopped dead still, realizing with a sudden horror that Whitey was playing the game, and she was the quarry. "You want to make it yourself?" she asked in a deadpan voice. "Why don't you just move aside a mite? I'll get these irons out of your way." She'd fooled him once, when she was new with the gang, and he hadn't forgotten. He kept a wary eye. Female rattlers bit, too.

He drew out the poker and spit on the end that had rested in the fire. The moisture sizzled and was gone. His eyes watched her over the iron. "Real hot, ain't it," he observed.

"So's the tea," she said, as though they were just making conversation. She knew what the slightest show of fear would do—she remembered the fat merchant, sweating, naked. And Whitey loved it—he fed on it.

It wasn't a matter of courage. It was survival. She served the tea and poured one for herself. Only biscuits and little sandwiches missing, she thought, and it could be the Taylor ranch in midafternoon. Her mother had never forgotten the ritual of England. *Ease and refreshment. A time for friends to call.*

Davy might return at any time. Hunting was never certain in the snow.

He read her mind. "When's he due back, Skinny? Your blond friend."

She shrugged. "He's gone to Sutter's for supplies. Couple days."

He chuckled. "Funny. I saw him headed north up the canyon trail. Looked set for hunting. No bedroll." He fondled his gun and swung it around his finger like a toy. "So we'll just sit tight here and wait for him.

"Now, I don't really mind your lying about little

things, Skinny," Whitey said, closing one eye and training the gun on the tip of her boot. He cocked the
trigger while she looked on unmoving, then slowly released it again. "But I do expect you to enlighten me on
certain matters. One certain matter in particular." He
began playing hammer and trigger again.

"If that gun should go off, *by accident,*" she said,
"he's gonna be coming back quick."

"Sorry if I make you nervous, Skinny," he said. The
gun rested again in his hand. *"Now, where's the
money?"*

She stared at him blankly.

"Twenty-five thousand in sweet solid currency. Your
old boyfriend Beau. He did me a bad turn, Skinny. A
bunch of bad turns. After keeping you all to himself
over that long cold lonely winter—you could have been
such a comfort to the boys—and he was there hogging
all the honey and playing sly. Then he has to go and
shoot down that poor old agent fellow—unarmed the
gent was. *Then* he runs out with that whole roll, and
Skinny, you know that just ain't fair. Wasn't kindly of
old Beau at all. *And then he comes to you."*

Beau had plenty of money. He had the payroll.

Lorelei smiled at Whitey. "That's a nice little nest
egg you're talking about, Whitey," she said, stalling for
time. "You think Beau dropped twenty-five thousand
on me as a present before he left? *He hadn't come for
the money. He had come to kill her.*

"The thought occurred to me," he said mildly.

"Why don't you search the place?"

"I don't think I'll have to do that, Skinny."

They both heard the unmistakable crack of a rifle
blast. Early hunting. If Davy made a kill, he'd be
coming back soon.

"Amazing isn't it, how sound travels from Sutter's,"
Whitey observed. She would have no chance to warn
him. She watched Whitey take the second rifle from its

place on the wall and load it. "You go through men awful fast, Skinny," he said. "Best you start thinking about that money, lessen you want to watch the end of another one!"

"He doesn't know about it!" she cried. "I buried it. I buried it before the snows!"

"Where?" His voice was like a pistol shot.

"Down by the lake." Her words were running as quick as her desperate thoughts. "Beside the big hemlock. *But there's five feet of snow over it!*" Time. Sweet time. It was their only chance.

"You best sit very quiet now, and don't move off that chair. Cause I'll shoot him when he comes through the door if you so much as twitch wrong."

They both heard the horse coming up to the cabin. Davy called to her. *Would he think it odd that she didn't come out?* Whitey signaled her to answer. *Or would he just walk in, a big, broad target for Whitey's amusement?*

"Davy, don't come in here!" she cried loud and desperately. How could she let him just walk in?

Whitey cuffed her and she fell back against the table. "Stupid bitch!" he said angrily. "I ought to just finish you up." But there was still the man outside. There were easier ways.

He used the butt of the rifle to break the cabin window. "I've got your girl friend inside," he called. "Be a cold bed with a dead lady!"

He didn't have to wait long.

"What d'you want with us?"

"Come out where I can see you."

A moment later Davy appeared, carrying his hunting rifle.

"Get rid of the gun and the knife." It was done. "Now come on in." He smiled to himself. Lovebirds. Well, that would make them easier to handle.

He gestured Davy to the cot. "See," he told Lorelei,

"It didn't make no difference nohow, did it? All I need is you and I've got your friend, free for the asking." He kept watch on Davy, but the gun stayed trained on Lorelei.

"Go get a shovel," he ordered.

Davy looked at him confused.

"Just get it," he growled. "We're going on a treasure hunt."

The shovel dug into the snow, lifted, and turned. Davy was sweating in his heavy jacket. The snow was heavy and wet and moved slowly.

Whitey looked on. The sun on the snow was bright and hurt his eyes. Davy saw him several times shading them with his hand. The other hand continued to hold the pistol unswervingly on Lorelei.

He had given them no chance to plot. Instead he had taken it upon himself to supply the entertainment— reciting Lorelei's exploits, both real and imagined. Lorelei cringed when he told of the stagecoach robbery. He said Lorelei handed him the gun to kill the merchant. He said she was Beau's whore, before the dandy who'd blown his brains out. He said. He said.

Some of it was true. But to everything, Davy replied the same. "That so?" he said softly, and continued to dig.

Her eyes met Davy's—they locked for a split second—then his glance flickered to Whitey's gun, trained midpoint on her body. Davy shifted position, hardly missing the rhythm of his labor. Dig. Lift. Turn. Dig. Lift. Turn. Dig. Lift.

"What's this?" he said aloud. Whitey's eyes shifted to the shovelful of snow. The white snow rose, smashing to his face, his eyes. Lorelei dived for the snow and the gun fired. It grazed her temple. Fired again before the shovel descended and knocked it across the ice.

She fought to stay conscious. Whitey had recovered and was racing for the gun. It was on the ice. And Davy

was going after him. "Davy, the ice!" She couldn't tell
whether or not he heard. The soft white snow seemed to
rise slowly to pillow her. Eyes opened. She had to stay
awake. Whitey had skidded toward the gun. Davy
pulled him down on the ice and the ice groaned under
the weight of his fall. Whitey clutched frantically at
Davy's arm as he felt the ice break. Davy tried to pull
back. Half of Whitey was in the water. His hands had
Davy in a death grip. Lorelei watched. She couldn't
walk—she chawled over the snow to the shovel, scut-
tling like a crab. She saw Davy struggle against the grip.
The water was drawing Whitey down. Davy couldn't
hold him up for long.

Safe ice. She felt her way. She knelt before the locking arms. "Lift up!" she cried to Davy and with the rest
of his strength and sinew he pulled the arm a few inches
from the water. Lorelei raised the shovel in two hands
and brought it down on Whitey's wrist. The fingers
broke open like a claw. Davy pulled free.

She tried to smile at Davy, but she failed. The dam
burst over her terrors and she began to tremble all
over. She felt Davy's arms wrap around her, and together, like one body, they staggered from the ice back
to the cabin.

"Lore!" His fingers traced the blood at her temple
where the bullet had caught.

"I'm all right!" she cried. "All right." She held his
hand to her face, wondering at the way he was looking
at her. He held her closer, tighter. She felt him pull her
down across the cot, his hands were searching inside
her clothes, and she heard his voice like a song against
her skin.

"Oh, God, I want you," he murmured. "Want you—
Lore."

His breath was warm and quick. This time it was
right. And Lorelei, laughing and crying all at once,
needed no spur. Her own fingers flew to his shirt,

loosened the buttons, crept inside. Their garments, wet
and cold, peeled from their flesh. The bodies made
tinder for the fire, meshing and merging, clinging to
each other. He pressed to enter and she parted like a
flower, like the first flower of spring.

"I've wanted you so much—so long," he groaned
against her shoulder, kissing the lovely neck, up to her
ear, across her beautiful eyes until they closed under a
fringe of lashes.

There was so much time to make up. They didn't stir
from the cabin until the next sun had risen. And a lifetime of new days to spend.

"Come out here and look!" Davy called to her.

The sun was warm and golden. And the ice on the
lake was breaking early.

Spring always comes as a shock to me now, Susanna
thought, pacing idly, purposelessly through the early
garden. The corn was up ankle-high. The boys were
grooming Ravensfire for the first full circuit of races
since the war. He had bred his first season last year, and
three mares would be foaling sometime soon.

A well-run ranch almost runs itself after a while.
Johnny Crandall and Ed knew the schedules. One turn
to plow, another to sow, slaughter time and breeding
season—just like in the Bible.

Jim Attaby was leaving for Hampshire in a fortnight,
to see his son. He had pressed her to go with him, and
she'd had a warm invitation from James, her half-
brother, the present Earl of Wye.

*You must know that this is your home too, at any
time you may desire it. I know it would have been
father's wish, and to it I add my own.*

> *I remain, your affectionate brother,*
> *James Hungerford, Earl of Wye*

A kind gesture from a man I've never met. I never knew any of them, really. I remember Father's eyes, green like mine, so many years ago. He wanted to be kind, but he didn't understand about Jed. And Jed really was my family. Jed and Benji and Lorelei. Now I'm the only one. I've buried my husband and my son. And I have probably destroyed my daughter. So it is no mercy that I am left, and yet I cannot leave.

She turned back toward the house. The sun played on the still-white peaks of the eastern mountain range, displaying in all its magnificence the land he had brought her to so many years before. *This is the land we settled, where our children were born. This is where I have buried my dead, and where I will be buried in my time.* She almost crushed a tiny purple crocus under her boot, and she stopped and gathered it up in her hands. *It shouldn't be like this. Spring's the wrong time to be thinking about dying.*

Susanna had topped the last veranda step when she heard the hue and cry break out down by the far corral. She turned, shading her eyes against the glaring sun. She saw two figures, double-mounted, coming up the drive.

BIG IN SIZE, BIG IN STORY, FROM DELL—

Nothing Could Stop
The Polreath Women
in their drive for
the ULTIMATE REWARD

ELIZABETH, the matriarch—her love for Lord John Polreath is surpassed by only one other passion . . .

PATIENCE, the scapegrace—she becomes the toast and the scandal of New York and London, and despair of her family, until one fateful night . . .

HOPE, the rebel—bearing her dead step-brother's child, she alone can save the Polreath heritage.

Set in England and America in the turbulent nineteenth century, embracing the Civil war, the rise of a great shipping empire and the emergence of women as a force in the world, here is a saga novel in the grand tradition of R.F. Delderfield's GOD IS AN ENGLISHMAN.